S tand still!" *Hollypaw was racing back* to help. Jaypaw froze, swallowing his frustration, and allowed Lionpaw to drag the tendrils from around his paws while Hollypaw gently guided him away from the prickly bush.

"Dumb brambles!" Jaypaw lifted his chin and padded forward, more unsure than ever of the terrain but trying desperately not to show it.

Wordlessly, Hollypaw and Lionpaw fell into step on either side of him. With the lightest touch of her whiskers Hollypaw guided him around a clump of nettles and, when a fallen tree blocked their path, Lionpaw warned him with a flick of his tail to stop and wait while he led the way up and over the trunk.

As Jaypaw scrabbled over the crumbling bark he couldn't help wondering: *Is the prophecy really meant for a cat who can't see?*

WARRIORS

THE PROPHECIES BEGIN

THE NEW PROPHECY

POWER OF THREE

OMEN OF THE STARS

DAWN OF THE CLANS

EXPLORE THE WARRIORS WORLD

MANGA

Also by Erin Hunter

SEEKERS

RETURN TO THE WILD

MANGA

SURVIVORS

NOVELLAS

POWER OF THREE

WARRIORS

ECLIPSE

ERIN HUNTER

HARPER

An Imprint of HarperCollinsPublishers

Eclipse

Copyright © 2008 by Working Partners Limited

Series created by Working Partners Limited

Map art © 2015 by Dave Stevenson

Interior art © 2015 by Owen Richardson

www.harpercollinschildrens.com

Library of Congress Cataloging-in-Publication Data

Hunter, Erin.

Eclipse / by Erin Hunter. — 1st ed.

p.   cm. — (Warriors, power of three ; bk. 4)

Summary: While Jaypaw, Hollypaw, and Lionpaw struggle to
understand their powers as warriors, the cats' faith in StarClan is tested
yet again.

ISBN 978-0-06-236711-2

[1. Cats—Fiction. 2. Brothers and sisters—Fiction. 3. Adventure
and adventurers—Fiction. 4. Fantasy.] I. Title.

PZ7.H916625Ec 2008   2008045060

[Fic]—dc22   CIP

                                                              AC

Typography by Ellice M. Lee

19   20 . CG/BRR   20   19   18   17

❖

Revised paperback edition, 2015

Special thanks to Kate Cary

ALLEGIANGES

THUNDERCLAN

LEADER   **FIRESTAR**—ginger tom with a flame-colored pelt

DEPUTY   **BRAMBLECLAW**—dark brown tabby tom with amber eyes

MEDICINE GAT   **LEAFPOOL**—light brown tabby she-cat with amber eyes
APPRENTICE, JAYPAW

WARRIORS   (toms and she-cats without kits)

SQUIRRELFLIGHT—dark ginger she-cat with green eyes
APPRENTICE, FOXPAW

DUSTPELT—dark brown tabby tom

SANDSTORM—pale ginger she-cat
APPRENTICE, HONEYPAW

CLOUDTAIL—long-haired white tom
APPRENTICE, CINDERPAW

BRACKENFUR—golden brown tabby tom
APPRENTICE, HOLLYPAW

SORRELTAIL—tortoiseshell-and-white she-cat with amber eyes

THORNCLAW—golden brown tabby tom
APPRENTICE, POPPYPAW

BRIGHTHEART—white she-cat with ginger patches

ASHFUR—pale gray (with darker flecks) tom, dark blue eyes
APPRENTICE, LIONPAW

SPIDERLEG—long-limbed black tom with brown underbelly and amber eyes

WHITEWING—white she-cat with green eyes
APPRENTICE, ICEPAW

BIRCHFALL—light brown tabby tom

GRAYSTRIPE—long-haired gray tom

BERRYNOSE—cream-colored tom

HAZELTAIL—small gray-and-white she-cat

MOUSEWHISKER—gray-and-white tom

APPRENTICES

(more than six moons old, in training to become warriors)

CINDERPAW—gray tabby she-cat

HONEYPAW—light brown tabby she-cat

POPPYPAW—tortoiseshell she-cat

LIONPAW—golden tabby tom with amber eyes

HOLLYPAW—black she-cat with green eyes

JAYPAW—gray tabby tom with blue eyes

FOXPAW—reddish tabby tom

ICEPAW—white she-cat

QUEENS

(she-cats expecting or nursing kits)

FERNCLOUD—pale gray (with darker flecks) she-cat, green eyes

DAISY—cream-colored long-furred cat from the horseplace, mother of Spiderleg's kits: Rosekit (dark cream she-cat) and Toadkit (black-and-white tom)

MILLIE—silver tabby she-cat, former kittypet, expecting Graystripe's kits

ELDERS

(former warriors and queens, now retired)

LONGTAIL—pale tabby tom with dark black stripes, retired early due to failing sight

MOUSEFUR—small dusky brown she-cat

SHADOWCLAN

LEADER

BLACKSTAR—large white tom with huge jet-black paws

DEPUTY

RUSSETFUR—dark ginger she-cat

MEDICINE CAT

LITTLECLOUD—very small tabby tom

WARRIORS

OAKFUR—small brown tom

ROWANCLAW—ginger tom

SMOKEFOOT—black tom
APPRENTICE, OWLPAW

IVYTAIL—white-and-tortoiseshell she-cat

TOADFOOT—dark brown tom

CROWFROST—black-and-white tom
APPRENTICE, OLIVEPAW

KINKFUR—tabby she-cat, with long fur that sticks out at all angles

RATSCAR—brown tom with long scar across his back
APPRENTICE, SHREWPAW

SNAKETAIL—dark brown tom with tabby-striped tail
APPRENTICE, SCORCHPAW

WHITEWATER—white she-cat with long fur, blind in one eye
APPRENTICE, REDPAW

QUEENS   **TAWNYPELT**—tortoiseshell she-cat with green eyes (mother of Rowanclaw's kits, Tigerkit, Flamekit, and Dawnkit)

SNOWBIRD—pure white she-cat

ELDERS   **CEDARHEART**—dark gray tom

TALLPOPPY—long-legged light brown tabby she-cat

WINDCLAN

LEADER   **ONESTAR**—brown tabby tom

DEPUTY   **ASHFOOT**—gray she-cat

MEDICINE CAT   **BARKFACE**—short-tailed brown tom
APPRENTICE, KESTRELPAW

WARRIORS   **TORNEAR**—tabby tom

CROWFEATHER—dark gray tom
APPRENTICE, HEATHERPAW

OWLWHISKER—light brown tabby tom

WHITETAIL—small white she-cat
APPRENTICE, BREEZEPAW

NIGHTCLOUD—black she-cat

WEASELFUR—ginger tom with white paws

HARESPRING—brown-and-white tom

LEAFTAIL—dark tabby tom, amber eyes

DEWSPOTS—spotted gray tabby she-cat

WILLOWCLAW—gray she-cat

ANTPELT—brown tom with one black ear

EMBERFOOT—gray tom with two dark paws
APPRENTICE, SUNPAW

QUEENS

GORSETAIL—very pale gray-and-white cat with blue eyes, mother of Thistlekit, Sedgekit, and Swallowkit

ELDERS

MORNINGFLOWER—very old tortoiseshell queen

WEBFOOT—dark gray tabby tom

RIVERCLAN

LEADER

LEOPARDSTAR—unusually spotted golden tabby she-cat

DEPUTY

MISTYFOOT—gray she-cat with blue eyes

MEDICINE CAT

MOTHWING—dappled golden she-cat
APPRENTICE, WILLOWPAW

WARRIORS

BLACKCLAW—smoky black tom

VOLETOOTH—small brown tabby tom
APPRENTICE, MINNOWPAW

REEDWHISKER—black tom

MOSSPELT—tortoiseshell she-cat with blue eyes
APPRENTICE, PEBBLEPAW

BEECHFUR—light brown tom

RIPPLETAIL—dark gray tabby tom

DAWNFLOWER—pale gray she-cat

DAPPLENOSE—mottled gray she-cat

POUNCETAIL—ginger-and-white tom

MINTFUR—light gray tabby tom
APPRENTICE, NETTLEPAW

OTTERHEART—dark brown she-cat

PINEFUR—very short-haired tabby she-cat
APPRENTICE, ROBINPAW

RAINSTORM—mottled gray-blue tom

DUSKFUR—brown tabby she-cat
APPRENTICE, COPPERPAW

<u>QUEENS</u>   **GRAYMIST**—pale gray tabby, mother of Sneezekit and Mallowkit

ICEWING—white cat with blue eyes, mother of Beetlekit, Pricklekit, Petalkit, and Grasskit

<u>ELDERS</u>   **SWALLOWTAIL**—dark tabby she-cat

STONESTREAM—gray tom

THE TRIBE OF RUSHING WATER

<u>PREY-HUNTERS</u> (toms and she-cats responsible for providing food)

BROOK WHERE SMALL FISH SWIM (BROOK)—brown tabby she-cat

STORMFUR—dark gray tom with amber eyes, formerly of RiverClan

CATS OUTSIDE CLANS

SOL—brown-and-tortoiseshell long-haired tom with pale yellow eyes

GREENLEAF
TWOLEGPLACE

TWOLEG NEST

TWOLEG PATH

TWOLEG PATH

CLEARING

SHADOWCLAN
CAMP

SMALL
THUNDERPATH

HALFBRIDGE

GREENLEAF
TWOLEGPLACE

HALFBRIDGE

CAT VIEW

ISLAND

STREAM

RIVERCLAN
CAMP

HORSEPLACE

MOONPOOL

ABANDONED
TWOLEG NEST

OLD THUNDERPATH

THUNDERCLAN
CAMP

ANCIENT OAK

LAKE

WINDCLAN
CAMP

BROKEN
HALFBRIDGE

TWOLEGPLACE

THUNDERPATH

KEY To The CLANS

THUNDERCLAN

RIVERCLAN

SHADOWCLAN

WINDCLAN

STARCLAN

NORTH

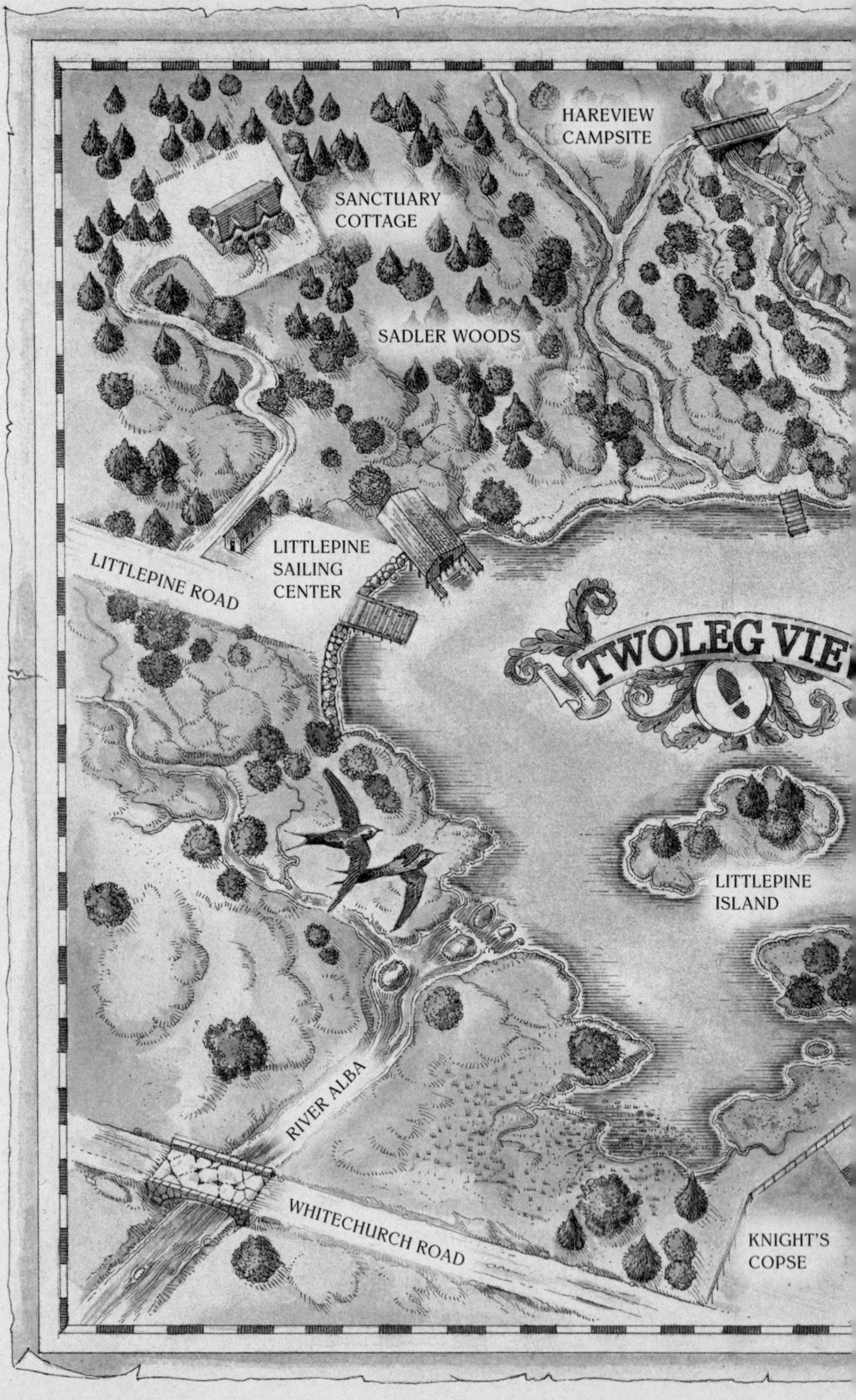
HAREVIEW CAMPSITE
SANCTUARY COTTAGE
SADLER WOODS
LITTLEPINE SAILING CENTER
LITTLEPINE ROAD
TWOLEG VIE
LITTLEPINE ISLAND
RIVER ALBA
WHITECHURCH ROAD
KNIGHT'S COPSE

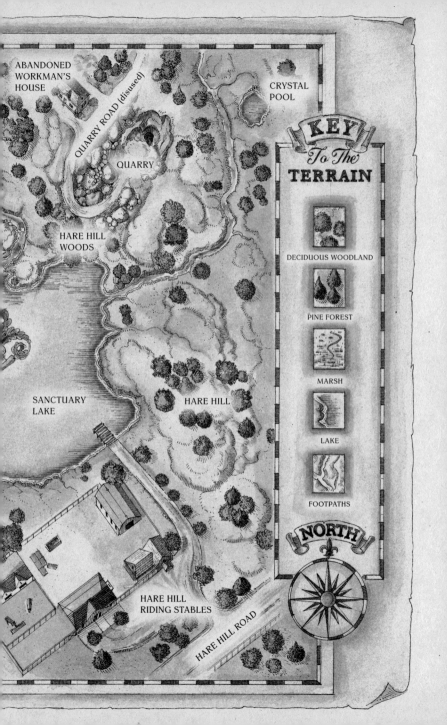

PROLOGUE

❧

The forest shimmered in bright sunshine, the undergrowth rustling with prey. Beneath an ash tree, a black tom stretched and let the sun slanting through the branches bathe his belly. With a purr, he lapped at his chest, paws curling in contentment.

Suddenly a tortoiseshell darted out of a bush and hurtled past him. The tom rolled onto his flank and called after her: "Mouse?"

"About to be fresh-kill!" the tortoiseshell answered. She plunged through a wall of ferns and disappeared into the greenery, her white-tipped tail whisking behind her.

Beyond the ferns, the forest floor sloped down into a grassy glade. At the bottom, a dark gray she-cat gnawed at a tick lodged at the base of her tail. She grumbled to herself as she tugged at the fat bug, then stopped and looked up the slope. The ferns at the top were shivering.

"Got you!" A triumphant mew rang out; then the ferns shivered again, harder than before, and the tortoiseshell popped out with a mouse hanging from her jaws. She blinked at the gray she-cat. "Hi, Yellowfang!"

"Good morning, Spottedleaf," Yellowfang called back. "A good day for hunting."

"The hunting's always good here." With a flick of her head, Spottedleaf tossed the fresh-kill down to Yellowfang before bounding after it.

Yellowfang sniffed at the fresh-kill and jerked backward. She rubbed her paw against her broad, flat muzzle as the dark shadow of a flea scuttled across her nose. "I thought these hunting grounds would be safe from fleas!"

"You probably brought them with you." Spottedleaf narrowed her eyes at Yellowfang's matted pelt. "When will you learn to groom yourself?" She leaned forward and began to lap at a large knot of fur on her Clanmate's shoulder.

"When *you* stop trying to take care of every cat," Yellowfang muttered.

A voice sounded at the top of the slope. "I can't imagine that ever happening."

Spottedleaf glanced up. A white tom was trotting down the slope toward them. "Whitestorm!" she purred. "Is Bluestar with you?"

"She was a moment ago."

"I still am!" Bluestar burst from the trees and raced after Whitestorm. "I would have kept up with you if Tallstar hadn't stopped me."

"What did he want?" Spottedleaf asked.

"He was fretting, as usual." Bluestar glanced at Yellowfang's flea-bitten nose and curled her lip. "Bad luck," she sympathized. "I didn't think there were any fleas here." Spottedleaf let out a soft *mrrow* and flicked the tip of her tail against Yellowfang's shoulder.

"Tallstar?" Yellowfang prompted, shrugging Spottedleaf away.

"He's worried about the kits," Bluestar explained.

Yellowfang's tail twitched. "Hollypaw, Lionpaw, and Jaypaw?"

"Who else?" Bluestar sighed. "The prophecy has gotten under his pelt like a tick."

"But their training is going well," Spottedleaf pointed out. "They each seem to be figuring out their path at last."

"That's true." Yellowfang stared at her paws and added quietly, "But there's so much they don't know."

"They're still very young," Bluestar warned.

Yellowfang looked up. "That doesn't mean we have to *deceive* them."

"Do you think it would help if they knew everything?" Bluestar countered.

Yellowfang's shoulders stiffened. "Lives begun in deception are always lived in shadow."

Bluestar sat down. "They cannot know the truth. We have kept this secret for a reason—one that we all agreed upon, Yellowfang. We have to do what is right for the Clan."

Yellowfang tipped her head to one side. "It's a *lie*. How can that be right?"

"It wasn't us who lied to them in the first place," Whitestorm reminded her.

"But we go on hiding the truth," Yellowfang argued. "I still think there's too much secrecy in their lives."

"They know about the prophecy," Spottedleaf put in.

Yellowfang shifted her paws. "The prophecy! I wish they'd never heard about it. I wish *I'd* never heard about it! Sometimes I think it would have been better if they hadn't been given their powers at all."

Spottedleaf brushed her tail along Yellowfang's flank. "You know we had nothing to do with that," she soothed. "We just have to hope they use their powers wisely, for the good of ThunderClan."

"Just ThunderClan?" Whitestorm looked thoughtful. "If their powers are so great, shouldn't they be used to help all the Clans?"

Bluestar widened her eyes. "These kits were born into ThunderClan! They have been raised as loyal ThunderClan warriors. Why should they feel responsibility toward any other Clan?"

Yellowfang narrowed her eyes at the old ThunderClan leader, but said nothing.

"Some things we must agree to differ on," Whitestorm meowed peaceably. "The most important thing is that the kits respect and listen to their warrior ancestors."

"Yes," Spottedleaf agreed. "We must make sure they take notice of what we tell them."

Whitestorm twitched his ear where it was being tickled by a blade of grass. "No cat is born so wise that it can't learn from its elders. We must guide them where we can."

"Easier said than done," Yellowfang muttered.

A butterfly flitted overhead, making jerky progress against the breeze. Spottedleaf's eyes flashed, and she suddenly reared up, clapping her paws together above her head. The butterfly surged upward and out of reach.

"Mouse dung!" Spottedleaf dropped back onto four paws. She noticed Bluestar padding away. "Are you leaving already?"

Bluestar glanced back at Yellowfang. "If I stay, we will argue."

Yellowfang flicked the tip of her tail. "So you still think we should keep the secret from them?"

"I understand your fears, Yellowfang," Bluestar murmured. "But for now this secret is safest kept with us."

Yellowfang looked away. "Nothing but stubbornness," she growled under her breath.

"Bluestar believes she's doing the right thing," Whitestorm told her. "You trusted her before, remember?" He nodded to Yellowfang and Spottedleaf, then followed Bluestar out of the glade.

"And what about you?" Yellowfang's pale stare rested on Spottedleaf. "Do you agree with all this secrecy?"

"Truth is a powerful weapon," Spottedleaf replied. "We must be careful how we use it."

"That's no answer!" Yellowfang snapped.

Spottedleaf searched Yellowfang's anxious gaze. "Why are you so worried?"

The fur along Yellowfang's spine rippled. "I don't know," she admitted. "I just have a feeling." Her gaze drifted toward

the trees, searching the forest. "Something's wrong. There is
a darkness coming that not even StarClan can prevent. And
when it comes, we will be helpless to protect the Clans. Helpless even to protect ourselves."

CHAPTER 1

Hollypaw crouched low, pressing her belly against the boulder. It was still warm from the sun, which was dipping behind the distant hills. A cold wind rolling from the mountains ruffled her fur. From here she could see green fields unfolding toward a swath of forest; somewhere beyond those trees lay the lake, and home.

Though the trees were still in full leaf, they were a shabby green, and the air had a new, musty taste that hadn't been there on the journey to the mountains. *Leaf-fall is coming,* she thought.

She couldn't wait to be home. It felt as though they had been with the Tribe for moons. At least they were safely out of the mountains. The ground would be softer underpaw from here on, the hunting easier, and the territory steadily more familiar than rock and water and stunted trees.

She glanced over her shoulder. Brambleclaw and Squirrelflight were talking in low voices with Stormfur and Brook. Tawnypelt and Crowfeather leaned in beside them. Were they saying good-bye?

Hollypaw was still shocked that Stormfur and Brook were

staying behind. Last night, at the farewell feast in the cave behind the waterfall, Stormfur had announced that he and Brook would accompany the Clan cats to the foothills, but no farther. Jaypaw, of course, had just shrugged and nodded, as though he'd known all along the two cats would not be returning to ThunderClan. But Hollypaw could only guess at why any cat would want to stay in the mountains when they could live by the lake. *Brook must feel the same way about the mountains as I do about my home. And Stormfur loves her enough to stay with her, wherever she is.*

Suddenly, a flash of brown feather caught her eye. An eagle was skimming over the rough slope below her. Ahead of it a hare pelted in terror, throwing up dirt and grass from its long back feet. Folding its wings deftly against its sides, the eagle attacked, tumbling the hare head over heels before pinning it to the ground with thorn-sharp talons.

Hollypaw envied the eagle's speed. To be able to fly like that! She closed her eyes and imagined skimming over the grass, paws hardly touching the ground, light as air, faster than the fastest prey. . . .

"I wish we could get moving again." Lionpaw's impatient mew broke into her thoughts. He padded onto the boulder and stood beside her, following her gaze toward the eagle feasting on its catch. "I wish I had something in *my* belly," he mewed.

"Do you suppose we'll ever be able to fly?" Hollypaw murmured.

Lionpaw turned and looked at her as though she'd gone crazy.

"I mean," she tried to explain hurriedly, "Jaypaw said we have the power of the stars in our paws." It still felt strange to say it out loud. "We don't really know what that means. I was just wondering if—"

"Flying cats!" Lionpaw scoffed. "What'd be the point of that?"

Hollypaw's ears were hot with embarrassment. "You've got no imagination," she snapped. "Here we are with more power than any other cat *ever*, and you act like it's nothing at all! Why shouldn't we be able to fly, or do *anything* we want to? And stop laughing at me!"

"I'm not laughing at you." Lionpaw flicked Hollypaw's flank with his tail. "I just think we'd look stupid with wings."

Frustration surged in Hollypaw's chest. She rounded on her brother, glaring. "You're not taking this seriously enough! We've got to figure out exactly what this prophecy means!"

Lionpaw blinked and took a step backward. "Keep your fur on. You know Jaypaw and his visions. They sound great, but we have to live in the real world."

"What does the real world mean, now that we have the power of the stars in our paws? We'll be able to do anything! Imagine how much we'll be able to help our Clan!"

Lionpaw frowned. "The prophecy didn't say anything about helping our Clan; it just mentioned the three of us."

Hollypaw stared at him. "But the warrior code says we must protect our Clan before anything else!"

Lionpaw's gaze drifted to the distant hills. "Are we bound

by the warrior code if we're more powerful than StarClan?" he wondered out loud.

"How could you say such a thing?" Hollypaw scolded, but a shiver of foreboding ran along her spine. If the prophecy meant that they had to live outside the warrior code, how would she know what was right? How would she know what she was supposed to do if it came to a choice between her own safety and her Clan's?

Jaypaw's pelt brushed hers as he jumped up beside them. "Could you two speak a bit louder?" he hissed. "I think some of the others didn't hear you." His blue eyes were flashing with anger. Blindness had not robbed them of showing feeling.

Hollypaw spun around to see if any of the other cats had been listening, but the warriors were still deep in their own conversation. "No one's taking any notice of us," she reassured him.

"Not every cat has got such good hearing as you," Lionpaw added.

"I'm just warning you to be careful, okay?" Jaypaw mewed. "We have to keep this a secret."

"We know," Lionpaw assured him.

"Actually, I don't think you do," Jaypaw argued. "How do you think the other cats would react if they found out we've been born with more power than StarClan?"

Lionpaw glanced at Squirrelflight and Brambleclaw. "They'd never believe it."

"I hardly believe it myself," Hollypaw admitted.

"They'd believe it, all right." Jaypaw's voice was icy. "But I don't think they'd like it."

"Why not?" Hollypaw felt a jolt of alarm. She hadn't thought about how her Clanmates would take the news. Surely they'd be glad? They must know she would only use her power to help them!

Lionpaw seemed to agree with her. "Won't they want us to be the best warriors we can be?"

"This prophecy isn't about being a good warrior!" Jaypaw warned. His claws scraped against the surface of the boulder in frustration. "It's about having more power than StarClan. Don't you think ordinary cats might find that a bit scary?"

"But we're not going to do anything bad," Hollypaw insisted. "This is a gift to our whole Clan, not just us." What did Jaypaw think they were going to do with their powers?

"Shh!" Jaypaw's hiss cut her off as Squirrelflight bounded toward them.

She halted at the edge of the boulder. "What are you bickering about?"

"Hollypaw and Lionpaw are just arguing about who's the best hunter," Jaypaw mewed smoothly.

Hollypaw opened her mouth to object, then stopped herself. She hated lying, but she couldn't give their secret away, not here.

"You shouldn't be standing around chatting," Squirrelflight told them. "Not when Brambleclaw has just told you to find fresh-kill. He wants to make sure Stormfur and Brook have something to take back to the Tribe."

They had been so busy arguing, they hadn't heard the order.

"You shouldn't *have* to be asked twice," Squirrelflight scolded.

Hollypaw hung her head. "Sorry."

Squirrelflight flicked her tail toward a cluster of trees at the side of the slope. "Try there, and hurry up!" The copse cast a long shadow that stretched up the hillside. The sun would be setting soon.

Lionpaw licked his lips. "There should be plenty of prey in there."

"Enough for everyone," Squirrelflight agreed. She turned to Jaypaw. "Will you come check Tawnypelt's pads? One of them is bruised where she trod on a sharp stone."

There had been enough sharp stones to bruise everyone's pads on the trek down from the mountain; Hollypaw guessed that Squirrelflight was finding Jaypaw something useful to do, since he couldn't hunt. She tensed, knowing how over-sensitive Jaypaw could be. But her littermate just nodded and followed Squirrelflight back toward the warriors. He didn't even bristle when his mother bent down to lick a grubby patch of fur behind his ear.

The gesture pricked at Hollypaw's heart. Squirrelflight still saw them as kits. It would be easier if they still were; kits didn't have to worry about having more power than their warrior ancestors. *But things change,* she told herself. She turned away, suddenly anxious. Would there come a time when Squirrelflight would be afraid of her own kits?

"What's ruffling your pelt?" Lionpaw asked.

Hollypaw licked the fur prickling on her shoulder. "It

doesn't matter." She nodded toward the copse. "Let's hunt."

She padded to the front of the boulder and let her paws slide over the edge. It was a short, steep drop, but the grass below looked like it would make a soft landing. She leaped. As she landed, a flurry of fur and paws knocked the breath from her body and sent her flying. *Who's attacking me?* Gasping, she scrambled to her paws and prepared to defend herself.

"Why did you get in the way?"

Breezepaw!

The black WindClan apprentice was shaking out his fur beside her. "I almost had that mouse!"

"Sorr—" she began to apologize, then bristled. Why didn't the dumb furball look where he was going? "I thought we were supposed to be hunting over *there*!" She flicked her tail toward the copse.

"*I* decide where I hunt!" Breezepaw snapped. He glanced up at Lionpaw, who was peering over the edge of the boulder. "At least I *was* hunting and not sitting around chatting with my denmates."

"Your denmates wouldn't want to sit around and chat with you even if they were here!" Hollypaw retorted. She felt instantly guilty. Even though he was as bad-tempered as his father and twice as smug, she had begun to feel sorry for Breezepaw. Crowfeather treated his son with such scorn that Breezepaw sometimes seemed a loner among his own Clanmates.

Lionpaw jumped down beside her. "Are you okay?"

"Of course she is!" Breezepaw snorted. "She'd be even

better if she were hunting like she's supposed to, instead of getting in my way. The sooner we get this fresh-kill, the better. Then we can go home."

It had been obvious from the start that Breezepaw hadn't wanted to come to the mountains. And Crowfeather hadn't acted like he was glad to have him along. He didn't seem proud of anything Breezepaw did, unlike Brambleclaw, who made Hollypaw feel like the best warrior in ThunderClan when he praised her. Compassion welled in her chest as she looked at the miserable WindClan apprentice. "We'll be back at the lake before long," she mewed gently.

Breezepaw glared at her. "Why do we have to find fresh-kill for the Tribe, anyway? Why can't they hunt for themselves?"

The compassion evaporated. Hollypaw wondered if she should remind Breezepaw that the Tribe cats were exhausted by their recent battle, and that prey was scarcer than ever in the mountains because of the gang of rogues who had invaded their land and forced them to set borders around their hunting grounds. But if he didn't know that already, she wasn't going to waste her breath. Let him figure it out. All she wanted now was to be back home, warm in her nest with a full belly and her denmates sleeping peacefully around her. She glanced at her brother. Would he set Breezepaw straight?

But Lionpaw just rolled his eyes at the WindClan apprentice. "Go catch a rabbit." He snorted and stomped away across the grass.

Breezepaw curled his lip. "ThunderClan cats think they're so special," he sneered before stalking down the slope.

Hollypaw hurried after her brother. He was muttering under his breath as she caught up to him.

"I wish I had the power to shut that furball up once and for all!"

Is he joking? Hollypaw looked sideways to see if Lionpaw's eyes were shining with their usual good humor, but they were half closed in a frown. She skipped in front of him and blocked his path. "You don't mean that, do you?"

Lionpaw flicked his tail. "Of course not," he grumped. "I'm just tired."

"But do you think that's what 'the power of the stars' means?" Hollypaw persisted. "The power to make any cat do what we want?"

Lionpaw shrugged but didn't meet her gaze. "I suppose," he answered. "I haven't really thought about it."

"You must have!"

Lionpaw padded around her and kept going for a few moments before he spoke again. "I hope it will make me stronger than any other cat, so that I can always win battles." He paused. "What about you?"

"I hope it means I'll know things other cats don't."

"Like what?" Mischief lit his gaze. "How to speak to Twolegs?"

"Don't be stupid!" Hollypaw's claws itched with impatience. "I mean the power to understand"—she groped for the words to explain—"*everything*," she mewed at last.

Lionpaw nudged her shoulder affectionately. "Is that all?"

Hollypaw flicked him away. "You know what I mean."

They had almost reached the trees before Lionpaw spoke again. "Perhaps each of us will feel the power differently," he ventured. "Jaypaw can already tell what cats are thinking, can't he?" He caught Hollypaw's eye. "He does it to you, right?"

Hollypaw nodded.

"Leafpool can't do that," Lionpaw went on. "None of the medicine cats can. Jaypaw is already making predictions about trouble in other Clans, too. That must be his power—to see things other cats can't."

"He's the least blind of us all," Hollypaw murmured, feeling her pelt prickle the way it did when Jaypaw said exactly what was running through her mind.

Thick foliage grew at the edge of the wood, and she halted to let Lionpaw take the lead. "Have you felt anything yet?" she ventured as he began to nose his way into the bushes.

To her surprise, Lionpaw spun around to face her. His eyes glittered with a strange intensity. "At the start of our journey, we stopped on the ridge to look down on the lake, remember? Then you went off to catch prey and rest, but I wasn't hungry." He blinked. "As I was looking at the territories, I started to feel . . . well, kind of strange."

Hollypaw leaned forward. "Strange? How?"

"I felt like I could do anything!" Her brother's eyes flashed. "Run to the farthest horizon without getting tired, fight any enemy and win, face any battle without being afraid."

Hollypaw shifted on her paws and realized that she was backing away from him. Something about him suddenly made her feel uncomfortable: the way he had tensed his shoulders so that he looked more powerful than before, the faraway look in his eyes, as though he could see beyond her, beyond the woods, to some distant place where he could take on enemies single-pawed. She thought back to how he had fought for the Tribe; how he had come staggering out of the battle covered in blood—none of it his own—still ready to fight until there were no cats left standing.

The fire in his eyes sent a shiver through her pelt.

How could she be scared of her own brother?

CHAPTER 2

Jaypaw touched his nose to Tawnypelt's pad. It felt hot and fat. "Swollen," he pronounced. "The skin's grazed but not bleeding. But you already know that." He could hear Hollypaw's and Lionpaw's faint mews as they headed away to find prey. Were they talking about the prophecy?

Tawnypelt pulled her paw from under his muzzle. "I knew I couldn't taste blood, but I wasn't sure if a stone had worked its way in." She licked it. "My pads have grown so hard from the mountains, I can't tell calluses from cuts anymore."

"No stones," Jaypaw reassured her. He nodded toward the sound of water babbling over rocks nearby. "That stream doesn't sound too deep. Go stand in it. The water should ease the swelling."

He padded after her and heard the splash as she leaped into the water.

She gasped. "It's cold!"

"Good," he mewed. "It'll take down the swelling quicker." He pricked his ears. Hollypaw's and Lionpaw's voices had faded into the distance. At last he had shared with them the secret he had kept to himself for so long. Telling it had felt like walking through unknown territory, each word falling like a paw step on uncertain ground. Lionpaw had accepted it as though something that had been confusing him had finally been explained. Hollypaw's reaction had been more frustrating: She only seemed concerned about how they could use their powers to help ThunderClan, and kept fretting about the warrior code. Didn't she understand that the prophecy meant more than that? They had been given a power that stretched far beyond the boundaries set by ordinary cats.

Tawnypelt's mew interrupted his thoughts. "This water's *very* cold."

"It's mountain water."

"I can tell," Tawnypelt meowed urgently. "My paws have gone numb!"

"Well, get out then."

With a gasp of relief, she landed beside him and began shaking the water from her paws, scattering icy drops on his fur.

Jaypaw shivered and moved away; mountain winds and cold water were a bad mix. "Does your paw still hurt?"

"I can't feel it at all," Tawnypelt replied. She paused. "Actually, I can't feel any of my paws."

Squirrelflight was padding toward them. "Any better?"

"I think so," Tawnypelt meowed.

Jaypaw felt his mother's tongue lap his ear. "Are you okay, little one?" she asked gently.

He ducked away, scowling. "Why shouldn't I be?"

"It's okay to be tired." Squirrelflight sat down. "It's been a hard journey."

"I'm fine," Jaypaw snapped. His mother's tail was twitching, brushing against the gritty rock. He waited for her to make some comment about how much harder the journey must have been for him, being blind and all, and then add some mouse-brained comment about how well he had coped with the unfamiliar territory.

"All three of you have been quiet since the battle," she ventured.

She's worried about all *of us!* Jaypaw's anger melted. He wished he could put her mind at rest, but there was no way he could tell her the huge secret that was occupying their thoughts. "I guess we just want to get home," he offered.

"We all do." Squirrelflight rested her chin on top of Jaypaw's head, and he pressed against her, suddenly feeling like a kit again, grateful for her warmth.

"They're back!"

At Tawnypelt's call, Squirrelflight jerked away.

Jaypaw lifted his nose and smelled Hollypaw and Lionpaw. He heard claws scrabbling over rock as Breezepaw arrived. The hunters had returned.

"Let's see what they've caught!" Tawnypelt hurried to greet the apprentices.

Jaypaw already knew what they'd caught. His belly rumbled as he padded after her, the mouthwatering smells of squirrel, rabbit, and pigeon filling his nose. If only it weren't going to be given to the Tribe.

Crowfeather and Brambleclaw were already clustered around the makeshift fresh-kill pile. Stormfur and Brook hung back as though embarrassed by the gift.

"This rabbit's so fat it'll feed all the to-bes," Squirrelflight mewed admiringly.

"Well caught, Breezepaw," Tawnypelt purred.

Jaypaw waited for the WindClan apprentice's pelt to flash with pride, but instead he sensed anxiety claw at Breezepaw. *He's waiting for his father to praise him.*

"Nice pigeon," Crowfeather mewed to Lionpaw.

Breezepaw stiffened with anger.

"And look at the squirrel I caught!" Hollypaw chipped in. "Did you ever see such a juicy one?"

"Come see!" Tawnypelt called to Stormfur and Brook.

The two warriors padded over.

"This will be very welcome," Stormfur meowed formally.

"The Tribe thanks you." Brook's mew was taut.

Jaypaw understood their unease. By accepting fresh-kill, they were openly admitting their weakness. Hunting was poor in the mountains now that two groups of cats were sharing the territory. And yet Jaypaw could feel fierce pride pulsing from Stormfur. *The mountain breeze stirs his heart as well as his pelt.* There was a core of strength within him, a resolve that Jaypaw had not sensed before, as though he were more rooted in the crags and ravines than he ever had been beside the lake. *He truly believes that this is his destiny.* The Tribe was Stormfur's Clan now. He had been born RiverClan, and lived with Thunder-Clan, but now it seemed that he had found his true home.

Jaypaw shivered. The wind had been sharpened by a late-afternoon chill.

A howl echoed from the slopes far above.

Brook bristled. "Wolves."

"We'll get this prey home safely," Stormfur reassured her. "The wolves are too clumsy to follow our mountain paths."

"But there's a lot of open territory before you reach them," Brambleclaw urged. "You should go."

"We should all head home," Crowfeather advised. "The smell of this fresh-kill will be attracting all the prey-eaters around here."

Alarm flashed from every pelt as Jaypaw detected a strange tang on the breeze. It was the first wolf scent he'd smelled. It reminded him of the dogs around the Twoleg farm, but there was a rawness to it, a scent of blood and flesh that the dogs did not carry. He was thankful it was faint. "They're a long way off," he murmured.

"But they travel fast," Brook warned. The rabbit's fur brushed the ground as she picked it up.

"We're going to miss you," Squirrelflight meowed. Her voice was thick with sadness.

Brook laid the rabbit down again, a purr rising in her throat. Her pelt brushed Squirrelflight's. "Thank you for taking us in and showing us such kindness."

"ThunderClan is grateful for your loyalty and courage," Brambleclaw meowed.

"We'll see you again, though, won't we?" Hollypaw mewed hopefully.

Jaypaw wondered if he would ever return to the mountains. Would he meet the Tribe of Endless Hunting again? He had followed Stoneteller into his dreams and been led by the Tribe-healer's ancestor to the hollow where ranks of starry cats encircled a shimmering pool. He shivered as he recalled their words: *You have come.* They had been expecting him, and they had known about the prophecy! Yet again, Jaypaw wondered where the prophecy had come from, and how the Tribe of Endless Hunting was connected to his own ancestors.

"There's no more time for good-byes!" Crowfeather's mew was impatient.

"Take care, little one." Brook's cheek brushed Jaypaw's before she turned to say good-bye to Hollypaw.

Stormfur licked his ear. "Look after your brother and sister," he murmured.

"Bye, Stormfur." Jaypaw's throat tightened. "Good-bye, Brook." He remembered the times when Brook had comforted and encouraged him. She had always seemed to understand what it felt like to be different. And Stormfur had never patronized him, but treated him with the same warmth and strictness as he had the other apprentices. He would miss them.

Lionpaw pushed in front of him. "Good-bye, Stormfur. Show those invaders that a Clan cat is never beaten."

"Good-bye, Lionpaw," Stormfur meowed. "Remember that even though our experiences change us, we have to carry on."

A rush of warmth seemed to flood between the warrior and apprentice, and Jaypaw realized with surprise that his brother shared a special bond with Stormfur, one he had not detected before. He stood wondering about it as his Clanmates began to head off down the slope, not moving when Stormfur picked up the freshly caught prey and started uphill after his mate.

"Stop dawdling!" Crowfeather nudged Jaypaw with his nose, steering him down a smooth rocky slope onto the grassy hillside.

Jaypaw bristled. "I don't need help!"

"Please yourself," Crowfeather hissed. "But don't blame me if you get left behind." He pounded ahead, his paws thrumming on the ground.

Imagine having such a sour-tongued warrior for a father. I'm glad I'm not Breezepaw!

"Hurry up, Jaypaw!" Lionpaw was calling.

Jaypaw sniffed the air. On this exposed slope it was easy to tell where the other cats were. Brambleclaw led the way downhill, Breezepaw at his heels, while Crowfeather had already caught up and was flanking Tawnypelt, keeping to the outside of the group. Squirrelflight padded alone, while Hollypaw and Lionpaw trotted behind.

Jaypaw raced after them. The grass was smooth and soft beneath his paws. "It feels strange leaving them behind," he panted.

"They chose to stay," Crowfeather pointed out.

"Do you think we'll ever see them or the Tribe again?" Tawnypelt wondered.

"I hope not," Crowfeather answered. "I don't want to see those mountains once more as long as I live."

"They might visit the lake," Hollypaw suggested.

A howl echoed eerily around the crags far behind them.

"They have to get home safely first," Lionpaw murmured.

"They will," Brambleclaw assured him. "They know their territory as well as any other Tribe cat."

Padding beside his littermates, Jaypaw caught the musty scent of forest ahead. Before long the ground beneath his paws turned from grass to crushed leaves. The wind ceased tugging at his fur as trees shielded him on every side. Hollypaw hurried ahead as though she already scented the lake beyond, but for a moment Jaypaw wished he were back on the open slopes of the foothills. At least there, scents and sounds were not muffled by the enclosing trees, and there was no undergrowth to trip him up. He felt blinder here in this unfamiliar forest than he ever had.

"Watch out!" Lionpaw's warning came too late, and Jaypaw found his paws tangled in a bramble.

"Mouse dung!" He fought to free himself, but the bramble seemed to twist around his legs as if it meant to ensnare him.

"Stand still!" Hollypaw was racing back to help. Jaypaw froze, swallowing his frustration, and allowed Lionpaw to drag the tendrils from around his paws while Hollypaw gently guided him away from the prickly bush.

"Dumb brambles!" Jaypaw lifted his chin and padded forward, more unsure than ever of the terrain but trying desperately not to show it.

Wordlessly, Hollypaw and Lionpaw fell into step on either side of him. With the lightest touch of her whiskers Hollypaw guided him around a clump of nettles and, when a fallen tree blocked their path, Lionpaw warned him with a flick of his tail to stop and wait while he led the way up and over the trunk.

As Jaypaw scrabbled over the crumbling bark he couldn't help wondering: *Is the prophecy really meant for a cat who can't see?*

CHAPTER 3

❧

Lionpaw twitched in his sleep. He was dreaming.

Standing on a craggy peak, he felt the mountain breeze tug at his fur. Above, a starless sky stretched black as a raven's wing to the distant horizon. In front of him ridge upon ridge lay like ripples on a wind-ruffled lake. Though no moon shone, the mountaintops glowed like moonstone. *All this is mine!* Exhilarated, Lionpaw bounded forward, his powerful hind paws sending stones cracking into the shadowy valleys below. He cleared the gorge in one easy jump, landing on the ridge beyond. His claws scraped the rock, holding his paws firm. He leaped again, light as air, the breath hardly stirring in his chest. His tail seemed to brush the pelt-soft sky and, with the blood rushing in his ears, he lifted his chin and yowled, his voice echoing like thunder around the empty mountains. *I have the power of the stars in my paws!*

"Lionpaw!" Ashfur's call jolted Lionpaw awake. "Hunting patrol!"

Lionpaw blinked open his eyes. Sunshine pierced the branches of the den, yellow sunbeams spearing straight downward. The other nests were empty. *It's sunhigh already!* Lionpaw clambered groggily to his paws. And then he remembered: They hadn't reached camp until well past moonhigh. Surely Ashfur wouldn't be angry with him for sleeping late today?

Arching his back in a trembling stretch, he yawned. His paws still ached from the long trek from the mountains, and he licked gingerly at a forepaw to check whether the grazing had begun to heal. No taste of blood. The scabs were hard. The soft forest floor would be no problem.

"Lionpaw!" Ashfur called again, more sharply. Lionpaw stumbled out of the den. Surely he deserved some rest! Heavy-pawed, he padded into the clearing, narrowing his eyes against the greenleaf sun. It flooded the camp and warmed his pelt. A light breeze stirred the trees encircling the top of the hollow. In the mountains, the only shelter from the wind had been in the damp and chilly cave behind the waterfall. How in the name of StarClan did the Tribe survive leaf-bare? Greenleaf had been cold enough!

"Awake at last!" Ashfur greeted him. "The prey's probably grown old and died while we've been waiting for you."

"Then it'll be easier to catch," Lionpaw grumbled.

"I know you're tired," Ashfur conceded. "But Icepaw is itching to get out into the forest, and I promised Whitewing we'd go with them."

Lionpaw noticed Icepaw for the first time. The young apprentice was bouncing around the clearing like a newleaf hare, leaping and twisting as she darted at invisible prey. Her prey might have been invisible, but Icepaw, with her sleek white pelt and bright blue eyes, certainly wasn't. Perhaps that was why Firestar had made Whitewing her mentor. The white she-cat knew what it was like to stand out like snow in greenleaf. She'd be able to teach Icepaw a few special stalking techniques. And she clearly needed to learn. As he watched Icepaw darting clumsily about, Lionpaw stifled a purr, remembering how excited he had been when he had started his training.

Whitewing padded across the clearing, one eye on her apprentice. "Can we go now?"

Lionpaw noticed her tail-tip twitching. Icepaw was Whitewing's first apprentice. Was she worried how to manage such a bundle of energy? Or did she think their matching snow-colored pelts would scare away all the prey as soon as they set foot under the trees?

"Where do you want to start?" Ashfur asked.

Whitewing eyed Icepaw thoughtfully as the little white cat hurled herself awkwardly at a pile of leaves, sending them scattering in all directions. "Do you think Icepaw would do better by the Ancient Oak or the Old Thunderpath?"

Lionpaw's belly rumbled. He gazed at the fresh-kill pile; a plump mouse was lying on top. But the Clan had to be fed before he could eat. It was the first rule apprentices had to learn, and the hardest. "There's usually more prey around the Oak," he suggested.

Ignoring Lionpaw, Ashfur dipped his head to Whitewing. "It's your decision."

Lionpaw felt a prickle of annoyance. Why bother waking him up at all? They clearly weren't interested in his opinion. And neither of them had asked about his journey to the mountains. He stared angrily around the camp. No cat seemed the slightest bit interested in his return. Mousefur was sunning herself outside the elders' nest. Ferncloud and Sorreltail were sharing a pigeon beneath Highledge, their hunting clearly finished for the day. Leafpool was disappearing into the nursery, holding leaves between her jaws. Weren't any of them curious about the mountains or his adventure?

"Hey, Lionpaw!" Icepaw called to him. "Am I doing this right?" She was creeping forward in a hunting crouch, her tail lashing.

"Yeah," Lionpaw mewed absently. *Doesn't anyone care about me?*

"You need to keep your tail still, Icepaw," Ashfur advised.

Lionpaw looked at his mentor in surprise. *I thought you weren't interested in apprentices.*

Ashfur met his gaze, eyes narrowed, then turned pointedly back to Icepaw. "If you stir up the leaves, the prey will know you're coming." Clearly he thought that Lionpaw should have pointed out Icepaw's mistake.

Lionpaw's fur bristled. Why did Ashfur expect him to mentor another cat's apprentice? That was Whitewing's duty. Then, with a flash of remorse, he remembered how grateful he'd been when Stormfur or Graystripe had gently pointed out his mistakes.

He padded over to the younger cat. "I'll show you what he means." He crouched beside her. "Keep your back down like this. The flatter you are, the less visible you'll be."

"Like this?" Icepaw squashed herself against the ground.

"Exactly."

Icepaw blinked up at him, her eyes like pools of sky. "Thanks, Lionpaw. I'm very nervous about hunting, actually."

Lionpaw brushed the tip of his tail over her back. "You'll be fine," he promised. "Just copy our mentors, and don't expect to make a catch on your first try. It took me ages to get it right," he added. Icepaw nodded, looking very earnest, and Lionpaw gave her ear a lick. Was this how it felt being a mentor? He liked the idea of teaching a young cat everything he knew about hunting and fighting, and watching them grow from a tumbling kit to a strong, quick-pawed warrior.

But what if the prophecy took him on a path away from being a normal warrior, mentoring apprentices and carrying out regular Clan duties? Looking down at Icepaw's glowing eyes, Lionpaw felt as if he were being asked to give up an entire way of life—and one that suited him very well.

"Can we hunt here?" Icepaw asked again. She'd wanted to hunt in every small clearing they'd passed on their way to the Ancient Oak. Now the great tree towered above them, the ground beneath littered with leaves and acorn cups. At the edge of the glade, ferns clustered together in pools of light filtering through the branches.

Whitewing glanced at Ashfur. "Should we keep going to the lake?" she asked. "There might be prey near the shore."

Ashfur gazed back at her, but didn't reply.

Why isn't he helping her? Lionpaw tried to catch his mentor's eye.

Whitewing scanned the clearing. "Here is fine," she

decided. "Perhaps that clump of ferns?"

Lionpaw noticed her tail twitching again. If Ashfur wasn't going to help her, perhaps he could. "There's a bramble—" His suggestion was silenced by Ashfur's tail flicking across his mouth. The warrior nodded at Whitewing. "Trust your instinct."

"Ferns." Whitewing led her apprentice toward a leafy thicket.

Ashfur murmured into Lionpaw's ear, "I know you're trying to help, but Whitewing needs to build her confidence on her own." They watched as Whitewing nudged Icepaw into a crouch and adjusted her stance with a touch of her muzzle. "She's doing fine."

The ferns quivered. The pale green stems trembled from the roots rather than the tips; it couldn't be the wind stirring them. Icepaw crouched and began to waggle her hindquarters, kneading the ground with her paws. Gently, Whitewing laid her tail over the apprentice's back until Icepaw grew still. Leaning forward, she whispered into Icepaw's ear, then sat back. It was up to Icepaw now.

Lionpaw watched as Icepaw darted forward and flung herself into the ferns.

A squeal from behind the fronds was quickly silenced, and Icepaw bounced out, a small vole dangling from her teeth. Her eyes shone with happiness.

Ashfur padded forward. "Well done!"

Whitewing fluffed out her chest proudly. "That was great, Icepaw!"

"Nice kill," Ashfur added.

So much excitement over a tiny vole! It was probably too young to run away even if it wanted to. Lionpaw's thoughts flicked back to the battle in the mountains. He was glad Icepaw had made her first kill so quickly, but what would they have said if they'd seen him fighting the mountain cats? Catching a bite of prey didn't compare to defeating a whole Clan single-pawed.

"Thrush!"

Hearing Ashfur's whispered alert, Lionpaw glanced over his shoulder, following his mentor's gaze. A fat thrush was pecking among the leaves beyond the wide trunk of the oak. Silent as a snake, Lionpaw slithered around until he was behind it. Crouching onto his belly, he began to steal toward the thrush, tail lifted slightly so it didn't stir the leaves. The thrush was searching for insects, unaware of the danger. Lionpaw felt a glimmer of satisfaction. Such a dumb bird deserved to be fresh-kill. He paused, judged the distance, then jumped. His massive leap cleared the tree roots and carried him three foxtails across the forest floor. The thrush spread its wings in panic, struggling to take flight, but it was too late. Lionpaw landed with deadly precision, flattening the bird with its wings outstretched, and killed it with a sharp nip to the spine.

"That was fantastic!" Icepaw was staring at him from the other side of the tree, her eyes wide with awe.

Whitewing's ears were pressed back in surprise.

Lionpaw felt something tickling his nose. One of the thrush's soft feathers had stuck to his muzzle. He swiped it away, feeling self-conscious.

Ashfur nodded. "Impressive."

"That was a huge leap!" Whitewing meowed. "You could have easily missed."

No, I couldn't. Lionpaw bit back the thought. Considering the surprise still lingering in his Clanmates' eyes, he decided it might be better to let them think it had been a lucky strike. Perhaps Jaypaw was right: They might not be too happy to know the truth behind his powerful kill.

As they headed back to camp, Lionpaw's nostrils filled with the mouthwatering aroma of the thrush. It bounced against his chest, its wings dredging leaves. Icepaw padded beside him, her small catch tripping her as she tried to match his pace.

"I wish my legs weren't so short," she complained, her words muffled by vole fur.

"They'll grow," Lionpaw promised.

Whitewing and Ashfur walked ahead, each carrying a catch of their own. This late in greenleaf, all prey was welcome. The Clan needed to gorge itself if it was to make it through leaf-bare. At least, that was what the older cats kept saying. Lionpaw couldn't remember leaf-bare, other than something beyond the nursery walls—a menace that worried the older cats and made the branches of the den rattle.

"That was such a great catch," Icepaw mewed.

Lionpaw grunted his thanks. He didn't want to swallow a feather and spend the rest of the day coughing.

"Why did you jump so soon?" Icepaw persisted. "Did you

think it might hear you if you'd gone closer?"

"I just thought I'd try." Lionpaw was sure he could have padded right up to the thrush if he'd wanted. But why waste time tiptoeing about?

"You're such a great hunter," Icepaw went on out of the corner of her mouth. "I thought Hollypaw was good, but you're amazing. Where did you learn to jump like that? Do you do extra practice to get so strong? Do you think I ought to be doing more training?"

"I'm sure Whitewing will give you all the training you need."

"I just hope she trains me as well as Ashfur trained you."

Lionpaw watched his mentor disappear behind a bramble spilling over the track ahead. Ashfur had taught him well. He had never wished for any other teacher. But Ashfur had not been his only mentor. Tigerstar had trained him, too. And he had been born with powers Icepaw could never dream of, even if she trained day and night every moon of her life.

As the path dipped down toward the hollow and home, Lionpaw felt a pang of loneliness. It was almost as though he belonged to a Clan of his own, distanced by the prophecy from the familiar faces waiting in camp to see what they'd brought back from their hunt.

Icepaw darted ahead of him and followed Whitewing and Ashfur through the barrier of thorns that sealed the camp from the forest. Lionpaw padded after, emerging into the clearing in time to see Icepaw drop her vole onto the fresh-kill pile and turn toward her denmates.

Cinderpaw, Honeypaw, and Poppypaw were sunning themselves outside the apprentices' den. Icepaw trotted over to them.

"Your first catch?" Honeypaw called.

Icepaw lifted her chin. "I got it first try!"

Lionpaw felt a pang of envy. He would never again feel so carefree, never again be thrilled by such a small success.

"Is Foxpaw back yet?" Icepaw asked, clearly eager to show off her catch to her brother.

"Squirrelflight took him on border patrol," Cinderpaw informed her. "They should be back soon."

As Lionpaw padded to the fresh-kill pile and dropped his catch, a pelt brushed his. He turned to see his sister.

"Nice catch." Hollypaw's mew was flat, as though she had something else on her mind. She was staring at the apprentices outside their den: Cinderpaw and Poppypaw were rolling a ball of moss to each other while Honeypaw leaped to try to catch it.

"Aren't you going to join in?" Lionpaw mewed.

Hollypaw blinked. "I don't feel like it."

That wasn't like Hollypaw. Especially if Cinderpaw was playing. "Something wrong?" Lionpaw asked.

"I'm just not in the mood."

Lionpaw searched her green gaze. Was Hollypaw feeling isolated, too? "It feels odd, doesn't it?" he ventured.

Hollypaw looked at him. "What?"

"Being different."

"We're not different on the outside."

"You know what I mean." Lionpaw felt a surge of impatience. He needed to talk to someone. All day he'd been clutching their secret like prey struggling to escape. Hollypaw didn't have to make it so hard. "Knowing something as huge as we do and not being able to tell anyone."

The fur on Hollypaw's shoulders bristled with alarm. "You're not thinking of telling, are you?"

"No, I—"

Hollypaw cut him off. "No cat must know! Not when we don't know exactly what the prophecy means." She lowered her voice, her gaze darting around the clearing. "We need to figure out what we're meant to do with our powers."

Lionpaw flexed his claws. "I wasn't planning on telling!" he snapped. Why did she have to be so bossy? He wasn't a mouse-brain! And why did she have to try to figure everything out all the time? The prophecy was simple: They were going to be more powerful than any cat. They just had to be ready to use their powers when they were needed. He turned and padded to the halfrock.

With the sun sliding toward the treetops, the Clan was beginning to take food from the fresh-kill pile. Cinderpaw snatched up Lionpaw's thrush and carried it to the nursery, where Millie, Daisy, and her kits would be growing hungry.

Poppypaw picked up a mouse and placed it outside the elders' den. "Fresh-kill!" she called.

Longtail emerged from the tangle of honeysuckle, nose twitching, and stood at the entrance, while Mousefur followed him stiffly out. The old she-cat grew more frail with each passing moon. Longtail waited until she had settled down next to the mouse, then sat beside her.

"You don't have to watch over me like I'm a helpless kit!" Mousefur snapped at him.

Longtail's whiskers twitched with amusement. "It's a shame your tongue's not as worn-out as the rest of you," he purred.

Mousefur swiped at him with her tail, catching him behind the ear. "Do you want some of this?" She nosed the mouse toward him.

"You can have this if you want!" Icepaw was trotting from the fresh-kill pile with her little vole swinging from her jaws. She dropped it at Longtail's paws. "I caught it myself!"

"Your first catch?" Mousefur's eyes glowed.

Longtail bent to sniff the small creature. "It smells delicious."

The brambles at the entrance to the medicine cat den twitched as Jaypaw slid out, a ball of moss held gingerly between his teeth. He padded over to Mousefur and Longtail and placed the moss on the ground. Turning his blind blue eyes on Icepaw, he mewed, "I've heard you've been busy today. You should get something to eat."

"I am pretty hungry," Icepaw admitted.

"Thanks for the vole!" Longtail called after the apprentice as she padded back to the fresh-kill pile.

Icepaw mewed happily over her shoulder, "Anytime!"

"Do you mind if I check for ticks while you eat?" Jaypaw asked Mousefur.

"If you must," Mousefur grumbled. "Though I don't know

why you had to wait until I was eating to bring that foul stuff over." She nodded at the moss. Lionpaw guessed that it was soaked in mouse bile.

"I thought you might be sleeping earlier, and I didn't want to wake you." Patiently, Jaypaw began to nuzzle through Mousefur's pelt. He paused to tear some moss from the ball and pressed it into the fur near the base of her tail.

Lionpaw watched his brother. He seemed completely different from the resentful young cat who had never wanted to be a medicine cat's apprentice. *And yet he's more powerful than any of his Clanmates.* Lionpaw climbed onto the halfrock and lay down, pressing his belly against the sun-warmed stone. *Perhaps knowing he's so powerful makes boring tasks easier to bear.* He wondered how many moons it had been since Jaypaw had crept into Firestar's dream and overheard the stranger predicting the birth of three kits with the power of the stars in their paws. Would the frustration gnawing in his own belly ease with time, once he'd gotten used to the prophecy, as Jaypaw had done?

He glanced up at Highledge as Firestar picked his way down the tumble of rocks, Sandstorm following. The ThunderClan leader had never given any clue that he knew of the prophecy. He had only ever treated Lionpaw, Hollypaw, and Jaypaw as if they were three ordinary apprentices. Lionpaw watched as Firestar picked a mouse from the pile and passed it to Sandstorm before taking a sparrow for himself. *What does he really feel?* Lionpaw suddenly wished he had Jaypaw's powers to see into Firestar's mind. Was he proud to have them as his kin? Pleased that his Clan would be safe forever, guarded by such powerful cats? Or was he anxious, as Jaypaw feared, about having cats more powerful than himself in the Clan?

The thorn barrier shivered as Squirrelflight and Brambleclaw padded through, followed by Foxpaw and Berrynose.

"The borders are quiet," Brambleclaw called to his leader. "But the sunset patrol should check the WindClan border closely. By the smell of it, they've been hunting in the woods on their side."

Firestar was settling down beneath Highledge, Sandstorm at his side. "It looks like they've developed a taste for squirrel," he remarked.

Cinderpaw, sharing a pigeon with Honeypaw, looked up eagerly. "Can I go out on sunset patrol?" Now that her injured leg was recovered enough to return to apprentice duties, she seemed keen to take on any task, as though making up for lost time.

"Yes." Brambleclaw nodded. "I was going to ask Graystripe to lead it."

"Did someone mention Graystripe?" Millie padded from the nursery, blinking sleep from her eyes.

Graystripe was repairing a tear in the nursery wall where winds had unraveled the carefully threaded brambles. "Are you okay?" He looked closely at Millie. She was fat with her kits, which were expected any day now.

"Fine." Millie picked up two mice from the fresh-kill pile. "I'd just rather share a meal outside with you." She carried the meal to where Firestar and Sandstorm lay. Graystripe tucked in a final tendril with his paws and hurried to join her.

A thrush thudded onto the ground beside the halfrock, surprising Lionpaw. Hollypaw stood over it, staring at him.

"I thought you might want to share," she mewed. Was this her way of apologizing? Lionpaw doubted it. He suspected that his sister didn't realize how bossy she could be. But he was grateful anyway. However alone he felt, knowing about the prophecy, he had to remember that Hollypaw and Jaypaw shared it too. As long as he had his littermates, he would never truly be alone.

"Thanks," he purred, settling down to eat.

Birchfall and Whitewing were sharing prey with Brackenfur, while Thornclaw and Spiderleg stretched out nearby, their meals already finished. This was the first time since the journey to the mountains that the Clan had eaten together, and Lionpaw began to feel more at ease. Nothing had really changed, he told himself hopefully.

"So how was the Tribe?" Firestar asked Brambleclaw.

The ThunderClan deputy swallowed a mouthful of fresh-kill. "They've a hard leaf-bare ahead of them," he meowed. "But I think they're going to be okay." Lionpaw narrowed his eyes. Was his father as confident as he sounded?

"Do you think they'll be able to defend the borders you made?" Thornclaw asked.

Squirrelflight shrugged. "We trained them as well as we could."

"Which will be very well, if I know you," Graystripe chipped in.

"They stand more of a chance now than they did when we

first got there," Brambleclaw meowed. "It was hard for them to get used to the idea of marking such distinct borders around a portion of where they hunted before, but I hope they understand how important it is for them to fight for what they have."

"And we certainly taught the invaders that they can't help themselves to anything they want," Squirrelflight added.

"Were many cats injured in the battle?" Sandstorm asked.

"Nothing serious," Brambleclaw informed her. "But it was a hard fight."

Which you would never have won without me. Lionpaw waited for his father to tell the Clan how well he had done.

"All the apprentices fought like true warriors." Brambleclaw glanced at Lionpaw. "They were a credit to our Clan."

Lionpaw's pads pricked with his frustration. "Isn't he going to mention how *I* fought?" he hissed under his breath.

"Shh!" Hollypaw warned him. "It's best if they don't know. We mustn't draw attention to ourselves."

Lionpaw bit angrily into the thrush. *What's the point of being so powerful if no cat ever knows?* He found himself half wishing for another battle this moon, so he could show his Clanmates just what sort of warrior he was going to be. *The other Clans had better watch out then,* he thought darkly.

Paws weary, muscles still aching from the journey, Lionpaw crept into his nest. Just one long sleep and he'd feel more like his old self. He spiraled down into the clean, dry moss and closed his eyes.

"You're not going straight to sleep, are you?" Poppypaw

called across the den.

"Don't you want to hear what Sandstorm said to me while we were training?" Honeypaw prompted.

"I'm tired," Lionpaw murmured. He wasn't in the mood to share Clan gossip with his denmates.

"Suit yourself," Poppypaw mewed.

Suddenly two small paws landed on his back, digging into his ribs.

"Sorry!" Foxpaw backed away as Lionpaw's head shot up.

Lionpaw glared at the young apprentice. "Watch out!"

"I was just showing Icepaw how I was going to catch a fox and earn my warrior name," Foxpaw mewed. "I want to be called Foxcatcher!"

"Well, you've proved you can catch a sleeping cat!" Honeypaw teased.

Icepaw jumped to her brother's defense. "He'll catch a real fox one day!"

"Yeah, right." Poppypaw tossed a wad of moss at the white apprentice.

Foxpaw leaped and caught the moss before it reached his sister, batting it back toward Poppypaw. "I will catch one; you just wait!"

"You couldn't catch greencough!" Poppypaw taunted him.

"Yes, I could!" Foxpaw argued.

The other apprentices purred with amusement.

"I mean I could catch anything I want," Foxpaw backtracked quickly. "If only Squirrelflight would stop fussing over me all the time."

"She might stop fussing if you stopped wandering off," Honeypaw pointed out. "We had to wait for ages while she went to look for you today. The squirrel I'd been tracking was in ShadowClan territory by the time she brought you back!"

"I was exploring!" Foxpaw protested.

"Well, come explore this." Cinderpaw had squeezed into the den. Lionpaw could smell honey, but he stayed where he was while the other apprentices scrambled from their nests to see what Cinderpaw had brought.

"Where'd you find it?" Icepaw gasped.

"Cloudtail found a hive in a hollow trunk while we were patrolling near the abandoned Twolegplace," Cinderpaw explained. "He managed to get his paw in and grab a chunk of the honeycomb."

"Did he get stung?" Foxpaw mewed.

"Only once."

"I haven't had honey for moons." Poppypaw sighed.

"Cloudtail gave most of it to Leafpool for her stores, but he said I could have this bit," Cinderpaw mewed.

"Can I have a lick?" Icepaw begged.

"Go on then, but not too much," Cinderpaw offered. "It's for everyone to share."

Icepaw closed her eyes as she swallowed, then blinked them open, surprised. "It doesn't taste of anything!"

Poppypaw purred. "Every cat knows that, mouse-brain." She licked at the honeycomb and sighed. "I like the way it soothes my throat and feels all warm in my belly. It reminds me of milk."

Lionpaw buried his nose under his paws, trying to block out the purrs of contentment as his denmates dug into the precious honeycomb. How easily pleased they were. One day all the honey in the forest would be his. He wasn't like them— pleased by any small treat. The pang of isolation returned, stronger than ever.

A warm body brushed against him. Hollypaw had crept into the den and was settling down beside him.

"Not joining in with the honey feast?" Lionpaw whispered.

"Let *them* enjoy it," she whispered back.

Suddenly feeling less alone, Lionpaw closed his eyes and slipped into sleep.

Dreaming, Lionpaw felt the forest floor cold beneath his paws, prickly with pine needles. A thin mist cloaked the ground and swirled around the lines of straight, bare trunks that stretched away into darkness.

"It's about time you came back to us," Tigerstar's low growl echoed from the shadows. Lionpaw saw the outline of massive shoulders as the warrior padded out from the trees.

Hawkfrost followed at his heels. "You need all the training we can give you."

Lionpaw bristled. "But didn't you see me fight in the mountains?" How much more training did he need? He was already a better fighter than any of his Clanmates. He had proved it!

"We're not concerned with past battles," Tigerstar meowed briskly. "Only the battles to come."

Lionpaw narrowed his eyes. That sounded like an excuse. *They couldn't see me in the mountains!* Even Tigerstar's powers had their limits.

"Let's see if you can use your brains as well as your strength." Tigerstar padded behind Lionpaw and nudged him toward Hawkfrost. "Try attacking Hawkfrost from his weaker side."

"But don't you want to hear about the mountain cats?"

Tigerstar lashed his tail. "They're no concern of mine."

He's not interested! Lionpaw stared at his ghostly mentor. Didn't he think Lionpaw could have learned something from going on the long journey and battling against different cats? Did Tigerstar really believe he knew everything about fighting? Well, he certainly didn't know everything about Lionpaw. Maybe it was about time he did.

"What are you waiting for?" Tigerstar snapped. "Attack Hawkfrost!"

Anger surged in Lionpaw's belly. He leaped for Hawkfrost and, unsheathing his claws, raked the striped warrior's flank so fiercely he felt the skin burst and blood spatter his paw.

Yowling in fury, Hawkfrost jumped away from him, hackles raised.

Lionpaw swung around to face Tigerstar. "Will you listen to me now? I've got something important to tell you. There's a prophecy! About me! That's why I can fight the way I can."

Tigerstar's eyes flashed. "What do you mean, a prophecy?"

"An old cat told Firestar in a dream: 'There will be three, kin of your kin, who will hold the power of the stars in their paws.'" Lionpaw recited the words just as Jaypaw had told him.

"Don't you see? It must be about us, because Squirrelflight is Firestar's kin."

Tigerstar snorted in disgust. "Firestar!"

"But it's true!" Lionpaw insisted. "If you'd seen me fight in the mountains you'd know. I defeated every cat who faced me. I felt like I could've fought forever and still defeated them all!"

"Only because *I've* trained you," Tigerstar growled.

"It's more than that!" Lionpaw argued. "I've got the power of the stars in my paws!"

"And Firestar told you this, did he?" Tigerstar sneered.

"No." Lionpaw dug his claws into the cold earth. "Jaypaw walked in one of Firestar's dreams. He overheard it."

Tigerstar's eyes suddenly glittered with amusement. "I see," he mocked. "A cat has a dream and that means you're the most powerful creature who ever lived."

Why wasn't Tigerstar taking this seriously? Wasn't he proud to have kin who might eventually rule the forest? Wasn't that what he wanted? Lionpaw felt a growl rising in his throat. Perhaps Tigerstar wanted that only for himself. "Don't laugh at me."

Hawkfrost's whiskers twitched. "Look at the little warrior! Pretending he's Firestar. All big and brave."

"How do you explain the battle in the mountains, then?" Lionpaw demanded. "I wasn't even hurt!"

"You beat a bunch of half-starved, untrained rogues," Hawkfrost taunted him. "Wow. That's a real sign of a great warrior!"

Lionpaw blinked. The ground suddenly felt colder under his paws. What if they were right? The mountain cats hadn't exactly been a Clan of highly skilled warriors. The Tribe could have beaten them with any of the Clan cats' help; they didn't need the most powerful cat ever to win the battle. What if the prophecy *was* just a dream?

"Not so sure now, are you?" Tigerstar flicked his tail. "I know it must be nice to believe you're the greatest warrior that ever lived, but would Firestar really have sent three such important cats to the mountains, where they might have been killed?"

Lionpaw's belly fluttered with doubt. Firestar had never said anything about the prophecy. If he really believed they were special he wouldn't have risked their lives. He would have kept them safe in camp, where they could take care of their Clan.

Tigerstar leaned forward, his breath stirring Lionpaw's whiskers. "There's only one path to power," he hissed. "*Training*. Practice your battle skills, practice hard, and one day you may well be the most powerful cat in the forest." He drew back, his voice hardening. "Now, repeat the battle move! But this time keep your claws sheathed. Unless *I* say otherwise!"

CHAPTER 4

Jaypaw pulled the sticky parcel of honeycomb onto the wide, flat leaf he had laid on the floor of the den. Already wrapped in dock leaves, the comb was still oozing honey. Fearing it would seep onto the other herbs stored in the rock cleft at the side of the den, Leafpool had found a wild rhubarb leaf and left Jaypaw to rewrap the honeycomb while she was out collecting cat-mint.

He folded over the sides of the leaf, hoping the gooey honey would hold them in place while he tied strips of bark around the wrap.

A squeal made him freeze. A kit was in pain. Pricking his ears, he recognized Toadkit's wailing mew. He turned and dashed toward the den entrance just as Daisy raced in. He smelled fear on her pelt and felt the lash of a flailing paw as she hurried past him. She must be carrying Toadkit by the scruff.

"Put him by the pool," he ordered.

"He was chasing a bee and jumped straight into the nettle patch," Daisy panted after setting down Toadkit.

"Dumb bee!" Toadkit yowled.

Jaypaw felt a wave of relief. *Nettle stings!* From the fuss he was making Jaypaw thought Toadkit had been savaged by a fox.

"Firestar should get those nettles pulled up," Daisy complained. "I knew they'd be trouble one day."

"Nettles aren't deadly." Jaypaw began sniffing Toadkit. A small paw swiped him across the muzzle. The young kit was twisting and fidgeting, trying to lick at his stings at the same time as he rubbed his nose with his paw. "Sit still!"

"But it hurts!" Toadkit complained.

His kit-soft pelt would have been no defense against the nettles' stinging barbs, and Jaypaw could feel heat pulsing from Toadkit's nose and ears, where the exposed skin had already swollen.

"I'll fetch some dock leaves," Jaypaw told him.

Daisy was anxiously circling her kit, and, as he dashed toward the medicine store, Jaypaw tripped over her tail. He stumbled to a clumsy halt at the store entrance and reached into the crack in the rock. Grabbing a pawful of dock leaves from where he knew they were stored beside the mallow, he gave them a quick sniff to make sure he had the right herb before chewing them into a pulp. The dock juice would work quickly on Toadkit's injuries as long as it got a chance to sink into his fur.

Still chewing, he returned to the wriggling kit and spat the ointment onto his paw, ready to rub it onto the kit's ears.

Instinctively, Toadkit shied away. "Don't touch me!" He swiped at the pulp, sending it flying into the pool. Jaypaw heard it drop into the water with a plop. Seething with frustration, he turned back to the pile of dock leaves. "The quicker I treat it, the sooner it'll stop hurting." He collided with Daisy, still pacing around her kit. *For StarClan's sake!* "Go check on Rosekit!" he snapped. "You don't want her ending up in the nettles too. I'll take care of Toadkit." He flicked his tail. "*If* he can sit still!"

"Are you sure he'll be okay?" Daisy fretted.

Jaypaw took a deep breath. *Staying calm is good for you and better for the patient.* Leafpool's words rang in his ears. "No cat has died of nettle stings yet," he mewed through gritted teeth.

"Try to sit still, dear," Daisy begged Toadkit as she padded out of the den. "I'll be back to check on you as soon as I know Rosekit's okay."

"Don't hurry!" Jaypaw muttered under his breath. He crouched to chew another mouthful of dock, then hurried back to Toadkit and began to lick the pulp onto his ears. Toadkit tried to duck away, but Jaypaw pressed his shoulders to the ground with his forepaws.

"Hold still," he mumbled between licks. Toadkit yowled, but Jaypaw continued until they were coated with bitter juice. "I know it hurts," he mewed, releasing the kit. "But you're not in any danger. Stay there while I fetch some more for your nose."

As Jaypaw turned away, he sensed anger flash in Toadkit's mind. Fur brushed the medicine cat den floor. Toadkit was lunging for his tail!

Jaypaw spun around quickly. "Don't you dare!"

Toadkit yelped in alarm as Jaypaw faced him, so close their whiskers were touching.

"H-how did you know what I was doing?" Toadkit squeaked.

Jaypaw narrowed his eyes. "I'm not as blind as you think."

Toadkit backed away. "I'm sorry."

"Now are you going to sit still?" Jaypaw demanded.

"Yes," Toadkit murmured.

Feeling a pang of guilt for frightening the kit, Jaypaw fetched another mouthful of pulp. This time he dropped it in front of Toadkit. "Spread this on your pads, then rub it into your nose and over your mouth," he ordered.

Jerkily, Toadkit smeared the pulp onto his stings. Jaypaw sensed his pain ease. The dock juice was working. Relieved, he fetched more pulp and helped Toadkit to rub it over his pelt until, between them, they had coated every sting. *I'll give Daisy a poppy seed when she gets back. She can give it to Toadkit before bedtime so he'll sleep through the itching.*

Brambles rustled. Jaypaw scented the air. Leafpool had returned, and she was carrying catmint.

"Daisy told me you've been stung." Leafpool dropped her bundle and padded over to Toadkit.

Jaypaw heard her sniffing as she checked him over. "Good job, Jaypaw," she pronounced. "Just the right amount of dock."

Jaypaw wondered whether to tell her what a difficult patient Toadkit had been.

"You should give him a small poppy seed," Leafpool advised,

"just to make sure the stings don't keep him awake tonight. They'll be sore and itchy for a while."

Thanks for the advice! Jaypaw bit back his reply. He was going to have to get used to listening to lessons he didn't need; unlike Hollypaw and Lionpaw, he would be treated as an apprentice for many moons yet. As a medicine cat, he would still be expected to learn from his mentor and follow her orders even after he was given his Clan name. He might as well get used to it.

"Thanks, Jaypaw." Toadkit's grateful mew took him by surprise. "Sorry I was such a mouse-brain."

Jaypaw felt a flood of sympathy for the young kit. "You were scared and hurt."

"I'm fine now, thanks to you." Toadkit began to head toward the entrance.

"Aren't you going to wait for Daisy to fetch you?" Jaypaw called.

Toadkit paused. "I *think* I can find my way back to the nursery."

Cheeky furball! Jaypaw felt a flicker of pride. Toadkit had been hard work, but Jaypaw had managed to earn his respect.

As the brambles swished shut behind the young kit, Jaypaw began clearing up the unused pulp. "I'll take the poppy seed over to the nursery before bedtime," he promised Leafpool before she could remind him.

But Leafpool seemed busy with her own thoughts. Jaypaw paused from his clearing up. *She's worried.* Her mind, though closed to him, seemed to prickle with uneasy energy, like lightning on the horizon. As she padded to where Jaypaw had left the half-wrapped packet of honey, her steps were heavy, as though weariness weighted her paws. *She must've worked twice as hard while I was away.* He quickly scraped up the last of the pulp and, flicking it into the corner of the den, hurried to help his mentor.

"Sorry I didn't have time to finish this." He pressed his paws down on the honey parcel, now well bundled in rhubarb leaf, and held it fast while Leafpool wrapped the bark strips around it.

She tucked the last one in place. "You had to look after Toadkit." Even her mew sounded tired. Why hadn't he noticed before?

"I'll check the stores," he meowed, licking the last of the dock juice from his paws. "You were saying that we need to find out what we've got before leaf-fall arrives, in case we need to stock up." He padded to the rock cleft and squeezed inside before Leafpool could offer to help.

They had only recently discovered this useful gap in the rock wall of the medicine cave. Leafpool had been clearing away the ivy that had gradually been creeping along the cave wall, threatening to dip its greedy roots into the precious supply of rainwater that pooled at the side of the den. The crack was narrow, wide enough for only a small cat to squeeze through, but inside it opened into a space large enough for a nest. Inside it now, Jaypaw had enough room to turn around, and he began sniffing the different piles of herbs, berries, and roots stacked along the wall.

"Pass them out," Leafpool called. "We can see what we've got."

One pile at a time, Jaypaw pushed them through the cleft. By the time he emerged, Leafpool had them ordered into neat rows. His sensitive nose placed each scent until he had built a picture in his mind of one small heap piled beside the next: comfrey, mallow, thyme, catmint, poppy seeds gathered in an expertly folded bark shell, and countless more.

"Not much mallow," Leafpool commented. "And I still want to get more catmint." Leaves rustled beneath her paw. "I brought back as much as I could carry today, but there's plenty more, and we should gather it while it's still in full leaf and dry it to be ready for leaf-bare."

Drying the leaves in the sun was the best way of making sure they didn't rot away in storage.

Jaypaw felt a bundle of thyme, tickly beneath his paw. It smelled stale. "How old is this?"

Leafpool bent toward him to sniff it. "Must have been gathered last greenleaf," she observed. "It'll have lost a lot of strength. We should get fresh."

"Do we have any deathberries?" Jaypaw had heard Littlecloud mention the fatal berry last time they were at the Moonpool. It was used only to save the sickest cats from a lingering death. A bushful of them grew on ShadowClan land, and Littlecloud had offered to share them. Leafpool had refused, and Jaypaw sensed a prickle of unease from her now.

"I don't use deathberries," she murmured. She began to pick through a pile of coltsfoot. "ShadowClan medicine cats keep them," she added. "They teach their apprentices how to use them." Her voice was thick, as though a dark memory filled her mind. "But I won't teach you."

Why not? Jaypaw was intrigued by the idea of having the power of life and death in his paws.

Leafpool clearly wanted nothing to do with it. "We must do all we can to help our Clanmates, but it's up to StarClan to choose the moment of death." She pushed a pile of leaves toward Jaypaw. Comfrey, by the smell of it. "Sort through these and throw out any that are musty or starting to lose their scent."

Jaypaw began to turn over each leaf, sniffing them closely and throwing to one side any that were no longer fresh or fragrant enough. Leafpool worked beside him, tearing coltsfoot and rolling it into bundles.

"I haven't had a chance to ask you since you got back," Leafpool began. "How was the journey?"

"It was okay." Jaypaw remembered the terrifying jump over the gap in the steep mountain path, not knowing where he would land, or how far was the drop below him. He shivered.

"What did you think of the Tribe?" Leafpool had met them on the Great Journey.

"They were odd." Jaypaw tried to fix on what he had found strangest about the mountain cats. "The mountains are tough. I thought the cats would be too, but they had no idea how to fight off the invaders." *They're like a Clan in hiding from something.* Jaypaw had pitied the Tribe, huddled in their cave behind their waterfall, always glancing nervously over their shoulders for danger. Even their ancestors had seemed fearful. "I met the Tribe of Endless Hunting," he ventured.

Leafpool kept on with her work. But the coltsfoot in her paws grew more fragrant, as though her pads were twitching with unease. "What were they like?" she mewed.

"They're a bit like StarClan." *They had known I would come. They knew about the prophecy.* "But they didn't try to help the Tribe to beat the invaders."

"Sometimes even our ancestors are powerless to help us." Leafpool sighed.

"But it was like they were lost." Jaypaw couldn't shake the idea that the Tribe hadn't always lived in the mountains; that they had lived far away from the bitter winds and craggy peaks, among cats who were the first to know about the prophecy of three.

Leafpool had paused in her task, and he could sense her watching him, curiosity flashing from her pelt.

"I was surprised Stoneteller was leader and medicine cat," he mewed before she could ask any more questions about the Tribe of Endless Hunting.

"It's a lot of responsibility for one cat," Leafpool agreed. She began rolling the coltsfoot again. "Great knowledge can be lonely."

Jaypaw's heart lurched. *Does she mean the prophecy? Does she know? She can't! She would have said something.* His heart began to slow as he reassured himself that Leafpool would never be able to ignore a secret like that. Nevertheless, he tried to search her thoughts for some clue. The usual fog barred his way. He could sense only wistfulness engulfing her like a cloud. She might not know about the prophecy, but *something* was troubling her.

Why did she often seem so unhappy? He wanted to cheer her up. "Can I get you some fresh-kill?" he offered.

"No." Leafpool gave herself a small shake, as though banishing her thoughts. "But you can start putting the comfrey back in storage."

As Jaypaw backed in through the cleft with a wad of comfrey between his jaws, a voice sounded at the entrance. "Leafpool?"

Jaypaw recognized Cloudtail.

"You're here." The warrior sounded relieved to find Leafpool in her den.

Jaypaw stayed where he was. He could busy himself rolling and stacking the comfrey at the back of the cleft while Leafpool and Cloudtail talked.

"Are you hurt?" Leafpool asked.

"No." Cloudtail was pacing the cave. "I'm worried about Cinderpaw."

Jaypaw pricked his ears. So far, only he and Leafpool knew that Cinderpaw had lived before as ThunderClan's medicine cat, Cinderpelt; that she had been given a second chance to live her life as she had always dreamed—as a warrior of ThunderClan. Cinderpaw herself didn't realize. But she sometimes showed flashes of knowledge that only memory could have taught her, and she talked about the old forest as though she had seen it with her own eyes. Was Cloudtail beginning to suspect that there was something unusual about his apprentice?

"Is she okay?" Leafpool's breathing had quickened with his own.

Jaypaw leaned closer to the opening.

"Do you think she's ready for her final assessment?" Cloudtail asked in a rush. "Honeypaw and Poppypaw are, but I don't want to put Cinderpaw through the test unless her leg is fully recovered."

Leafpool hesitated.

Why isn't she answering? Alarmed, Jaypaw groped for her thoughts. This time he was determined to make it through the fog. His breath caught in his throat. A memory lit Leafpool's mind, a memory so strong that it couldn't be hidden.

Walls of rock enclosed a snow-filled ravine. At once Jaypaw recognized the old forest camp he had visited in Cinderpaw's dream. Snow blanketed the dens and bushes, but a hollow had been cleared in the center, and here limped a gray she-cat, tail down, whiskers white with frost. She was so thin Jaypaw could see her bones like the branches of a leafless tree. A biting wind sent flurries of powdery snow scudding across the makeshift clearing. Jaypaw shivered with cold, caught in Leafpool's memory like fur in a thistle.

Leafpool was padding toward the gray she-cat, snowflakes dappling her coat. She looked young, with the rounded face of a kit and her fur fluffed up against the cold. "Cinderpelt, let me fetch you some fresh-kill," she begged. "A hunting patrol has just returned with a blackbird."

Hope sparked in Cinderpelt's dull eyes. "A blackbird?" she murmured. "We haven't seen prey like that for a while."

"Let me bring you some," Leafpool insisted.

Cinderpelt's expression changed abruptly. Now her eyes were like chips of ice. "Don't waste it on me!" she snapped. "The elders and queens must eat first. And the warriors and apprentices. They need their strength if they are to find more food."

"But you need strength, too," Leafpool argued. "You're looking after the cats with whitecough. What if it turns to greencough? They'll need you even more."

Cinderpelt dipped her head, then spoke more gently. "With this leg, I can't walk far. Especially when the cold makes it ache. I can get by on less food than the others." There was grief and longing in her voice. Jaypaw could hear the words Cinderpelt did not speak: *If I weren't crippled, I could be out there too, finding food for my Clanmates. . . .*

"She's fine." Leafpool's bright mew jolted him back into the present. His mentor was reassuring Cloudtail enthusiastically. "Nothing will stop her from becoming a warrior."

"I've noticed her leg is stiff in some of her battle moves." Cloudtail sounded uncertain. "I'm worried she's not telling me when it hurts."

"Then it probably doesn't hurt," Leafpool mewed.

"Perhaps you could watch her next training session?" Cloudtail ventured. "To make sure?"

"No need." Leafpool was brisk. "She's going to make a great warrior. You should be proud of her."

"I am," Cloudtail assured her. "But I don't want to push her. If she needs more time to recover I'm happy to wait."

"You're not pushing her, I'm sure," Leafpool insisted.

Jaypaw sensed Cloudtail's doubt melt away.

"I'm relieved to hear it," the warrior meowed.

"I'm glad I could help."

"Are you coming to eat?" Cloudtail asked. "A hunting party's just returned."

Jaypaw waited for the two cats to leave before he hopped out of the cleft in the rock. He could still feel Cinderpelt's grief like a wound in his mind. How had Leafpool pushed it away so easily? She must have felt it; the memory was hers. Yet she had sounded so bright when she had spoken to Cloudtail. *Unnaturally* bright, as though covering doubt. Jaypaw picked up a bundle of coltsfoot and headed back into the store. He hoped that Leafpool was right about Cinderpaw's injury.

CHAPTER 5

Leafpool was sharing a mouse with Cloudtail when Jaypaw nosed his way out of the medicine cat den and padded to the fresh-kill pile.

There was plenty of prey to choose from. Hunting patrols had already stacked it full, and it was hardly sunhigh. As he dragged a shrew from the bottom—so fresh it still felt warm— the image of Cinderpelt starving in the snowy camp flashed in his mind. Was Leafpool thinking of her old mentor as she ate her meal?

"Jaypaw!" Graystripe was bounding across the clearing toward him. The warrior skidded to a halt. "Eat up! We're going hunting."

"Me?" Jaypaw's heart soared.

"Sorreltail, Mousewhisker, and I will be hunting," Graystripe corrected him. He must have realized Jaypaw's disappointment. He whisked his tail along Jaypaw's flank. "You've got a more important job. Leafpool wants you to come with us to gather herbs."

Great. Jaypaw suddenly didn't feel hungry anymore. He shoved the shrew back under the pile. "I'll eat when I get back."

"We're going down to the lake," Graystripe went on.

"The lake?" Jaypaw felt a glimmer of interest. The notched stick was on the shore; it was his link to the ancient cats from the tunnels. Maybe to even greater mysteries, if he could just understand what all the claw marks meant. "I guess it'll be good to get out of camp and stretch my legs."

"That's more like it." Graystripe turned and headed toward the thorn tunnel. Jaypaw could hear Sorreltail and Mousewhisker pacing there impatiently. He hurried after Graystripe, and together the patrol headed out into the forest.

Mousewhisker—only recently made a warrior—was buzzing with excitement. "I hope I catch something good! Maybe a squirrel."

Graystripe purred. "Look out, squirrels!"

The woods were drowsy with heat, the undergrowth limp and fragrant as Jaypaw brushed past it, the air humming with bees. Mousewhisker's paws thrummed on the leaf-strewn floor as he dashed on ahead. Graystripe hurried after him.

"I wish it could be greenleaf forever." Sorreltail was padding beside Jaypaw, letting her pelt brush his.

"Yeah." He drew away from her. He knew this part of the forest well enough not to need guiding. Pushing hard against the leafy forest floor, he broke into a run and charged along the familiar track.

"Wait for me!" Sorreltail called in surprise.

They caught up to Graystripe and Mousewhisker at the top of the rise. The trees ended here as the forest turned to grassland, sloping down to the lake.

Mousewhisker was panting.

"He almost got his squirrel," Graystripe meowed proudly. "But it scooted up that tree."

Leaves rustled overhead.

"If that dumb blackbird hadn't called the alarm," Mouse-whisker grumbled.

"You'll get the next one," Graystripe told him encouragingly.

Sorreltail kneaded the ground. "I can't wait to hunt with my kits when they're warriors." Pride warmed her mew. "Honeypaw, Poppypaw, and Cinderpaw will be having their assessment any day now."

Jaypaw tensed. Was Cinderpaw's leg really strong enough?

"It'll be great having them in our den," Mousewhisker put in. "It might stop the old warriors from hogging the best nests and stealing all the softest moss."

Graystripe purred with amusement. "We *old* warriors need the soft moss for our poor ancient bones."

"I didn't mean *you* two!" Mousewhisker mewed, sounding embarrassed.

"I'm sure Thornclaw and Dustpelt will be pleased to hear that," Sorreltail teased.

"You won't tell them?" Mousewhisker squeaked in alarm.

"Of course not!" Sorreltail called over her shoulder as she darted down the slope. "Besides, we're not old. And once Millie's kits are born, Graystripe will feel younger than ever."

Jaypaw hurried after her, enjoying the breeze ruffling his fur. It smelled of the lake.

At the shore, Graystripe paused. "Is this a good place for herbs?"

Jaypaw nodded. "I can get mallow down by the water."

"Mousewhisker can help you," Sorreltail volunteered her denmate.

"But what about my—"

"Your squirrel can wait," Graystripe meowed.

"I guess so." Mousewhisker swished his tail. "Besides, if we're going down to the water, I might catch a fish!"

Unlikely, unless you've had a RiverClan mentor as well. Jaypaw picked his way down onto the shingle. It shifted satisfyingly beneath his paws.

Mousewhisker padded after him. "The lake's as smooth as a laurel leaf."

Jaypaw had guessed that already. He could hear the sound of lazy ripples lapping the shore.

"What does mallow look like?" Mousewhisker asked.

Jaypaw shrugged. "Never seen any."

Mousewhisker squeaked in dismay. "Sorry!"

"Forget it." It was just a dumb slip. "It *feels* soft and kind of furry. The leaves are big." Jaypaw sniffed the air. He remembered gathering mallow here before. Sure enough, a sweet smell filled his nose. Jaypaw flicked his tail toward the water's edge. "See that plant over there? That's mallow."

"Really?" Mousewhisker sounded impressed.

Jaypaw didn't bother to reply. His paws had started to tingle. The stick must be just along the shore. "Would you go and gather some leaves?" Jaypaw asked. "There's something farther up the shore I want to check."

"Okay." Mousewhisker began to hurry down to the water. "How much do you want?"

"As much as you can carry!" Jaypaw veered away, heading along the beach. He padded to the tree line, where twisting roots spilled over onto the pebbles, and sniffed around the gnarled bark until he scented the stick. It was still where he had wedged it, beneath the root of a rowan, safe from the pull of the lake.

He dragged it out, relief flooding his paws as they felt the smoothness of the exposed wood. This was definitely the right stick. Running his pads along its length he felt the familiar scratches. He knew so much more about what they meant than when he had first found it: They marked the successes and failures of countless cats—of Fallen Leaves and his Clanmates. And yet there was so much more to know; this stick only hinted at the lives of the cats who came before him. He wondered about the Clan who had used the tunnels as the test of a warrior. And the Tribe. Were they somehow linked? Were all Clans, Tribes, whatever, however different, somehow connected?

Mousewhisker was splashing toward him, reeking of mallow. Jaypaw, clumsy with haste, shoved the stick back behind the tree root. The shingle crunched as the warrior climbed the beach.

"What are you doing?" Mousewhisker's mew was muffled by mallow leaves.

"Just checking something."

Mousewhisker spat the leaves onto the shore. "A *stick*?"

"It's not important," Jaypaw lied. "It's medicine cat stuff, nothing you'd understand." He braced himself for a flurry of questions.

But Mousewhisker simply began scraping the mallow leaves into a pile. "Whatever you say. I'm not an apprentice anymore," he meowed. "I'm a warrior—I hunt and fight. I'll leave the weird medicine stuff up to you." His mew grew muffled again as he began to gather up the leaves. "I'm just glad I don't have to remember everything you do."

You don't know the half of it. . . .

Graystripe's mew sounded from up on the bank. "Did you catch your fish, Mousewhisker?"

"No, but I caught some mallow!"

Leaves sprayed Jaypaw as Mousewhisker answered. Jaypaw stifled a frustrated hiss and collected the dropped leaves in his mouth. Then he followed Mousewhisker onto the bank, where Graystripe and Sorreltail were waiting. From the smell of it they'd caught mice. Jaypaw's belly grumbled, and he wished he'd eaten when he'd had the chance.

"Let's get these back to camp," Sorreltail meowed. "It sounds like someone's hungry." She turned and darted up the grassy hillside, back toward the forest.

As they topped the ridge and began to head home, Jaypaw halted.

"What is it?" Graystripe asked.

"A patrol, heading this way." The air was filled with their scent. A moment later Jaypaw heard Thornclaw and his apprentice,

Poppypaw, crashing through the undergrowth. Brightheart and Birchfall were close behind. Excitement pulsed from them.

They burst out of the bushes onto the ridge.

"WindClan has crossed the border!" Brightheart burst out.

Graystripe dropped his mouse. "Are they in ThunderClan territory now?"

"No," Thornclaw growled. "But the scents are fresh. It looks like they didn't listen to Firestar's last warning, and they've been hunting in our territory again."

"Have you remarked the borders?" Graystripe asked.

"We did it straightaway." Birchfall was pacing agitatedly around his Clanmates.

"Good." Graystripe's claws scraped the ground. "We must report this to Firestar at once."

The camp was wrapped in the same greenleaf sleepiness as the forest, and hardly any cat stirred as the patrol rushed into the clearing.

"Brightheart?" Cloudtail's dozy mew sounded from outside the warriors' den. "Where are you going?"

"I'll be right back," Brightheart promised as she scrambled up to Highledge after Thornclaw.

Mousewhisker dropped his mouthful of mallow leaves beside Jaypaw. "Can you manage these?" he asked. "I want to go tell Berrynose and Hazeltail what's happened."

This was the first crisis since Mousewhisker had been made a warrior. Jaypaw didn't begrudge him his excitement. "No problem."

As Mousewhisker hurried away, Jaypaw dropped his own mouthful of leaves onto the pile and began to bundle them together, ready to take to the medicine cat den.

"Can I help?" Hollypaw was padding toward him.

"Yes, please." Jaypaw was sick of the taste of mallow.

"What's all the fuss about?" Hollypaw pawed some leaves into a pile of her own.

"WindClan has crossed the border again."

Hollypaw's pelt bristled. "I would have thought after last time . . ."

Jaypaw shrugged. Clearly, rescuing WindClan kits wasn't enough to appease their increasingly hostile neighbors. He braced himself for an indignant speech about how true warriors respected borders, and was surprised to find something else was on Hollypaw's mind.

"Cinderpaw just told me her assessment's tomorrow," she mewed.

Jaypaw stiffened. *So soon?* "Has Cinderpaw ever complained about her leg hurting?" he asked quietly.

"What?" Hollypaw leaned in closer. "Why? What's the matter? She's better, isn't she?"

Jaypaw nodded. "Leafpool says she is."

"Well, there's nothing to worry about then." Hollypaw sighed. "I wish I could watch."

"Cinderpaw's assessment?" An idea sparked in Jaypaw's mind.

"Of course!"

Jaypaw thought fast. He could keep an eye on her while she

was tested. Check that everything was really all right. "Why don't we?"

"Watch her assessment?" Hollypaw gasped. "But that's not allowed, surely?"

"Is that part of the warrior code?"

"What are you two talking about?" Lionpaw padded up behind Hollypaw.

"We were thinking about watching Cinderpaw's assessment tomorrow," Hollypaw explained.

"Is that allowed?" Lionpaw echoed his sister.

"I doubt it," Jaypaw mewed. "But we weren't planning on announcing it from Highledge."

"Let's do it!" Lionpaw decided.

"If anyone catches us," Hollypaw mewed, "we can say we were just trying to get some tips before our own assessment. No warrior could object to that."

Birds chittering in the trees above the hollow woke Jaypaw. Dawn. He stretched and climbed out of his nest, shivering. Early morning had brought a chill to the hollow, reminding him that leaf-fall would soon be here. He gave his paws and face a quick wash. The assessment would start early, and he had promised to meet Lionpaw and Hollypaw outside the camp.

"Where are you going?" Leafpool's mew startled him as he headed for the den entrance.

"I left some leaves behind," he lied.

"Will you be able to find them by yourself?"

"I was only there yesterday," he snapped. "I know exactly where to find them. I'm not a mouse-brain." He figured Leafpool would be too worried about offending him to ask him any more questions.

He padded out of the den and through the thorn tunnel.

Brightheart was guarding the entrance. "You're out early."

"I'm fetching herbs for Leafpool."

"Do you need an escort?"

"No," Jaypaw mewed quickly. "Thanks."

"The dawn patrol's out," Brightheart informed him. "And the assessment's going to start soon. So there'll be plenty of your Clanmates around if you need help."

"I won't," he assured her.

He padded away, relieved that he knew this part of the forest so well. He didn't want Brightheart to see him fall flat on his nose. He headed up the track until he was sure he was out of sight, then ducked into the bushes. Lionpaw had said to meet by the oak where the mushrooms grew. It would be easy to find; this time of year the mushrooms were strong enough for even a sighted cat to smell. He could detect their musty odor from here, and, treading carefully through the undergrowth, he followed his nose until he felt the peaty soil of the mushroom bed beneath his paws.

There was no sign of Lionpaw and Hollypaw.

Then the stench of dirtplace hit his nose. The bushes rustled beside him.

"Sorry we're late," Hollypaw panted.

"We couldn't think of an excuse for leaving the camp,"

Lionpaw added. "So we sneaked out through the dirtplace tunnel."

Jaypaw wrinkled his nose. "I can tell." They smelled stronger than the mushrooms budding around them.

"And I've got prickers in my fur," Hollypaw complained.

"Try rolling in the soil here," Jaypaw suggested. "It'll get rid of the smell and the prickers."

"Good idea!"

Jaypaw leaped backward as Hollypaw sent gritty earth spraying up into his face. "Thanks!" he muttered.

"It was your idea," she retorted, scrambling to her paws. She sniffed loudly at her fur. "It worked!"

"Don't sound so surprised," Jaypaw mewed.

"Let me try." Lionpaw copied his sister.

"Now you smell like a couple of mushrooms," Jaypaw complained.

"It'll be good camouflage," Hollypaw pointed out.

"Poor Cinderpaw'll think she's being stalked by toadstools," Lionpaw mewed.

Jaypaw pricked his ears. "Shh!" He could hear the undergrowth rustling in the distance. The scents of Sandstorm, Cloudtail, and Thornclaw drifted on the early-morning breeze. "Follow me, and keep quiet."

He began to creep forward as though stalking prey, but a tree root snagged his paw and he stumbled.

"I'll lead," Lionpaw whispered. "Tell me which way to go."

"Straight ahead," Jaypaw muttered, letting Lionpaw slide past him. "Thornclaw and the others are right in front of us."

After crawling a few tail-lengths through the under-growth, Hollypaw tugged on Jaypaw's tail. "I can hear them," she hissed.

Jaypaw had already heard Thornclaw's deep mew. "I hope you're ready," he was telling Poppypaw.

"There's a bramble bush here," Lionpaw warned. "Stay close behind me and keep low."

Ducking, Jaypaw crawled after his brother, feeling the barbs scrape his pelt.

Cloudtail's voice was clear now. "I know you will all do your best. But remember, you are not competing against one another, only yourselves."

"You can't help one another, either," Sandstorm warned. "This is a test of your solo hunting skills."

"And we shall be watching you, though you may not see us," Thornclaw meowed.

Lionpaw halted, and Jaypaw wriggled alongside him, feeling the brambles pressing down on his back. Hollypaw pushed in as well. "This is so exciting!"

"Shh!" Lionpaw hissed.

From the sound of it, the warriors and their apprentices were only a foxtail ahead of them. Jaypaw trusted that Lionpaw had chosen a spot where they were still well hidden, and hoped the mushroom dirt was enough to hide their scents. The air pricked with the excitement of the three apprentices waiting to begin their assessment.

"Cinderpaw can hardly sit still," Hollypaw commented.

"Poor Honeypaw looks petrified," Lionpaw whispered.

"But Poppypaw looks as calm as a vixen."

"Nothing fazes Poppypaw," Hollypaw mewed.

Hopefulness and determination mingled in the air like meadow scent.

"Good luck," Thornclaw meowed.

The three warriors melted into the forest, leaving the apprentices alone.

"Where shall I hunt?" Honeypaw mewed nervously.

"Trust your instinct," Poppypaw advised. "I'm heading this way."

Jaypaw heard Poppypaw's paw steps heading toward the bramble where he and his littermates hid. Not daring to back away in case he set the bush shivering, he flattened himself against the ground. Lionpaw and Hollypaw tensed beside him, holding their breath as Poppypaw's pelt brushed the leaves of the bush.

Don't let her see us!

Hollypaw dug her claws into the soft earth.

Shh! Jaypaw stiffened. Then he let out a relieved sigh as the apprentice's paw steps scuffed away up the slope.

"She's heading to the shore," Hollypaw guessed.

"Honeypaw's going the other way," Lionpaw mewed.

"What about Cinderpaw?" Jaypaw asked.

"She's tasting the air." Hollypaw's breath tickled Jaypaw's ear fur. "She must have caught a scent. She's on the move."

"Come on," Lionpaw hissed. "Let's follow her." He began crawling out from under the bush.

Jaypaw followed, his brother's tail brushing his nose. Out

in the open, he soon recognized the ground beneath his paws; they were following the bottom of the slope. Keeping close to Lionpaw's tail, and with Hollypaw's fur brushing his flank, he found it easy to keep up with Cinderpaw as she began to pick up speed.

"She looks confident!" Hollypaw mewed. "Her tail is up."

Lionpaw stopped without warning. "She's turning around!" he hissed.

Jaypaw skidded to a halt just before he crashed into his brother. He felt Hollypaw's teeth grasp his tail and drag him backward; then Lionpaw bundled him sideways and the three of them tumbled through a wall of ferns in time to hear Cinderpaw's paw steps thrumming past.

"That was close!" Lionpaw panted.

In the distance, a screech split the air and Jaypaw heard the fluttering of wings.

"Mouse dung!" An angry mew rang through the trees.

"Sounds like Honeypaw's missed her first catch," Lionpaw guessed.

"Never mind Honeypaw," Hollypaw mewed. "Cinderpaw's getting away!" She pushed her way out of the ferns and began to give chase. Lionpaw nudged Jaypaw after her, and they were once more hurrying through the forest after the apprentice.

Jaypaw recognized a scent. "Squirrel!"

Cinderpaw's footsteps grew quicker.

"She's following it," Lionpaw mewed.

"I can see her!" Hollypaw whispered. "She's definitely stalking it. She's keeping lower than a snake."

"Has the squirrel seen her?" Jaypaw asked.

"It's fleeing," Lionpaw answered. "But it's still on the ground. I think it knows something's up, but it's not climbing yet."

"It's trying to escape," Hollypaw hissed to Jaypaw. "Cinderpaw's going to have to make her move soon."

"It's running along a fallen tree," Lionpaw mewed, "heading for an oak. Cinderpaw's got to attack now or she'll lose it."

"There she goes!" Hollypaw mewed triumphantly. "What a leap—" Her voice broke off.

"What's the matter?" Jaypaw felt a flash of alarm. Through the bushes, he heard a scraping sound, followed by a dull thud.

"She mistimed the jump!" Lionpaw gasped.

"She's crashed on top of the fallen tree!" Hollypaw yelped.

The air was suddenly thick with pain.

"She's hurt!" Hollypaw screeched. But Jaypaw was already racing for Cinderpaw, praying nothing would trip him up.

Hollypaw pelted past him and leaped up to her friend, who was helpless and moaning with pain on the trunk. Jaypaw clawed his way up the trunk, the rotting bark splintering beneath his paws. Panting, he crouched beside Cinderpaw.

Cloudtail exploded from the bushes. "Is she hurt?"

Waves of agony flooded from Cinderpaw's injured leg. Jaypaw pressed his cheek to it. It was swelling already, hot and trembling. "It's her bad leg!" he called.

Cinderpaw's breathing was sharp and shallow. "It just

buckled as I jumped," she croaked.

Cloudtail scrabbled onto the trunk, pushing Hollypaw to one side. "I knew she wasn't ready!"

"We need to get her back to camp," Jaypaw told him. "Hollypaw, you go on ahead and warn Leafpool."

Hollypaw hesitated, not wanting to leave her friend.

"Go on!" Jaypaw ordered.

Hollypaw scrambled away, the undergrowth rustling as she disappeared into the forest.

"It's okay, Cinderpaw," Cloudtail soothed. "We'll get you home." He called to Lionpaw, who was still on the forest floor. "I'm going to hold her by her scruff and jump down. I need you to make sure her injured leg doesn't hit anything, or touch the ground. Do you think you can do that?"

"Yes."

Cinderpaw moaned as Cloudtail lifted her carefully by the loose fur at the back of her neck.

Lionpaw's hind paws stumped heavily on the forest floor as he reached up to help. Jaypaw leaped down beside him, his pelt brushing Cinderpaw's as she dangled in midair. Carefully, Cloudtail slid down from the tree. Cinderpaw wailed as they landed and Cloudtail laid her on the ground.

Jaypaw pressed his cheek to her trembling flank. Her heart was steady and strong. "Can you walk on three legs?"

"I think so," she groaned.

"We'll help you," Lionpaw promised.

Fur scraped the leafy floor as Cinderpaw dragged herself onto three paws. Jaypaw scuttled out of the way to let

Lionpaw and Cloudtail press against either side of her. Slowly, the injured apprentice limped forward, her paws thudding unevenly on the ground.

Every step stabbed Jaypaw like a thorn. "Can't you carry her?" He bristled with frustration. "Leafpool needs to check her over." *What if she goes into shock?*

"Steady, there." Cloudtail wouldn't let him hurry them. "We could damage her leg more."

At last they reached the thorn barrier and made the final snail-slow steps through the tunnel.

Hollypaw was waiting for them inside, her pelt bristling with worry. "She's walking!"

"Not exactly," Cinderpaw grunted.

"How bad is it?" Graystripe called across the clearing.

Daisy was at the nursery entrance. "Is it broken again?"

"We don't know yet." Jaypaw circled his patient anxiously as Lionpaw and Cloudtail helped her to hobble across the clearing. Hollypaw held the brambles to one side as they reached Leafpool's den.

"Lie down here," Leafpool told Cinderpaw as soon as they entered. From the smell of it she had already prepared a bed of fresh moss in a quiet corner of the cave.

Cinderpaw grunted with pain as her fur brushed the moss.

"Outside, please." Leafpool shooed Hollypaw and Lionpaw away.

Hollypaw objected. "But I want to stay with Cinderpaw!"

"You can visit her later." Leafpool was adamant. The two

apprentices were bundled out of the entrance. "What happened?" Leafpool's mew was brittle as she turned to Cloudtail.

The warrior began to explain. "She was jumping over a fallen tree—"

Cinderpaw butted in. "My stupid leg gave way! And now I've failed my assessment!"

"It doesn't matter," Cloudtail tried to reassure her, but Cinderpaw was pulsing with anger.

"Of course it matters!" she snapped. "I don't want Honeypaw and Poppypaw to move to the warriors' den without me. I wanted to sit the warriors' vigil with them, not on my own!"

"I know you're upset," Leafpool soothed. "Let's just see if we can make you more comfortable." Her mew was calm, but Jaypaw could sense distress crackling beneath her pelt as she began to run her pads over Cinderpaw's leg. "Nothing broken," she mewed. "It's not as bad as before."

"Feels like it's worse," Cinderpaw grumbled.

"You've just wrenched the muscles," Leafpool assured her. "They'll heal with rest."

"But why did it give way?"

Leafpool didn't answer but spoke instead to Cloudtail. "Leave her to me," she mewed softly. "I'll let you know how she is as soon as I've finished treating her."

Jaypaw ducked out of the way to let Cloudtail pass as the warrior padded out of the den. He wondered whether he should offer to help, but Leafpool seemed so caught up in Cinderpaw's injury that he remained quiet, crouching near the entrance, ready if she needed him.

"Why did it give way?" Cinderpaw repeated her question more fiercely. "Didn't it heal properly last time? Will it always be weak? What if I can never be a warrior?"

Jaypaw felt Leafpool's rush of panic like a hot wind flattening his pelt.

"You'll be fine," Leafpool soothed. "I've made a poultice." She padded to the back of the den. Jaypaw smelled the tang of nettle and comfrey in the ointment she brought back and began smoothing over Cinderpaw's leg. "Take these poppy seeds," Leafpool advised. "They'll help you to rest."

Jaypaw listened as Cinderpaw's breathing slowed and deepened. Leafpool sat motionless beside her, and only when Cinderpaw finally drifted into sleep did she turn away.

Surprise pricked from her when she saw Jaypaw. "Are you still here?"

Jaypaw sat up, stiff from crouching so long. "I wouldn't leave while we had a patient."

"I thought you'd gone out with the others," Leafpool murmured absently.

"You shouldn't have told Cloudtail she was ready for her assessment."

"That's not for you to judge." Leafpool's voice quavered.

"You didn't even watch a training session to make sure she was fully fit."

"You don't understand!"

"I do," Jaypaw answered quietly. He nodded toward the cave entrance, beckoning Leafpool outside. She followed him to the bramble patch. No one would overhear them there.

Jaypaw took a deep breath. "I know that you want Cinder-paw to become a warrior as soon as possible. You don't want her to suffer the same fate as Cinderpelt."

"What's wrong with that?" Leafpool demanded. "Not being able to become a warrior broke Cinderpelt's heart."

There are worse fates. "You're obsessed with the past," Jaypaw warned her. "You want to make sure everything turns out the way you think it should."

"I just want to do what's right."

"You can't always do the right thing. No matter how much you want to."

"I know." Grief pulsed from his mentor, sharper and deeper than Jaypaw expected. "But I'll always try."

CHAPTER 6

❧

Hollypaw watched the dawn sky lighten. Was it too early to visit Cinderpaw? Leafpool had shooed her away the night before; her patient had been sleeping.

The thorn barrier rustled. The dawn patrol was returning.

Graystripe and Dustpelt padded into the camp, followed by Whitewing and Icepaw. Whitewing was trying to persuade her apprentice to be quiet. "You've been chattering nonstop since we left," she scolded. "We're home now, and your Clanmates are still sleeping."

"But I was only asking Graystripe if I could go with him to tell Firestar." It had been Icepaw's first dawn patrol, and the young apprentice was fizzing with energy.

"This is serious news." Graystripe flicked Icepaw's ear gently with his tail. "I'm not sure Firestar will want you bouncing around his den while he hears it."

Hollypaw pricked her ears. "What news?" She padded forward.

"You'll know soon enough," Graystripe called as he followed Dustpelt up the rocks to Highledge.

Disappointed, Hollypaw turned away and stared at the medicine cat's den. *I'll just peek in and see if anyone's awake.* She padded to the cave and nosed her way through the brambles that covered the entrance. Blinking to adjust to the half-light, she saw Leafpool mixing herbs by a cleft in the rock.

Hollypaw entered the den. "Is that for Cinderpaw?" she whispered.

Leafpool nodded without looking up. "Yes, it is."

"I've come to see her," Hollypaw explained. "Is she awake?"

A croaking mew sounded from a nest in the shadows. "I've been awake for ages." Cinderpaw sounded in pain. Hollypaw hurried over to her friend's nest. The gray apprentice lay awkwardly on the moss, her injured leg sticking out, her eyes dull.

Leafpool padded across the cave and dropped a mouthful of leaves beside the nest.

Hollypaw gazed anxiously at the medicine cat. "Is she okay?"

"She's wrenched the muscles in her leg."

"In that case, she just needs to start using it," Hollypaw mewed brightly. "To build up her strength."

"Easy for you to say," Cinderpaw grumbled.

"Come on, try stretching it," Hollypaw encouraged.

Trembling, Cinderpaw strained to move her leg. "I *can't!*"

Hollypaw's heart lurched. Cinderpaw had never sounded so miserable.

"It's bound to be stiff," Leafpool told her.

Hollypaw narrowed her eyes. There was sharpness in the medicine cat's voice. Was she frustrated that Cinderpaw was making such a fuss?

"Try stretching it again," Leafpool meowed.

"Yes," Hollypaw agreed. "The sooner you start moving around, the better."

Screwing up her face, Cinderpaw struggled to her feet.

"Try putting a little weight on it," Leafpool suggested.

Cinderpaw gingerly pressed her paw to the ground. "Ow!" She flopped back into her nest. "It hurts too much, and I'm too tired."

"Eat these herbs." Leafpool nosed the pile of leaves close to Cinderpaw's face. "I'll fetch some more ointment to soothe the swelling." The medicine cat was frowning. Was she worried, or upset?

As Leafpool padded to the other side of the cave, Hollypaw decided to try to distract her friend. "Icepaw's been on her first patrol."

"Really?" Cinderpaw sounded uninterested.

Hollypaw searched for something else to tell her. Should she share what Brambleclaw had told her last night? *She's going to find out anyway.* "Firestar's giving Poppypaw and Honeypaw their warrior names today."

Cinderpaw turned her head away and closed her eyes.

"It'll be your turn soon," Hollypaw promised.

"I just want to sleep," Cinderpaw muttered, without opening her eyes.

"Okay." Feeling wretched, Hollypaw padded to the entrance. "Don't forget to eat those herbs!" she called over her shoulder.

Cinderpaw merely grunted, and Hollypaw pushed her way

out through the brambles.

Jaypaw was heading toward the den.

Hollypaw greeted him. "You're up early."

"I've been checking on Millie." He halted beside her. "Were you visiting Cinderpaw?"

"Yes." Hollypaw sighed. "She seems even worse than the last time she hurt her leg."

"She'll feel better once the swelling goes down."

"Will she be able to walk again?" Hollypaw's ears twitched. She realized with a jolt that she was terrified of the answer.

Jaypaw blinked. "Of course she will! She's only wrenched her leg. She should heal quicker this time."

Is that true? Hollypaw searched his face. "But Cinderpaw won't even try to move. Last time, we could hardly keep her still."

"She's just upset," Jaypaw mewed. "She was so close to making warrior, and now she's got to wait."

"But Leafpool seemed really worried."

"Leafpool!" Jaypaw snorted angrily and padded past her into the den.

Surprised, Hollypaw watched him go. Had he fallen out with his mentor? *But what have they got to fall out over?*

"Hollypaw!" Foxpaw's excited mew made her spin around. The young apprentice nearly crashed into her as she skidded to a halt. "Firestar's about to give Poppypaw and Honeypaw their warrior names!"

Hollypaw looked up at Highledge and saw Firestar gazing down at the clearing. "Let all cats old enough to catch their own prey gather together!" he called.

Thornclaw and Sandstorm were already waiting below Highledge with Honeypaw and Poppypaw. The young cats looked sleek and shiny from close grooming, and their eyes sparkled.

Hollypaw hurried to join Lionpaw at the edge of the clearing. Her paws were tingling. She was only a moon younger than Poppypaw and Honeypaw. It would be her turn next.

"Can you imagine what it feels like to be made a warrior?" she whispered to Lionpaw.

Lionpaw puffed out his chest. "Every cat will take us seriously then," he meowed.

Millie, swollen-bellied, padded from the nursery and looked hopefully around the camp. Her eyes lit up when she spotted Graystripe gulping down a mouse beside the halfrock.

He looked up, swallowing. "Sorry." He burped, hurrying to her side. "I was hungry after the patrol." He looked anxiously at her. "Have you eaten?"

Millie licked his cheek. "Poppypaw brought us fresh-kill earlier," she assured him.

They padded to the edge of the clearing, which buzzed with chatter as the Clan gathered for the naming ceremony. Mousefur padded stiffly from the elders' den, Longtail beside her. It was hard to tell who was guiding whom.

"At this rate, there won't be any apprentices left to fetch moss for my nest," Mousefur complained.

Icepaw was bouncing past the elder and stopped to gaze earnestly up at her. "I'll always fetch you the softest moss,

Mousefur," she promised. "Even when I'm a warrior."

Mousefur purred. "Get away with you!" She affectionately shooed the young apprentice away with her muzzle.

Hollypaw nudged Lionpaw. "Icepaw must be crazy."

Lionpaw's whiskers twitched with amusement.

Cloudtail and Brightheart had settled in the shadow beneath Highledge. Thornclaw and Sandstorm nodded a greeting to them. The two mentors had backed away from Poppypaw and Honeypaw, and their fur splayed untidily against the rock face. They clearly wanted to give Sorreltail and Brackenfur room to fuss over their kits.

Sorreltail was giving Poppypaw's ears a fierce lick. "I want you looking nice," she meowed as Poppypaw scooted backward, out of reach.

Brackenfur purred. "She looks fine." His proud gaze switched to Honeypaw. "They both do."

Sorreltail looked at her paws, sadness glazing her eyes. "Molepaw should be here too." Her only tom-kit had died of greencough.

"And Cinderpaw." Cloudtail glanced toward the medicine cat den.

The white warrior's whiskers twitched as the brambles at the entrance stirred, then drooped as Leafpool emerged. Hollypaw guessed he had been hoping that Cinderpaw would come to watch the ceremony.

Tail flicking, Sorreltail left her kits and hurried to Leafpool's side. "Is she okay?"

"She's fine," Leafpool assured her friend. "Otherwise I

wouldn't have left her." Hollypaw noticed that the worry in the medicine cat's eyes didn't match the lightness of her tone.

To Hollypaw's surprise, Sorreltail nuzzled Leafpool's flank. "It must remind you of Cinderpelt's accident," she murmured.

Leafpool's eyes grew round, as though she'd never noticed the connection before. She blinked. "That's exactly why I won't let the same thing happen to Cinderpaw."

"I hope Leafpool's right this time," Cloudtail muttered to Brightheart.

Brightheart pressed her muzzle against his cheek. "She will be. It'll be Cinderpaw's turn before you know it."

Icepaw still hadn't settled. "I can't wait till it's my turn!" She was padding excitedly around her brother outside the circle of cats. "I want to be called Icestorm. Do you think we get to choose?"

"Firestar chooses," Foxpaw mewed. "But I hope he chooses Foxcatcher for me."

"That's a terrible name." Icepaw gasped.

"No, it's not!"

"Is so!"

Ferncloud padded over to her two kits. "Are you arguing again?" She licked Icepaw's head, flattening a bit of fur that was sticking up like a tuft of grass.

"Foxpaw started it," Icepaw accused.

"I don't care who started it," Ferncloud meowed. "Be quiet and let Firestar speak."

Icepaw looked up in alarm to find Firestar staring sternly

down at her. Quickly, she hurried around the edge of the clearing with Foxpaw on her tail, and sat down beside Hollypaw. Hollypaw stifled a purr as Icepaw folded her tail over her paws and tried to sit still.

Firestar stepped to the edge of Highledge. "I, Firestar, leader of ThunderClan, call upon my warrior ancestors to look down on these two apprentices." Hollypaw could feel Icepaw trembling with excitement as Firestar went on. "They have trained hard to understand the ways of your noble code, and I commend them to you as warriors in their turn." He bounded down the tumble of rocks and padded to the center of the clearing. Sandstorm nodded encouragement to Honeypaw, whose eyes were wide with apprehension. Thornclaw nudged Poppypaw forward, and the two apprentices stepped into the clearing.

"Poppypaw and Honeypaw, do you promise to uphold the warrior code and to protect and defend this Clan, even at the cost of your lives?"

"I do," Honeypaw breathed.

"I do!" Poppypaw's mew nearly drowned out her sister's reply.

Envy made Hollypaw's claws itch. She pushed it away. *Not long to wait.*

"Then by the power of StarClan I give you your warrior names." He beckoned Poppypaw with a flick of his tail. She padded toward him, chin high.

Touching his muzzle to her head, Firestar pronounced, "Poppypaw, from this moment you shall be known as

Poppyfrost." He stepped back. "StarClan honors your courage and initiative."

He glanced at Honeypaw, who stepped forward in her turn. "Honeypaw, you shall be known as Honeyfern. StarClan honors your intelligence and kindness." He pressed his nose between her ears.

"Poppyfrost! Honeyfern!" The Clan raised their voices to welcome the new warriors.

Hollypaw cheered as loudly as she could, proud of her denmates. But her mew died away as she noticed Honeyfern glance shyly at Berrynose; it was as if she wanted his approval above anyone's.

She hissed into Lionpaw's ear, "I wish Honeypaw—I mean Honeyfern—would stop mooning over that know-it-all!"

Lionpaw snorted. "She'll be worse now that they're sharing a den again."

Hollypaw glanced at her brother, surprised to hear him so scornful. After all, he'd had his fair share of heartache. *Does he ever think about Heatherpaw?* If only Honeyfern were looking at him instead. A relationship with her would tie him even more tightly to the Clan. She remembered with a pang how close his love for Heatherpaw had come to tearing him away from them. Had he truly forgotten her? He certainly never mentioned her. That was a good sign. But then, he hadn't mentioned her when he was sneaking off to meet her in the tunnels.

"Cats shouldn't get so sappy over each other," Lionpaw interrupted her thoughts. "It distracts them from trying to be the best warriors they can be."

Relieved to hear that he finally seemed to have worked out where his loyalties lay, Hollypaw pressed closer to him. She knew how hard it had been for him to say good-bye to Heatherpaw. But it was the right thing to do. It was the *only* thing to do.

As the cheering died away, Firestar lifted his voice once more. "I'm sorry that I cannot give Cinderpaw her warrior name today. But once her leg has healed, I know the whole Clan will be pleased to welcome her as a warrior."

"Cinderpaw!" Honeyfern and Poppyfrost led the cheering this time, and Hollypaw glanced hopefully at the entrance to the medicine cat den. Had Cinderpaw peeked out to watch after all? There was no sign of the injured apprentice. Hollypaw sighed. Had she even heard the ceremony?

"Brambleclaw!" As the cats began to melt away, returning to their duties or to their dens, Firestar called to his deputy. "Bring Sandstorm, Brackenfur, and Hollypaw with you."

Hollypaw didn't wait to be summoned by her father. She hurried over to the Highledge. Graystripe was already there; Sandstorm and Brackenfur padded beside Brambleclaw to join them.

"What is it?" Brambleclaw asked.

Hollypaw leaned forward, her whiskers twitching with worry. Graystripe's warning flashed in her memory. *This is serious news.*

Firestar's tone was grave. "The dawn patrol picked up WindClan scent on our side of the border again."

Graystripe nodded. "And this time we found proof that

they're not just chasing prey over the border, but killing it there too."

A growl rumbled in Brackenfur's throat. "Proof?"

"There was squirrel fur and blood at the bottom of a tree inside our territory."

Sandstorm bristled. "How dare they, after the warnings we've already given them?"

"We don't know why they're doing it," Firestar meowed. "But we must find out before we react."

"It's obvious why they're doing it!" Brambleclaw burst out. "They're *greedy*."

"We can't be sure of that." Firestar remained calm.

"We should post a patrol at the border," Sandstorm declared, "and attack them next time they cross."

Firestar glanced at his mate, narrowing his eyes. "I know how you feel, Sandstorm. But that's not the best way to deal with this. I want to avoid bloodshed if we can."

Sandstorm's hackles rose. "They're stealing our food!"

"And we're not going to let them get away with it," Firestar insisted. "But there's no point rushing into battle before we know what's going on."

Sandstorm glared back. "Don't you fight *anyone* anymore?"

"I'll fight if I have to!" Firestar held her gaze. "But I won't spill blood if reason can solve the problem."

"We've tried reasoning with WindClan before," Brambleclaw argued. "You act like they're still our allies."

Firestar shook his head. "I know they stopped being our allies long ago." Wistfulness clouded his gaze. "The Clans are all rivals now."

Hollypaw stared at her leader. *Is he remembering the Great Journey?* Six cats from the Clans traveled together to save them all. Or perhaps he was thinking of their most recent trek into the mountains. Hollypaw felt a tremor of doubt. Perhaps that journey hadn't been such a good idea. Perhaps the blurring of the Clans led to the blurring of borders. And if borders were blurred, how could prey be shared fairly? There *had to* be rules, or only those who were prepared to fight all the time would survive! That was why StarClan wanted them to live by the warrior code. *We need the warrior code as much as we need food and water!* Hollypaw dug her claws into the ground. The Clans depended on the code; it was as simple as that.

"So what's your plan?" Brambleclaw asked.

"I want you to go to Onestar," Firestar told him. "Take Sandstorm, Brackenfur, and Hollypaw. Find out why he's doing this. Tell him we're increasing border patrols, and that if we catch any prey-thieves, we'll deal with them, claws unsheathed."

"Very well," Brambleclaw agreed. "We'll leave at once." The deputy turned and headed for the gorse tunnel, Brackenfur and Sandstorm at his heels.

I've got to tell Lionpaw what's happening! Hollypaw scanned the clearing. Her brother's tail was sticking out of the elders' den. He must be cleaning out their nests.

She darted toward him.

His backside wriggled as he flung old bedding over his shoulder. Balls of moss showered around him, and he was grumbling to himself: "Mousefur was right." A wad flew past Hollypaw's ear. "There aren't enough apprentices to do all the chores, and it'll be ages till Rosekit and Toadkit are made 'paws!"

"I'm going to WindClan territory," Hollypaw hissed.

Lionpaw's tail disappeared as he whipped around. "Why?"

"We're going to warn Onestar to keep out of our territory."

He flexed his claws. "I wish I were going!"

Brambleclaw's impatient mew sounded from the thorn tunnel. "Hollypaw!"

"I'll tell you all about it when I get back." Hollypaw dashed away and followed the patrol through the tunnel.

The forest was gloomy. No sunlight flickered through the trees; the sky hung dull and gray above them. The air tasted musty, of dying leaves and rotting bark, and the ground was soft and mushy beneath Hollypaw's pads. Leaf-fall was closing in. As Brambleclaw and Sandstorm charged ahead, Hollypaw stopped to clean the mud from between her claws on the deeply ridged bark of a fallen tree.

Brackenfur halted beside her. "You're wasting your time," he meowed. "We've still got to cross the moor."

"But it feels icky," she complained.

"You can give them a good cleaning when we get home." Brackenfur flicked his tail toward Brambleclaw and Sandstorm as they disappeared over the crest of the slope. "Hurry up; we don't want to get left behind."

Hollypaw raced after her mentor, and they caught up to the others at the edge of the forest. As they padded out from the trees, the wind flattened Hollypaw's fur. It tasted of rain. She narrowed her eyes against the buffeting breeze. Below them the land sloped down to the border; clumps of heather dotted the hillside as woodland gave way to moorland.

"Why didn't we go to the border inside the forest?" she asked.

"We'll get a better view this way," Brambleclaw told her. "We should be able to spot a WindClan patrol far inside their territory and call to it without setting paw on their land."

As he led the way to the border, Hollypaw opened her mouth, tasting for the scent of WindClan markers. The grass beneath her paws grew coarse. She tried to detect the scent line, but a tangier smell was filling her nose. Hollypaw curled her lip. "What's that stench?"

"Sheep." Brackenfur plunged through a swath of heather crossing their path.

Of course. As Hollypaw struggled through the heather and emerged on the other side, she recognized the fluffy shapes on the hillside. "Why are there so many?" They swarmed across the moor like clouds across a dusty green sky.

"Must have been a good season for them," Brackenfur guessed.

Brambleclaw halted. "Here's the border."

Hollypaw sniffed at the heather and detected the stale scent of WindClan.

Sandstorm's ears pricked. "Dogs!"

Hollypaw stiffened. Half-blinded by the piercing wind, she peered at the distant hillside rising up to the gray horizon. She could make out the shape of black-and-white dogs streaking over the heather. A Twoleg stood close by, waving its forelegs and whistling like a shrill bird giving an alarm.

Are the dogs hunting the Twoleg?

She watched more closely. *No.* The Twoleg seemed to be using the dogs to hunt the sheep; when it pointed with its forelegs, the dogs chased the animals across the grass, sending them into a frightened, bleating huddle. With any luck, the sheep would keep the dogs distracted long enough for the patrol to make it to the WindClan camp.

Brambleclaw was scouring the slope. "No sign of Wind-Clan," he meowed. "And judging by the markers, they haven't been here for a while."

"That's because they've been too busy hunting in our forest," Sandstorm growled.

"Should we go back and tell Firestar?" Brackenfur wondered.

Brambleclaw flexed his claws. "Not without speaking to Onestar." He padded across the border and, with a flick of his tail, ordered the patrol to follow.

Hollypaw's heart was racing as she followed Brackenfur through the heather into WindClan territory. The wind tugged at her fur as Brambleclaw led them on, chin high, ears pricked for danger.

As they crossed a muddy dip and began to climb the slope beyond, Hollypaw felt more and more wary. Something was wrong. She tasted the air, wrinkling her nose against the sheep stench. Where were the birds and rabbits? She sniffed again. No WindClan, no birds, no rabbits. It was as though the land had been deserted by everything but the sheep and the dogs.

Brambleclaw halted suddenly, his hackles rising. Alarmed, Hollypaw looked up. A boulder rose like a giant paw from the grassy slope, and on it she saw the shape of a cat silhouetted against the hillside. WindClan!

"Stay where you are!"

Hollypaw recognized Harespring, a young brown and white tom.

He crouched, bristling, and glared down at them. "Isn't there enough prey in ThunderClan territory?"

"How dare *he* accuse *us*?" Sandstorm hissed.

"Careful," Brambleclaw whispered. "We *are* on his territory."

Two more cats appeared beside Harespring—Ashfoot, the WindClan deputy, and Owlwhisker. The wind slicked their fur, but there was no doubt they were angry. Their eyes glittered with rage.

Before Ashfoot could speak, Brambleclaw took a step forward. "We've come to speak with Onestar."

"We come in peace," Sandstorm assured her.

"Go back to your own territory!" Ashfoot ordered.

Brambleclaw held his ground. "Not until we've seen Onestar."

Owlwhisker narrowed his eyes. "ThunderClan should stop thinking they can come and go on WindClan territory as they please!" The light brown tom drew back his lips, his teeth yellow beneath. "I bet you don't visit Blackstar this often!"

"Just go home," Ashfoot growled. "Onestar doesn't owe you any favors." Her unsheathed claws scratched white marks into the stone.

Brambleclaw took another step forward. "We promised Firestar we'd speak to Onestar. We only want to talk!"

Harespring streaked from the boulder, hurling himself through the air and skidding to a halt in front of Brambleclaw. "Not another paw step!"

Hollypaw let her claws slide out, her muscles tensing to defend her Clanmates.

"We want to see Onestar," Brambleclaw repeated evenly. He lifted his paw to take another step forward.

Harespring lunged at him, forepaws slashing.

With one swipe of his paw, Brambleclaw knocked the young warrior to the ground without unsheathing his claws. Pinning him there, Brambleclaw glared up at Ashfoot. "We come in peace," he growled through clenched teeth.

Ashfoot leaped down, staring in dismay at her fallen Clanmate. "Please let him go!" she begged.

Hollypaw was startled by the desperation in her voice.

Brambleclaw stepped back and let Harespring scramble to his paws. The young warrior hissed at the ThunderClan deputy.

Panic flashing in her eyes, Ashfoot weaved between the two warriors. "You really have to go," she meowed, half-pleading. "Onestar has nothing to say to you."

Brambleclaw hesitated, then nodded. Turning away, he flicked his tail. At his signal, Hollypaw fell in beside her

Clanmates, and the patrol headed back toward the border.

Hollypaw was bristling with indignation. "It's so unfair," she snapped at Brackenfur. "*We* haven't stolen any prey. We only came to give Onestar a chance to explain himself."

Brackenfur didn't respond. "Don't you think they seemed thin?" he wondered out loud.

"WindClan cats are always thin." And yet, thinking back, Hollypaw realized he was right: The three WindClan warriors had seemed even skinnier than usual.

Brambleclaw glanced back at Brackenfur. "Could they be in trouble?"

"It would explain why they turned us back," Sandstorm meowed.

"They didn't want us to see how weak the Clan was," Brambleclaw guessed.

Hollypaw remembered the absence of rabbit scent and birds. "But what's happened to all their prey?" No other Clan was fast enough to steal rabbits from WindClan territory.

Brackenfur tipped his head toward the sheep and dogs mewling and barking on the distant slope. "Perhaps *they* scared the rabbits and birds away."

Hollypaw felt her belly tighten. "That doesn't mean Wind-Clan can steal our prey." Things couldn't change. There had to be four Clans around the lake. If WindClan's territory couldn't support them, what would happen to the other boundaries?

As soon as they reached camp, Brambleclaw and Sandstorm leaped up to Highledge to report what they'd found.

Hollypaw spotted Lionpaw, tail-down at the edge of the clearing. A large wad of tatty moss hung from his jaws, and scraps clung to his pelt.

"You're not still cleaning out the elders' den, are you?" she mewed.

Lionpaw spat out the moss. "I finished that ages ago," he snapped. "I'm doing the nursery now."

"Let me help you," Hollypaw offered.

"I thought you were too busy going on border patrols."

Hollypaw flicked her brother's ear with her tail. "Don't be grumpy! I've cleaned out my fair share of nests."

"I guess." Lionpaw grunted.

"Let's get this dirty moss out of the camp and gather some fresh." She picked up a mouthful of the old moss and padded out through the thorn tunnel. Stopping at a bramble bush not far from the entrance, she dropped it.

Lionpaw flung his wad down beside hers. "I'm sick of moss!"

"We'll be finished in no time," Hollypaw soothed. "Look! There's fresh moss between the roots of that tree."

Lionpaw joined her as she began clawing pawfuls of soft, green moss away from the rough bark.

"Aren't you going to ask me what happened?" Hollypaw mewed.

Lionpaw sighed. "Sorry. I've been in a foul mood since you left. I'm no better than a jealous kit."

"Well, ask now," Hollypaw prompted. She was dying to share her news.

"Okay. What happened?" Lionpaw peeled a long strip of

moss and let it dangle from his claw.

"Ashfoot turned us back before we got anywhere near the camp."

Lionpaw dropped the moss. "Turned you back?"

"We didn't even get a chance to explain," Hollypaw told him. "They accused us of coming to steal prey."

"But they've been stealing *our* prey!" Lionpaw was furious.

"I know!" Hollypaw clawed a lump of moss from the root and flung it onto the pile. "But I think we found out why they're doing it."

"Who cares *why*?"

Hollypaw ignored his comment. "Their own prey has disappeared."

"That's no excuse."

"But at least we know what's wrong now." *We can solve the problem before it spoils everything.*

"I hope Firestar sends a patrol to teach them a lesson."

Hollypaw fought the urge to agree. She must think logically. WindClan had to be stopped from stealing prey, but not weakened. There had to be four strong Clans. "Firestar doesn't think we should attack them," she mewed. "He's just going to post more border patrols."

Lionpaw lashed his tail. "We've done that before. This time we need to show them once and for all that they can't hunt on our land." He glared at her so fiercely that Hollypaw found herself leaning away.

"Do you want a battle?" She gasped. Was he even thinking about Clan boundaries?

"Don't you?"

"I want WindClan to keep to their own territory," Hollypaw replied. "Boundaries are boundaries." *And if they disappear, what will become of the Clans? Would the warrior code disappear next?* Hollypaw's pads prickled with fear.

Lionpaw turned away and dug his claws into a fresh patch of moss. The bark shredded beneath it and filled the moss with splinters.

That moss will be used for newborn kits! Hollypaw stared at him, shocked by his recklessness. She could tell by the muscles flexing beneath his pelt that he was thinking of battle, not kits. Was this what power meant to him? The need to fight for the smallest reason?

Hollypaw shivered. If it did, would any cat be able to stop him?

CHAPTER 7

❧

Lionpaw tugged another sprig of moss from his pelt. Hauling the stuff in and out of dens had left his fur itching. His muscles were knotted from the tedious work. Sighing, he watched the sun sliding behind the trees. The sunset patrol had left without him.

What a boring day! Frustrated, he headed to the apprentices' den. There was nothing left to do but sleep, though he longed to run through the forest, stretch his legs, and feel the wind in his fur.

He ducked under a branch of the low-spreading yew. Inside, Foxpaw and Icepaw were chattering like sparrows.

"Whitewing taught me how to do a roll," Icepaw boasted.

"I can fight on my hind paws," Foxpaw countered. "Do you want to watch me?"

Lionpaw realized the young apprentice was talking to him. Wearily, he nodded and watched Foxpaw rear up on wobbly back legs and stagger around his nest before toppling onto the moss.

"I was better this afternoon!" Foxpaw scrambled to his paws, looking flustered.

"I'm sure you were," Lionpaw mewed. He was jealous of Foxpaw's excitement. Since he'd returned from the mountains it seemed as though life were entirely made up of dull chores. It was all very well feeding the Clan and clearing out its dens, but when would he have a chance to use the power he felt pulsing through his paws?

He curled into his nest.

"Look!" Foxpaw called. "I'm doing it properly this time!"

Lionpaw didn't bother lifting his head.

"Show him your new hunting crouch," Icepaw encouraged.

Moss rustled, and Lionpaw jerked as Foxpaw pounced on him, grappling with his tail as though it were a snake. Crossly, Lionpaw heaved the apprentice out of his nest with a shove of his hind paws.

"Hey!" mewed Icepaw, protective of her littermate.

"Keep to your own nest and let me sleep!" Lionpaw growled.

"You're no fun anymore!" Foxpaw sulked.

The yew rustled as Hollypaw padded into the den.

"Lionpaw's been pushing Foxpaw around!" Icepaw appealed to Hollypaw.

"I can look after myself," Foxpaw objected.

"I think Lionpaw's tired," Hollypaw soothed. "I'm sure he'll want to play in the morning."

She curled in beside Lionpaw, and he felt the gentle lap of her tongue on his pelt. Gratefully he let her wash the last scraps of moss from his fur, calmed by the rhythmic licking.

"Cheer up," she mewed. "Brackenfur just told me we're both going out on patrol in the morning."

Lionpaw pricked his ears.

"Firestar's sending extra patrols to the WindClan border to check for invaders," she explained.

At last! Lionpaw felt a dark thrill at the thought of confronting the prey-thieves.

"We'd better get some sleep," Hollypaw advised. "We have to be at the border by dawn."

Lionpaw closed his eyes, relieved that at last he could be useful to his Clan in the only way that made sense.

"Lionpaw!" Tigerstar's deep yowl roused him. He blinked open his eyes to find himself lying on bare ground, surrounded by close, whispering pine trees.

He was dreaming.

Scanning the gloomy forest, he spotted his nighttime mentor padding from the trees. Hawkfrost was already sitting in the needle-strewn hollow, his ice-blue eyes glowing in the half-light.

"I hope you're ready," Tigerstar warned. "I'm going to teach you how to knock any warrior off his paws, no matter how big." He beckoned Hawkfrost forward with a flick of his striped tail.

Lionpaw stretched his claws. "What do I do?"

"You don't have the weight yet to overpower every cat," Tigerstar told him. "That will come in time. Until it does, use your size to your advantage. You'll have to be fast. Dart underneath your enemy's belly, slashing the back of their forepaws as you go. They'll twist, expecting you on one side, but you'll be at the other to catch them off balance."

"How do I get to the other side before they slash me?" Lionpaw wondered.

"I told you. Be fast!" Tigerstar padded around Hawkfrost. "Try it on him."

Lionpaw dropped into a crouch as Tigerstar stepped out of the way. He focused on the gap beneath Hawkfrost's white-furred belly, letting energy build in his muscles. Then he shot forward. Darting underneath the long-legged warrior, he drew a paw, claws sheathed, across his forepaws, as Tigerstar had instructed. He felt Hawkfrost twist above him. The warrior was rearing, ready to crash down on him as soon as he emerged. But Lionpaw backed sharply, pulling out the way he had come, like a rabbit backing out of its hole. He hooked his claws into Hawkfrost's fur, careful not to prick the skin, and dragged Hawkfrost, now unbalanced, down onto the ground.

"Excellent," Tigerstar purred.

Hawkfrost scrambled to his paws, shaking pine needles from his fur.

Lionpaw lifted his chin and gazed proudly at Tigerstar. "Not bad, huh?"

Paws slammed into his side, knocking him to the ground. Lionpaw struggled, gasping in surprise, but Hawkfrost held him down, his massive paws pressing hard into Lionpaw's flank.

"Never assume you've won until your enemy is dead!" Tigerstar called.

Hawkfrost leaned in close. "Found out any more about that prophecy?" he sneered.

"I don't think about it anymore," Lionpaw lied.

Hawkfrost gave him a pitying look. "Hasn't StarClan made you leader of the forest yet?"

Pain seared his side. Hawkfrost's claws tore his flesh, then let go.

Jumping to his paws, Lionpaw felt blood welling in his fur. Anger swelled in his belly. Why didn't they take the prophecy seriously? It could be his greatest weapon. A shiver of uncertainty ran down his spine. *Unless they were right and it was nothing more than Firestar's dream.*

"Wake up!"

Lionpaw felt a muzzle nudging his flank where Hawkfrost had clawed it. He winced in pain and struggled to his paws.

Hollypaw was sitting beside him. "The patrol will be leaving soon."

The den glowed faintly in predawn light. Light rain pattered on its branches.

Hollypaw licked her nose. "Blood?" She licked it again, glancing anxiously at Lionpaw's flank where she had nuzzled him.

Shocked, Lionpaw licked the wound Hawkfrost had left. He hadn't realized the line between dream and reality was quite so blurred.

"There must be a thorn in your nest," Hollypaw decided. She pushed Lionpaw out of the way and began picking through the moss.

Paws began to pace the clearing outside.

"We'll have to find it later," Lionpaw mewed. "It sounds like the patrol's getting ready to leave."

Hollypaw looked up, eyes shining in the half-light. "Let's go!"

Lionpaw was already heading out of the den.

Ashfur and Brackenfur waited in the clearing, their fur slicked flat by the rain.

"You're awake." Ashfur shook drops from his whiskers. "We can leave."

"Wait." Firestar bounded down from Highledge. "Remember," he warned, "you're only going to look for signs of prey-stealing. I don't want you fighting any trespassers. If you find intruders, come back and report it." His eyes glittered with worry. "This is more serious than a simple border skirmish. If there is to be a battle, it must be decisive." He looked from one cat to another. "Understand?"

Lionpaw nodded along with his Clanmates.

"Good." Firestar turned and began to climb the rocks back to Highledge.

Brackenfur weaved between Lionpaw and Hollypaw. "Are you two ready?"

Ashfur was already darting through the tunnel. Lionpaw raced after him, his paws slapping the rain-muddied ground. The tunnel sheltered him briefly; then he was out in the dripping forest. Hollypaw and Brackenfur pounded behind; he could hear their paws skidding on the slippery leaves. He unsheathed his claws, gouging the earth as he ran. Energy surged through him.

Ashfur, streaking through the forest ahead, seemed small among the trees. Lionpaw stretched out, gaining on him. *I could reach the border in one leap if I wanted.* Power pulsed in his blood. *And if we meet WindClan, I could beat every one of them.* The pain from the gash in his flank eased, as though it were healing already. Rain washed the blood from his pelt. *Hawkfrost had better watch out next time.*

In front of him, Ashfur swerved. He was following the track. But Lionpaw knew a better way. He ran straight on, crashing through a wall of fern. As he exploded from the undergrowth, Ashfur stared in surprise. Lionpaw was ahead now, veering back onto the track and lengthening his stride.

"Get back!" Ashfur ordered. "I'm leading this patrol."

Lionpaw slowed and let Ashfur shoulder past him. The warrior's blue eyes flashed with anger. Lionpaw fell in behind, a flash of satisfaction warming his pelt. He'd let Ashfur lead— for now. One day he'd be at the head of every patrol.

Ahead, the border stream glimmered between the trees. Ashfur quickened his pace, leaping a patch of ground elder before pulling up at the water's edge. Lionpaw slid to a halt behind him, raindrops dripping from his pelt.

"What in StarClan did you think you were doing?" Ashfur demanded. "You could have run into an ambush! We'd no idea what was waiting for us."

Hollypaw and Brackenfur caught up.

"I was just taking a shortcut," Lionpaw defended himself.

"Well, next time, just stay back!"

"Problem?" Brackenfur asked.

"Nothing I can't handle," Ashfur snapped.

Hollypaw threw her brother a warning glance.

Lionpaw shrugged. *I haven't given our secret away.*

Brackenfur was sniffing the air. "The rain has gotten rid of any scents."

"There may be other signs," Ashfur guessed. "Let's split up and search."

"Okay." Brackenfur nodded. "But stay within earshot. We don't know what we might find."

While the others padded away, sniffing every leaf and twig, Lionpaw peered downstream. Bushes crowded the bank. Was it possible a WindClan cat had sheltered there from the rain? If so, the scent might not have been washed away yet.

He padded beneath a dripping red currant bush. The soil was drier inside. He sniffed around the stem. No scent. As he pushed his way out through the soft leaves, holly leaves jabbed his nose. A dense bush spread up the bank, its glossy leaves gleaming with raindrops. Narrowing his eyes against its prickles, he lay flat and wriggled inside. Mud smeared his belly as he squirmed around the branches. Sharp leaves scraped his back.

"What are you doing?" Hollypaw hissed to him from outside. "Hiding from the rain?"

"Shh!" Lionpaw could smell the faintest hint of WindClan scent. He rummaged carefully through the barbed leaves clumped around the roots.

"I've found something!" he mewed, wriggling out backward with his pelt ruffled and muddy. "Look!" He dragged out the remains of a blackbird.

"What is it?" Ashfur came hurrying to see, Brackenfur on his heels. He curled his lip as he stared at the carcass. The tangle of bloody bones and feathers was still warm. The scent of WindClan mixed with the scent of fresh-kill: This had been taken by a WindClan warrior and eaten where it was caught, in the shelter of the holly bush.

"We must have just missed them," Brackenfur growled.

Hollypaw was gazing in silent dismay at the blackbird.

Lionpaw nudged her. "Pretty good find, huh?"

"They're breaking the warrior code!" She gasped. "They should be taking their fresh-kill back for their elders and queens. Not stuffing their faces as soon as they've caught it."

Lionpaw snorted. "I don't think cats who steal care much about the warrior code."

"They must be pretty desperate," Brackenfur commented.

Ashfur pawed the remains toward Brackenfur. "Take this back and show Firestar. I'll take Hollypaw and Lionpaw to check upstream."

"Is there any point?" Brackenfur flicked his tail. The bank behind them was crowded with bushes, most of them bramble. "WindClan isn't used to fighting their way through that kind of stuff."

Lionpaw wasn't ready to go back to camp yet. "They managed to get under that holly bush." He could still feel the scratches along his spine.

Ashfur nodded. "It's worth checking."

"Don't be too long." Brackenfur picked up the carcass in his teeth and disappeared into the trees.

Lionpaw gazed along the bank, squinting his eyes against the rain. It was a jungle of brambles from bottom to top, but he was ready to search every tail-length of it. A WindClan warrior might be hiding there. He headed toward a tiny opening in the prickly thicket, tensing his shoulders, ready to batter his way through.

"Wait!" Hollypaw tugged on his tail. "You'll get torn to shreds if you try squeezing along that mouse path! Let me go. I'm smaller. I can get through."

"I won't get hurt," Lionpaw assured her. "It's only thorns." *Don't forget the battle in the mountains*, he wanted to say. He stopped himself in time, suddenly conscious of Ashfur hovering behind them.

"Come on, Lionpaw," Ashfur meowed. "Let her pass."

Frustrated, Lionpaw stepped back and allowed Hollypaw to push her way carefully into the brambles.

"We'll go this way." Ashfur led him around the edge of the thicket and started sniffing the rain-slicked roots of a beech clinging to the bank.

"I'll check closer to the water." Lionpaw scrambled down the slippery bank. The stream spat and gurgled, splashing his paws as he picked his way along the edge. He sniffed every tuft of grass and pushed back the leaves of each plant to check that nothing was concealed underneath.

A clump of ferns blocked his path. He opened his jaws, letting its scent lick the roof of his mouth. As he reached a paw in among the dripping fronds, a mew came from above him.

"Nothing in the brambles!" Hollypaw's head was peeping

over the top of the bank. Her eyes were wide, her fur fluffed up despite the rain.

"Are you sure?" Lionpaw narrowed his eyes. She seemed pretty excited for a cat who had found nothing.

"Just brambles," Hollypaw insisted. "Ashfur says we're to go back to camp."

Still suspicious, Lionpaw scrabbled up the bank.

Ashfur was waiting there. "WindClan has obviously gone home," the gray warrior meowed. "We're wasting our time."

"Yeah," Hollypaw agreed quickly. "Let's go."

Lionpaw glanced sideways at her. *What's she up to?*

But Ashfur was already trotting away through the trees. Hollypaw chased after him. *She found something. But why's she hiding it?* The thought nagged as Lionpaw pounded after his Clanmates.

"Wait!" he called to Ashfur, a few tail-lengths ahead.

Ashfur halted and turned.

Hollypaw spun around, her pelt bristling. "What is it?"

"I heard something on the border," Lionpaw lied. "I want to go back and check."

Ashfur tipped his head to one side. "What did you hear?"

"I can't be sure," Lionpaw mewed. "Probably nothing, but I'd like to be certain."

"I'll go with you," Hollypaw offered, tail-tip twitching.

"I'll be fine on my own," Lionpaw promised.

Hollypaw looked skeptical.

Lionpaw didn't meet her gaze. "I'll probably have caught up with you by the time you reach camp."

"Go on, then," Ashfur meowed. "But if you see anything suspicious, come and report it at once. No silly heroics. This is too serious."

"Okay," Lionpaw promised. He turned tail and raced back to the thicket of brambles. Hollypaw had made the tiny opening larger. It was easy for him to wriggle inside, but the thorns still tugged his pelt as he followed the twisting path his littermate had made through the bush. At least it was dry inside.

A smell hit his nostrils. *Fox!* Was that what Hollypaw was so worried about? Why didn't she tell Ashfur? He pushed on more cautiously through the thicket, remembering the time he had sneaked out of camp with Hollypaw and Jaypaw. They had been only kits, but they had been determined to find the fox threatening their Clan. They had tracked it all the way to its den. He shivered at the memory. How did they possibly believe they could have chased it away when they were so small? In the end, it had chased them.

As the scent grew stronger now, he realized that it was stale. No fox had been here for a while. Suddenly the brambles thinned out and the ground opened into a smooth-edged hole. *Hollypaw had found a fox's den!* It hadn't been used in a while, by the smell of it.

Creeping forward, Lionpaw peered into the darkness. Hollypaw's scent mixed with that of the fox. She had gone inside! Impressed by her courage, he crept into the gloom, his heart quickening. The tunnel was narrow, and cold earth brushed his shoulders. It snaked steeply downward almost at once, and Lionpaw's whiskers twitched as he felt his way through the darkness. The soil beneath his paws was damp and clung to his pads. The tunnel must open out soon, he guessed. The fox's lair could be only a few steps ahead. The hole plunged onward, and Lionpaw began to wonder if he was wasting his time. But *something* had spooked Hollypaw, and he had to find out what. He padded on, unnerved by the silence. What could live this far underground?

Suddenly a breeze tickled his nose. There was an opening ahead. He followed the tunnel around a bend, his paws sliding on polished rock. Cold, fresh air spilled over him, stirring his whiskers. The tunnel opened around him, and Lionpaw realized, with a shiver of surprise, that this wasn't merely a fox den. Light filtered behind him through the tunnel, enough to see that the walls were stone too, and a jagged roof arched high over his head. The air smelled of rock and water, a scent never found in the forest but achingly familiar all the same. *This must lead to the dark river!* Memories of Heatherpaw and the flood washed over Lionpaw's pelt. The fur bristled along his spine. Hollypaw had found another way in!

Why hadn't she told him? Lionpaw's claws scraped furrows in the stone beneath his paws. He knew why. Oh, yes, it was as plain as Icepaw's fur at dusk.

She's scared I'll start seeing Heatherpaw again! Anger burned in his belly. *I'm a loyal ThunderClan warrior! Won't she ever trust me?*

CHAPTER 8

"My kits!"

Jaypaw felt a prickle of annoyance. Daisy only ever worried about her kits. The rest of her Clanmates could starve, for all she cared. It was obvious she wasn't Clanborn. Firestar's announcement that WindClan were definitely stealing prey had set the camp fizzing with worry and excitement. The remains of the blackbird lay in the center of the clearing where Brackenfur had dropped it.

Daisy swept her bushy tail around Rosekit and Toadkit.

"Get off!" Toadkit's tiny paws scraped against the ground as he struggled out of his mother's clutches.

Good for you! Jaypaw padded away from the nursery, where he had been checking on Millie.

"We need to teach them a lesson about boundaries," Thornclaw growled.

Dustpelt's tail swished over the ground. "I hope I meet Onestar in battle," he growled. "He's stolen from us too many times, the fox-hearted thief."

Mousefur was pacing outside the elders' den. "WindClan has changed so much since Tallstar was leader," she meowed wistfully.

Firestar was standing on Highledge with Brackenfur at his side, still panting after his dash through the forest. "There'll be extra patrols," he reassured his Clan, "including a predawn patrol to protect our prey."

His voice was steady, but Jaypaw could feel waves of anxiety pulsing from him, bouncing off the walls of the hollow like distant thunder.

WindClan! Jaypaw bristled. They might be struggling to feed their Clan, but stealing was the cowardly solution. Onestar was a leader of *warriors*. How could he make thieves of his Clan?

He padded back to his den, relieved to find that Leafpool was gone. She must have left the camp to search for herbs. He wasn't surprised that she hadn't asked him to join her. Since their argument, they had spoken only when necessary. Why did she have to be so obsessed with making Cinderpaw a warrior? She was just being stubborn. And Cinderpaw still lay in the den, a constant reminder of their quarrel.

As he nosed his way in through the brambles, a voice called weakly to him from inside.

"Can you fetch me some water?"

Cinderpaw hadn't even tried to leave her nest since she'd been brought in. Not even when Firestar had summoned the Clan to share the news about WindClan's prey-stealing.

"You can drink from the pool yourself," he mewed crossly.

There was a moment's silence, then, "Please!"

How could she beg like that? She was almost a warrior! Jaypaw padded to her nest and leaned in till he felt his whiskers brush hers. "Your leg's going to be fine," he snapped. "But only if you use it!"

"But what if it isn't?" Cinderpaw mewed pitifully.

As she spoke, Jaypaw's mind filled with a violent swirl of images and noise. His heart seemed to pitch in his chest like a leaf tossed on waves. He was standing on a thin strip of grass, a Thunderpath as wide as the lake stretching in front of him. A roar filled his ears, and he crouched in terror as a silver monster hurtled by, so close its wind flattened his fur. Another roared in the opposite direction. His eyes stung with their choking scent as monster after monster howled by.

Suddenly one broke from its path, careering toward him. He struggled to flee, but his paws wouldn't grip the slippery grass. Then a lightning bolt of pain pierced his leg and the world turned black.

He blinked open his eyes. Brightness flooded his gaze, sharper than sunlight. Ferns sprang around him, and the ground was soft with fragrant grass. He was lying in a glade, the clear blue sky glittering through the leaves overhead. Squinting, he recognized Bluestar and Yellowfang muttering together near the entrance to a narrow tunnel. Every now and then one of them would steal an anxious glance toward him. A dull pain throbbed in his leg and when he tried to move, it felt limp and lifeless.

"You're doing really well." Firestar was leaning over him, his face framed with soft fur like that of a much younger cat. His green eyes were round with grief. "No, you'll never be a warrior," he whispered suddenly. "I'm sorry."

This is Cinderpelt's memory! Jaypaw fought the pain that seemed to crack his heart. Despair and panic clawed his belly.

I've lost everything. Everything!

"Jaypaw!" Cinderpaw's worried mew jolted Jaypaw back to the present.

"I thought you didn't know . . ." Jaypaw breathed, trying to scrabble back to his own reality.

"Know what?" Cinderpaw sounded puzzled.

"Cinderpelt . . ." Jaypaw began unsteadily. He paused, feeling Cinderpaw's whiskers brush his paws.

"She was the medicine cat before Leafpool, right?" she prompted.

"What's going on?" Leafpool burst into the den. "What are you talking about?"

Jaypaw turned, battered by the storm of fear and anger flooding from his mentor. "She knows about Cinderpelt," he breathed.

The moss in Cinderpaw's nest rustled. "Knows what?"

But Jaypaw hardly heard the apprentice. He could feel Leafpool's hot breath on his face.

"She does *not* know," she hissed. "She must *never* know, understand?"

He flattened his ears, drawing back. "But . . . but . . . she remembered!" he stammered.

Leafpool shouldered past him. "Don't worry, Cinderpaw," she soothed. "Jaypaw was just wondering if Cinderpelt might have tried a different remedy for your leg."

Liar! Jaypaw flushed hot with anger. Why was she so determined to keep this secret?

Leafpool's tail swished over her patient's pelt.

"I knew you couldn't make it better." Cinderpaw's mew was barely more than a whisper. "I'm never going to be a warrior, am I?"

"You need to rest," Leafpool told her. "Your ears feel hot." Moss rustled as she fussed with Cinderpaw's nest. "Jaypaw?" she called over her shoulder. "Bring Cinderpaw some water, please."

Jaypaw stomped to the pool, picked a wad of moss from the pile kept beside it, and dipped it into the cold water. *If she spoils her like this, of course her leg'll never get better.* Leafpool was wrong about *everything*! He dropped the soaking moss beside Cinderpaw's nest and padded out of the den.

Frustration with Leafpool tangled with the vision of monsters and the echo of pain in his leg. He stood beside the bramble patch and breathed deeply, hoping the fresh air would clear his thoughts.

"Jaypaw?" Leafpool's mew surprised him.

"I thought you'd still be fussing over your patient," he snapped.

"I'm sorry I was short with you," Leafpool apologized. "But she mustn't find out."

"Why not?" Jaypaw demanded.

"Because it isn't fair." Leafpool sat down heavily. "She can't be influenced by her last life; don't you see?"

"But you're influenced by it," Jaypaw argued. "Are you really treating her the same way you'd treat Poppyfrost or Honeyfern? Every time you go near her, your thoughts are filled with Cinderpelt."

Even as he spoke, he glimpsed memories flashing through Leafpool's mind: of a badger forcing its way into the nursery and snapping at Cinderpelt as she stood in front of Sorreltail's newborn kits. "You're doing it now!" he accused. "It's not *your* fault Cinderpelt died."

"But it is!" Leafpool's mew was thick with grief. "If I hadn't left the Clan . . ."

Fog instantly shrouded her thoughts, shutting Jaypaw out. "You mustn't keep doing that!" she snapped. "It's not fair!"

"I can't help it," Jaypaw told her. "It just happens."

"Nothing ever 'just happens' with you, Jaypaw," she mewed.

"What's that supposed to mean?" Jaypaw could feel Leafpool struggling to push away her anger.

"Nothing," she mewed. Weariness suddenly seemed to engulf her. "StarClan sent Cinderpelt back to live the life she always wanted. As a warrior of ThunderClan. I just wanted to make sure that it happened."

"Then why are you letting her lie in her nest like a cripple?"

"I don't want her to suffer any more."

"You've given up on her," Jaypaw accused. "She's too scared to move, and you're too scared to let her!"

"That's not true," Leafpool hissed.

"Really?" Jaypaw lashed his tail. "Then why don't you go in there and tell her to get her own water next time?"

"Because I don't know if that would help her or harm her."

Jaypaw could hardly believe his ears. How could his mentor have lost so much faith in her own judgment? "You've examined her leg! You know it's just her muscles that are hurt!"

"But I was wrong last time," Leafpool pointed out. "I said she was ready for her assessment and I was wrong." Her voice dropped to a whisper. "I've failed her, and I've failed StarClan."

Frustration welled in Jaypaw's belly. "Do you always give up so easily?" he growled. "I thought this mattered to you, but maybe it doesn't matter enough!"

Without waiting for her reply, he turned and padded across the clearing. He wanted to get out of the hollow and as far away from Leafpool as possible. He pushed his way through the thorn tunnel.

Birchfall was guarding the entrance. "Hey, Jaypaw. Do you want someone to go with you?"

"No!" Jaypaw headed into the trees.

Following the scent and direction of the breeze, he headed for the lake. The air felt cool and damp, with a chill that hadn't left it since the recent rains. He picked his way through the woods, following a path he knew well. Emerging from the trees, he padded down the slope toward the beach. Wind ruffled the water, which sounded surprisingly close. Perhaps the damp air carried the sound more easily. Jaypaw stepped down off the bank, his paws sinking into the shingle. He padded forward.

Splash!

His paw plunged into water, not deep, but enough to make him leap back, trembling. Since his fall into the lake as a kit, he was terrified of water. He scrambled up the bank, heart thumping. The lake must have risen from all the rain.

My stick! Alarmed, he skirted the edge of the lake, keeping to the grassy bank until he reached the line of trees edging the shore. Weaving among the trunks, he tried to guess which one held the stick in its roots. Sniffing carefully, he recognized with a burst of relief the rowan where he'd wedged it. He scrambled onto a thick root and leaned over the edge. The water was lapping the bank. He dug his hind claws into the bark, reached a forepaw down into the water, and felt for his stick.

It's not there! He flapped his paw in the space beneath the root. With panic rising in his throat, he leaned farther out, planting his other forepaw on the muddy bank so water lapped his claws as he dangled over the edge. Reaching as far as he could, he splashed his paw in the lake, feeling desperately for the sleek piece of wood. The waves licked his muzzle, making him splutter.

Where is it? Had the lake taken it back? He might never see it again!

Something hard bumped his muzzle. Something floating on the waves. He sniffed, coughing as water shot up his nose. But he recognized his stick at once. Flailing with his paw, he tried to drag the stick closer, but it bobbed out of reach each time he tried to hook it with a claw. Why was it so smooth? Why couldn't it have bark for him to grip? Fear and frustration stormed in his chest.

"What in the name of StarClan are you doing?" Teeth

grasped his tail, and Jaypaw was jerked backward onto the top of the bank.

It was Firestar.

"I was just . . ." Jaypaw searched for the right words. How could he explain his need for the stick? But it might be floating out of reach while he stood here trying to tell Firestar. "I have to have that stick!" He prayed that the desperation in his mew would be enough. Hope flashed in his heart as Firestar brushed past him to peer over the edge of the bank.

"What? That smooth stick floating near the bank?"

"Yes!" Jaypaw almost wailed.

"It won't sink, you know," Firestar informed him. "Wood doesn't. Will it matter if it does?"

Jaypaw took a deep breath. "Yes," he mewed. "It matters very much . . . to me." He fought to keep calm as Firestar's curious gaze warmed his pelt.

"Okay," Firestar meowed, after what seemed like moons. "I'll get it."

The ThunderClan leader's claws scratched the tree roots as he leaned out and fished in the water. Jaypaw could hear splashing and Firestar's grunt as he grasped something in his jaws.

He's got it!

The stick scraped against the muddy bank as Firestar heaved it out and dropped it onto dry land.

"Thank you!" Jaypaw sighed, pressing his paw to the wet wood.

"Do you want me to carry it back to camp for you?" Firestar puffed.

"No!" The word blurted out before Jaypaw could think. This was his secret. The fur along his spine rippled at the thought of Leafpool asking questions, of his Clanmates staring at his stick, seeing what he could not see, touching what was his.

"Well, it's safe now," Firestar meowed. He leaned closer to the stick. "It's got some unusual scratches on it. Did you put them there?"

"No," Jaypaw answered honestly, his pelt burning. He curled his claws, hoping Firestar wouldn't ask any more questions.

"Come on," Firestar meowed. "Let's head back."

Thank you, StarClan! Jaypaw rolled the stick to the nearest stubby bush and pushed it close to the trunk, wedging one end under a gnarled root. He didn't think the water would ever rise this high, but even if it did, the stick shouldn't float away again. *Good-bye*, he whispered before turning and following his Clan leader up the grassy slope that led to the forest.

As they entered the trees, Jaypaw tried to pick up Firestar's thoughts. He wanted to know what the ThunderClan leader truly felt about him, knowing the prophecy. But, like Leafpool's mind when she was on her guard, Firestar's thoughts were clouded and impossible to read.

"How's Cinderpaw?" Firestar asked. There was worry in his voice. Jaypaw remembered his vision: Firestar had been the one to tell Cinderpelt she'd never be a warrior. He felt a rush of pity for his leader. Cinderpaw's latest injury must have scratched old wounds.

"She'll be okay, won't she?" Firestar pressed.

Jaypaw answered cautiously. "She's in a lot of pain. It's hard to tell how bad the injury is." He didn't want to contradict anything Leafpool might have said to Firestar.

"That name must bring bad luck," Firestar murmured, half to himself. Jaypaw had to fight the urge to tell him that Cinderpaw didn't just share Cinderpelt's name, but her spirit.

They walked in silence to the hollow, and, as they entered the camp, Leafpool trotted up, breathless. "Are you okay?" she asked Jaypaw.

"He's fine," Firestar told her. "I met him in the woods and we walked back together."

Jaypaw was grateful that Firestar hadn't mentioned the stick.

"Come fetch some mouse bile with me," Leafpool ordered Jaypaw. "Daisy has a tick."

As Jaypaw headed for the medicine cat den, Leafpool padded beside him, not speaking. Was she still angry after their quarrel? He tried to read her thoughts, but his own kept interfering. He pictured the stick floating in the water. It hadn't sunk. According to Firestar, it *couldn't* sink. Jaypaw had always thought of water as a treacherous creature, sucking whatever it touched to its freezing depths. It had tried to swallow him when he was a kit. But it hadn't sucked the stick down. It had held it. Kept it on the surface, next to the air.

RiverClan cats could swim. Jaypaw had even heard stories of Firestar and Graystripe swimming through a flood to rescue a nest of kits. And after the tunnels had flooded, they'd all managed to get to land, hadn't they?

He remembered that night, flailing in the water with nothing to cling to. The water had dragged at his pelt until he had stopped fighting it. Then he had floated, like his stick. He remembered the sensation of his paws churning, the water pushing and pulling at him like wind. He had felt as light as thistledown.

He halted.

"What's the matter?" Leafpool stopped beside him.

"Nothing," Jaypaw answered. But an idea was forming in his mind.

A screech made him jump. Poppyfrost was yelping in pain beside the nursery.

"A thorn's poked her eye!" Honeyfern yowled. "A branch was sticking out of the nursery wall!"

"I thought I'd weaved them all back in!" Graystripe came pounding across the clearing.

"Don't panic!" Leafpool darted from Jaypaw's side. "The thorns aren't big. At worst it'll be a scratch."

Jaypaw raced to the medicine cat's den. Poppyfrost would be fine. He had something more important to do.

He burst through the brambles and heard moss crackle as Cinderpaw stirred in her nest.

"What is it?" she called in alarm.

"You have to swim!" Jaypaw mewed excitedly.

"Swim?" Cinderpaw gasped. "But I can't swim!"

"You could if you tried." Jaypaw hurried to her nest. "River-Clan cats do it all the time."

"But they're RiverClan."

"Don't you see?" Jaypaw paced beside her, unable to keep still. "You can practice using your leg in water. That way you won't have to put any weight on it, but it'll get stronger."

"Stronger?" Cinderpaw echoed, sounding dazed.

"It'll be like walking on it, but easier," Jaypaw pressed.

"Where will I swim?"

"In the lake, of course!"

"How will I get there?"

"You managed to walk back to camp, didn't you?" Jaypaw reasoned. "And you've rested since then."

"How will I know what to do?"

"I'll teach you." Jaypaw ignored the fear pricking in his pelt at the thought of getting his paws wet.

"*You?*" A purr of amusement rumbled in Cinderpaw's throat. It was the first time she'd purred since her accident.

Jaypaw knew he could convince her now. "I'll do my best," he promised.

"Leafpool will think we're crazier than hares."

"Let's not tell her, then. It can be our secret. Think how surprised she'll be when she sees you walking on four paws again."

Cinderpaw didn't speak, but Jaypaw could detect a small flower of hope budding in her mind.

"Okay," she agreed at last.

"We'll start tomorrow." Jaypaw felt jubilant. "You'll be better in no time."

Cinderpaw flicked his ear with her tail. "If I don't drown first."

CHAPTER 9

Jaypaw blinked open his eyes. He could hear Leafpool stretching in her nest. It must be dawn. The medicine cat sat up and yawned. Jaypaw waited for her to leave the den to make dirt, as she always did first thing.

The moss from his nest was tickling his nose. He sneezed, then sniffed the air. It was dry and warm and promised sun. It would be a good day to take Cinderpaw to the lake. Padding from his nest, he tried to ignore the doubt rumbling in his belly. Even if teaching Cinderpaw to swim didn't heal her leg, it would prove to Leafpool that *he* hadn't given up on their patient.

"Jaypaw?" Cinderpaw was calling him. "Leafpool's gone out." She sounded nervous. "But she'll probably be back in a moment. Perhaps we should leave this swimming idea for another time."

"If we hurry, we can be gone by the time she gets back." He was nervous too, but he refused to let it stop either of them. "We have to try this."

Cinderpaw gave a resigned sigh, and her nest rustled as she struggled to her paws. "Ow!"

"Your leg's just stiff," Jaypaw reassured her.

"Could I have a couple of poppy seeds, just to ease the pain?" Cinderpaw begged.

"No." Jaypaw was firm. "They'll make you sleepy, and you'll need all your wits about you if you're going to learn to swim."

A pause. Then determination hardened Cinderpaw's mew. "Okay."

Jaypaw slid beside her, pressing his shoulder to hers so that she could lean on him. She was heavy, and he struggled to help her out of the den.

Once outside the bramble-covered entrance he checked the clearing, tasting the air and pricking his ears for any sign of life. Squirrelflight was padding sleepily from the thorn tunnel. She must have been on guard overnight. "Don't move," Jaypaw warned Cinderpaw. The pair stood still as Squirrelflight padded into the warriors' den.

The entrance would be unguarded for a few moments while Squirrelflight woke her replacement. The dawn patrol was due back, and Leafpool was sure to return from the dirtplace before long.

"Come on." He nudged Cinderpaw forward, and they made awkward progress across the clearing. Jaypaw tensed every time Cinderpaw stumbled and growled with pain. He willed her on, praying her courage would hold and hoping no one could hear her. As they reached the thorn barrier, it rustled.

Jaypaw sniffed the air and froze. "Leafpool." The medicine cat was returning through the dirtplace tunnel at the far end of the barrier.

Quickly, he pressed Cinderpaw against the thorny hedge and flicked his tail across her mouth to silence her gasp. Leafpool's paws scuffed across the clearing as she headed back to her den. The moment the bramble-covered entrance swished shut, Jaypaw steered Cinderpaw into the thorn tunnel and nudged her onward. "You're doing really well," he encouraged.

"I'm not getting much choice," she grumbled.

She was panting with effort by the time they had cleared the camp. Once they reached the trees, Jaypaw relaxed a little. They would be out of sight of the camp guard and any patrol here.

"Rest a moment," he mewed.

Cinderpaw sat down, relieved. "Where are you going?"

"Just scouting for the best route." He felt his way carefully forward, testing the ground for slippery leaves, checking that no fallen branches blocked the path. Cinderpaw was in a lot of pain, and he wanted to make the journey as easy as possible for her.

When he returned, she had flopped onto her side, but her breathing had eased. Jaypaw sniffed her leg, touching his nose to her fur. It didn't feel too hot, and the swelling hadn't grown any worse.

"Your leg's doing great," he mewed.

"Doesn't feel like it," Cinderpaw moaned.

"Imagine we're going to save a drowning kit," Jaypaw suggested.

Cinderpaw lifted her head.

"You wouldn't let a sore leg stop you from getting there."

She heaved herself to her paws. "No way!"

That's more like the old Cinderpaw! "Come on, then." Jaypaw pressed in beside her once more, taking her weight the best he could.

Her whiskers twitched, tickling his cheek. "A blind cat leading the way!"

"I bet you never thought it was possible." Jaypaw was glad to hear her joking.

The smooth grass beyond the trees was slippery, and they slid and stumbled down the slope toward the lake.

"Are you sure you're not trying to make me worse?" Cinderpaw mewed through gritted teeth as they fell for the third time.

"It'll be worth it, I promise." Jaypaw hoped it was true. Was swimming really the answer? *StarClan, let me be right!*

A cool breeze lifted their fur as he finally helped Cinderpaw onto the beach. The shingle crunched under their paws.

"The lake's beautiful today," Cinderpaw breathed. "With the wind ruffling the water, it looks like soft gray fur."

Jaypaw padded cautiously forward, expecting to find himself wading at any moment. But the water level had fallen since yesterday. He remembered with a twinge how close he'd come to losing his stick, then hopped backward as the waves lapped unexpectedly at his paws.

"Is it cold?" Cinderpaw mewed anxiously.

"Not too bad." Jaypaw's fur along his spine rippled. He'd have to wade in with her. How else could he persuade her there was nothing to worry about? Tensing against the tug of the lake, he padded a tail-length out, trying not to show how much he hated the feel of the water soaking his leg fur. "Come on!"

Water splashed as Cinderpaw limped out after him. "Now what?" she asked, pausing beside him.

"Just keep walking until you can't feel the stones under your paws anymore."

Cinderpaw's fur bristled. "You make it sound so simple."

"It is." Jaypaw remembered struggling to shore after he was washed out of the tunnels, the terrifying sensation of water dragging him down, how he'd fought to stay afloat. "You'll know what to do," he promised Cinderpaw. After all, *he'd* managed to stay afloat, hadn't he?

Cinderpaw pressed against him, fear pulsing beneath her pelt. "I can't."

Jaypaw tried to picture the lake stretching before her, but his mind was swept into a vision of thick woodland. Vibrant green ferns circled a gray she-cat. Cinderpelt sat inside the medicine cat's den at the old camp. The night sky arced over her head, flecked with stars. "I'll do anything to be a warrior," she whispered, gazing up at the sparkling heavens.

Jaypaw blinked away the vision. "Do you want to be a warrior?" he asked Cinderpaw.

Cinderpaw didn't hesitate. "Of course."

Jaypaw didn't need to say another word. Cinderpaw was wading deeper into the lake. She gasped as the fur lapped her belly. "You told me it wasn't cold!" she squeaked.

"You'll get used to it!"

"The water's pulling at my fur!" Cinderpaw called.

"You won't have to wash for days!" Jaypaw joked. He hoped she didn't hear the tremble in his mew.

"It's over my back."

"Keep going, but slowly."

"It's soaking through my pelt. I feel heavy as a stone!"

Jaypaw heard splashing. Had he sent her to drown?

"I can't touch the bottom! Help!"

He rushed forward through the waves till the water soaked his chest. "Cinderpaw!" Blood pounded in his ears. "Come back!"

He could hear Cinderpaw flailing, and water spattered his nose. "What should I do?" She gave a spluttered cry; a wave must have washed straight into her mouth.

"Keep moving your legs!" Jaypaw yowled. "Imagine you're running. Use your tail for balance." *Anything to keep your nose above water.*

The splashing stopped suddenly.

"Cinderpaw!"

No sound. Only the gentle splash of the waves on the shore. Had she been sucked into the depths?

"Cinderpaw! Are you okay?" he called more desperately.

"I'm swimming!" Cinderpaw's reply made him gasp with relief.

"Really?"

"What do you mean, *really*?" Her reproachful mew was drowned as a wave slapped her muzzle and she started to cough.

"Keep moving your paws!" Jaypaw urged.

"I am!" Cinderpaw spluttered. "And it works. It really works! I'm floating!" She coughed again.

"Concentrate on swimming!" Jaypaw ordered. He could hear her rhythmic passage through the water. She was heading along the shore. He splashed through the shallows, keeping level with her.

Suddenly a yowl from the bank made him freeze. "Cinderpaw! What are you doing?"

Leafpool was calling from the beach.

"I'm swimming!" Cinderpaw splashed back toward the shore and padded, dripping, into the shallows beside Jaypaw. "Jaypaw taught me!"

Jaypaw flattened his ears, waiting for Leafpool to lecture him. But her gaze warmed his pelt. She was intrigued, not angry.

"Go on," she prompted.

"I figured the water would support her," he ventured. "So she could strengthen her leg without putting too much weight on it."

"And how does your leg feel now?" Leafpool asked Cinderpaw.

"It aches," she mewed. "But it doesn't hurt like it does when I walk on the ground." She began to wade back out into the lake. "Can I try some more?"

She didn't wait for an answer, but plunged into the waves.

The shingle shifted as Leafpool reached Jaypaw. "Well done," she murmured.

He dipped his head. "Cinderpelt couldn't be a warrior, but Cinderpaw *can.*"

Leafpool ran her tail along his damp flank. "I hope so." Her mew became brisk. "You should come out now, Cinderpaw, before you're too tired to walk back to camp." She turned to Jaypaw. "Bring her back slowly; then get some rest. It's half-moon time, and we're going to the Moonpool tonight."

Jaypaw scrambled upward, his claws scraping on the smooth boulders. *A few more tail-lengths and I'll reach the hollow.* His paws were aching, heavy as stones, and his head buzzed with tiredness. He had walked Cinderpaw carefully back to camp as Leafpool had asked, and their Clanmates had gathered around them, shocked by Cinderpaw's dripping pelt.

"You're wet!" Sorreltail had meowed.

Hollypaw had paced around her friend, prickling with worry. "Did you fall in the lake?"

"I've been swimming!" Cinderpaw told them proudly. She was still limping, but she could walk without help now.

"Swimming!" Hollypaw sounded astonished.

"She's going to swim every day to strengthen her leg," Jaypaw explained. He guided his patient away from the noise of the clearing and settled her back into her nest.

"Thank you, Jaypaw." Cinderpaw's mew was heartfelt. "Being a warrior is so important to me."

Jaypaw nodded. "I know."

"Hurry up!" Leafpool's mew jolted him back to the present. He scrambled over the rim of the hollow, a rush of cool mountain air flattening the fur on his face. Following Leafpool, he padded down the well-trodden path to the Moonpool. As usual, the smooth stone, dimpled by the paw steps of ancient cats, felt warm and comforting beneath his paws.

Barkface had hardly spoken during the journey. Leafpool had been no better. The tension between her and the Wind-Clan medicine cat had made the air crackle as though a storm were brewing. Barkface hadn't brought Kestrelpaw with him, claiming the WindClan apprentice had hurt his paw on a sharp thorn. But Jaypaw could sense a defensive shield around Barkface, as though he'd wrapped himself in brambles. He guessed that the WindClan medicine cat wanted to protect his apprentice from any difficult questions Leafpool might ask about the prey-stealing.

Mothwing, Willowpaw, and Littlecloud seemed oblivious to the tension.

"Next time we come, it'll be leaf-fall," Mothwing commented.

Willowpaw shivered. "I'll miss the warm nights."

"It's been a fine greenleaf," Littlecloud meowed. "But the halfbridge has been crowded with Twolegs. Why do they have to be so noisy?"

"At least leaf-fall will mean they'll stop coming," Mothwing soothed.

"That is the one comfort of the cold seasons," Littlecloud agreed.

"Have you chosen your apprentice yet, Littlecloud?"

Willowpaw sounded eager to have a new set of paws join them on this journey.

"I have someone in mind," Littlecloud purred.

Jaypaw waited for Leafpool to make a comment. Did she long for an apprentice who had always wanted to be a medicine cat? She knew Jaypaw had wanted to be a warrior first. *Or maybe one who can see?* he thought with a flash of bitterness. But Leafpool said nothing, just swept the tip of her tail lightly over his ears as she passed. Jaypaw felt hot with shame. Sometimes he wasn't the only cat who could tell what others were thinking.

The cats fanned out around the edge of the Moonpool, Jaypaw padding in Leafpool's paw steps until she settled at the far side. He sat down beside her, eager to touch his nose to the water. He wanted to talk to StarClan about the prophecy. He wanted to find out if they knew of the Tribe of Endless Hunting. Would StarClan be able to explain how the Tribe knew about the prophecy?

Jaypaw lifted his muzzle. Another cat was bristling with anticipation. *Mothwing.*

The RiverClan medicine cat cleared her throat. "Before we share dreams with StarClan, I wish to give Willowpaw her full Clan name."

"Already?" Willowpaw was thrilled. "Oh, wow! How can I thank you, Mothwing?"

"You have earned your name," Mothwing replied gently. "This is nothing but what you deserve."

"Only thanks to you," Willowpaw mewed. "You've been a great mentor."

"And I hope I shall continue to be so."

Jaypaw knew that Willowpaw would be an apprentice to Mothwing for as long as the RiverClan medicine cat lived, but her new name would give her a respect and status in her Clan she had not had before. His tail twitched. How long before Leafpool gave him his Clan name?

Then a thought crossed his mind: How could Mothwing perform the naming ceremony when she didn't believe in StarClan?

Leafpool's whiskers brushed his cheek as she leaned close. "StarClan will hear her, even though she refuses to hear them."

Jaypaw gasped. "How—"

"I know you better than you think, Jaypaw," Leafpool purred.

Jaypaw pulled away. He didn't like the idea that his mentor could second-guess his thoughts.

Mothwing began the ceremony. "I, Mothwing, medicine cat of RiverClan, call upon my warrior ancestors to look down on this apprentice. She has trained hard to understand the way of a medicine cat, and with your help she will serve her Clan for many moons."

Was it his imagination or did the starlight feel warm on his pelt? Jaypaw closed his eyes and reached into Willowpaw's mind. Her joy flooded over him.

"Willowpaw, do you promise to uphold the ways of a medicine cat, to stand apart from rivalry between Clan and Clan, and to protect all cats equally, even at the cost of your life?"

"I do." Stars swirled in Willowpaw's mind.

"Then by the powers of StarClan I give you your true name as a medicine cat. Willowpaw, from this moment you will be known as Willowshine. StarClan honors your loyalty and your compassion. May you use them to serve your Clan for endless moons."

Jaypaw heard Willowshine's tongue lap Mothwing's fur.

"Willowshine! Willowshine!" Leafpool, Barkface, and Littlecloud raised their voices to Silverpelt.

"Willowshine!" Jaypaw joined them, caught up in their excitement.

Jaypaw heard the Moonpool ripple as Willowshine's paw tips touched the water's edge.

"Thank you—all of you," she meowed. "My paws were guided by StarClan in everything I have done, and I hope they will continue to guide me for the rest of my life."

"May StarClan grant that it is so," murmured Barkface.

"Congratulations, Willowshine," Leafpool meowed warmly.

"Well done," Littlecloud purred. He lay down beside the Moonpool. "StarClan will be eager to share tongues with you, I'm sure." He touched his nose to the water and grew still.

Fur brushed stone as the other cats followed his lead and lay down to share dreams with StarClan. As Jaypaw rested his belly on the cool rock, Leafpool whispered in his ear.

"Don't walk in Willowshine's dreams tonight," she warned. "Let her meet StarClan alone."

I wasn't going to! He felt a flash of satisfaction. She wasn't a mind reader after all. Jaypaw had no intentions of sharing any other cat's dream tonight. He wanted his own meeting with StarClan, to ask them about the prophecy.

He touched his nose to the chilly water, and his mind instantly filled with lush greenery as he entered StarClan's hunting grounds. There was no hint of leaf-fall in the air here, only trees in full leaf and undergrowth burgeoning with life.

Cats moved through it, some talking, some chasing prey, others simply basking in the sunshine. An orange pelt shimmered beyond a swath of ferns. A tabby groomed a tortoiseshell, while a cat with a black-and-white pelt crept through the long grass, stalking prey. Jaypaw didn't recognize anyone. *Ancestors from the other Clans.* Jaypaw was frustrated. He wanted to talk to someone he knew.

His hopes lifted as he recognized a pelt weaving through the long grass ahead of him. Then, with a sigh, he realized it was Littlecloud. He hadn't meant to be here, in Littlecloud's dream. He was about to turn away when he noticed a small gray-and-white tom padding toward the ShadowClan medicine cat. The tom's pelt was flecked with grizzled strands of fur. *He must be ancient!*

Littlecloud dipped his head in greeting. "Runningnose."

The tom blinked in reply, his nose glistening between sniffs.

I'm not surprised they don't touch muzzles. Jaypaw slipped behind a tree and listened. He knew Runningnose had been a Shadow-Clan medicine cat many moons ago. *What kind of medicine cat can't cure his own cold?*

"How are things?" Runningnose asked.

Littlecloud hesitated, and Jaypaw could sense that he was groping for an answer.

"Is the prey running well?" Runningnose pressed. His eyes narrowed as Littlecloud fidgeted in front of him, shifting his weight from one paw to another.

"Prey's running fine," Littlecloud answered.

"Are the Twolegs bothering you?"

Littlecloud shook his head.

"What about Tawnypelt's kits? Are they healthy?" Runningnose sat down, clearly puzzled as Littlecloud's gaze darted to his paws. "What's *wrong*?" he demanded.

"It's Blackstar!" Littlecloud blurted out his leader's name with a guilty glance over his shoulder. He dropped his voice to a whisper so Jaypaw had to prick his ears to catch the rest. "He's so . . ." Littlecloud was still searching for words. "So . . . distant."

"Distant?" Runningnose echoed. "Do you mean he's left the Clan?"

"No!" Irritation edged Littlecloud's mew. "Distant, as in *distracted*. He lets Russetfur organize all the patrols, and he's started to say things." Littlecloud flicked his tail.

"What sort of things?"

"He says he wonders if StarClan meant to bring us to the lake at all!" Littlecloud burst out.

Runningnose's gaze darkened. "Then you're right to be worried."

"I am?"

"Blackstar is losing his faith," Runningnose meowed.

Littlecloud's ears twitched. "How can that be? He's always believed."

"It doesn't matter why or how." Runningnose rubbed a paw across his muzzle. "You must help him to find his faith again."

"But how?" Littlecloud sounded dismayed. "What can I do?"

"Help him find his faith again," Runningnose repeated. The old tom was fading, growing transparent like the forest around him.

"Help me!" Littlecloud begged. But the forest had disappeared.

Jaypaw blinked open his eyes and found himself in darkness beside the Moonpool. He got to his paws, frustrated. What did it matter to him if Blackstar was turning into a birdbrain? Surely it was better if ShadowClan was led by a senile old fool?

Leafpool was stirring beside him. "Did you dream of anything?" she whispered.

"No," Jaypaw replied, still feeling out of sorts. "Nothing that matters."

CHAPTER 10

A *fox screeched from deep in* the forest. Hollypaw stirred in her nest as its bark echoed around the walls of the camp and crept into her dreams. "Not in the tunnels," she murmured.

"What?" Lionpaw rolled over beside her, but Hollypaw didn't answer. She had fallen back into sleep, slipping into the dream again.

A tunnel stretched away in front of her, disappearing into shadow. The dark river frothed and swirled at her tail. Heavy paws padded down the tunnel toward her, claws scraping against the rock floor. The stench of fox filled her nose. Her pelt pricked in terror as she saw a shape forming from the shadows, eyes glowing in the dark. *Fox!* She backed away, feeling the river tugging at her hind paws. The shape kept coming, eyes unblinking, until it emerged into the half-light.

It was Lionpaw.

She leaped up with a start as a paw touched her shoulder.

"Hollypaw?" Brackenfur was standing beside her nest. The den was in darkness, weak moonlight washing through the branches of the yew. "Are you okay?"

She was trembling, her pelt hot with panic. "It was just a dream." Relief washed over her like a cool wind.

"Can't you dream more quietly?" Lionpaw grumbled beside her. "I was out on the midnight patrol while you were snoring." He rolled over and tucked his muzzle under his paw.

"It's your turn now, Hollypaw," Brackenfur meowed softly.

Foxpaw and Icepaw were fast asleep in their nests.

"Is it dawn?" Hollypaw asked, trying to rub the sleep from her eyes.

"Not for a while yet," Brackenfur whispered. "We're doing the predawn patrol."

The extra patrols had drained the Clan and left its warriors and apprentices tired, but Firestar's plan seemed to be working. There had been no sign of intruders or prey-stealing in days. Hollypaw stretched and followed her mentor out of the den. Her paws felt numb with sleep, and even the early-morning chill couldn't chase away her weariness.

A sharp white moon lit the camp. Thornclaw sat in the clearing, holding his tail down with a paw while he washed the tip.

Sorreltail paced around him. "It's too cold to sit still," she complained.

"There'll be more warm nights before greenleaf is gone," Brackenfur promised, padding up to the tortoiseshell and brushing his muzzle against hers.

"Is Hollypaw awake?" Thornclaw asked.

Hollypaw stepped from the shadows. "Almost."

"Good." The golden brown tabby got to his paws. "We can go."

A small squeak sounded from inside the nursery. "Has the fox gone?" Rosekit mewed anxiously. "I heard it barking, and it sounded really close!"

"It's far away in the forest, dear," Daisy soothed. "Now go back to sleep."

Hollypaw fell in behind Brackenfur as the patrol padded single file out into the forest. It was dark beneath the shelter of the trees, and Hollypaw stumbled over a root as they headed up the slope toward the WindClan border.

Brackenfur glanced back at her. "Are your paws still asleep?"

"I'll wake up soon," she promised.

They trekked to the border stream, slowing as they neared it. Sorreltail, leading the patrol, signaled with her tail for them to halt and lifted her nose to taste the air. "No fresh scents here."

Thornclaw scrambled down the bank, and Hollypaw heard bushes rustle as he checked beneath them. He emerged with leaves caught in his pelt. "No signs there."

Padding quietly through the trees, they followed the stream along the border. Brackenfur pushed through a clump of ferns, sliding out the other side with a shake of his head. "All clear."

Thornclaw left a scent marker at the roots of an oak.

"We'll follow the stream out of the trees," Sorreltail decided. "Then we can reset our markers along the moorland border." She led the way out of the forest and into moonshine.

The hillside glowed eerily white, and the silence of the moor and the forest set Hollypaw's pelt prickling.

"It's so quiet," she murmured.

"Dawn's coming," Brackenfur meowed. "The birds will be waking soon."

A breeze rustled the heather.

"Thornclaw, Brackenfur, you reset the markers," Sorreltail ordered. "Hollypaw and I will scout around and check for any WindClan scents." She nodded to Hollypaw. "Follow me."

Hollypaw padded down the slope after the tortoiseshell, her sleep-clumsy paws slipping on the coarse grass. Sorreltail beckoned her onward with her tail, and Hollypaw weaved ahead through the heather while Sorreltail headed back up the slope. Sniffing her way from bush to bush, she followed the curving ground through a dip and up onto a shallow hillock. The borderline lay here, detectable more from recent ThunderClan markers than the stale WindClan scent. It was as if this border hardly mattered to WindClan anymore. They must have been too busy hunting in the forest.

Hollypaw gazed at the hillside beyond. The hill arched like the spine of a giant cat against the sky. It stretched to the horizon, creamy with the coming dawn. Cream gave way to yellow as the sun began to push against the darkness, driving back the night and staining the hilltop a soft pink.

As the sky lightened, Hollypaw noticed a shape silhouetted on the crest. She narrowed her eyes, trying to make it out. She could not gauge its size. But as the dawn light washed over the hilltop, she recognized the shape as feline, with a face that tapered at the muzzle, a long, smooth back, and a curving tail, bushed at the tip. There was something proud and magnificent about the way it held its head; the large, wide-spaced ears prickled as it surveyed the lake below.

Hollypaw stiffened. "It's a *lion*!"

"A lion?" Sorreltail dashed to join her. "Where?"

Hollypaw pointed with her nose at the figure standing motionless on the hill.

Sorreltail shook her head. "It's just a cat." She peered harder. "Doesn't look like WindClan, though. It's far too stocky and long-haired."

Hollypaw blinked, realizing Sorreltail was right. But for a moment it really had looked like a lion; she'd heard of them in stories whispered in the nursery when she was a kit—huge and fierce, rising like the sun to defeat all their enemies.

"We've reset the markers!" Brackenfur called from the treeline. "We should head back so the dawn patrol can leave."

Sorreltail turned and dashed away to join him. Hollypaw dragged her gaze from the strange cat still standing on the horizon. Was it watching them?

"Hollypaw reckons she saw a lion," Sorreltail told Brackenfur and Thornclaw as they padded back to camp. "On the moor."

"A lion?" Brackenfur's eyes glittered with amusement. "Are you sure you weren't still dreaming?"

"No, I wasn't!" Hollypaw mewed defensively. "And it did look like a lion."

"It did look strange," Sorreltail agreed. "Not a WindClan cat, that's for sure."

"Just so long as it doesn't cross our border," Thornclaw growled.

Cinderpaw was nosing her way out of the medicine cat's den as Hollypaw padded into camp. She limped around the clearing, heading for the thorn tunnel.

Hollypaw fell in beside her. "Where are you going?"

"Swimming."

"On your own?" Hollypaw asked in surprise.

"Jaypaw's busy sorting herbs, and Leafpool says I'll be okay if I take it slowly."

Hollypaw noticed that Cinderpaw's words were no longer punctuated with gasps of pain. "Is it feeling better?"

"Lots." Cinderpaw stopped and stretched. Her injured leg trembled with the strain, but she didn't flinch.

"Can I come with you?" Hollypaw asked.

"Aren't you tired?"

"Not anymore." The sight of the "lion" on the moorland had jerked her wide-awake.

Cinderpaw purred. "I'd love the company." She glanced sideways at Hollypaw. "Do you want me to teach you how to swim?"

Hollypaw shivered at the thought of a cold, wet pelt. "No, thanks!"

They padded nose-to-tail through the thorn tunnel. The sun was climbing the sky, warming the forest, and birds chattered in the trees. Hollypaw loved how the woods had lost the neat crispness of early greenleaf and had grown unkempt and disheveled, the undergrowth spilling over paths and trees sending willowy shoots out from among their roots. It seemed that the forest was fuller and lusher than ever.

She slowed as they climbed the slope toward the lake, so that Cinderpaw could match her step for step despite her limp.

"Have you seen how Honeyfern keeps following Berrynose with that drippy look on her face?" Cinderpaw mewed.

"Oh, yes!" Hollypaw agreed. "Anyone would think he was StarClan's gift to the Clan!"

"Can't she see what a bossy know-it-all he is?"

"I think she likes him almost as much as he likes himself."

"Then it must be love!" Cinderpaw's whiskers twitched. "That reminds me! Have you noticed how Birchfall has started sharing tongues with Whitewing?"

"The nursery could start getting crowded," Hollypaw purred.

"I don't know if there'll be room once Millie has her kits," Cinderpaw mewed. "Leafpool says there're going to be at least three."

"Has Millie chosen names yet?" Hollypaw wondered if Cinderpaw had heard any gossip while she'd been confined to Leafpool's den.

"Leafpool says a kit needs to be seen before it can be named."

"Then I must have been a prickly kit," Hollypaw joked.

It was good to talk about nothing in particular. It was like things used to be, before the prophecy. For the first time since returning from the mountains, she felt like an ordinary apprentice again.

But she wasn't. A stab of envy jabbed her belly. Cinderpaw could chat like this forever, with no worries about being more powerful than her Clanmates. Her only ambition was to become a warrior and do the best she could for her Clan.

I have so much more to aim for. Hollypaw frowned. *And I don't even know for sure what that could be.*

CHAPTER 11

A *warm breeze circled the hollow,* drawing the night scents of the forest into the camp. The moon was high; Jaypaw could feel its light wash his pelt. He shifted his paws, stiff from waiting.

"Are you sure there's nothing I can do?" he whispered to Leafpool through the brambles covering the entrance of the medicine cats' den. She'd sent him outside when his pacing had knocked the poppy seeds flying across the floor. She was gathering them up now.

"I could help you clean up," he offered.

"No, thanks," Leafpool called back. "You just keep your ears pricked for any noise from the nursery."

Millie had been circling her den restlessly since sunhigh, and, though her pains had not started properly, Leafpool had warned her the kittens might come anytime. The rest of the camp was asleep, except for Graystripe, who kept his own vigil outside the nursery. Jaypaw tried not to let the fear drifting from the gray warrior taint his own thoughts.

Millie will be fine.

The nursery brambles shivered, and paws pattered over the clearing.

"The kits are coming!" Daisy called, keeping her voice low.

Leafpool darted out of her den. "Follow me," she hissed to Jaypaw.

Jaypaw hurried after her, his heart racing as Leafpool and Daisy squeezed into the nursery.

"Look after Millie." Graystripe's anxious growl made him jump. The warrior was so close their pelts touched. "If you have to choose which life to save, save hers."

Before Jaypaw could answer, he was swept into Graystripe's memory. A silver tabby she-cat lay in a pool of blood at the bottom of a ravine. Grief wrenched Jaypaw's heart, and he fought to escape the vision, relieved when he blinked and found the world black once more.

"Leafpool won't let anything bad happen," he promised as he scrabbled inside the nursery. He was scared of sensing any more of Graystripe's pain. He must have loved the silver she-cat very much.

Millie was panting hard. She yowled low and long as Jaypaw slid in beside his mentor. "Is she okay?" he whispered. He had missed the birth of Daisy's kits and was excited to be witnessing Millie bringing new life into the Clan.

"She's doing fine," Leafpool soothed.

"If this is what *fine* feels like," Millie croaked, "StarClan save me from—" Another spasm silenced her.

Rosekit and Toadkit were wriggling in the corner of the den, their paws scrabbling on the moss.

"Stay back!" Daisy mewed sternly, her fur brushing theirs as she held them.

"I want to see the kits!" Rosekit complained.

"Is there any blood?" Toadkit squeaked.

"Shh!" Leafpool hissed.

Millie was panting again, hard.

"You're doing well," Leafpool assured her.

"Where's Graystripe?" Millie begged.

"He's just outside," Jaypaw told her.

"Good." Millie sighed as the spasm left her. "Don't let him come in, not yet."

Leafpool wrapped her tail over Jaypaw, drawing him closer. "Here," she mewed, grasping his paw gently between her jaws and resting it on Millie's swollen flank. "Another spasm is coming. They come like waves lapping the shore, one after another, growing faster and stronger." Jaypaw felt a thrill of anticipation as Millie's flank tensed and rolled beneath his paw.

"Her muscles are working to push the kits out," Leafpool explained. "In a moment she's going to have to help by pushing too."

"Now?" Millie asked.

"Not yet." Leafpool rested her paw beside Jaypaw's as the spasm subsided. Calm radiated from the medicine cat like moonbeams. Jaypaw was impressed. His own heart was pounding so hard he was sure the others must be able to hear it.

"Now!" A new spasm gripped Millie, and Jaypaw felt the queen tense and tremble as she pushed with all her might.

"The first one's coming," Leafpool encouraged. "I can see it."

Millie pushed again, and Jaypaw smelled a new scent, warm, both musky and fresh at the same time.

Leafpool shuffled along until she was crouched at Millie's tail. "Look," she whispered to Jaypaw. He leaned over and sniffed the damp bundle wriggling under his nose. Leafpool's cheek brushed his as she lapped at the newborn kit. "I've opened the sac so it can breathe air for the first time."

Millie gasped.

"The next one's coming," Leafpool announced. Daisy pushed past Jaypaw and dragged the first kit out of the way. Jaypaw could hear her tongue scraping the kit's soggy pelt. "Are you washing it?" From the sound of it she was licking the fur the wrong way.

"This will warm it and help it start breathing," Daisy told him. Jaypaw leaned in close and heard a tiny gasp as the kit drew in its first mouthful of air.

Millie gave a low moan, and another damp bundle fell onto the moss. "Here." Leafpool nosed Jaypaw toward it. "Nip open the sac to release it."

Suddenly feeling nervous, Jaypaw licked at the wriggling mass, feeling the membrane slimy on his tongue. Careful to avoid the soft flesh beneath, he nipped at the delicate sac. It split between his teeth and tore open so that the kit tumbled out, squeaking and struggling. "This one's breathing already," he told Leafpool.

"Good," she mewed. "Now lick it like Daisy is doing."

Sniffing first to find the kit's head, he began licking it from tail to ear. Soaked to the skin, it had grown cold quickly, but it soon began to grow warm and dry beneath his tongue.

Millie shifted behind him, and her nose pushed past to sniff at her kits. Then she fell back again with a groan.

"Another one's coming," Leafpool announced.

Millie yowled, softer this time, as though the pain were easing.

"There we go," Leafpool murmured as a new bundle plopped out. "That's the last one." Millie turned and released it from the sac. She started to purr, lapping at its wet body.

"One male and two females," Leafpool told her.

Millie sank back into her nest, still purring, and Leafpool lifted the two female kits and laid them at the queen's belly. "They need milk," she explained to Jaypaw.

Jaypaw picked up the kit he'd been washing and laid it beside the others; it immediately wriggled toward the warmth of its mother, scrabbling to latch on. He sat back and listened to them suckling, their tiny purrs drowned by their mother's, and a wave of wistfulness swept over him as he smelled the warm, milky scent.

"You're lucky to be born in ThunderClan," he whispered to them, thinking of the prophecy for the first time that night.

The brambles rustled as Graystripe pushed his way in. Leafpool must have called him. He crouched beside Millie, and Jaypaw heard him snuffling the queen's fur, relief flooding from his pelt.

"You have two daughters and one son," Millie told him, sounding tired.

"They're perfect," Graystripe replied softly.

Millie struggled to prop herself up so that she could look down at her suckling babies. "The tom looks just like you," she commented. "Big and strong already, though he has more black stripes than you."

"He looks like a bumblebee," purred Graystripe. "How about we call him Bumblekit? And the dark brown she-cat could be Briarkit."

"That sounds good," Millie agreed. "I'd like to call the littlest one Blossomkit. The white patches on her tortoiseshell fur look just like fallen petals."

"Bumblekit, Briarkit, and Blossomkit," Graystripe murmured. "Welcome to ThunderClan, my precious children."

"They'll be all right now," Leafpool mewed to Jaypaw. "Daisy will keep an eye on them and call us if they need anything."

She wriggled out of the den, and Jaypaw followed her into the moonlight. As they padded back to their den, he felt a surge of pride—for Millie, for himself, and for Leafpool.

"You did well." Leafpool brushed her muzzle against his cheek as if she could tell how he felt inside.

"Thanks." Jaypaw licked her ear. Their quarrel was a long way from his mind right now. "That was the most amazing thing ever!"

"Yes, it was," Leafpool murmured.

Was that sadness in her mew? Jaypaw wondered. She certainly didn't seem as elated as he was; his paws felt lighter than the breeze, as if he could fly right out of the hollow and over the trees. Perhaps Leafpool had helped so many cats give birth that it didn't stir her anymore. Or perhaps she was envious of the way the tiny kits knew instantly who their mother was, and loved her fiercely from their very first breath. Jaypaw's paw steps slowed as he tried to imagine how Leafpool really felt watching new lives being born. Did she feel sorry that she would never have kits of her own?

Jaypaw slept late. When he finally padded out into the clearing, his thoughts bleary with sleep, hot sunshine warmed his back. The fresh-kill pile smelled delicious, and, hungry after his night's work, he dragged a mouse from the top and began to eat.

"I heard you delivered your first kits!" Hollypaw hurried up to him and rubbed his cheek with her muzzle. "I wish I could have been there."

"It was great," Jaypaw mewed between mouthfuls.

Graystripe squeezed out of the nursery. Happiness shone from him warmer than the sun as he padded across the clearing.

"Congratulations, Graystripe!" Longtail called.

Cinderpaw paused from her washing as Graystripe passed the apprentice den. "Is Millie all right?"

"She's *perfect*," Graystripe answered. "And so are the kits."

"I can't wait to see them!" Icepaw was bouncing around the clearing.

"We've seen them already!" Toadkit boasted. "Bumblekit is going to play with me when he's a bit bigger."

"They're really cute!" Rosekit added. "Especially Blossom-kit. She's so tiny!"

Jaypaw could hear Graystripe nosing through the fresh-kill pile.

"Millie will be hungry," Mousefur called from outside the elders' den.

"And she's going to eat the best piece of prey I can find," Graystripe called back.

Sorreltail kneaded the ground. "What do the kits look like?"

"Briarkit is dark brown, Blossomkit is tortoiseshell and white," Graystripe reported, "and the tom, Bumblekit, is gray with black stripes."

Dustpelt was washing beside the halfrock. "At least they'll have proper *warrior* names," he muttered. He had clearly not forgotten that Millie had refused a Clan name.

Graystripe took no notice of the brown tabby warrior. He returned to rummaging through the fresh-kill pile until Firestar bounded down from Highledge.

"You chose fine Clan names." The ThunderClan leader sounded excited for his old friend, though Jaypaw detected sorrow running like a spider's web between the two warriors, as though they shared a sad memory. Was it connected with the silver tabby Jaypaw had seen in his dream?

"You should have called Blossomkit Squealkit, because that's all she does!" Toadkit mewed.

"Don't be mean!" Rosekit gasped. Fur brushed the dusty ground as the two kits tumbled into a fight.

"Stop it, you two!" Spiderleg's stern mew echoed around the hollow as he separated his kits.

"We were just playing," Toadkit complained.

"Well, play something quieter!" Spiderleg snapped. "I don't envy you, Graystripe. Two kits are hard enough." Then he yelped in pain. "When I told you to play something else, Toadkit, I didn't mean attacking my tail!"

The thorn barrier rattled. Jaypaw swallowed the last of his mouse and tasted the air. Brambleclaw, Ashfur, and Lionpaw were padding into the camp. They headed to the fresh-kill pile and dropped their prey.

"Where's the dawn patrol?" Brambleclaw called. "They should be back by now."

"Who was on it?" Spiderleg asked.

"Thornclaw, Poppyfrost, and Birchfall." Guilt was prickling Firestar's pelt. *He should have noticed they were missing.*

Jaypaw concentrated on the camp, scanning it for signs or smells of the three missing warriors.

"Perhaps they decided to hunt," Graystripe suggested.

"They're supposed to report straight back," Brambleclaw pointed out.

"It must be quiet in the forest," Spiderleg guessed.

Jaypaw could smell only stale scents of the three warriors. He cast his mind farther, beyond the walls of the camp. If they were close to the hollow he might be able to pick up a stray thought or feeling. He could picture trees and bushes, a landscape built of images glimpsed in his dreams. But no sign of his Clanmates.

Suddenly his mind emptied and blackness crowded in, smothering his thoughts. Coldness gripped him, seeping into his flesh, chilling his bones. He tried to breathe, but the emptiness choked him, crushing him like water, drowning him in its terrible darkness.

Then it vanished, and he could picture the forest again, green and quiet.

Jaypaw gasped for breath, his flanks heaving as he sucked in clean, bright air.

"Are you all right?" Leafpool was crouching beside him.

Hollypaw pressed against his pelt. "What's wrong with him?" she wailed.

How much time had passed?

Graystripe was still standing at the fresh-kill pile with a vole dangling from his jaws. Spiderleg was still chasing Toadkit away from his tail. The vision had only overtaken him for a heartbeat or two.

"Something's coming," Jaypaw croaked. "Something"—he broke off as terror seized him again—"something dark!"

Leafpool didn't comment. Her attention had been snatched away by the rustling of the barrier.

"Poppyfrost!" Firestar greeted the young warrior as she padded out of the thorns. Then the ThunderClan leader's mew sharpened. "Are you okay?"

Poppyfrost was ruffled and nervous. Birchfall followed her, his paw steps hesitant. Jaypaw leaned forward, every hair on his pelt tingling. Unfamiliar paw steps were padding through the tunnel. A new scent filled his nose as a strange tom entered the hollow.

"Who is it?" Jaypaw demanded under his breath.

"I don't know," Hollypaw whispered back.

"What does he look like?"

Hollypaw didn't answer, her thoughts drawn to the stranger. Jaypaw tasted the air. The tom carried the scent of heather on his pelt, and the clean smell of wind and water, but nothing else familiar. He tried searching the tom's mind but found himself dazzled by countless thoughts and images: trees, sky, lightning, roaring monsters, and vast stretches of rolling green water, but none of them stayed still long enough for Jaypaw to see them clearly. It was like trying to gaze at broken water flashing with sunlight.

He nudged Hollypaw. "Well?"

"H-he's tall," she mewed distractedly. "Taller than Firestar. His head narrows toward his chin, and his ears are large and wide spaced. His fur is longer than ours—dark brown and white with splashes of bright tortoiseshell—and his tail . . ." Her mew trailed away. "I've seen him before! It's the lion."

Jaypaw stiffened in alarm. "What?"

Her voice dropped even more. "On the moor, with the sun rising behind him. He looked like a lion."

Jaypaw wanted to know everything, but Firestar was padding toward the stranger. The air in the hollow crackled with tension.

"Thornclaw." Firestar's voice was sharp as he addressed the senior warrior. "Why have you brought this cat here, into our camp?"

"I-I . . ." Thornclaw seemed lost for words, and Jaypaw sensed confusion clouding the warrior's thoughts. He was no longer sure why he had led a perfect stranger to the heart of Thunder-Clan territory. It had just seemed like the right thing to do.

"Firestar." Unexpectedly, the stranger broke in. "I am honored to meet you. I have long looked forward to see-ing ThunderClan." His mew was deep but his tone light, as though promising honesty.

"How does he know us?" Spiderleg hissed.

"Where's he from?" Leafpool breathed.

"You've looked forward to seeing ThunderClan?" Disbe-lief edged Firestar's meow as he echoed the stranger's words. "What do you want with us?"

"What do *we* want with *him*?" Mousefur growled. "Send him away!"

"I want nothing from you." The stranger's mew echoed around the hollow.

Wariness flashed from Firestar. "Then why are you here?"

"I came because it was time."

"Time for what?" Spiderleg called.

"Time to come," the stranger replied. Jaypaw shivered. How did this cat make such simple words sound so powerful?

Firestar shifted his paws.

"He's talking nonsense," Mousefur muttered. "Tell him to leave."

"But he just got here!" Toadkit skipped excitedly across the clearing. "Who are you?" he asked, stopping in front of the stranger.

WARRIORS: POWER OF THREE: ECLIPSE   165

A purr of amusement rumbled in the stranger's throat. "I am Sol."

Brambleclaw padded quickly forward. "You and Rosekit should be resting in the nursery," he told Toadkit. "You couldn't have gotten much sleep last night."

"There was trouble?" Sol meowed.

"No." The ThunderClan deputy followed Rosekit and Toadkit as they padded, grumbling, to their den. He waited while they scrambled inside, then called to Thornclaw, "Where did you find this stranger?"

"On the WindClan border," Thornclaw explained. "He wasn't stealing prey, or even trying to cross into our territory. He was just . . . waiting."

"I was waiting for a patrol," Sol told them.

How does a loner know about borders and patrols?

"Why?" Firestar sounded baffled.

"So that they could escort me here."

Jaypaw focused on Sol, groping for a reason why he had come. But he still couldn't make any sense of the glittering shoal of thoughts.

His Clanmates seemed to have been lulled into a bewildered, ruffled silence.

When no one spoke, Sol meowed again. "I have intruded." The tip of his tail brushed the earth. "I thought that Thunder-Clan above all would welcome me." His attention fixed on Firestar like a shaft of light. "You like to help cats less fortunate, don't you?"

Firestar bristled. "We don't turn away cats who are in need," he meowed carefully. "But you say you need nothing."

"You want me to go," Sol concluded. But he made no move to leave. Instead, he sniffed as though tasting the air for more information. "May I meet your Clan first? I have traveled far, and alone, and I would be grateful to brush pelts with other cats for a few moments."

"Very well." Firestar padded across the clearing. "This is Brambleclaw, my deputy." His tail swished the air. "And that is Leafpool, our medicine cat."

"So *you* are the medicine cat." Sol sounded pleased.

"Y-yes," Leafpool meowed, shifting her paws.

"This is Thornclaw, Graystripe, Sandstorm, and Dustpelt," Firestar meowed quickly.

"And I'm Icepaw!" The young apprentice bounded forward. "And that's my brother, Foxpaw."

"Ah, 'paws," Sol meowed thoughtfully. "You are learning to be warriors, yes?"

"That's right," Brambleclaw answered for her. "In fact, they should be training now." He addressed the apprentices. "Shouldn't your mentors have you out in the forest?"

Whitewing darted forward. "Yes, come on, Icepaw, let's go do some battle training. Foxpaw, you can train with us until Squirrelflight gets back from hunting."

"Can't we stay here?" Foxpaw whined. But Whitewing was already shooing them out of the camp.

With a squeak, Rosekit and Toadkit tumbled out of the nursery.

"I thought I told you—" Brambleclaw began, then stopped

as Daisy followed them out, scolding.

"I told you, Millie's kits are too young to play! Even if you were just tickling them with a feather!" The queen's angry mew trailed off abruptly. She must have spotted Sol.

"Away with you!" she whispered to her babies, her mew brittle with embarrassment. She hurried Rosekit and Toadkit toward the apprentice den. "Play over here, and don't make any noise. Firestar is busy."

"She isn't Clanborn, is she?" Sol commented.

Spiderleg growled. "She's part of ThunderClan now!"

"Of course," Sol meowed smoothly.

Spiderleg shuffled his paws. "I meant she's one of us, that's all."

Jaypaw smelled fresh prey as the barrier rustled. Squirrelflight and Sandstorm were returning from their hunt. They slowed when they spotted Sol, surprise pulsing from them.

"More prey?" Sol queried as they dropped their catch self-consciously on the fresh-kill pile. "Do you ever run out?"

Brambleclaw crossed the clearing to join Squirrelflight. Jaypaw didn't catch what he whispered in his mate's ear before turning back to Sol. "Prey is scarce in leaf-bare, but we survive," he meowed.

"I can see," Sol meowed approvingly.

"Perhaps we can offer you a meal before you continue your journey," Firestar offered.

Sol sat down. "I catch my own prey."

"Can't he take a hint?" Hollypaw whispered.

Jaypaw felt Sol's gaze hot on his pelt.

"You have blind cats in the Clan?"

Leafpool stepped in front of Jaypaw. "Jaypaw's my apprentice," she meowed protectively.

"*Two* medicine cats," Sol observed. "Even better. I have something to share that I think a medicine cat will appreciate more than a warrior."

"So you *have* come for a reason!" Firestar challenged.

"I am just passing through," Sol meowed lightly. "But while I'm here I may as well share." He paused. "Would you rather I left immediately?"

"No!" Leafpool darted forward. "Let him share what he knows with me," she begged to Firestar.

"It is not for all ears," Sol warned.

"We can go into the forest," Leafpool suggested.

She feels his power too! Why else would she be so eager to share with him?

Firestar hesitated.

"Very well," the ThunderClan leader agreed cautiously. "But take Jaypaw with you."

Leafpool led Sol out of the camp, and Jaypaw followed, padding in their paw steps until they reached a mossy clearing not far from the camp entrance.

"What is it that you want to tell us?" Leafpool seemed determined not to be intimidated.

Sol crouched, energy surging from his pelt. "Darkness is coming," he hissed.

Jaypaw held his breath. *The choking blackness!* He pushed the memory away. He had to hear everything that this cat said.

"What do you mean?" Leafpool's mew was taut.

"A time of great emptiness lies ahead," Sol warned. "Nothing will be the same again."

Sol's voice was hypnotic, and his words seemed to echo with the wisdom of the ancient Clans. Jaypaw leaned closer as Sol's voice grew softer.

"The sun will go out."

What does he mean? Jaypaw struggled to see beyond the words, into Sol's thoughts, but it was like trying to catch fish too slippery to grip.

Leafpool shifted her paws. "StarClan hasn't given me any signs."

"Dear Leafpool." Sol sighed. "Your faith is noble, but can StarClan really know everything?"

"But—" Leafpool tried to object, but Sol pressed on.

"They are only the spirits of ordinary cats like you and me, aren't they?"

That's what I think! Jaypaw's fur stood on end. *But he's brave enough to say it out loud.* He wanted to ask Sol how he knew. Had he met StarClan? The Tribe of Endless Hunting? *Rock?* But Leafpool flicked the tip of her tail across his mouth to stop him from saying anything.

"We have been guided by StarClan in many things," she meowed firmly. "They found us a new place to live after our forest was destroyed by Twolegs. We will continue to trust in them for all the moons to come."

Sol sat up. "I was only thinking of the Clans," he meowed. Had Leafpool offended him? "But no doubt they can take care of themselves, as they always have."

"Yes, they will." Leafpool stood and began to head back toward the thorn barrier. Clearly she didn't care whether she'd offended him or not.

Sol padded slowly after her. Was that satisfaction warming the stranger's pelt?

Jaypaw began to follow.

"Hush!"

A hiss from the undergrowth made him stop in his tracks. He sniffed the air.

Foxpaw and Icepaw!

"I thought you were training," he mewed sternly.

Ferns swished as the apprentices slid out from where they'd been hiding.

"Whitewing sent us off to practice stalking," Foxpaw mewed sheepishly.

Icepaw showed no sign of embarrassment. "Is it true?" she squeaked. "Is the sun really going to die?" She was quivering with a mixture of excitement and horror. "Why hasn't StarClan warned us?"

"Be quiet!" Jaypaw pricked his ears, afraid Whitewing might be close. "None of the others must know!"

"But we should warn them!" Foxpaw mewed.

"Who do you trust more?" Jaypaw snapped. "This stranger? Or StarClan? Spreading gossip like this will only cause panic. You must think like warriors, not kits." Praying this would be enough to keep them quiet, he shooed them toward camp and followed them as they scampered through the thorn barrier.

Lionpaw, with the scent of trees lingering on his pelt, hurried to greet Jaypaw. "What did you find out about him? Hollypaw told me you've been into the forest to talk."

"Leafpool and Sol did the talking."

"What did they say?"

Jaypaw pricked his ears. Firestar was speaking to Sol.

"A patrol will escort you to the border," the ThunderClan leader meowed.

"We'll make sure he crosses it," Dustpelt growled from the barrier, where he waited with Sandstorm and Spiderleg.

Jaypaw felt his paws grow hot as Sol began to pad toward them.

"Well?" Lionpaw pressed.

Sol's faint, unfamiliar scent filled his nostrils.

"Don't forget." Sol leaned close as he passed. "Darkness is coming."

"What did he say?" Lionpaw demanded as Sol headed out through the tunnel.

Jaypaw stifled a shiver. "It doesn't matter," he mewed.

CHAPTER 12

"Why don't you two go to sleep?" Lionpaw grumbled, circling in his nest yet again.

Icepaw and Foxpaw had been whispering in the dark ever since Whitewing had sent them to their nests. With only five apprentices left in the den, the noise seemed louder than usual. Hollypaw was asleep with her tail covering her ears, and Cinderpaw snored gently beside her. Didn't Icepaw and Foxpaw need rest, too? Lionpaw tried to make himself comfortable, but his moss felt lumpy.

"What are you whispering about, anyway?" he hissed at the two young apprentices.

"Nothing important," Foxpaw mewed.

Lionpaw wriggled, feeling a pebble deep in his nest. Perhaps that was what was making him so uncomfortable. He rooted down through the moss, feeling for the stone and wishing he were asleep.

The whispering started again.

"Shut up!" Lionpaw hissed.

"It wasn't us!" Icepaw retorted indignantly.

Lionpaw tensed. Who was it then? He sat up in his nest.

Something was moving outside. A faint shadow flickered over the branches of the den. Lionpaw tasted the air. A musky tang filled his mouth. Not ThunderClan.

He froze.

WindClan!

Had they come to ask for help? But why now, under cover of darkness? He crept to the entrance of the den.

"Where are you going?" Foxpaw whispered.

"Shh!"

Peering out, Lionpaw saw thin shadows streaming through the thorn tunnel. The light-footed shapes were filling the clearing, hardly visible under the moonless sky.

He blinked in disbelief. An invasion?

"Attack!" Lionpaw screeched the alarm and shot from the den. He slammed into a WindClan cat, surprised that the wraithlike warrior felt so real. Noise exploded around him as, snarling and hissing, the WindClan invaders turned on him. He lashed out at the barrage of paws, keeping his hind paws firmly planted against the onslaught.

Then he dropped and crouched, letting the attackers fall in upon themselves, and wriggled out of the melee.

ThunderClan warriors were streaming from their den, pelts bristling, eyes wide with shock. Hollypaw raced into the clearing with Cinderpaw, Icepaw, and Foxpaw at her heels. "Why are they attacking us?"

This was no time for questions.

"Circle the clearing and pick off the outsiders!" Lionpaw ordered.

He ducked as a WindClan warrior leaped for him, then arched his back. His attacker rolled clumsily over him, landing wrong-footed as Lionpaw spun and leaped for his throat.

Only just in time, he re-aimed his attack, biting the WindClan warrior sharply behind the ear and rolling him to the ground. *I nearly killed you!* Lionpaw realized how close he'd come to tearing this warrior's throat out. "Get out of my camp!" he hissed, hooking the warrior with his forepaws and raking his belly with his hind. *Or I will kill you!*

The WindClan warrior wriggled from his grasp but didn't flee, only disappeared into the throng of cats fighting in the clearing. Lionpaw tried to follow him, but the WindClan warrior's pelt disappeared into the gray, writhing mass.

A flash of white! Cloudtail was shouldering his way through the crowd. Sandstorm's pelt glowed at the far side of the battle; close by, Lionpaw could make out the white-patched pelts of Sorreltail and Brightheart. Whitewing was outside the elders' den, slashing side by side with her apprentice, Icepaw, at an advancing line of WindClan warriors. Graystripe reared up at the entrance to the nursery, battering a WindClan cat with such force that it scrambled backward, hissing, into the crowd.

Brightheart rolled past him, grappling with a spitting WindClan tom.

Graystripe grabbed the tom, hooking him away from his Clanmate and tossing him aside like fresh-kill. "Get inside the nursery!" he yowled.

While Brightheart slid inside the nursery to defend the

queens and kits, Graystripe planted his paws at the entrance, his glittering eyes daring any cat to come close.

"Lionpaw!" Ashfur's yowl sounded from the elders' den. "Get over here!"

Lionpaw scooted around the edge of the battle, ducking past flailing paws. Whitewing and Icepaw were still fighting the oncoming WindClan warriors, their fur darkened with blood.

"We've got to get Longtail and Mousefur onto Highledge," Ashfur growled. "I'll help Whitewing and Icepaw hold this lot off." He rolled onto his back and shoved a WindClan warrior away with his hind paws. "You guide Longtail and Mousefur up the rocks to the ledge."

Lionpaw glanced at Icepaw, grappling with a young Wind-Clan tom. Her eyes shone with fury as she battered his ears with blow after blow.

"Get on with it!" Ashfur screeched.

Lionpaw darted into the elders' den. Longtail and Mousefur were crouching at the back of the honeysuckle cave, fur bristling, claws unsheathed.

"You need to follow me to Highledge."

"We should be fighting," Mousefur spat.

"You may have to," Lionpaw told her. "But for now, it'll be easier to chase WindClan off if we don't have to worry about you." He knew it was blunt, but there was no time for tact. All their lives were at stake. He checked the den entrance. Ashfur and Whitewing were pushing WindClan back. Icepaw, her muzzle glistening with fresh blood, had fought off the tom.

She narrowed her eyes, then lunged at the hind legs of the WindClan warrior battering Whitewing.

They'd created a gap in front of the den big enough to guide the elders through. Lionpaw turned and nudged Mousefur out, then Longtail. He slid alongside them, shielding them from lashing tails and thrashing paws as they made their way to the tumble of rocks leading to Highledge.

Hurry up! He willed Mousefur on.

Longtail was already climbing the rocks, but Mousefur was hobbling as though each step was a struggle. Leaning against her, Lionpaw took her weight and guided her upward.

"Stop!" Firestar stood on the ledge above them, eyes blazing with rage. His yowl rang like thunder around the walls of the hollow.

Lionpaw halted and the cats grew still, all eyes turning to the ThunderClan leader.

"How dare you?" Firestar roared.

The mass of cats parted to reveal Onestar in the midst. The WindClan leader had led the attack himself! Lionpaw stiffened. This was no raiding party. This was war.

Starlight glittered in Onestar's eyes. "We *dare* because we are true warriors," he meowed evenly. "This battle has been too long coming. ThunderClan must learn that they are not the most important Clan in the forest."

Firestar listened, still as rock.

"You watch the suffering of others, waiting to be begged for help like you belong to StarClan." Onestar lashed his tail. "We will not beg. We are *warriors*! We will fight for the prey and the territory we need to survive."

Firestar's eyes grew wide. "So you invade our *camp*?" The ThunderClan leader was outraged.

"We want to make sure you get the message," hissed Onestar. "You think being a warrior means saving mountain cats and rescuing strays. We think it's about taking care of our Clan."

That's unfair! Where would *any* of the Clans be now if it weren't for Firestar? Lionpaw dug his claws into the loose rock to stop himself from leaping at the WindClan leader's throat.

Firestar leaped down from Highledge, landing lightly, and padded toward Onestar. The Clans drew back to let him pass. He stopped, unblinking, a whisker away from the WindClan leader. "If you want a battle," he growled, "then you have one."

Onestar flicked his tail and Lionpaw tensed, ready to push Longtail and Mousefur up to safety when the camp exploded once more into battle. But, to his astonishment, the WindClan cats turned and swarmed out through the thorn tunnel, their paw steps fading into the forest as the barrier grew still.

"Ha!" Icepaw bounded forward. "They're too scared to fight us!"

Dustpelt narrowed his eyes. "It doesn't make sense," he growled. "Why go to the trouble of attacking at night and then leave? They had the advantage. We were totally unprepared."

"We're not unprepared now," Foxpaw mewed, flicking his back legs out in a well-rehearsed battle move.

"I want a patrol to follow them," Firestar ordered. "I want to be sure they've left our territory."

"I'll go!" Dustpelt volunteered at once.

Firestar nodded. "Take Birchfall, Cloudtail . . ." He glanced around his Clan.

Lionpaw leaned forward.

". . . Ashfur and Lionpaw, you go with them."

Yes! Lionpaw bounded down the rocks.

"Is anyone wounded?" Firestar called. Leafpool and Jaypaw were already weaving among the warriors, bundles of herbs in their jaws.

Whitewing was licking the blood spatters from her pelt.

Firestar looked at her anxiously. "Whitewing?"

"Just a few scratches," she meowed. "Mostly WindClan blood."

"Good." Firestar nodded. "I want you to lead a patrol to the ShadowClan border to make sure all's quiet there. Take Brackenfur and Sorreltail."

Hollypaw padded forward. "Can I go?"

"Yes," Firestar agreed. "Icepaw, you go with them too." He looked at Graystripe, who was still guarding the nursery.

"Do you want me to go?" Graystripe volunteered.

"No," Firestar answered. "We need strong warriors to protect the camp in case WindClan return, and I can't think of anyone who would defend the nursery more fiercely than you.

"Brambleclaw!" He turned to his deputy. "Why wasn't the entrance guarded tonight?"

Brambleclaw's gaze darkened. "The extra patrols have stretched us to the limit."

"Guard it now," Firestar told him. "From now on, it will be guarded day and night, patrols or no patrols. We shall just have to manage on less sleep till this danger passes."

Mewling sounded from the nursery, and Graystripe stiffened. Brightheart popped her head out. "The kits are frightened but they're all okay."

Toadkit slid out beside her. "I wanted to see the battle!"

Brightheart grabbed him by the scruff and scooped him back inside.

"Sandstorm." Firestar turned to his mate. "The thorn barrier must be strengthened. We'll weave in all the extra brambles we can find. I want everyone working together."

Sandstorm dipped her head.

Lionpaw raced to the entrance, where Dustpelt was already waiting with Cloudtail. Ashfur and Birchfall joined them.

Dustpelt flicked his tail. "Ready?"

Cloudtail nodded. Birchfall kneaded the ground. Lionpaw could hardly keep his paws still. He wanted to watch Wind-Clan as they fled like cowards over the border.

"Come on." Dustpelt turned and pounded into the forest, and Lionpaw followed, blood roaring in his ears.

The woods smelled of WindClan, and Lionpaw wrinkled his nose. *Warriors?* They were nothing but thieves and bullies. *Perhaps we'll catch them before they reach the border.* His paws itched for battle. He would beat WindClan just like he'd beaten the mountain cats. They were both scrawny bunches of prey-stealers.

Cloudtail raced into the lead, signaling for the patrol to slow down. He was the Clan's best tracker; no WindClan scent would escape him. He led them straight for the border, stopping and sniffing at twigs and leaves before nodding and moving on to the next scent.

As they neared WindClan's part of the forest, he halted beside a low-spreading yew. He sniffed it and then turned his head, ears pricking. Padding into a dip, he sniffed at a bramble and frowned. He jumped onto the bank, which led down to the border stream, and opened his mouth to draw in scent. Shaking his head, he glanced back at his Clanmates.

"What is it?" Dustpelt demanded.

"They split up here," Cloudtail meowed.

Dustpelt flattened his ears. "They did *what*?"

Cloudtail flicked his tail toward the yew. "One group went that way."

Toward the old Thunderpath! An ominous feeling rumbled in Lionpaw's belly.

"Another went that way." Cloudtail was pointing his nose toward the lake. "And the other—"

Birchfall cut him off. "The *other*?"

Cloudtail was looking upstream. "The *other* group has gone deeper into the woods," he finished.

Lionpaw gulped. That was where the tunnel entrance lay.

"Then *none* of them have crossed back over the border?" Ashfur circled his Clanmates, pelt bristling.

"Not as far as I can tell," Cloudtail meowed. "This is as close to the border as the scents go."

"Isn't there any fresh scent on the border at all?"

Cloudtail shook his head.

Ashfur narrowed his eyes. "So they didn't come *in* this way either."

"They must have crossed the moorland border," Birchfall guessed.

Lionpaw prayed it was true. But he couldn't forget the fox den he had found. Had WindClan found it too? Had they used it to invade ThunderClan territory? He fought down the urge to race to the thicket and check for WindClan scents. How would he explain his suspicions to the others?

"We should get back to camp," Birchfall warned. "Wind-Clan is still on our land." Eyes round with worry, he glanced at his Clanmates before bounding away. Lionpaw raced after him, Cloudtail and Dustpelt on his heels. The forest floor blurred beneath his paws as they sped for home.

"Firestar!" Dustpelt exploded through the thorn tunnel and called to the ThunderClan leader.

Lionpaw saw with relief that the camp was the same as when they had left. Foxpaw and Icepaw were passing up brambles to Brightheart, who stretched up to weave them into the thorn barrier. Spiderleg was dragging more branches out from behind the medicine den, while Berrynose and Honey-fern pressed mud and leaves around the bottom of the barrier to root it more firmly into place. Graystripe paced outside the nursery, the fur bristling along his spine. Mousefur and Long-tail crouched on Highledge.

Firestar looked up sharply. "Have they left?" He had been talking with Brambleclaw in the middle of the moonlit clearing.

Dustpelt shook his head.

"What?" Firestar dug his claws into the soft earth.

"They've split up into three groups and disappeared."

Graystripe hurried from the nursery. "Split up?"

"They must be trying to weaken us by dividing us up," Brambleclaw growled.

"The attack on the camp was just to get our attention," Firestar concluded. "They want to draw us out into the forest."

"If they've split up, they've weakened themselves too," Dustpelt pointed out.

"But they have the advantage of surprise," Graystripe muttered. "They know we're coming."

"And we don't know where they're hiding," Dustpelt finished.

Brightheart left her work at the barrier and padded into the clearing. Spiderleg, Berrynose, and Honeyfern joined her, ears pricked and tails flicking nervously.

"We know which way they headed," Cloudtail meowed. "One group went up toward the top of the territory, one went down toward the lake, and it looks like one doubled back and headed for the old Twoleg path."

"How in the name of StarClan did they know which way to go?" Dustpelt wondered.

Firestar frowned. "It looks like they know our territory better than we imagined."

"That's impossible!" Brambleclaw insisted. "Our patrols have kept them from crossing the border."

Lionpaw listened silently, his belly churning as he pictured

WindClan warriors creeping night after night from the fox hole, past the patrols, and into the very heart of ThunderClan territory to scout for places to fight.

The thorn barrier shook as Whitewing charged into the camp. "No sign of trouble on the ShadowClan border!"

Brackenfur and Hollypaw raced in after her, Icepaw and Sorreltail on their heels.

Firestar faced them. "WindClan has split up and are still on our territory."

Hollypaw's eyes widened.

"They didn't *leave?*" Sorreltail gasped.

"No." Firestar paced the clearing. "We need three battle patrols to go out and find them. A fourth patrol will stay behind to defend the camp." He swung his head toward his old friend. "Graystripe, that will be your duty."

Graystripe nodded.

"I'll lead one patrol. Brambleclaw, you lead the second, and Dustpelt will lead the third."

By now the whole Clan was gathered around their leader. Leafpool and Jaypaw listened from outside the medicine den. Firestar scanned the anxious faces. "ThunderClan will defend its territory," he promised. "Ashfur, Lionpaw, Berrynose, Spiderleg, Poppyfrost, you'll follow me." He turned to Brambleclaw and Dustpelt. "Pick your own warriors. Leafpool and Jaypaw will stay in camp with the queens and elders. Brightheart and Whitewing, you stay with them. Cinderpaw, Ferncloud, and Icepaw, you stay too."

Cinderpaw looked ready to argue, but held her tongue.

Icepaw wasn't so wise. "But I—" she began to complain.

Firestar glared at her. "Do you think kits and elders aren't worth defending?"

"Of c-course!" Icepaw backed away.

Dustpelt and Brambleclaw began to gather their patrols, choosing cats with a flick of their tail. The Clan divided like water around rocks, pooling behind the two warriors.

"Are we ready?" Firestar asked.

Brambleclaw beckoned Mousewhisker and Hazeltail, then nodded.

"What about me?" Foxpaw mewed.

"You'll be with us, of course," Squirrelflight called from beside Dustpelt.

The apprentice hurried to his mentor.

"I'll head into the woods near the border," Firestar declared.

Lionpaw pricked his ears. Would he have a chance to check out the fox hole? He might even be able to seal it up.

"Brambleclaw," Firestar went on, "you go to the Shadow-Clan border. Check the abandoned Twoleg nest. And Dustpelt . . ."

The tabby warrior leaned forward.

". . . you head for the lake."

Lionpaw darted to Hollypaw's side. "You'll be careful?"

"I'll do what I have to," she answered.

Jaypaw's gray pelt shimmered in the moonlight as he hurried from the medicine den. "You must *both* come back," he told them. His blind blue gaze sparked with fear.

The prophecy! Was that all he cared about? Their territory was at stake.

"Of course we'll come back," Hollypaw promised, her voice catching in her throat. She brushed her cheek against Jaypaw's.

Lionpaw felt a prickle of guilt. Perhaps he *was* just worried about them.

At the entrance to the nursery, Millie pressed her muzzle into Graystripe's pelt. She looked weary, but as she stepped back Lionpaw could see her eyes glittering with determination. She would die to save her kits.

Daisy squeezed out behind her and called across the clearing, "Take care, Spiderleg!" But the warrior was talking to Berrynose and didn't turn. Had he heard?

Ferncloud weaved around Dustpelt, then nodded a brisk farewell to her mate before turning to Foxpaw. "Be strong and brave, and do exactly as you're ordered."

"Of course." Foxpaw nodded.

Ferncloud opened her mouth to say more but turned away, her eyes clouding for an instant. She had watched her mate, Dustpelt, leave for battle many times, but it was harder to say good-bye to one of her kits.

Icepaw scampered to her mother's side. "I'll be strong and brave too!"

Ferncloud touched her muzzle to the little cat's ear. "I know."

"Lionpaw!" Firestar called from the mouth of the thorn tunnel. His patrol was already filing out into the forest.

"Good luck!" Lionpaw whispered to Hollypaw and Jaypaw before running out of the camp after his Clanmates.

Firestar led them quickly through the woods, keeping to the undergrowth. No cat spoke as they moved through the bushes. In the darkness, Lionpaw stumbled over roots and tripped on stones. They were heading into battle, but the familiar tingle of excitement was dulled by worry. What if his hunch was right? Had WindClan really been sneaking through the fox hole he'd discovered?

Berrynose was jostling behind him, but Lionpaw refused to let him pass.

"Mouse dung!" The cream-colored tom suddenly cursed.

Lionpaw turned to see him hopping about, flapping his paw.

"What happened?"

"A dumb mouse hole tripped me."

"Are you okay?"

Berrynose pressed his sore paw carefully to the ground, then sighed with relief. "Nothing sprained."

The rest of the patrol had pushed on ahead.

"We'd better catch up," Lionpaw whispered.

He quickened his pace, glancing back to make sure Berry-nose was keeping up.

The scent of WindClan soured the air. Worse, it was growing stronger as they neared the border, until it seemed every leaf and twig were tainted by their stench. Lionpaw's heart was racing. Why hadn't he done something about the tunnel? He should have told Firestar, or blocked it up.

An angry yowl made him jump.

"The fox-hearted cowards!" Firestar was furious.

Lionpaw burst from the undergrowth to see the Thunder-Clan leader standing at the edge of the thicket where the fox hole lay concealed. The patrol gathered around it and, even in the moonlight filtering through the trees, the WindClan paw prints were obvious. The forest floor had been trodden to mud by the comings and goings of the WindClan intruders.

"They must have been using this for ages!" Ashfur growled.

Firestar stooped to sniff the prints. "They used it tonight; that's for sure."

Spiderleg was squeezing out of the thicket, using the same gap Lionpaw had wriggled through days earlier. "There's a tunnel in here," he confirmed. "I didn't go down too far, but it stinks of WindClan, and leads toward their territory."

"Then we must block it up," Firestar ordered. "No more WindClan warriors will be coming in this way."

"Or leaving," Ashfur hissed.

Poppyfrost glanced around nervously. "But they're here already."

"Then we'll deal with them next," Firestar promised. He grabbed a dead branch in his jaws and rammed it into the gap in the thicket. "We can seal off the entrance to the tunnel later," he meowed. "Blocking this opening should be enough for now."

Ashfur turned and began kicking mud against the gap in the brambles. The others followed suit. Lionpaw grabbed a broken branch and shoved it in beside Firestar's, churned-up earth spattering his flank. Why hadn't he done this days ago?

Firestar nudged him out of the way. "You and Poppy-frost stand guard." He nodded to the others. "We'll continue checking the border." He led them away from the thicket in silence, each cat prowling now as if hunting for prey. *WindClan prey.*

Standing by the heap of branches blocking the way into the thicket, Lionpaw scanned the forest, whiskers stiff.

Poppyfrost paced a little ways from him, nose twitching.

He glanced at her. "Any sign?"

She opened her mouth to answer, but a bush rustled a few tail-lengths ahead of them. She froze.

A shadow streaked toward her.

Nightcloud!

"Attac—" Lionpaw's warning was cut off as Harespring shot from beneath a bramble and slammed him to the ground. Struggling to his paws, Lionpaw screeched again as Wind-Clan warriors swarmed from the shadows on every side.

CHAPTER 13

♣

A rising wind stirred the forest. Branches rattled and leaves showered down onto the patrol as Hollypaw followed her Clanmates through the woods.

It's so dark!

She glanced up. No starlight glittered through the leaves, and clouds had hidden the moon.

Brackenfur's tail brushed her cheek. He was only a few paw steps ahead of her, but she could hardly see him.

"Stay close," he whispered.

The patrol was moving slowly, picking its way through the forest. WindClan might be hiding anywhere, waiting for them to pass by.

"Ow!" Mousewhisker's muted yelp from behind made Hollypaw jump.

"Are you all right?" she hissed over her shoulder.

"Scratched my eye on a bramble."

Hollypaw stopped and peered through the darkness at Mousewhisker's cut. Blood was welling around his eye and it was already puffed up.

Mousewhisker brushed away the drips with his paw. "I'll be okay," he mewed.

"Keep up!" Brackenfur called to them.

Falling in beside Mousewhisker to guide him, Hollypaw quickened her pace. It was like running blind. Her paws fell on leaves, then mud, then tangled roots. She sniffed the air, her heart racing as she tried to picture where she was. This was how Jaypaw must feel all the time.

Only when her paws scraped against stone did she realize they had reached the old Twoleg path. It was dotted with tufts of weeds, and she had to be careful not to trip.

"Stay close together," Brambleclaw warned. Hollypaw could only just make out his shadow in the darkness. "It'll be easy for WindClan to surprise us."

What does WindClan want? The question whirled in Hollypaw's mind. *All of our territory? But where would we go? We don't deserve this!* Only ThunderClan had tried to help when other Clans refused. Daisy, Millie, Stormfur, and Brook would have had to survive as loners if ThunderClan hadn't welcomed them. And Firestar would never have been able to save ThunderClan—to save *all* the Clans—if Bluestar hadn't taken him in as a kittypet all those moons ago.

Why did the other Clans make such a fuss about it?

Because the warrior code rejects kittypets, loners, and rogues.

As the grim answer flashed in Hollypaw's mind, the ground seemed to rock beneath her paws. Her Clan had been ignoring the warrior code forever! Glancing ahead, she could just make out the abandoned Twoleg nest looming darkly against the black sky. It seemed to sway in front of her.

"Ambush!"

Brambleclaw's yowl snapped her back to alertness and she realized the nest was not swaying, but swarming with the shadows of WindClan warriors. They streamed from the openings, their night-grayed pelts ghostly in the darkness.

"Spread out!" Brambleclaw ordered.

Where? Hollypaw tried to make out the signal he must be making with his tail, but it was too dark. Then WindClan was on him, and he disappeared altogether in a mass of shadowy pelts. She stared in terror as two warriors—Weaselfur and Emberfoot—streaked from the gloom, heading straight for her. Their eyes gleamed with hunger for blood. Her paws felt frozen. Then she was tumbling to the ground while claws raked her side like fire in her flesh.

Remember your training!

Anger shot through her like lightning, and she leaped to her paws, claws unsheathed, and lashed out at her attackers. She caught Weaselfur across the muzzle and felt his blood spatter her fur.

Mousewhisker appeared beside her, his injured eye half-closed, and lunged for Emberfoot, while Hollypaw swiped again at Weaselfur. She had to jump back as Brackenfur rolled past, grappling with Tornear. Weaselfur saw his chance and leaped for her, sending her staggering back with a heavy blow to her cheek. Her paws skidded on the stone path, and she fell. The WindClan warrior's eyes flashed with triumph as he dropped on her, lips drawn back in a snarl. Blood roared in Hollypaw's ears as she fought panic. She twisted just in time to avoid the warrior's sharp teeth, and pushed out with her hind legs.

Yes! She'd caught him in the belly and sent him lurching backward. Leaping onto her paws, she ducked forward and sank her teeth into his hind leg.

"Well done." Brackenfur was beside her. He reared up and slammed Weaselfur to the ground. Hollypaw lunged again, tasting blood as she sank her teeth into his other hind leg. The WindClan warrior yowled in agony and streaked away into the shadows.

Hollypaw reared up to scan the battle.

Thornclaw was fighting off two WindClan cats. As he batted one away, the other dived in low, nipping at his legs.

Cloudtail's white fur glowed in front of the Twoleg nest. WindClan warriors surrounded him. *His pelt is giving him away!*

Beside her, Mousewhisker suddenly shrieked. Emberfoot had pinned him to the ground. Mousewhisker was flailing desperately, half-blinded by the scratch to his eye.

"I'll help him," Brackenfur hissed. "You help Cloudtail."

Hollypaw pelted forward, but Brambleclaw was already beside the white warrior. The ThunderClan deputy dragged two WindClan cats from Cloudtail's back and flung them away like dead leaves. His eyes sparked as he spotted Hollypaw.

"We're outnumbered," he hissed. "You'll have to ask Blackstar for help!"

"Me?" Hollypaw gasped. How could she persuade the ShadowClan leader to fight on behalf of ThunderClan?

"Just do it!" Brambleclaw yowled. "Blackstar would rather have *us* on their borders than this fox-hearted bunch!"

The two WindClan warriors had scrambled to their paws and were diving back for revenge. Before Brambleclaw disappeared beneath a fury of bristling pelts, he glanced at her. "Go!"

She turned and fled. Fear pulsed in her blood. How would she make it through ShadowClan territory alone? *My Clanmates need help.* The thought gave her courage. And her black pelt would hide her.

She slid through the shadows along the Twoleg path, veering into the woods when she scented the ShadowClan border. She had never been this way. *How will I find their camp?*

Sniffing, she scented her way along, feeling the forest floor change underfoot from broad, slippery leaves to prickly needles. The undergrowth grew sparse around her, the trunks thin and smooth as the territory passed from lush woodland to pine forest. Strong ShadowClan scents made the fur along her spine prickle. She must be crossing the border. Ducking low, she thanked StarClan for the darkness. She didn't want to be caught by a suspicious patrol; she wanted to get right into the camp to speak directly to Blackstar. She weaved through the woods, staying close to the trees, praying that their shadows would be enough to hide her.

Where's the camp? Her heart pounded harder. She tasted the air. ShadowClan scent flooded her mouth. Hope fluttered in her belly as she ducked to sniff at the forest floor. *A trail!* Countless ShadowClan paws had passed here. It must lead to the camp!

She followed the scent trail on trembling paws and, glancing up, saw a shadow looming ahead. A swath of brambles blocked the path. Could this be the camp? She slowed, pricking her ears. She could hear muffled mewing. A kit cried and the bramble leaves rustled.

This *must* be the camp.

She padded closer, skirting the brambles, wondering how she could find the entrance.

"Who's there?" A snarl startled her. She blinked into the gloom as pine needles shifted ahead of her. A cat blocked her path. It was Ivytail; Hollypaw recognized her white-and-tortoiseshell pelt from Gatherings.

Breathing hard, she tried to explain. "I'm Hollypaw of ThunderClan," she mewed. "Brambleclaw sent me. I must talk with Blackstar."

Ivytail approached cautiously, whiskers twitching as she sniffed at Hollypaw. She scanned the forest. "Where's the rest of your patrol?"

"There's only me." Hollypaw spotted a gap in the wall of brambles. The entrance? Was Ivytail guarding it?

"No warriors would send an apprentice into enemy territory alone," Ivytail growled.

Hollypaw dug her claws into the needle-strewn ground. "I must talk to Blackstar," she repeated. *My Clanmates are being torn to shreds.*

"Are you planning to distract him while your Clanmates attack?" Ivytail sneered. "How stupid do you think we are?"

Hollypaw's patience snapped. She shouldered past the ShadowClan warrior and darted for the gap in the brambles.

Ivytail raced after her as she tore through the tunnel and burst into the ShadowClan camp.

"What in the name of StarClan . . . ?" A large tabby tom spun around to face Hollypaw as she skidded to a halt in the clearing.

"Where's Blackstar?" she demanded.

The tom bristled, his eyes round with surprise.

"Hollypaw!" A familiar voice sounded beside her.

Hollypaw turned, relieved to see Tawnypelt. "You've got to help me!" Her mew was choked with desperation.

"Slow down," Tawnypelt soothed.

"There's no time to slow down," Hollypaw panted. "WindClan is attacking, and Brambleclaw's patrol is outnumbered. He sent me to get help!"

Tawnypelt stiffened. "Come with me." She led Hollypaw across the clearing and beckoned her to follow her through a gap in the brambles. Inside, Hollypaw blinked, trying to see in the gloom.

"Blackstar." Tawnypelt addressed a shadow at the back of the den. "ThunderClan needs our help." She brushed Hollypaw's flank with her tail and Hollypaw guessed she was inviting her to speak.

"Blackstar." She dipped her head low. "I'm sorry for breaking into your camp, but it's a matter of life and death. WindClan has invaded our territory. They're all over our forest, and we're outnumbered. You have to help us or they'll drive us away."

Blackstar stepped from the shadows, his eyes wide with

worry. "Fetch Russetfur," he whispered to Tawnypelt.

The ShadowClan she-cat slipped from the den, leaving Hollypaw alone with Blackstar.

"How many WindClan warriors?" he asked.

"It seems like all of them, except the elders and kits."

"Where are they?"

"Brambleclaw's fighting a patrol at the abandoned Twoleg nest." Hollypaw tried to stop her voice from shaking. "Firestar followed some to the border, and Dustpelt went to follow another patrol by the lake."

A voice sounded at the entrance. "It sounds like a well-planned invasion." Russetfur slid into the den, Tawnypelt at her side.

Hollypaw turned to face the ShadowClan deputy. "It is. We were totally unprepared."

Russetfur's whiskers twitched. "ThunderClan caught off guard, eh?" Was that amusement in her mew?

Hollypaw bristled with rage. "My Clanmates might be dying while you talk!"

Russetfur blinked. "Yes." She sat down beside her leader. "This is serious. We can't let one Clan be driven out."

Hollypaw stared at Blackstar. Wasn't he going to say anything?

Russetfur went on. "There have always been four Clans. Onestar seems to have forgotten that. We will all be more vulnerable if one disappears." She narrowed her eyes. "But should ShadowClan risk its warriors to fight ThunderClan's battle?"

Yes! Hollypaw stared at Blackstar. *Oh, please say yes!*

Blackstar stood up. "We will come."

Relief flooded Hollypaw.

"Russetfur will organize the patrol."

Don't be long! Hollypaw longed to beg him to hurry, but Tawnypelt brushed her lips with the tip of her tail. "I'll go with Hollypaw now," she suggested, "and give what help I can till the others arrive."

Blackstar narrowed his eyes. Did he suspect that Tawnypelt was just worried about her brother, Brambleclaw, and her former Clanmates?

Who cares? Let's just go!

Blackstar nodded. "Very well."

Tawnypelt dipped her head and backed out of the den.

"Thank you so much!" Hollypaw burst out before scooting after the she-cat. She almost tripped over the kits tumbling around Tawnypelt's paws just outside Blackstar's den.

"Dawnkit, Flamekit, stay out of the way!" Tawnypelt scolded.

A third kit stomped up and down in front of her. "We want to go to the battle!" he squeaked.

"Tigerkit! Have you been eavesdropping again?" Tawnypelt glared at her dark tabby kit, but it was easy to see the fondness in her gaze.

Hollypaw felt a purr rumble in her throat at the sight of their short, fluffy tails.

"Sorry about my kits," Tawnypelt apologized. "They can't wait to become warriors."

"I remember feeling just the same way," Hollypaw mewed.

Tawnypelt hustled the kits toward a yew bush. A white queen waited at the entrance.

"Look after them, Snowbird," Tawnypelt meowed as the queen swished them into the den with her tail. "Make sure they don't leave camp."

Snowbird nodded. "I know all their tricks," she promised.

"Bye, Tawnypelt!" Dawnkit's mew was muffled by Snowbird's fur.

"I'll be back before you know it," Tawnypelt promised. She glanced at Hollypaw and added under her breath, "StarClan willing."

She darted out of the camp like a shadow. Hollypaw paused, glancing up at the sky. The clouds were thinning, scudding across the moon. "StarClan help us!" she whispered.

Tawnypelt was waiting outside the camp. "Follow me."

She led Hollypaw through the woods and into a sloping field. A stream cut through it. This was the land Thunder-Clan had given to ShadowClan moons ago. Twolegs lived here in strange, flapping nests, but only in greenleaf.

"Keep low," Tawnypelt warned. She ducked and streaked across the grass, leaping the stream where it narrowed near the top of the field. A few Twoleg nests rustled in the breeze, but there was no sign of life apart from a gentle growling from inside.

They were in the ThunderClan forest within heartbeats. Tawnypelt clearly knew the territory well. She headed straight for the Twoleg path and followed it, her paws almost silent on the stone.

Hollypaw pricked her ears, suddenly terrified. Had she been gone too long? Had WindClan chased off her Clanmates already?

A screech told her that the battle still raged. Tawnypelt began to run, and Hollypaw hared after her. The Twoleg nest loomed ahead of them, yowls splitting the air. Cloudtail's white pelt was stained and ragged as he struggled with the shadowy shapes of two WindClan warriors. Brackenfur screeched in fury as he threw a tabby tom from his back. Brambleclaw and Mousewhisker fought side by side, driving a line of WindClan cats back against the stone side of the Twoleg nest. With a battle cry, Tawnypelt flung herself into the fray.

Hollypaw stared. Would this battle never end? Unsheathing her claws, she raced to defend her Clanmates.

CHAPTER 14

"I can't stand hearing it and doing nothing." Ferncloud crouched in the clearing beside Jaypaw. Distant wails and screeches echoed from the forest.

"We need you here in case the camp is attacked again," Jaypaw pointed out.

"Waiting is worse than fighting," Ferncloud growled.

"Concentrate on noises inside the camp."

"What noises?" Ferncloud stiffened beside him as she strained to listen. Couldn't she hear the murmuring and shuffling from inside Firestar's den?

Longtail and Mousefur were sheltering there with Millie, Daisy, and the kits. From the sound of it, they were having trouble finding room.

"Where am I supposed to sit?" Longtail complained.

"Just stay where you are," Mousefur croaked. "If you move, you might tread on another kit."

Another bout of mewling started, followed by Millie's soothing mew. "It's all right, little ones. Isn't it fun to be in the leader's den?"

"I want to be outside fighting!" Toadkit squeaked. "Not stuck in this hole."

"You'll turn your mother's fur white with talk like that," Mousefur scolded. "You're too young to fight. Stop complaining and make yourself useful, like Rosekit."

Rosekit was mewling softly to the younger kits, helping to quiet them.

"Do you think they'll attack the camp again?" Daisy fretted.

"Whatever happens, no cat's going to harm our kits," Millie growled. But Jaypaw could hear fear in her mew. There was nothing she could do to help her Clanmates fighting out in the forest.

Graystripe, Whitewing, and Icepaw paced outside the barrier, guarding the entrance. They were too busy listening for danger to speak. Icepaw's fur scuffed against the forest floor from time to time, and her paws scrabbled on the fallen leaves. *She must be practicing battle moves.*

Inside the hollow, Brightheart restlessly circled the camp. Occasionally she stopped, and Jaypaw guessed she was scanning the ledges along the steep rock walls in case any WindClan warriors were trying to sneak down in a stealth attack. Jaypaw trusted her senses; her one eye made her hearing and sense of smell almost as good as his own. No cat could steal past her. And even if they did, Cinderpaw was prowling the clearing, every hair on her pelt bristling.

"Are you sure your leg's okay?" Jaypaw was worried she'd been pacing on it too long.

"It's much stronger with all the swimming," Cinderpaw promised.

"Just rest awhile," Jaypaw advised.

"I'll rest on Highledge."

Jaypaw wondered whether to stop her from struggling up the tumble of rocks, but there was such determination in her voice that it seemed pointless to argue. Leafpool's memory of the badger flashed in his mind, part of his own memories now—black-and-white fur crashing through bramble walls, snapping jaws, the stench of blood, kits mewling in terror. Cinderpelt had died to protect them. Was Cinderpaw's mind echoing with that memory now? If it was, then *nothing* he could say would stop her from guarding the kits.

He listened to her scrabbling up to Highledge, praying her leg wouldn't slip on the loose rocks, relieved when she mounted the ledge and settled at the mouth of Firestar's cave.

Leafpool was in her den, sifting through leaves and sorting herbs. Jaypaw could smell their pungent aromas mingle as she mixed poultices and ointments, ready for the wounded.

"We've got everything covered," Jaypaw comforted Ferncloud. "ThunderClan won't be taken as easily as Onestar thinks."

Ferncloud shifted on her paws. "Now tell me what you *really* think."

"What do you mean?" It wasn't like Ferncloud to be skeptical.

"It's your duty to encourage your Clanmates, but what has StarClan told you about this battle?"

Jaypaw shook his head. How could he tell her that they'd had no warning? Yet he wouldn't lie to defend his ancestors. Why *had* they let ThunderClan down? "StarClan didn't tell us anything," he murmured.

"Nothing at all?"

"No."

Ferncloud huddled into a tighter crouch, her whiskers trembling.

Was StarClan as surprised as ThunderClan by this attack? Or were they simply on WindClan's side?

Brambles swished.

"How did Cinderpaw get up there?" Leafpool's mew was taut with worry.

"She climbed up," Jaypaw replied.

Leafpool bristled.

"I told her to rest her leg," Jaypaw explained. "It was the only place she would settle." Hadn't he proved already that he knew what was best for Cinderpaw? Why couldn't Leafpool believe that Cinderpaw's leg was healing?

Leafpool called up to Cinderpaw, "Don't try to climb down without help!"

"I don't *need* help!" Cinderpaw mewed. "My leg's fine!"

"She's smart enough to be careful," Jaypaw pointed out. "She's worked hard to recover, and she knows better than both of us what she can and can't manage." He pressed on. "Don't forget that she *wants* to become a warrior. She's not going to do anything that will threaten that."

Leafpool didn't reply.

"Just trust her," Jaypaw urged. *And trust me!*

Leafpool sighed. "Can you tell what's going on in the forest?"

Relieved to change the subject, Jaypaw cast his hearing beyond the confines of the hollow, concentrating on the faraway shrieking, and gradually began to recognize yowls and screeches.

"Dustpelt's patrol is fighting by the lakeside," he told her. "Firestar's patrol has been ambushed near the WindClan border. Brambleclaw's patrol is under attack near the Twoleg nest."

He wished she hadn't asked him. Now his mind swirled with images of cat fighting cat, of blood-soaked pelts, of flesh ripping between teeth. He shivered. "Let me go out there," he begged.

Leafpool stiffened. "No way!"

"Our Clanmates are getting injured," he protested. "I could bring them back to the hollow." He had to do something to help his Clan. He was no use here, even if WindClan attacked.

"But it's dark," Leafpool argued.

"Do you think that makes a difference to me?" Jaypaw let his wide, blank gaze rest on her. "In fact, it'll help. I'll be able to hear cats when they can't see me."

He sensed Leafpool soften. "You will be careful, though?"

"I'm not going to get myself hurt." *I'm too important to let that happen.*

"It would be good to start treating the wounded as soon as we can."

Jaypaw sensed a tremor beneath her mew. There had never been a battle like this before, fought in so many places within a single territory. He reached into her mind and found her thoughts swathed not in fog, but in darkness.

They were all flailing around in the unknown.

Jaypaw stood up. "The sooner I get going, the better."

Leafpool leaned forward and pressed her muzzle to his cheek. "Be careful," she whispered.

Outside the thorn tunnel, Jaypaw sensed Graystripe tense with surprise.

"Where are you going?" the gray warrior demanded.

"Leafpool says I can go look for wounded cats."

Graystripe hesitated.

"Do you want an escort?" Whitewing offered.

"It'll be easier to stay hidden if I'm on my own," Jaypaw reasoned.

"Keep low," Graystripe advised. "If you hear trouble, head away from it."

"I will," Jaypaw promised. He padded away from the hollow.

"StarClan be with you!" Whitewing called.

As he weaved through the trees, picking his way over roots and around trailing bushes, Jaypaw wondered if *any* cats were with him. What about Fallen Leaves' ancestors? Or the Tribe's?

He paused. Which battle was closest? Pricking his ears, he heard a wail from the shore. The lake. He'd check there first. With all that screeching, there were bound to be injuries.

He headed toward the scent of water, his paws slipping on the slope as it steepened toward the top of a low ridge. As he neared the crest he heard a grunt on the other side. A body smacked onto the ground. Jaypaw tasted the air, recognizing the scents of Sorreltail and Honeyfern. Honeyfern hissed, and claws scraped fur. A yowl split the air, and paws scrabbled against the leafy forest floor. Who were they fighting?

He tasted the air again, expecting to smell WindClan. But this scent was different. Watery, with a hint of fish.

RiverClan!

Two of them, by the smell of it.

What in StarClan's name are they doing here?

Ducking low, he crept forward, nosing his way under a red currant bush. Its soft leaves stroked his pelt. It should give him good cover. He pulled himself forward, careful not to make the bush rustle.

One of the RiverClan cats was taunting Honeyfern. "Call yourself a warrior?"

"Call yourself a cat?" Honeyfern retorted. Pelt brushed pelt, and the two cats rolled, tussling on the ground.

"This is too easy," the other RiverClan cat hissed.

Sorreltail yelped in pain.

Fresh air bathed Jaypaw's muzzle. Then a strong smell of fish as a RiverClan pelt brushed his nose. Screeching a battle cry, he shot forward with his claws unsheathed and sank them into the glossy pelt in front of him.

The RiverClan tom screeched in surprise.

"Thanks, Jaypaw!" Sorreltail called.

Jaypaw ducked back as his Clanmates fell upon their attackers. Paws scrabbled in sudden desperation. The RiverClan cats were on the defensive now.

"Thought we were easy prey, didn't you?" Honeyfern's growl was followed by a yowl of pain from one of the River-Clan warriors.

"They're running away!" Sorreltail cheered.

"Let's chase them home!" Honeyfern yowled. Her paws thrummed the earth as she hared in pursuit of the fleeing warriors.

"Argh!" Sorreltail squealed as she tried to give chase and stumbled to a clumsy halt.

Jaypaw darted out from the bush. "What's wrong?"

"I've twisted my paw!"

He sniffed at the forepaw she held gingerly out. It was hot but not swollen. Gently he grasped it between his jaws and lifted it. Then he gave it a soft shake.

Sorreltail gasped but didn't screech.

Placing it carefully down, Jaypaw told her, "It's sprained, not broken. But I need to get you back to camp."

"I can't go now!" Sorreltail gasped. "RiverClan has joined the attack! There are more of them down on the shore. They attacked us from behind while we were fighting WindClan." Her mew was filled with outrage. "What did we ever do but help them? Why are they trying to drive us out of our home?"

Jaypaw couldn't answer. He didn't know why any of this was happening, and StarClan wasn't giving any answers.

"Is Honeyfern all right?" he asked.

"Just a few scratches," Sorreltail replied. "Once she's seen those two off, she'll rejoin the patrol." She turned to go. "I should get back to them too."

Jaypaw darted in front of her, ready to block her path, but it wasn't necessary. She gasped in pain when she tried to put weight on her sprained paw.

"Let's get that seen to," he mewed. He pressed against her shoulder and began to guide her up the slope back toward camp. With a pang, he remembered helping Cinderpaw this way after her accident in her warrior assessment. That seemed moons ago now.

Panting, they neared camp, Jaypaw stumbling under her weight. He was relieved when he heard Graystripe pounding toward him.

"Here, let me take over." The gray warrior nosed him out of the way and supported Sorreltail for the last few paw steps into camp.

Leafpool hurried across the clearing to meet them, comfrey leaves bundled between her jaws. "Lay her here," she ordered, dropping the comfrey.

She's in safe paws now. Jaypaw turned, preparing to go out again.

"Wait!" Graystripe blocked his path. "What's it like out there?"

"RiverClan is fighting with WindClan," Jaypaw told him. "I'll try to find out how far they've gotten into our territory." He padded past Graystripe, feeling the warrior's tail touch his back.

"Try to reach Firestar," Graystripe meowed. "Warn him about RiverClan, but don't take any risks."

Jaypaw pushed his way out through the thorn barrier once more and headed inland, toward the border, where he could hear Firestar's patrol battling the WindClan ambush. Ashfur's yowl rang through the trees, desperate but determined. They hadn't been beaten yet.

Jaypaw weaved through the trees, feeling his way with his whiskers, keeping low. His pelt bristled as he remained alert for any sound other than the distant cries of battle.

"Stupid brambles!"

A sudden unfamiliar mew sent Jaypaw scooting backward into a clump of ferns. They swallowed him and he froze, relieved to be hidden.

"Did you hear that?" The mew was only a few tail-lengths away.

Jaypaw tasted the air. *RiverClan again!*

"Hear what?"

"That rustling."

"Everything rustles in this dumb place."

Four RiverClan cats were making clumsy progress through the woods. One of them tripped, setting a whole bramble bush rattling.

"Could you make any more noise, Reedwhisker?"

"Shut up, Mosspelt! You're the one that yelped like a kit when you fell down that rabbit hole!"

Jaypaw's whiskers twitched. *Like fish out of water.* He waited for them to pass. *They're heading for the WindClan border.*

Firestar's patrol!

He had to get there first. He backed out from the ferns as

quietly as he could and darted along a fox trail. He knew it led directly to the border stream. For once he was grateful for the stench of fox; it made it easy to follow the trail and would hide his own scent. The sound of battle grew louder. Jaypaw smelled blood and sensed fear and pain flooding the forest. He slowed as he heard scuffling ahead and tasted the air.

Lionpaw.

The scent of his brother was strong.

He pricked his ears. Lionpaw was fighting two WindClan warriors single-pawed. Jaypaw unsheathed his claws, wishing he could help. But Lionpaw sounded as though he was doing okay by himself. One of the WindClan warriors was already hopping on three legs, and the other was scrabbling on the ground, backing away in a hurry.

"Run home, cowards!" Lionpaw sneered as the bushes beside Jaypaw exploded and the two WindClan warriors pelted past him.

"Lionpaw?" Jaypaw hissed.

"Jaypaw? Is that you?" Lionpaw darted toward him. "Are you okay?" He was breathing hard, and his pelt smelled of blood. Energy was pulsing from him as though a fire raged in his belly, and Jaypaw could sense that his mind was caught in a whirl of exhilaration.

"Four RiverClan cats are heading this way to help Wind-Clan," Jaypaw warned.

"RiverClan?" Lionpaw sounded shocked for a moment. Then his mew hardened. "I'll sort them out." He hurried away, leaving Jaypaw blinking in surprise.

"You can't tackle them on your own!" Jaypaw called after him.

But Lionpaw had vanished among the trees.

"Jaypaw?" Firestar's mew sounded close to his ear. "What are you doing here?"

"RiverClan has joined WindClan in the battle."

Firestar drew in a sharp breath. Fear flickered from his pelt for an instant. "Go tell Brambleclaw." The ThunderClan leader's mew was grim. "Can you find the way?"

Jaypaw nodded.

"We're outnumbered here," Firestar went on. "We may need to retreat to the hollow and defend ourselves there."

Jaypaw's heart lurched. That would give WindClan control of the rest of the territory. It would no longer be a question of protecting their borders. They would be fighting for their lives. He longed for Firestar to tell him it would be all right, but the ThunderClan leader had plunged away, back into battle.

Jaypaw lifted his muzzle, finding his bearings. The lake breeze was blowing from behind him. The sound of Brambleclaw's patrol screeched somewhere ahead. He pushed on through the undergrowth, heading for the noise, whiskers twitching, paws feeling gingerly ahead with each step. He couldn't risk tripping and hurting himself. He had to warn the Clan deputy about WindClan's RiverClan allies.

Birds were stirring in the trees, chattering anxiously as the sound of battle unsettled the forest. The air began to taste warm. Dawn must be on its way.

Jaypaw's forepaws slipped as the ground dipped down steeply in front of him. Unsheathing his claws, he skittered down the slope, half running, half falling into a soft swath of ferns at the bottom. Only tail-lengths ahead, claws scraped against stone. Cats hissed and yowled, and the air smelled of blood.

And of fish. RiverClan was here already.

He'd found Brambleclaw's patrol too late!

Jaypaw trembled as he sensed exhaustion flooding from his Clanmates. They couldn't hold out much longer.

"Jaypaw?" Hollypaw was backing through the ferns toward him. "I thought I smelled you." Her words were slurred, and her pelt was sticky with blood. She was as close to being beaten as he'd ever known. And yet determination still stiffened her battered body.

I should have brought traveling herbs to give her strength.

"What are you doing here?" she panted.

"I came to warn you that RiverClan has come to help WindClan."

"Thanks, but we know," she mewed grimly. Suddenly she pushed him back. "Stay out of the way!" Paws were padding toward them. Jaypaw smelled a RiverClan tom advancing.

A growl rumbled in Hollypaw's throat. Jaypaw sensed the power and energy rippling beneath the RiverClan warrior's pelt. It was an unfair match! Hollypaw was exhausted. He had to help her. Crouching beside her, he faced the tom and ripped at the ground with his claws.

Then he froze. Another scent was tainting the air.

ShadowClan!

Tawnypelt was fighting close to Brambleclaw. Was ShadowClan battling them too?

Paws pounded up the Twoleg path. More ShadowClan!

Jaypaw felt a wave of despair break over him. How could they possibly fight three Clans? Had StarClan given up on them entirely? He stumbled back into the ferns. There was nothing he could do now to save his Clan.

Fur brushed his pelt. Tawnypelt was beside him. "What are you doing here?" she demanded.

Jaypaw lashed out with a forepaw, aiming for her muzzle, rage burning in his belly. "How can you attack your own kin?"

She blocked his blow with her paw. "We've come to help," she hissed. "Hollypaw fetched us!" She shoved him farther back into the ferns. "Get back to the hollow and stay out of trouble!"

"What about Hollypaw?"

"Snaketail and Scorchpaw will help her."

Jaypaw tasted the air. Two ShadowClan warriors were fighting alongside Hollypaw now, their scents mingling with the tang of fish-foul blood spraying from her RiverClan attacker. Her paws scrabbled against the path as she leaped forward and, with a yowl of rage and pain, the RiverClan cat pounded away into the forest.

"Go now!" Tawnypelt urged. She turned to head back into the fight, but Jaypaw pressed his paw to her flank.

"Firestar's outnumbered by the WindClan border, and

Dustpelt's struggling beside the lake."

"I'll send warriors to help them," Tawnypelt promised. The ferns rustled as she hesitated. "Wait," she hissed. "Take Mousewhisker with you. His eye's hurt." She leaped away and returned a moment later with the young warrior.

"I want to stay and fight," Mousewhisker was protesting.

"Not with that eye," Tawnypelt told him.

"I can see out of the other."

"That's not good enough."

Jaypaw smelled blood. "You can come back when I've cleaned it up, and fight even better," he promised.

Mousewhisker hesitated. "Okay," he agreed. "But we have to be quick."

Tawnypelt plunged back into battle.

"Come on," Mousewhisker prompted.

Side by side, they ran along the edge of the Twoleg path, back toward camp. Mousewhisker pressed against him, steering him through the undergrowth spilling from the edge of the forest. Jaypaw's head was full of the sounds of horror and spilling blood. The whole forest seemed alive with wailing and clawing and the ripping of fur.

All four Clans were fighting, and StarClan had told him nothing.

CHAPTER 15

❧

Lionpaw lunged at the last RiverClan warrior. The other three had fled wailing into the forest already, but this one was cornered, backed up against a bramble so tangled that even a Thunder-Clan cat would think twice about trying to escape through it.

Mosspelt. Lionpaw recognized the blue-eyed tortoiseshell from Gatherings. But this wasn't a Gathering, and he was going to make her sorry she'd ever set paw on his land.

She crouched, trembling, in front of him as he padded toward her, rage darkening his vision until all he could see was her round, frightened eyes.

"Lionpaw!" Firestar's sharp mew made him freeze.

Mosspelt darted past him and disappeared into the trees.

"Now look what you've done!" Lionpaw turned on his leader. "I could have finished her off."

Wariness glittered in Firestar's eyes. "I think she knew she was beaten."

Lionpaw glanced down at his fur, clumped with blood, some fresh, some drying. What had he done? In the heat of battle he wasn't always sure how he fought. He simply smelled blood and felt flesh tear beneath his claws.

"What about WindClan?" Lionpaw wondered if the rest of the invaders had been beaten yet.

"We've just seen the last one back over the border," Firestar told him.

Ashfur and Berrynose slid from the undergrowth, Spiderleg and Poppyfrost beside them. Ashfur was sticky with blood. One of Berrynose's ears was shredded at the tip. Spiderleg was limping badly, and Poppyfrost, ruffled and bleeding, was round eyed with shock.

"What about the other patrols?" Lionpaw insisted. "We should go help them now that we've finished here."

Firestar flicked his tail. "Spiderleg's got a bad belly wound. We need to get him back to camp before we check the rest of the territory."

Spiderleg was lying down, flanks heaving and blood oozing onto the forest floor. Ashfur dug his nose under his denmate's shoulder and pushed him to his paws. "Come on," he encouraged. "We'll get you back to Leafpool." Berrynose pressed against Spiderleg's other flank, and, between them, the two warriors began to half guide, half carry their injured Clanmate back toward the hollow.

"I'll go see if I can help the other patrols while you take Spiderleg back." Lionpaw wasn't ready to return home. He could hear the other battles raging in the distance. He ought to be there, fighting.

"I can't let you go into the forest alone," Firestar told him. Was that fear in his eyes?

Frustrated, Lionpaw joined his Clanmates as they headed

for home. He tried to hurry them on by padding ahead, but Firestar kept calling him back. Spiderleg was panting, groaning with each step. *Hurry up!*

At last they headed down the slope toward the thorn barrier. Lionpaw halted at the entrance to let Ashfur and Berrynose help Spiderleg through. Firestar followed them in, but Lionpaw hesitated. He could hear rustling in the bushes behind him.

He stared in surprise. "Jaypaw?" His brother was trotting out of the trees with Mousewhisker.

"Are you okay?" Jaypaw called. His nose was twitching. "I can smell blood."

Lionpaw shrugged. "It's not mine."

Mousewhisker's eye was closed and swollen to the size of an apple.

"Is he okay?" Lionpaw asked.

"The cut just needs cleaning," Jaypaw told him.

"Apart from a few scratches, it's my only injury," Mousewhisker meowed proudly. Jaypaw guided the injured warrior into camp, and Lionpaw trailed after them. His claws itched to be fighting again.

"RiverClan has come to help WindClan," Jaypaw was reporting to Firestar. "But Blackstar has sent some cats to help us."

Surprise lit Firestar's eyes. "Blackstar's helping us?"

"He sent a whole patrol."

Firestar drew in a deep breath. "Then all four Clans are fighting on our territory."

Jaypaw nodded.

"You'd better help Leafpool treat the injured."

Leafpool was already crouching over Spiderleg, pressing leaves to his belly to stanch the bleeding.

Firestar turned back to the entrance, signaling to his patrol with his tail.

At last! Lionpaw flexed his claws and followed his leader through the barrier, refusing to step aside when he felt Ashfur pressing on his heels.

His mentor slid past him as they emerged from the tunnel. "You should clean yourself up," he meowed, glancing at Lionpaw's sticky pelt.

"There'll be plenty of time for that after the battle," Lionpaw replied.

Ashfur veered away from the patrol, shadowing its flank, his dark pelt rippling as he slid through the undergrowth. The sun was up now, rising above the trees into a pale, empty sky. Ashfur paused, pricking his ears, and Firestar signaled for the rest of the patrol to halt.

"Cats approaching from WindClan's direction," Ashfur hissed.

Lionpaw tasted the air.

WindClan.

A whole patrol.

He stiffened, tasting the air again to be sure.

Heatherpaw!

He bolted toward the approaching patrol, ignoring Firestar's cry for him to stop. As he darted like a bird through the undergrowth, his paws skimmed the ground. The sunlight glittered golden through the trees, making it easy to spot the WindClan patrol slinking like weasels through the forest. They were heading for the lake, hoping to finish off Dustpelt's patrol, no doubt.

Lionpaw could hear his Clanmates' paws thrumming after him. They exploded from the bushes around him as he reached the WindClan cats.

The enemy patrol scattered in panic, but not quickly enough. Ashfur knocked a brown tabby warrior to the ground, while Firestar flung himself at a black tom. Lionpaw charged through two WindClan apprentices, shoving them aside. Behind them Heatherpaw reared up on her hind legs, her blue eyes wide with shock. Lionpaw lunged at her and grasped her scruff between his teeth. She struggled, wailing, as he dragged her through a wall of ferns and flung her to the ground in the small clearing beyond. Enclosed in the pale green cave, he pinned her down, letting his paws prick her skin.

"You told them about the tunnels!" he hissed. "I can't believe you betrayed me. I thought I could trust you to keep your mouth shut."

"It wasn't me!"

Rage surged beneath his pelt. "So why is my forest filled with your Clan?"

Heatherpaw struggled to escape from his grasp, twisting and biting him hard on the foreleg.

"I don't lie," she growled. "It wasn't me! It was Sedgekit!"

"Why would he do that?" Lionpaw couldn't believe it. "I saved his life!"

"He was boasting to Weaselfur about the tunnels he found, and then every cat in the Clan knew."

Lionpaw stared down at her, stifling the urge to shred her fur. "I don't believe you," he breathed. "You've never forgiven me for wanting to be a loyal Clan warrior." He leaned closer and dug in his claws as she tried to wriggle away from his hot breath. "I'll never forget this, Heatherpaw. I will be your enemy *forever*."

He released her and turned away, swishing through the ferns with his paws trembling with rage. Had he really loved her once? He had been a different cat then. Now he was one of the three, and he walked a path Heatherpaw couldn't even dream of.

Blue eyes flashed in front of him. "Where's Heatherpaw?" Crowfeather was blocking his path.

"Get out of my way!"

The WindClan warrior peered past Lionpaw. "What have you done with her?"

"*Get out of my way!*" Lionpaw lunged at Crowfeather. Hooking his claws into the dark gray warrior's neck, he flung him through the ferns and thumped him onto the ground. Still gripping his throat, he leaped on top, tearing at his flesh in a frenzy.

Suddenly teeth sank into Lionpaw's shoulder and claws dug into his flank.

Heatherpaw was dragging him off. "Stop it!" she shrieked. "What are you doing?"

Startled by the terror in her voice, Lionpaw froze. Crowfeather lay among the green ferns by his forepaws, bright red blood bubbling at his throat.

Heatherpaw crouched over her mentor. "Crowfeather!"

"I'm okay." He lifted his head. Heatherpaw backed away as he staggered, spluttering, to his paws.

Shame seared Lionpaw's pelt. The warrior code told him he didn't need to kill a cat to prove the battle was won. If Heatherpaw hadn't stopped him, he would have left Crowfeather dead.

What have I become?

Suddenly the light changed.

The bright morning air softened into shadow. Dawn seemed to give way to dusk. The birds fell silent. The screeching and wailing of battle ceased. Even the buzz of insects quieted as darkness seeped through the trees.

Lionpaw looked up.

The sun was disappearing, swallowed by a great black disk, darker and more sharply defined than any cloud.

"What's happening?" Heatherpaw's terrified mew hissed in Lionpaw's ear, but he couldn't answer. His voice was trapped in his throat, and his claws rooted him to the ground. Around him the air chilled. And above, the sun vanished completely, plunging the forest into night.

"StarClan's killed the sun!" The shriek of a WindClan warrior rang through the forest. Instantly cats began wailing, and the woods shivered as they fled, their paws thrumming through the pitch-black forest.

"We've got to get home." Crowfeather coughed. He dragged at Heatherpaw's scruff as she stood petrified beside Lionpaw. "Come on!"

Wild-eyed, Heatherpaw turned to follow her mentor.

"I won't forget," Lionpaw hissed in her ear.

As she disappeared into the forest, he watched the sun's dying rays bleed from the edge of the wide black circle.

CHAPTER 16

❧

Jaypaw pressed his nose to Sorreltail's paw. Leafpool had swathed it in damp comfrey leaves, and it seemed cooler already. "How does it feel?"

Sorreltail lifted it. "Much better." She glanced toward the barrier. "I should get back to the fighting."

"No." Leafpool was cleaning up Mousewhisker's eye beside them, soaking away the blood with wet moss. "ShadowClan is helping us now and, by the sound of it, there are going to be enough injuries to treat without you getting another."

"But the fighting's getting closer," Sorreltail argued.

Leafpool shook water from the moss. "In that case we might need you here."

Although the camp felt empty, the forest rang with the chilling sounds of battle. Jaypaw pricked his ears to listen more closely. Firestar's patrol was fighting WindClan just above the hollow. Had they really been driven back that far?

"Shouldn't we take the injured cats into the den?" he prompted. Spiderleg was already resting there, calmed by poppy seeds, his bleeding stanched by cobwebs. "It'll be safer." *If the camp is overrun.*

"The light's better out here now that the sun's up," Leaf-pool meowed. "Besides, I think *they* like to see us."

He knew she meant Daisy and the kits. Millie was organizing them on Highledge.

"Now, who can remember what we do if strangers come into the camp?" Millie prompted.

"Take Millie's kits to the back of Firestar's cave," Rosekit squeaked.

"Then what?" Millie was drilling them carefully.

"We stay with them inside in case strangers come in," Toadkit mewed.

"Where will I be?"

"Just outside the cave, keeping guard with Daisy," Rosekit mewed.

Mousefur's pelt brushed the rock beside Millie. "Longtail and I will be defending the top of the rocks, to stop any cat from getting onto Highledge."

"And I'll be at the bottom!" Brightheart called up from the clearing.

Graystripe and Whitewing were still on guard outside the thorn tunnel. Icepaw had come inside the camp to practice battle moves with Cinderpaw and Ferncloud.

"You will be careful of your leg, won't you?" Leafpool warned Cinderpaw. "No heroics."

"No heroics," Cinderpaw promised. "But if we're invaded, I'm not hiding inside the medicine den!"

Fear flashed from Leafpool's pelt. "We won't be invaded, I'm sure."

Would the ThunderClan patrols really be able to hold WindClan and RiverClan at bay?

"Don't forget ShadowClan is helping us now!" Mousewhisker meowed. "I was fighting beside one of their apprentices when Tawnypelt dragged me away. They're pretty good fighters. We were about to overpower a WindClan warrior." His tail swished over the ground.

"Sit still," Leafpool chided.

Mousewhisker was obviously itching to get back into battle. Didn't he understand how serious this was? All four Clans fighting. No warning from StarClan. No clear reason for the battle.

Jaypaw headed for the medicine cats' den to soak more leaves for Sorreltail's dressing, but as he neared the entrance, the air grew chilly around him. His fur fluffed, prickling along his spine.

"Why is it getting dark?" Rosekit's mew echoed around the hollow from above his head.

Was a storm coming?

Graystripe and Whitewing were hurrying through the tunnel.

"What's happening?" Graystripe called.

"Why's the camp getting dark?" Daisy's mew trembled. "The sky's still light."

"The sun's disappearing!" Brightheart's terrified wail made Jaypaw stiffen. This couldn't just be a cloud passing over the sun. The birds in the forest had fallen silent. Even the fighting had stopped. What was going on?

He darted back to Leafpool. "What does she mean?"

"Something's swallowing the sun!" Leafpool whispered.

Millie's kits started mewling, their cries muffled as their mother gathered them to her.

Leafpool pressed against Jaypaw. "We have to stay calm." Her body was shaking but her mew was steady. "It's probably a message from StarClan. It will pass."

"What message?" Ferncloud demanded.

Graystripe leaned closer. "Are they trying to stop us from fighting?"

"I-I don't know," Leafpool stammered. "They've never hidden the sun, only the moon."

Why send a message now? They hadn't given any warning before.

Jaypaw's blood turned to ice.

This was nothing to do with StarClan. It was *Sol* who had warned them about this. *Sol* who had told them a darkness was coming, a darkness that was beyond the control of StarClan, beyond even their powers of sight. Sol had tried to warn them that the sun would disappear, but they hadn't listened to him.

Wailing swept down toward the camp, and paws thundered near the barrier.

Were they being attacked?

Graystripe's claws sprayed earth as he dashed to the camp entrance. Brightheart hurtled after him.

Jaypaw held his breath as the thorn barrier rattled and cats exploded into the clearing.

ThunderClan.

Jaypaw smelled the raw fear-scent of his Clanmates returning from battle, along with the stench of blood. Wounded cats, too scared to worry about their injuries.

"Why is this happening?"

"Where's the sun gone?"

"Has StarClan abandoned us?"

Terror pulsed from every pelt.

"Can we hide in the nursery?" Icepaw begged Ferncloud.

Lionpaw tore through the thorn tunnel and skidded to a halt beside Jaypaw. Hollypaw was at his heels.

Jaypaw sniffed them quickly, relieved to find they weren't badly wounded. "Has the sun really gone out?"

"Yes." Lionpaw kneaded the ground.

"Is it dark like nighttime?"

"More like dusk." Hollypaw weaved around him, her fur bristling.

"But the sun's really gone?"

Lionpaw brushed his tail against Jaypaw's shoulder. "There's a thin circle of flame in the sky, where it used to be. But the rest of the sun has been covered up."

Why can't I see?

"Is everyone safe?" Firestar demanded.

"As safe as any cat," Graystripe growled. "Where are the other Clans?"

"Fled back to their territories," Brambleclaw called from the barrier.

Whimpers and yowls rippled through the Clan.

"Ferncloud!" Icepaw mewled. "Where are you? I can hardly see!"

"Everybody keep calm!" Firestar ordered. "I don't know what's happening. But we are warriors, and we must face it with courage."

Slowly the Clan began to quiet.

He padded toward Leafpool. "Can you tell us what is happening?"

Will she mention Sol's warning?

"StarClan hasn't spoken to me directly," she mewed.

Jaypaw flexed his claws. *Because they didn't know. . . .*

"This must be an omen," Leafpool continued. "To stop the battle."

"But the battle wasn't our fault!" Hazeltail wailed.

"WindClan started it," hissed Whitewing.

"Why do *we* have to suffer?" Ferncloud yowled.

Leafpool's tail stirred the air. "But it *has* ended the battle. That must be what StarClan intended."

"Are we going to live in darkness from now on?" Thornclaw sounded more outraged than scared.

"Wait!" Leafpool called. "It's getting lighter. The sun's coming back!"

CHAPTER 17

❧

Hollypaw gazed at the trees above the hollow as the sun bleached away the half-light. The sky paled to blue and the air began to warm. Beside her, Lionpaw shifted on his paws, and Jaypaw tasted the air. The birds began to sing again. Late-season bees began to rise sleepily from the grass around the edge of the camp and buzzed away on heavy wings. But, despite the sun on her pelt, Hollypaw was still shivering, her scratched and aching body trembling beyond her control.

What just happened?

She turned to ask Jaypaw. If StarClan had hidden the sun, surely he must know something. But he was hurrying away to join Leafpool as she weaved among the anxious and wounded cats.

"Can you stretch out your forepaws?" Leafpool asked Brackenfur. The golden tom winced as he tried.

"Shoulder wrench," Leafpool concluded. "Go and wait by the halfrock. I won't be long." She moved on to Whitewing. The warrior's snowy pelt was darkened by patches of blood. "Any sprains or wrenches?"

"Just scratches," Whitewing answered.

"Then wait beside the warriors' den," Leafpool ordered. "We'll bring you ointment as soon as we can."

"Thornclaw's sprained a hind paw," Jaypaw called.

"Help him over to the far end of the clearing and let him rest below Highledge," Leafpool told him. She moved on, sending Hazeltail and Poppyfrost to wait with Whitewing.

Hazeltail dropped into a crouch beside Whitewing. "How could the sun disappear?"

"The sky was clear blue, so it couldn't have been a cloud," Poppyfrost breathed.

"Clouds never make it dark and cold like that," Whitewing added.

Leafpool looked at them sharply. "You should be licking those scratches, not chattering like finches!" She nudged Birchfall and then Berrynose toward Thornclaw. "Wait over there."

Birchfall limped across the clearing, keeping his swollen forepaw off the ground. "I don't see why StarClan should hide the sun from *us*!" he meowed indignantly.

Berrynose hopped alongside him, a hind paw held out gingerly behind him. "WindClan should never have started the battle. It serves them right if StarClan is angry with them."

Hollypaw glanced at her brother. He was watching the Clan. "Are you okay?"

"Fine," he mewed.

Didn't he want to talk about the vanishing sun? "You're very quiet."

"Yeah." Lionpaw glanced up at Highledge, where Millie

was picking her way down the tumble of rocks. Briarkit swung from her jaws. Daisy followed, holding Toadkit.

"Let's help them," Lionpaw suggested. He darted away toward Highledge.

How did he have so much energy left? Hollypaw felt weighted with exhaustion, and the scratches and bites that covered her body, though not deep, were stinging. Sighing, she followed.

"I could have walked down myself!" Toadkit flailed his paws crossly.

"Keep still, or we'll both fall!" Daisy's rebuke was muffled by his scruff. She jumped down the last few paw steps and looked back at Millie. "Are you okay?"

Millie nodded. Briarkit was dangling wide-eyed under her chin.

It isn't always like this, Hollypaw wanted to tell the tiny kit, not sure if he was old enough to understand.

Lionpaw reached out a forepaw to steady Millie as she scrabbled down into the clearing, stones cracking behind her. "We'll bring the others," he promised.

"Thanks." Daisy put Toadkit down and he bounced away, fluffing up his fur.

"Watch out!" Daisy shut her eyes as he careered straight toward Graystripe.

The gray warrior sidestepped him. "Why don't you go make sure there's enough moss in Millie's nest, little one?" he meowed.

"Okay!" Toadkit raced away to the nursery.

Graystripe blinked at Daisy. "He's obviously not too shaken."

Daisy's pale eyes darkened. "He just thinks it's an adventure." She sighed.

"Perhaps it's better that he does." Graystripe took Briarkit from Millie and followed Daisy to the nursery. Millie padded beside him, pressing her pelt to his.

Lionpaw was already bounding up the rocks. Hollypaw scrambled wearily after him and followed him into Firestar's den.

It was dark inside. Hollypaw almost tripped over Rosekit, crouched in the entrance. Behind her, Longtail was trying to hush Bumblekit. The tiny gray-and-black-striped tom was wailing for his mother.

Longtail ran his tail gently over him. "Shh, you'll wake your sister."

Hollypaw could just make out Blossomkit curled against Mousefur's belly, sound asleep.

"Don't disturb her." Mousefur waved Hollypaw away with her tail. "Graystripe can fetch her down later."

Longtail nudged Hollypaw's shoulder with his nose. His blind eyes were round with worry. "Did you see it happen?"

He meant the vanishing sun.

"Yes."

"What does Jaypaw say?" Mousefur asked, her eyes gleaming in the half-light.

Lionpaw shrugged. "He doesn't always tell us what he learns from StarClan."

Hollypaw caught his eye. *Is he thinking what I'm thinking?* If they were really more powerful than StarClan, Jaypaw should know what the vanishing sun meant. Lionpaw looked away.

"Perhaps he'll share dreams with them tonight," she mewed hopefully.

Mousefur wrapped her tail around Blossomkit. "I hope so."

Hollypaw grabbed Bumblekit by the scruff and swung him into the air. He squeaked with surprise and churned the air with his tiny paws.

Rosekit backed away. "I'm not being carried down!"

"Oh, yes, you are!" Lionpaw scooped her up and headed out of the cave.

Her paws scuffing the ground with tiredness, Hollypaw followed him to the nursery, where Graystripe was waiting to bundle the kits inside.

"Blossomkit's sleeping," she told him as she passed Bumblekit over. Pain flashed from a scratch on her neck. "Mousefur said you can fetch her later."

Graystripe nodded and disappeared into the brambles.

Cinderpaw trotted over. "Are the kits all right?"

"Lionpaw!" Leafpool called from across the clearing. "Take Foxpaw out to fetch more cobwebs." She was smearing pulp over a cut on Honeyfern's shoulder.

Foxpaw came bounding over at the mention of his name. "I know where there are some really big cobwebs," he mewed. "There's a hollow log just outside the entrance. It's full of them."

Lionpaw glanced at Brambleclaw. The ThunderClan

deputy was standing below Highledge while Jaypaw pressed a sticky poultice onto a wound in his side. "Is it okay to go out?" he called. "Leafpool needs cobwebs."

"Yes, but be careful," Brambleclaw warned.

As Lionpaw and Foxpaw headed away, Leafpool turned to Hollypaw. "There are herbs piled beside the pool in my den," she meowed. "Take them to Whitewing and the others. You've had enough training to show them how to chew them up and lick them into their scratches."

"*I* know how to do that!" Cinderpaw mewed suddenly.

Hollypaw blinked. "How? You're not a medicine cat's apprentice."

Leafpool stopped wrapping cobwebs over Honeyfern's wound. "She's spent so long in the medicine den, she must have picked it up." She waved Cinderpaw away. "Go with Hollypaw and help her. Just be careful of your leg."

"I will."

As they headed for the medicine cat den, Hollypaw noticed that Cinderpaw was hardly limping. "How's your leg?" she asked.

"Much better," Cinderpaw mewed. "I don't think I could do *every* battle move yet, but it won't be long till I can. The swimming helped just in time," she added somberly.

They padded past Squirrelflight. The dark orange she-cat was sitting awkwardly at the edge of the clearing, her haunches drawn up, with one hind paw jutting out.

Hollypaw nodded a greeting, but Squirrelflight only stared dully back.

Hollypaw felt uneasy. "Has Leafpool checked you?"

"Not yet." Squirrelflight's mew was taut.

Something's wrong.

Hollypaw glanced down and saw that the sand around Squirrelflight was stained dark red. *Blood.* "You're hurt!" Her tiredness forgotten, she darted to her mother's side and sniffed at her pelt. Fresh blood was oozing from below her chest. Squirrelflight's forepaws trembled, and she dropped into a crouch, a groan jerking from her as she moved.

Paws pattered behind Hollypaw.

"What's wrong?" Sandstorm was pressing in beside her.

"She's bleeding," Hollypaw whispered, feeling her paws go numb with alarm.

Groaning again, Squirrelflight rolled onto her side, revealing her blood-soaked belly.

Sandstorm gasped. "Why hasn't this been seen to?" She flicked Hollypaw with her tail. "Fetch Leafpool!"

Hollypaw stared at her mother. Squirrelflight was panting, her flanks fluttering unevenly.

"Now!" Sandstorm shoved Hollypaw away.

Leafpool was squatting down at the far side of the clearing, chewing herbs.

"Squirrelflight's hurt!" Hollypaw didn't have to say any more. Leafpool was already on her paws and racing toward the she-cat.

Hollypaw chased after her, skidding to a halt as Leafpool crouched and rolled Squirrelflight over with one paw. With her other she carefully parted the dark orange belly fur. A deep claw gash ran from Squirrelflight's chest to the top of her hind leg. Blood was flooding from it, pooling on the sand beneath her flanks.

Hollypaw pressed her muzzle against Squirrelflight's cheek. "She's hardly breathing." Her mother's eyes were beginning to close. "Stay awake!" Hollypaw begged. She spotted Lionpaw and Foxpaw returning with wads of cobweb hanging from their jaws. *Thank StarClan!* "Over here!"

Lionpaw darted to his mother's side.

"Give me those." Leafpool dragged the cobwebs from his mouth and began padding Squirrelflight's wound. She beckoned Foxpaw over, taking his cobwebs too. "Go to the pool in my den," she told him, not looking up. "Fetch soaked moss. Quick as you can."

Lionpaw was staring at his mother in horror.

"You too!" Leafpool growled. "Quickly!"

Lionpaw and Foxpaw darted away.

Jaypaw must have heard the commotion. He left Brambleclaw, his paws still wet with ointment, and began weaving his way through the wounded warriors.

Brambleclaw watched him go, surprise lighting his eyes, then looked past him and saw Squirrelflight. He charged around the clearing, Jaypaw's poultice crumbling from his flank as he ran. He stopped beside Hollypaw. "What's wrong?"

"Belly wound," Hollypaw whispered.

"How'd it happen?"

Sandstorm shook her head. "She was fighting beside me on

the shore, but I thought she was okay. She was never down for more than a moment."

Brambleclaw crouched beside his mate. "Don't leave me," he begged.

Squirrelflight's eyes flickered open at the sound of his voice, then closed again.

He nudged her with his muzzle. "You'll be okay. Leafpool won't let you die."

Hollypaw stared hopefully at Leafpool, but the medicine cat was too busy working on Squirrelflight's wound to look up. Jaypaw slid in beside her and began holding cobwebs in place as Leafpool applied fresh padding.

Lionpaw returned and dropped a wad of dripping moss beside her. She snatched it up and began washing away the blood. "Fetch more!"

Squirrelflight didn't flinch at the cold water. She was too deeply unconscious.

Hollypaw leaned in closer. "She's going to be all right, isn't she?"

Brambleclaw started to lick Squirrelflight's cheek. "Sleep well, my lovely. I'll be here when you wake up."

"What's happened?" Firestar was staring down at Squirrelflight, his eyes round with shock.

"Get back, all of you!" Leafpool suddenly snapped.

Blood roared in Hollypaw's ears. *She's going to die!* She stepped back, numbly, and brushed against Brambleclaw. Her father was trembling.

"Hollypaw!" Leafpool was staring directly at her. "Go to

my den and fetch oak leaves."

Oak leaves. Oak leaves. She tried to focus, terrified she'd forget, her mind in a whirl of panic.

In the medicine cat's den, she reached into the gap in the rock and dragged out a pawful of leaves. Sifting through them, she separated out the oak leaves. At least they were easy to recognize. She picked them up in her jaws and hurried back to Leafpool.

"Do you want me to chew them up?" she offered, dropping them beside Leafpool.

"Jaypaw can do that."

Hollypaw stepped out of the way. Lionpaw was staring down at his mother, his eyes lit with fury. *He wants to know who did this.*

She realized she was trembling like a kit. She closed her eyes and felt Sandstorm press against her.

"If anyone can save her, Leafpool will."

Hollypaw leaned against Sandstorm, thankful for her warmth, while Leafpool and Jaypaw finished packing Squirrelflight's wound.

Leafpool looked up. "I've done all I can," she meowed. "It's in the paws of StarClan now." She picked up a wad of moss and held it to Squirrelflight's lips, letting the water drip into her mouth.

After a few moments, Squirrelflight swallowed. Was that a good sign?

"She needs a warm nest," Leafpool explained. "But I daren't move her yet in case her wound opens up again." She gazed at

Hollypaw and Lionpaw. "Can I rely on you to build a nest around her?"

Hollypaw nodded. Of course they would!

"Fern, moss, feathers, whatever you can find," Leafpool went on. "She needs to stay warm and still." She got to her paws. "Jaypaw, watch her, and report to me if there's any change. I have to see to the other wounded cats." She looked at Brightheart, who was moving among the warriors with a bundle of herbs in her mouth. "Brightheart can't manage all this alone."

Firestar stepped forward and rested his muzzle on Leafpool's head. "I'm proud of you."

"I just hope I've done enough," Leafpool murmured.

Firestar turned to his mate. "You must be exhausted. You should eat and rest."

Sandstorm's green eyes flashed. "She's my kit! I'm not leaving her!"

Hollypaw felt a thorn-sharp stab in her heart. *She's my mother, too! She can't die!*

"Come on." Hollypaw felt Lionpaw's tail brush her flank. "Let's build her a nest."

Foxpaw and Icepaw sat huddled a tail-length away. Had they been watching all the time?

"Can we help?" Foxpaw mewed.

"We need to find stuff for a nest," Lionpaw told them. "Anything soft and warm will do."

As Foxpaw and Icepaw hurried away, Hollypaw noticed that Firestar and Brambleclaw were already below Highledge in deep conversation with Graystripe, Dustpelt, and Thorn-claw. Their eyes were dark and their voices low. She pricked her ears, but she couldn't make out what they were saying.

"Surely the battle is over?" she mewed. "What's left to talk about?"

"The battle wasn't won or lost," Lionpaw pointed out. "The vanishing sun stopped it. Now that the sun's back, WindClan might return to finish what they started."

"They can't!" Hollypaw bristled in shock. "StarClan has told us that we mustn't fight!"

"If it was StarClan who hid the sun," Lionpaw muttered.

Foxpaw came hurrying back with a large feather fluttering from his mouth. "Will this do?" He sneezed, and the feather shot into the air and drifted onto the ground.

"It's a start," Lionpaw mewed. "But I think we should look outside the camp. We'll need a lot of bedding."

Hollypaw glanced at Squirrelflight, lying on her side. Her flanks were hardly moving, and she looked small and cold. Jaypaw was pressed close to her, his muzzle resting beside hers as though he were listening to her breathing.

"Come on," Lionpaw urged. He led the way through the entrance and out into the forest.

Hollypaw gazed around in surprise. *It's so peaceful. As if nothing's happened.* The sun streamed through the branches, and birds sang in the trees. A few leaves drifted down. Leaf-fall drew closer by the day. Many of the ferns were browning into bracken, too brittle and hard for a nest.

She padded after Lionpaw, her exhaustion returning. Here

and there a flattened clump of grass or a scrap of fur caught on bramble reminded her of the battle just fought, and the sting of her wounds began to prick her once more.

"These ones are soft." Lionpaw stopped beside a green swath of ferns. He began to tug at a frond with his teeth, hauling it out of the ground.

Hollypaw grabbed another in her jaws and heaved it out of the clump. They worked steadily until they'd gathered a thick pile.

"Foxpaw!" Lionpaw called to their denmate.

"We're coming!"

The undergrowth rustled, and Foxpaw and Icepaw appeared with great wads of moss hanging from their jaws.

"I think we've got enough," Lionpaw decided. He hooked his paw over the pile of ferns and began to drag them back toward camp. Hollypaw followed, shoving the fronds together when the pile began to loosen and scatter. She was so tired that the edges of her vision blurred, and the forest seemed to sway about her.

"We would have won anyway," Lionpaw puffed as they neared the barrier.

Really? Hollypaw wasn't so sure. Swerving wearily to avoid a thin trail of blood, she felt as though all four Clans had lost something, though she wasn't sure what.

Squirrelflight hadn't moved when they reached her. Jaypaw was still curled beside her. He looked up as they neared, then stood and stretched. "Put the moss underneath her," he instructed. "The ground's very hard."

Hollypaw pushed one bundle under Squirrelflight's shoulders, another under her haunches, then gently patted a swath around her belly. Her mother's fur was stiff with dried blood and smelled of herbs. Daisy had brought feathers from the nursery, and, while Lionpaw bunched ferns around Squirrelflight, Hollypaw laid the feathers over her to keep her warm. When they'd finished, Jaypaw settled beside her again, resting his chin on her shoulder.

"Come and eat!" Brambleclaw called them over to the fresh-kill pile. Only a few morsels remained. There hadn't been time for hunting today.

Lionpaw padded away, but Hollypaw stayed where she was. She was too tired to eat, her belly hard with grief. She wasn't going to leave her mother's side again. She curled up beside Squirrelflight's head and, breathing softly against her mother's cool ear, closed her eyes.

Please don't let this battle take her away from me.

CHAPTER 18

♣

Lionpaw swallowed his last mouthful. He had hardly tasted the mouse, but it had quieted his rumbling belly. He glanced up at the sun shining high in the clear blue sky. Would it disappear again?

What's happening? Heatherpaw's terrified mew echoed in his mind.

He could not trust her.

He could not trust the sun.

He could only trust himself and his Clan.

The clearing was slowly emptying as Firestar moved from cat to cat, sending them to their dens to rest.

Squirrelflight lay in her makeshift nest with Hollypaw and Jaypaw curled beside her. Leafpool was checking her again.

"You must rest," Firestar urged the medicine cat.

Leafpool was swaying on her paws. "What about the other injuries?"

"Brightheart will see to them and fetch you if you're needed." Firestar looked at the one-eyed she-cat who was prowling from den to den, peering in to check on the cats inside.

"She'll need rest too," Leafpool argued.

"And she'll get it, once you've had some sleep."

Leafpool blinked, her whiskers trembling as she stifled a yawn. "Okay," she agreed. "But wake me if there's *any* problem." She was looking at Squirrelflight.

Hollypaw nuzzled closer to her mother, pressing her nose against Squirrelflight's ear as though she could make her better by wishing it so. Lionpaw's shoulders tensed, and he dug his claws into the soft earth. If he could fight Squirrelflight's battle for her, he knew he would win. Frustration stung his paws. This was a battle she must fight alone.

Firestar's muzzle brushed his ear. "Shouldn't you be resting too?"

"I'm not tired." He stared into Firestar's clear green gaze.

Firestar blinked first. "Come on, then. We need to decide what happens now."

Lionpaw followed him to where Dustpelt, Ashfur, and Brambleclaw were sharing a rabbit with Cloudtail and Sandstorm.

Sandstorm looked up as they approached, and nudged a mouthful of the prey toward Firestar. "You must be hungry."

"I'll eat once the fresh-kill pile's been restocked," Firestar replied.

Sandstorm stared at him, then glanced down at the morsel she'd offered. "You need your strength as much as any cat."

Firestar sat down, his shoulders sagging, and took the piece of rabbit. "Thank you."

Brambleclaw was sitting uncomfortably, the thorn stab in his side clearly hurting. Lionpaw swallowed the growl rising in his throat. No other cat was going to suffer because of Heatherpaw's betrayal! He sat down. Now they would plan revenge on WindClan and RiverClan. The cowards! Their sneaky attack wasn't worthy of true warriors. ThunderClan would make them pay for what they'd done.

"Do you think it'll disappear again?" Dustpelt's tail was bushed out.

Ashfur hadn't washed the blood from his paws yet. He scored a line in the dust with one red-stained claw. "This might just be the start."

"We mustn't panic," Firestar meowed, swallowing. "We have to believe this was simply a message, nothing more."

Is that all they're going to talk about? The vanishing sun? Lionpaw could hardly believe his ears.

"But what if it wasn't a message?" Dustpelt argued. "What if the sun is starting to fail?"

"It's never failed before," Sandstorm argued. "Why should it fail now?"

"It's never disappeared before," Ashfur pointed out. "But it just did."

"Surely it must just have been StarClan's way of warning us to stop fighting?" Brambleclaw meowed.

"Why warn *us*?" Dustpelt growled. "We didn't start the battle!"

"Perhaps it was just a strange cloud that hid it," Cloudtail reasoned. Lionpaw knew the warrior had been born in a Twoleg nest and had never really believed in StarClan.

"Where did the cloud come from?" Ashfur challenged.

"Where did it disappear to? The sky was clear."

Cloudtail shrugged. "There must be some explanation."

Dustpelt flicked his tail. "StarClan," he insisted. "Who else could it be?"

What does it matter? Lionpaw's belly churned with fury. The battle with WindClan hadn't been won. It had to be finished once and for all if they were ever to sleep soundly in their dens. The sun didn't matter. Enemies had to be dealt with. He scraped the ground with his claws.

"Have you got something to say?"

Lionpaw realized that Brambleclaw was staring at him.

I've got plenty to say! He got to his paws. "We need to teach WindClan a lesson!" he declared. "They can't invade us without suffering the consequences."

Brambleclaw shook his head. "Enough blood has been spilled, Lionpaw."

"The battle's finished," Firestar agreed. "We need to find out what the vanishing sun means."

"Will Leafpool go to the Moonpool and share tongues with StarClan?" Sandstorm asked.

Firestar glanced at Squirrelflight on the far side of the clearing. "Once our wounded cats are well enough to manage without her."

"I hope that's soon," Dustpelt muttered.

Ashfur's pelt smoothed. "The sooner the better."

Lionpaw pawed the ground. Why wait to find out if their ancestors knew the answer? This wasn't the time for questions. This was the time for action! There was a battle to be fought. A betrayal to avenge. "Why can't we just—"

He stopped.

He'd interrupted Sandstorm. She was staring at him with her mouth open.

"Sorry." Lionpaw backed away, suddenly conscious that he was only an apprentice.

"Perhaps you should rest," Firestar suggested gently.

Lionpaw nodded and turned away, leaving the circle of warriors to fret and worry without his interruptions. He kicked sand out behind him with every paw step. One day they'd listen to him.

Hollypaw and Squirrelflight were sleeping. He stopped beside them, watching their flanks rise and fall together as though they shared a single breath. Jaypaw had gone. The ferns beside Squirrelflight were crumpled where he'd slept.

As though summoned by Lionpaw's thoughts, Jaypaw emerged from the medicine cat's den. He was carrying dripping moss. Lionpaw watched him pick his way from the den to his mother's side and press the wet moss to Squirrelflight's lips.

"Will she live?" Lionpaw whispered.

"I think so." Jaypaw didn't look up. "There's no sign of infection."

"Did StarClan warn you she'd be injured?" *Did they warn you about any of this?* Lionpaw's heart quickened as he waited for an answer.

Jaypaw put down the moss. "No." He smoothed down a frond of fern curling near Squirrelflight's nose. "And before you ask, they said nothing about the vanishing sun or the battle, either."

Lionpaw narrowed his eyes. He knew when his brother had

something on his mind. "You don't think this has anything to do with StarClan, do you?"

Jaypaw sat down. "No."

Well? Why did Jaypaw have to be so mysterious about everything?

"I think . . ." Jaypaw began tentatively.

"What?"

He looked up. "I think I know someone who can give us answers."

The fur along Lionpaw's spine lifted. Jaypaw's pale blue eyes seemed to be watching him, as though he could actually see.

"We need to find Sol," Jaypaw meowed. "He predicted that the sun would vanish. He told Leafpool a great darkness was coming, and the sun would disappear. I think he would have told us more, but Firestar sent him away."

Disappointment flooded Lionpaw. Jaypaw was no better than the warriors. "Why are you all obsessing over the sun?" He lashed his tail. "It doesn't matter. It's back now, and we're okay. But we still have to deal with WindClan. They're going to come back if we don't show them they can't—"

Jaypaw cut him off. "It *does* matter," he growled. "Wind-Clan is nothing more than a thorn in our flesh. We can pull it out anytime we want. But the sun *disappeared*, and *Sol* knew it would happen. StarClan didn't! Don't you realize what that means?"

Lionpaw didn't, but he wasn't going to admit that. "What can we do about it?"

"We have to find Sol."

Lionpaw leaned back in surprise. "Don't be silly! He left yesterday. He could be anywhere by now. And Firestar's not going to let us wander off to look for him. There's been a battle. Half the warriors are injured, and who knows when there'll be another invasion."

Jaypaw flattened his ears. "Remember the prophecy!" he snapped. "We have the power of the stars in our paws! That makes us more powerful than Firestar, more powerful than StarClan! If Sol knows why the sun vanished, we have to find him!"

CHAPTER 19

Jaypaw wanted to claw his brother's ears to make him listen. Please understand! "We have to find Sol!"

Squirrelflight stirred beside him. "Who?" she breathed.

She's awake!

Jaypaw leaned down and pressed his nose to his mother's pelt. She felt warmer. Not hot, though. No infection. He laid his pad on her flank. Her breathing was steadier, not too fast. She was recovering from the shock of her injury.

"How's Lionpaw?" Squirrelflight asked faintly.

"I'm right here." Lionpaw brushed her ear with his nose.

"What about Hollypaw? Was she wounded?"

"Hollypaw's fine too," Jaypaw reassured her. "We're all fine."

The ferns rustled as Squirrelflight lifted her head. "Has the sun vanished again?"

"Look!" Jaypaw encouraged her to open her eyes. "It's still shining."

Squirrelflight rested her head down. "StarClan must be angry with us."

"Not *us*," Lionpaw mewed. "It's WindClan they're angry with."

It's got nothing to do with StarClan. Jaypaw patted the ferns around his mother's head. It was like taking care of an anxious kit.

Hollypaw stirred. "Is she awake?" She jumped to her paws. "Squirrelflight?"

"Is that you, Hollypaw?"

Hollypaw buried her nose in her mother's fur. "I was so scared you were going to die!"

Squirrelflight managed a soft purr. "I'll never leave you, little one," she promised.

Paw steps scuffed toward them, and Jaypaw scented Brightheart.

"I saw her move!" The one-eyed warrior's mew was filled with hope.

"She's awake," Jaypaw told her. "No sign of fever, and her breathing's strong."

"Shall I fetch Leafpool?" Brightheart offered.

Jaypaw shook his head. "She's sleeping. I think we should wake her only if the bleeding starts again or Squirrelflight starts to get restless."

"How did these feathers get here?" Squirrelflight was sniffing at the soft blanket covering her. She pawed weakly at her bedding. "And the ferns?"

"We built a nest around you," Hollypaw told her.

"Thank you." Pride warmed Squirrelflight's mew. "I have such brave, kind kits."

"You should rest, Squirrelflight," Brightheart warned. "You lost a lot of blood."

"Yes," Squirrelflight breathed, the ferns rustling around her.

"She's closing her eyes," Hollypaw whispered. "We should leave her to sleep."

"You three should be resting too," Brightheart advised. "I'll watch Squirrelflight until Leafpool wakes up."

Jaypaw's fur tingled. This could be their chance to go look for Sol. "Thanks, Brightheart." He forced his voice to sound tired. "Come on," he called to Lionpaw and Hollypaw. "Let's go get some sleep."

He paused as soon as he was sure they were out of earshot of Brightheart.

"What is it?" Hollypaw stopped beside him. "You're all jumpy."

"We have to find Sol!"

"What?"

Lionpaw sighed. "Jaypaw's got it into his head that this stranger knows why the sun vanished."

"How?" Hollypaw's breath stirred Jaypaw's whiskers.

"Because he warned us it was going to happen!" Jaypaw didn't wait for another of Hollypaw's dumb questions. "We've got to go *now*, while the Clan thinks we're sleeping."

Lionpaw padded around his sister. "We have to go with him," he warned. "He'll only go by himself if we don't." He stopped and looked at her. "Are you fit enough?"

"Yes." Hollypaw nodded. "My rest did me good. But wait." She hurried away and returned a few moments later with a stale shrew.

Jaypaw wrinkled his nose. "You're not going to eat that?"

"I'm starving. Aren't you?"

"No." Jaypaw was too anxious to bother with food. He could eat later. "Just hurry up."

Hollypaw began to gulp down her meal.

"Is Brightheart watching us?" Jaypaw asked Lionpaw.

"She's watching Squirrelflight," Lionpaw told him. "She's got her back to us."

"Who else is in the clearing?"

"No one else," Lionpaw told him. "They're all in their dens." He paused. "Firestar's on Highledge."

"But he's sleeping."

Surprise bristled from Lionpaw's pelt. "How did you know?"

"I can hear his breathing." Jaypaw sniffed the air. Gray-stripe was guarding the camp entrance. "We'll have to sneak out through the dirtplace tunnel."

"Not *again*!" Lionpaw sighed. "Are you sure we really need to find this Sol?"

Jaypaw clawed the ground. "He could hold the answer to *everything*!"

Lionpaw leaned closer. "You mean the prophecy, don't you?"

And StarClan. And the Tribe of Endless Hunting. Who else might share the secret? "I'm just guessing," Jaypaw admitted. "But I've got to find out."

Lionpaw nudged Hollypaw. "Are you finished?"

"Yes!" Hollypaw answered, still chewing. She belched

loudly as Jaypaw led them along the thorn barrier toward the dirtplace tunnel.

Jaypaw flicked her nose with his tail. "Hush!"

"Sorry."

"Wait!" Lionpaw warned. He pressed Jaypaw down behind a clump of grass. "Brightheart's looking around."

"Has she seen us?" Jaypaw whispered, heart thumping.

Lionpaw held his breath. "No," he mewed at last. "She's watching Squirrelflight again. It's safe to go." He straightened and began to pad forward.

"Wait!" Jaypaw hissed, and dragged him back by his tail. There were more cats coming.

Lionpaw ducked down beside him. "What is it now?"

Birchfall and Berrynose were padding one after the other through the dirtplace tunnel, back into camp.

"I beat off two WindClan warriors single-pawed," Berrynose boasted.

"They may be fast, but they're small," Birchfall meowed. "Once you get hold of them, it's easy to knock them off their paws."

"Unlike RiverClan," Berrynose sneered. "They must do nothing but eat. They're more like fat, furry fish than cats!"

Jaypaw held his breath as their paw steps passed and disappeared into the warriors' den.

"How was I meant to know they were coming through the tunnel?" Lionpaw muttered. "I can't see through thorns."

"Try using your ears!" Jaypaw snapped.

They squeezed through the dirtplace tunnel, and Jaypaw

felt a wave of relief to be safely out in the forest, even though the stench of dirtplace lingered in his nostrils. He led Hollypaw and Lionpaw up the slope toward the lake. There was a patch of brambles they could hide behind while they decided which way to head.

"So?" Hollypaw prompted once they'd halted behind the bush.

Jaypaw sniffed the air. He had a faint hope that he could still pick up some of Sol's scent. After all, it hadn't rained since his visit. But the battle had drowned the forest in unfamiliar scents. Four Clans had fought here. No trace of Sol remained.

"Dustpelt took him back to the WindClan border," Lionpaw reminded him.

"That's where I saw him," Hollypaw mewed excitedly. "On the moorland."

"He won't be there now then," Jaypaw mewed.

Lionpaw's tail swished the leaves. "Why not?"

"Because he's *been* there." Jaypaw felt certain that Sol knew about all four Clans. He'd sought out Firestar on purpose. He'd been on WindClan's land. It made sense that he would want to make contact with the other Clans as well. Jaypaw just hoped he hadn't gone looking for RiverClan. That was on the other side of the lake, too far to go and come back before their Clanmates noticed they were missing. "He would have gone to ShadowClan next," he mewed firmly, though he wasn't completely certain. He was worried that his littermates wouldn't follow him if they thought he hadn't a clue where he was leading them.

"How can you be sure?" Lionpaw asked.

"I just am," Jaypaw lied.

"But we can't go onto ShadowClan's territory!" Hollypaw gasped.

"*You* did," Jaypaw reminded her.

"That was an emergency," Hollypaw argued. "I had to go."

"This is an emergency too!"

"But we don't know he's there. Not for certain." Hollypaw sat down. "I didn't see any strangers in the camp when I was there."

"Maybe he hadn't arrived by the time the battle started," Jaypaw mewed.

Lionpaw rubbed a paw through his whiskers. "Hollypaw's right. We can't risk crossing into ShadowClan territory. There's just been a battle. They'd shred us."

"It's not like you to be scared," Jaypaw taunted.

"I'm not scared for me; I'm scared for the Clan," Lionpaw snapped.

Hollypaw let out a long breath. "He's right," she mewed. "ShadowClan was our only ally. We can't risk annoying them."

Jaypaw flicked a paw crossly through the leaf litter. They were getting nowhere.

"Why don't we head up through *our* territory?" Hollypaw suggested. "We might find some trace of Sol near the border. If you're right and he *is* trying to get to ShadowClan, he has to cross our territory to go the quickest route."

"That makes sense," Lionpaw agreed. "And a loner like him

would have steered well clear of the battle."

"Okay," Jaypaw agreed. He padded out from the shelter of the bramble, and promptly tripped over a fallen twig.

"I'll lead the way," Lionpaw offered.

Jaypaw felt a familiar flicker of frustration, but pushed it away. This was too important. He was closer than he'd ever been to getting answers about the prophecy.

They trekked away from the lake, pushing deeper into the woodland than any of them had ever been. The forest floor became unfamiliar beneath their paws. The broad oak and beech leaves, so smooth on their pads, gave way to small, scrunched-up hazel. Jaypaw couldn't even scent the lake any- more, and the woodland became denser. Smaller trees clustered closer, and they had to weave along a winding path. The soft foliage of ferns and berry bushes gradually petered out, and the smell of prey became fainter. Twigs scratched their pelts.

The land was sloping steadily upward, and Jaypaw could smell mountain air drifting down through the trees.

"We've reached the edge of our territory!" Lionpaw announced.

Jaypaw sniffed. A few stale ThunderClan scent marks dot- ted the trees, and beyond them, no ThunderClan scent at all. His heart began to pound as he followed Lionpaw across the scent line, relieved to feel Hollypaw's pelt brushing his. It felt like stepping off the edge of the world.

Lionpaw stopped. "I can smell something."

Jaypaw hurried to catch up and sniffed the twigs beside Lionpaw. "That's him!" He recognized Sol's scent straightaway.

"He's been here." The tom's smell was faint, worn away by the breeze, but unmistakable. Jaypaw padded forward, letting his nose lead him. Another scented twig! They had found Sol's path.

"He was definitely heading toward ShadowClan," Hollypaw observed.

"What if he's crossed into their territory?" Lionpaw asked.

"Let's deal with that if it happens," Jaypaw urged. He couldn't lose Sol now.

They trekked onward, following Sol's trail as it skirted the top of ThunderClan's border. Suddenly Jaypaw scented ShadowClan. He halted and pricked his ears. There was no sound of a patrol, no cats rustling the undergrowth.

"It's just their scent markers," Lionpaw reassured him. "We've reached the top of ShadowClan's border."

Jaypaw felt a surge of triumph. He'd been right. Sol *had* been seeking out ShadowClan. But fear also stirred in his belly. What if Sol's trail veered down into ShadowClan territory? Would Lionpaw and Hollypaw agree to cross the border with him? How would he find his way without them? He padded on, acutely aware of the ShadowClan scent line as it followed their path through the forest.

The trail drew them onward, a twig here, a leaf there, each lightly brushed by Sol's pelt. Jaypaw felt excitement growing with each discovery until, suddenly, the scent ended. He spun around, tasting the air.

Nothing!

Lionpaw pushed on, sniffing the undergrowth. "No sign here!" he called back.

No!

Jaypaw darted forward, desperate to find another clue. He tripped on a rock sticking out of the ground. Pain seared his paw, and he licked at it furiously.

"Are you okay?" Hollypaw was beside him.

"Fine," he replied through clenched teeth. The pain was easing. No damage.

"I guess we've lost him." Hollypaw sighed.

Panic fluttered in Jaypaw's belly. "Let's try another direction."

"He might have headed across the ShadowClan border," Lionpaw mewed grimly.

"Let's look!" Jaypaw urged.

Lionpaw stiffened. "No."

"Wait!" Hollypaw darted away.

"Where are you going?"

She was back at his side by the time Jaypaw had finished his question.

"I've found a piece of fur," she mewed. "It's long, with a mixture of tortoiseshell and white hairs. It must be Sol's."

Jaypaw sniffed at the hairs she'd dropped on the ground beside him. It *was* Sol's! "Where did you find it?" he demanded.

"In the grass over there," Hollypaw mewed. "You can even see where he's walked. The grass is crushed."

"But the path leads away from ShadowClan's border," Lionpaw pointed out. "I thought you said he'd be heading for their camp."

"I must have been wrong." Jaypaw shrugged. He didn't care where Sol was going. He just wanted to find him. He plunged into the grass, sniffing as he went, following the scent trail of pawprints. He let his mind reach out into the forest, hoping to pick up some sense of the stranger. But he found nothing but unknown smells and unfamiliar territory.

A thorn scratched his cheek. Jaypaw leaped back. Brambles were trailing across the path.

"Careful." Lionpaw slid past him, pressing back the tendrils to let Jaypaw pass.

Hollypaw tugged his tail gently with her teeth. "Let me go in front," she suggested. "There are brambles everywhere."

Jaypaw let her pass without arguing. His pelt was tingling. They must be near Sol now! The scent from the trail had grown stronger ever since they left the ShadowClan border. At last he was going to find out why the sun vanished. Was it connected to the prophecy?

"Ow!" Hollypaw yelped, and jumped backward, crashing into Jaypaw.

Lionpaw stumbled behind them. "Watch where you're going!"

"A thorn scratched my nose," Hollypaw whimpered.

Jaypaw could smell blood. "Are you okay?"

"Yes," she mewed. "I just didn't see it. It's getting dark."

Jaypaw suddenly realized how late it must be. He'd thought the air had chilled because they were closer to the mountains here. But the sun must be sinking in the sky. He felt a jolt of guilt as he detected waves of exhaustion flooding from Hollypaw. She'd fought a battle already today, and now they'd traveled far from the hollow. He focused on Lionpaw, who had pushed on ahead. His brother seemed as strong as ever, untouched by tiredness.

"Perhaps we should stop for a while," Jaypaw called. "So Hollypaw can rest." For the first time he noticed how weary he felt too. His paws ached, their pads raw from walking, and his muscles were tender from being tense for so long. *So much for being more powerful than StarClan!* He felt like any other apprentice, rooted to the earth by the need for sleep and food.

"Lionpaw?" he called again, suddenly anxious. He turned to Hollypaw. "Can you see him?"

"He's only a few tail-lengths ahead," she mewed. "He's crouching down. . . ." Her voice trailed away.

"What is it?" Jaypaw's heart leaped. Had Lionpaw found something?

Hollypaw lowered her voice. "A Twoleg nest," she hissed. "Through the trees. I can just make it out."

Jaypaw hurried to catch up to Lionpaw, Hollypaw matching him step for step.

"It's abandoned," Lionpaw reported as they crouched beside him. "Like the one in our territory." He sniffed. "Half the walls are down, and there's no roof at all."

Hollypaw bristled. "I can smell Twolegs."

Jaypaw wrinkled his nose. The stench was stale and old. "They've not been here in a while," he mewed.

"Come on," Lionpaw urged. He began to creep forward, keeping low. "Stay close."

Jaypaw followed, pressing against Hollypaw, conscious of how much he needed her to guide him along the tangled path. He struggled to build an image in his mind of the forest around him, but he could picture only darkness. The wind hissed through the trees, rattling the branches. Jaypaw pricked his ears, hoping for birdsong. Nothing. *They must be asleep.* He sniffed. No prey scent at all, not even mouse. Frustrated and confused, he followed Lionpaw, feeling utterly blind.

The ground beneath his paws turned to pebbles and then smooth stone. The breeze stopped ruffling his ear fur.

"Are we inside the Twoleg nest?" he asked Lionpaw. His mew echoed strangely.

"In the entrance," Lionpaw whispered.

"Can you see anything?" Jaypaw's whiskers twitched in disgust at the foul-scented air ahead of them.

"It looks empty," Lionpaw murmured.

Jaypaw's heart sank. How much farther were they going to have to travel in search of Sol? He jerked in surprise as Hollypaw spun around beside him, pelt bristling.

A deep voice sounded behind them.

"Are you looking for me?"

CHAPTER 20

♣

Hollypaw stared at Sol, suddenly aware of how untidy she and her littermates looked. Their pelts were ruffled, with crumbs of leaf and scraps of moss sticking out, and she and Lionpaw were bloodstained around their claws. Sol gazed at them, his elegant tricolored head tilted, the white patches on his pelt tinged pink by the late-afternoon sun. His eyes shone, amber as sunlit sap.

Would he be angry they'd tracked him down?

He didn't look angry.

He didn't even look surprised, just blinked calmly at them and dipped his head in greeting.

"I thought you would come." His mew was as rich and smooth as high-season honey. He was looking at Jaypaw. "I knew you'd be curious after the great darkness came."

Jaypaw padded forward. "How did you know it was coming?"

Sol's whiskers twitched. "Did it frighten you?"

"Of course!"

"Even though I told you it would happen?"

His gaze was unwavering, and so intense that Hollypaw

found her sight glazing until the forest blurred around her and all she could see was Sol's eyes.

She blinked, shivering. She was just tired.

Jaypaw lifted his chin challengingly toward Sol. "Is that why you came to ThunderClan? To warn us?"

The tip of Sol's tail twitched. "It's not my business to give warnings." He padded onto the unkempt grass at the side of the pebbly path, flattening a patch with his paws before sitting down. He swept his thick brown-and-white tail over the grass and rested it in front of him.

"Come." He tipped his head to one side, indicating that they should sit down too. "If we are going to talk, we may as well be comfortable."

Jaypaw padded forward, feeling for the grass. Hollypaw followed a little self-consciously. Sol was watching them closely. The grass was long but soft, and she flattened a spot to sit on, as Sol had done.

Lionpaw hung back in the doorway, his fur bristling.

"Come on," Hollypaw called, smoothing a space next to her with her tail.

Lionpaw padded forward with his eyes fixed on the stranger and sat down beside her.

"Your brother looks as if he doesn't trust me," Sol observed.

"You're not a Clan cat," Lionpaw answered.

Sol blinked. "Do you trust every Clan cat?"

"Of course not!" Lionpaw snapped. "But I can make a pretty good guess at what they're thinking."

"You came looking for me, don't forget," Sol chided. "Is it

fair to disturb me, then reproach me because you can't read my thoughts?"

Lionpaw narrowed his eyes. "I guess not."

Hollypaw felt Jaypaw fidgeting beside her, running his forepaws over the grass.

Sol must have noticed too. "You have something you want to ask me, yes?" he prompted.

"Do you know about the prophecy?" Jaypaw burst out.

Hollypaw stretched her eyes wide. No cat knew about the prophecy except Firestar—and he didn't know that they knew. Beside her, Lionpaw's ears were twitching. Why was Jaypaw sharing their deepest secret with a complete stranger?

But he had known the sun would vanish.

Sol flicked the tip of his tail. "It concerns all three of you, doesn't it?"

Jaypaw nodded. "'There will be three, kin of your kin, who hold the power of the stars in their paws.'"

"And you are the kin," Sol murmured. He dipped his head with respect.

Jaypaw was trembling like an excited kit. Hollypaw glanced at him in surprise. He really believed that this cat held answers StarClan would not give him. Or *could* not give him. A shiver rippled down Hollypaw's spine. Maybe the prophecy did lie beyond anything StarClan could predict.

She felt sick, and pushed away the thought as her heart began to race. There was nothing beyond StarClan! Nothing beyond the warrior code!

Sol interrupted her thoughts. "The prophecy is a grave

responsibility for three such young cats to bear." His amber eyes were round with sympathy.

Jaypaw clawed at the grass. "I can walk in other cats' dreams, and in their memories."

But Sol was staring at Lionpaw. "And you? I can see something burns within."

Lionpaw's tail quivered.

Sol's voice softened. "Something that maybe frightens you a little?"

"I can fight in battles without getting hurt," Lionpaw confessed, sounding very young and small.

Hollypaw stared at her paws. What was her special power? She knew it was there. She could feel it inside her. But the only thing she felt certain of—so certain it felt like a thorn-sharp stab in her side—was the need to defend the warrior code, the absolute faith that it was vital for the Clans' existence.

Would Sol understand? He was a loner. How could he appreciate the importance of something that held the four Clans together? She looked up at him, expecting to see his amber gaze on her, but Sol had tipped his head to one side again and closed his eyes.

"Of course, you must nurture these powers." His mew was light, as though this were a small matter to him. "Listen to your inner voices, to the instinct that in every other cat would merely help them find food or shelter. Who's to say that in you, these instincts won't help you achieve more?"

Jaypaw flicked a mosquito from his nose. "Did the vanishing sun have anything to do with us?"

Hollypaw blinked. It hadn't occurred to her that the prophecy and the sun's terrifying disappearance might be connected. She leaned forward, paws prickling.

"Maybe it did." Sol swept his tail over the grass.

Hollypaw felt Lionpaw stiffen beside her. "How?"

"Maybe you are like the shadow covering the sun, and one day you will cover the stars in the sky, so that the cats see you instead of StarClan."

Hollypaw gasped. "Does that mean we'll be *dead*?"

Sol shook his head. "Of course not," he meowed. "You'll just be more powerful than your warrior ancestors. The light will return, just like the sun came back, but it will be *your* light, and yours to control."

Our light?

Jaypaw looked like a startled mouse, his tail sticking straight out behind him.

"B-but if we control the light . . ." Hollypaw searched for the words to describe the fear rising inside her. Nothing made sense right now. It was all upside down. "If we control the light . . ."

Sol leaned forward, as though willing her to speak.

"What about the warrior code?" she mewed at last. "How will it fit in?"

"However you want it to," Sol meowed simply. "You will have the power to destroy the code, or preserve it. It's up to you."

Destroy the code!

Hollypaw felt dizzy. "We can't be more powerful than the

code," she whispered.

Jaypaw padded in front of her. "Sol." He looked up at the tom. "You must come back with us." His mew was urgent. "We need you to be our mentor."

"Me?" Sol paused for a moment to wrap his tail neatly over his paws. "You don't need me. The prophecy will take care of itself." He made it sound like the simplest thing in the world.

"But you know so much more than the others," Jaypaw insisted. "You knew the sun was going to vanish. You must be able to help us."

"But I can't possibly live in your territory," Sol pointed out. "Firestar would never allow it."

Lionpaw stepped forward, eyes shining. "You could live just outside it, though." A bat fluttered above them. "We could build you a den and visit you every day and bring food."

Hollypaw was still swimming against the tide of fear lapping at her. *More powerful than the code!* She felt Jaypaw nudging her.

"You want him to come, don't you?" he mewed.

She heard herself answer. "W-won't it be hard to keep up with our apprentice duties?" Her common sense worked her tongue while her mind still reeled. What might this stranger show them? They had learned nearly everything their mentors had to teach, yet there was room for so much more. And if they were really destined to be more powerful than the warrior code, they were going to need much greater guidance.

"Please come!" Jaypaw begged.

Sol glanced at the Twoleg nest, wrinkling his nose. "Very well."

Hollypaw stared at him in surprise. How had he changed his mind so quickly? "Really?" She gasped, relief flooding her.

Sol nodded. "How can I ignore the prophecy? You have asked for my help to walk your true path."

Jaypaw bounced onto the stone trail. "Let's go!"

Lionpaw took the lead, and Sol fell in behind. Jaypaw skittered after Lionpaw like a kit, trying to make him go faster, as if he couldn't wait to have his first lesson from Sol. Hollypaw was used to seeing her brother stomping reluctantly about the camp as he carried out his apprentice duties. Now he was so excited, she wondered why she felt only fear.

But it *was* exciting, wasn't it? Just because she would be more powerful than the warrior code didn't mean she'd have to destroy it. She would have the power to preserve it forever. Sol had said so. It was more than she had ever hoped for: the ability to secure the future of all four Clans for all the moons to come.

They retraced their steps to the ShadowClan border, then followed the scent markers toward their own territory. It was late, the sun sinking toward the treetops and Lionpaw was pushing the pace, clearly keen to get Sol settled and return to camp. Had they been missed? How would they explain their disappearance?

A rustle in the bushes on the other side of the border made Hollypaw jump.

Jaypaw halted, pulling on Lionpaw's tail. "Shh!"

The cats ducked, trying to hide, but it was too late.

"What in the name of StarClan are you doing there?" Russetfur's eyes burned in the shadows, wide with astonishment.

"Don't worry," Hollypaw whispered to Sol. "ShadowClan was our ally in the battle today."

"Are you spying on us?" Russetfur's mew was sharp. "Did Firestar send you?"

Jaypaw straightened up and faced the ShadowClan deputy across the scent line. "Like Firestar would send *me* to spy," he meowed sarcastically.

"Then what are you doing here?" Russetfur demanded.

Smokefoot padded out of the shadows behind her. He was staring at Sol, his gaze lingering on the cat's soft fur and blunt claws. "Looks like Firestar's adopting *another* kittypet," he declared.

Sol frowned. "Kittypet?"

Lionpaw glanced at him. "He means a cat born in a Twoleg nest." He turned to Smokefoot, eyes gleaming. "Sol isn't a kittypet."

"Then he's a loner," Smokefoot growled. "And no more welcome in a Clan than a kittypet."

A tabby she-cat with long unkempt fur slid in beside her Clanmates. "Oh, but ThunderClan welcomes *everyone*," she sneered.

Lionpaw unsheathed his claws.

Russetfur stiffened. "Shut up, Kinkfur," she hissed. "I don't want any more fighting today." Her mew seemed edged with fear. Hollypaw noticed for the first time how tatty the Shadow-Clan deputy's pelt was. Dried blood crusted the tip of one ear, and Smokefoot's eyes were dull with tiredness. The battle had taken its toll on ShadowClan, too. She spotted Owlpaw behind his Clanmates. The apprentice was gazing fearfully up at the sun, fiery now as it slid behind the treetops. Were they afraid that StarClan would hide it again if they started fighting?

"They won't attack," Hollypaw whispered. She nudged Lionpaw and tipped her nose toward the sun.

He seemed to understand. "Come on." He beckoned Sol and his littermates with a flick of his tail. "Let's go home."

"Wait!" Russetfur ordered.

Hollypaw froze. They weren't going to get away so easily after all.

"You're coming to explain to Blackstar what you're doing on our borders."

Jaypaw spat, "We haven't even crossed the scent line!"

"You're close enough." Russetfur flicked her tail, and her patrol dashed over the border and surrounded the Thunder-Clan cats.

Lionpaw arched his back, hissing. Hollypaw unsheathed her claws, but Sol just stared at the ShadowClan cats. His calm gaze seemed to unnerve them, and they backed away.

"What kind of loner are you?" Russetfur looked him over, her pelt ruffled. "Don't you know we're warriors?"

"Yes, I know." Sol kept staring at her. "Blackstar is your leader, right?"

Russetfur flattened her ears. "Yes," she answered warily. "I'd be interested in meeting him."

Hollypaw's heart sank. There wasn't time to go to the ShadowClan camp! Firestar was sure to notice they were missing any moment now.

Jaypaw began to pad toward the ShadowClan border. "We might as well go," he mewed. "Think how much Sol can learn from another Clan."

He can teach us ShadowClan's secrets! Perhaps this wasn't such a bad idea after all. And compared with what they could learn about another Clan, Firestar's anger didn't seem so important. Hollypaw followed Jaypaw, enjoying the puzzlement clouding the eyes of their ShadowClan captors. She guided her brother through the unfamiliar woods, pressing against his shoulder to keep him on the faint path. Lionpaw walked a few paces ahead, calling out every time there was a twig to trip on or a prey-hole to stumble into. Sol padded alongside them, gazing around the forest with fascination.

Russetfur didn't take her eyes off the stranger. Was she regretting bringing him into the heart of her territory?

After a while, Hollypaw began to recognize the landscape. A slope led up to a small ridge. She had followed this path when she had come to beg Blackstar for help. A few more paw steps through the trees, and she spotted the great bramble wall of the ShadowClan camp.

Rowanclaw was guarding the entrance this time, his dark ginger pelt the only color in the darkening forest. He stared in surprise at the approaching patrol, but Russetfur simply swept past him with her prisoners.

Ivytail and Toadfoot leaped to their paws as the Thunder-Clan cats entered the camp. A half-eaten mouse lay between them. Snaketail and Scorchpaw stood in the middle of the clearing, staring in unconcealed shock at Sol.

"Who is he?" Scorchpaw whispered.

Snaketail tasted the air. "Not a Clan cat, that's for sure."

"Where is everyone?" Lionpaw hissed in Hollypaw's ear.

Hollypaw looked around the camp. It was strangely empty. "They must be resting after the battle," she guessed.

"Wait there," Russetfur ordered, and disappeared into Blackstar's den.

The brambles rustled at one side of the camp. Hollypaw recognized the nursery entrance, where Snowbird had gathered Tawnypelt's kits. Flamekit, Dawnkit, and Tigerkit were tumbling out now, their eyes bright with excitement.

"Hollypaw!" Flamekit reached her first and started jumping up to grab her tail. She spun around and greeted him with a playful cuff over his ear.

Tigerkit was bouncing around Lionpaw. "Have I grown?" the kit demanded, stretching himself up to his full height.

Dawnkit leaped on her brother, bowling him over. "You *must* have grown, the amount you eat!" She pummeled his back with her hind paws, then stopped when she spotted Sol. She scrambled to her paws and stared at the stranger. "Who's he?"

Tigerkit followed her gaze. "What's he doing here?" He frowned and gazed up at Hollypaw. "Why are *you* here?" Was he worried they'd come to take his mother away again?

Flamekit was padding around Jaypaw. "Who are *you*?"

"He's Jaypaw, our brother," Lionpaw told her.

Jaypaw stared blankly ahead as Flamekit circled him.

"Why isn't he looking at me?" he asked.

Jaypaw leaned down suddenly. "Do you want me to look at you?" His nose was a whisker away from Flamekit's eyes.

Flamekit leaped back with surprise. "His eyes are all stare-y!"

Hollypaw glanced nervously at Jaypaw.

"I'm blind," he explained more softly.

Flamekit padded closer. "How did you get here, then?"

"I walked," Jaypaw mewed.

"Without bumping into anything?" Tigerkit sounded impressed.

"I hope you're not being rude!" Tawnypelt's stern mew sounded from the nursery. The ShadowClan she-cat padded out, yawning and ruffled. She blinked in surprise as she caught sight of Hollypaw. "You're back again!" Then her gaze flicked to Jaypaw, Lionpaw, and finally Sol. "What in StarClan's name are you doing here?" She pawed her kits back toward their den. "And who's he?" Tigerkit tried to leap out of the way, but she caught him with an expert flick of her tail and sent him bundling toward the den. "Go inside," she ordered. "You can come out and say good-bye when they leave."

"But—" Dawnkit began to argue.

"But nothing." Tawnypelt gave the kits a final gentle shove, and they disappeared into the brambles.

Tawnypelt looked warily at Sol. "Who are you?"

"I've come to meet Blackstar."

As he spoke, Russetfur appeared from Blackstar's den and stood to one side to let her leader pass. Blackstar's white pelt was unwashed. His long tail drooped behind him, and he padded across the clearing as though his soot-black paws were too heavy for him.

"Russetfur tells me there is a stranger among us," he growled. He glanced at Hollypaw, Lionpaw, and Jaypaw. "She said you were showing him around our border."

"We weren't showing him anything!" Jaypaw mewed hotly. "We were on our way home."

"Why were you there at all?" Blackstar sat down and looked at them. His eyes were strangely dull, considering he was the leader of a Clan who'd just been involved in a terrible battle.

Hollypaw stepped forward. "We went to find Sol."

Blackstar looked at the stranger for the first time. "And this is Sol, I suppose."

"It is." Sol dipped his head. "I'm honored to meet the leader of ShadowClan."

"You know about ShadowClan?" A glimmer of interest sparked in Blackstar's eyes.

"I have heard much about you."

Blackstar tilted his head. "From these three trespassers?"

"We never crossed your border!" Jaypaw growled. He stared toward Russetfur as though challenging her to deny it.

Lionpaw moved closer to his brother. "We were looking for Sol."

"So you said. But why? He's just a loner, isn't he?"

"A traveler," Sol corrected him.

Blackstar blinked. "Why would three apprentices be so interested in a *traveler*?"

Jaypaw flicked his tail. "Because he told us the sun was going to disappear and it did!"

Russetfur's pelt bristled. Behind her, Ivytail and Toadfoot stared wide-eyed.

Tawnypelt shifted on her paws. "You *knew* it would happen?"

Sol nodded. "I saw a great darkness fall over the Clans."

"Did StarClan tell you?" ShadowClan's medicine cat, Littlecloud, had come out of his den and was staring at Sol.

Sol swung his head around to face the medicine cat. "The great darkness had nothing to do with StarClan."

Silence gripped the camp as the setting sun turned the brambles to liquid amber.

"Then who made the sun disappear?" Blackstar growled.

Sol padded across the clearing and turned so that his tail swept a rainbow shape on the needle-strewn ground. "It was a sign." He lifted his chin, the dark patches on his fur shining in the last rays of sunshine. Lean, hard muscles rippled under the thick-furred pelt on his shoulders. "A sign of change that will come whether you want it or not."

Are we part of that change? Hollypaw glanced at Lionpaw, anxiety stirring in her belly. Lionpaw gave a small shake of his head. She understood.

Say nothing about the prophecy.

Blackstar padded toward Sol, his eyes gleaming. "What sort of change?"

"Do you *want* change?" Sol lowered his voice to barely a whisper.

Blackstar stepped closer. "I'm not sure the Clans should be here," he confessed.

Hollypaw wondered if the ShadowClan leader had forgotten where he was. Should he be sharing his fears so openly?

But Blackstar's eyes were brimming with hope as he gazed at Sol as though here was someone who finally understood. "Could StarClan have made a mistake by telling us to settle by the lake?"

Smokefoot shot an astonished glance at Ivytail, who shrugged. Littlecloud was leaning forward, as if he were finding it hard to hear—or finding it hard to *believe* what he was hearing.

Or perhaps he was simply waiting for Sol's answer.

Hollypaw's heart began to race. Was ShadowClan about to reject StarClan? And the warrior code?

"Change is not necessarily a bad thing," Sol murmured.

Yes, it is! She dug her claws deep into the ground, desperate to root herself in something solid.

Sol's voice chanted on, soft, yet loud enough to reach to the edges of the clearing. "Especially if we anticipate what's coming and prepare for it."

Blackstar was nodding as Sol continued. "There is more than one path to tread in this life."

"There must be an easier one than this," Blackstar agreed.

"Life here is so hard. There is great hunger in leaf-bare, and in greenleaf the Twolegs drive us farther and farther from our hunting grounds."

Sol closed his eyes as Blackstar went on, as if he were picturing Blackstar's description of life in ShadowClan's new home.

"We are plagued by battle after battle, and even the moon-high trek to the Gatherings is longer and harder than in the forest."

"You are greatly troubled," Sol sympathized without opening his eyes.

"My troubles are endless," Blackstar told him.

Tawnypelt stepped forward. "Night is falling," she meowed briskly. "The ThunderClan apprentices should be on their way home." She flashed a knowing look at Hollypaw. "Their Clanmates will be wondering where they are."

She's guessed we shouldn't be out of camp. Hollypaw stared at her paws, feeling hot and guilty. *And she doesn't want us to hear what Blackstar is saying.*

Blackstar turned from Sol, blinking as if he were surprised to find them still there. "Of course." He beckoned Smokefoot and Ivytail with his tail. "Take them to the border."

Lionpaw tipped his head to one side. "What about Sol?"

"I must stay here." Sol's answer was soft but firm. He gazed at the ShadowClan leader. "That is, if Blackstar will have me."

Blackstar did not hesitate. "Of course!"

Hollypaw stared at him. "But he was coming with us!" They had so much to learn from him. He was going to be *their* mentor, not Blackstar's. Why did a Clan leader need a mentor? Outrage shot through her. Sol knew about the prophecy! *He promised he'd come with us!*

Jaypaw stepped forward. "You promised—"

Lionpaw cut him off. "Let's go, before we get into more trouble," he hissed into Jaypaw's ear.

"Kits!" Tawnypelt called to the nursery and Flamekit, Dawnkit, and Tigerkit charged out. "I promised you could say good-bye."

Dawnkit held her muzzle up to Hollypaw, purring when Hollypaw ran her cheek along the top of her head. "Good-bye."

Tigerkit arched his back and bounced toward Lionpaw. "Next time we meet, I'll be even bigger!"

Flamekit approached Jaypaw a little cautiously. "Bye."

Ivytail marched past, sweeping the kits out of the way. "Go play with your own Clanmates," she growled.

As Hollypaw followed her escort through the tunnel, she glanced back into the clearing. Blackstar and Sol were sitting with their heads close together, talking too quietly to hear.

CHAPTER 21

"Stop!" Jaypaw swerved in front of Hollypaw and Lionpaw as they began to head down the slope toward the thorn barrier.

He ignored the surprise flashing from their pelts. "We can't tell any cat what's happened or where we've been."

"Of course not," Lionpaw agreed.

"Not about Sol, or being in ShadowClan's camp. Not *anything*!" He had to know that they understood.

"I wasn't going to," Hollypaw mewed. He could sense her puzzlement and hurt—directed not at him, but at Sol. The stranger had abandoned them.

Jaypaw was confused by Sol's change of heart too, but he refused to let Sol's behavior change what he believed. It wasn't Blackstar who was more powerful than StarClan. *They* were.

Evening shrouded the camp as they padded through the entrance. Jaypaw was relieved to hear the Clan only just beginning to stir. The warriors' den rustled as Brambleclaw and Graystripe padded out. Kits mewled inside the nursery, and Icepaw and Foxpaw were nosing through the few remaining morsels on the fresh-kill pile.

"Where've you been?" Foxpaw called.

"Out," Lionpaw replied.

"Did you bring back any prey?"

Jaypaw could hear Foxpaw's belly rumbling. "Afraid not."

Graystripe padded, yawning, across the clearing toward them. "Have you been out long?" he asked sleepily.

"No," Jaypaw lied. He hoped no one noticed their nests hadn't been slept in.

"Any sign of prey out there?" Brambleclaw put in.

Jaypaw shrugged. He had been too lost in his own thoughts to notice.

"Lionpaw!" Ashfur was stretching outside the warriors' den. "I think we should hunt for our Clan, don't you? Hollypaw? Why don't you go wake Brackenfur? You might as well come with us."

Jaypaw sensed Hollypaw's heart sink. He felt sorry for his littermates. They'd managed to sneak out of camp unnoticed, but it seemed they were going to be punished anyway. "You'll soon be in your nests," he whispered to them.

"Not soon enough," Hollypaw hissed back.

Jaypaw padded to his den, feeling a twinge of guilt. He was the one who'd made them leave camp, after all. He nosed through the brambles, breathing in the comforting smells of home—Leafpool's scent, herbs, the damp rock where water dripped into the pool. Spiderleg was snoring in Cinderpaw's old nest. And another cat scent drifted from the back of the den.

"Jaypaw? Is that you?"

"Squirrelflight?"

"We moved her inside." Leafpool padded from beside the pool. "It was too cold to leave her out all night."

Jaypaw stiffened. "What about her wound?"

"We moved her slowly," Leafpool reassured him. "There was a little fresh bleeding, but I treated it once we'd got her settled."

Ferns rustled around Squirrelflight. "Have you eaten, Jaypaw?"

"Not yet." He was starving.

"Make sure you do." Squirrelflight's mew sounded a little stronger.

Leafpool's tail brushed the ground. "I know how to take care of my apprentice."

Jaypaw was surprised. There was a sharp edge to his mentor's mew. She was never bad-tempered with her patients. But he was too tired and hungry to figure out what was bothering her. His mother sounded better, and that was all he cared about right now.

He padded to the fresh-kill pile and gulped down a dry sparrow, coughing as the feathers caught in his throat. Swallowing, he returned to the den. He padded to his mother's nest and pressed his nose to her pelt. "See you later, Squirrelflight. I'll be right here if you need anything."

She stirred sleepily. "Okay, Jaypaw."

Jaypaw crawled into his nest and closed his eyes.

"Jaypaw!"

A harsh mew woke him.

Branches crisscrossed overhead, glimmering silver in the starlight. *StarClan's hunting grounds.* He got to his paws, feeling soft, moon-washed grass caress his pads.

"You've been looking for answers again, haven't you?" Yellowfang was sitting beside him. Her eyes gleamed accusingly.

Jaypaw stretched and yawned. "I wouldn't be much of a medicine cat if I didn't."

Her paw clouted his ear.

"Ow!"

"I'm still your elder!" Yellowfang glared at him. "And I'm trying to teach you something important."

Jaypaw rubbed his ear, indignant. "What?"

"Be patient!" She shook out her disheveled fur. "Answers will come to you in time."

"Why shouldn't I know what's going on?" Jaypaw dug his claws into the grass. "It's not fair if I can't even be curious!"

"Curiosity must be tempered with patience," Yellowfang insisted. "Knowledge is wasted on those without the wisdom to know how to use it. And wisdom comes only with time."

The same old excuses. Frustration welled in Jaypaw's belly. *You think you know everything, but one day I'll be more powerful than you.* He stared at the battered old she-cat, the words ready on his tongue. She stared back, her chin high, her gaze unflinching. Jaypaw let his fur lie flat. He couldn't bring himself to tell her about the prophecy now.

Yellowfang leaned closer, and Jaypaw had to force himself not to duck away from her foul breath. "Serve your Clan," she murmured. "Trust StarClan, and everything will be revealed in good time."

Jaypaw looked up. The glade was crowded with cats, their fur sparkling with starlight.

"Listen to Yellowfang," Bluestar urged him.

Whitestorm gazed down at him, his eyes glowing with warmth. "She's telling you the truth."

"All will be revealed in time." Lionheart swished his thick tail.

"We are watching you," Yellowfang reminded him.

Jaypaw snorted softly. What was starry fur but a trick of the light? They were just a bunch of dead cats. *He* was alive. So were Lionpaw and Hollypaw. And Sol. Didn't that make them stronger than StarClan already?

Yellowfang leaned forward, hissing as though she could tell what he was thinking. "You don't know what's best for your Clan, Jaypaw! Just remember that!"

CHAPTER 22

❧

The sun woke Lionpaw. He blinked open his eyes, his pelt hot from the rays streaming through the den roof. Flinching from the brightness, he rolled over in his nest. His muscles were stiff. Ashfur had kept him out hunting all day, and when he'd finally reached camp, already weary from the battle and the hunt for Sol, he had sunk into his nest, too tired to do anything but close his eyes.

Hollypaw was still sleeping. She had been stumbling with exhaustion by the time they'd got back.

He checked his pelt for scratches. The only trace of the battle was the blood and fur still wedged in his claws.

"Hollypaw!"

Cinderpaw was calling into the den. Lionpaw scrambled from his nest and slid out of the entrance. "What is it?" he whispered.

"Brackenfur wants her to help me clean out the nursery," Cinderpaw mewed.

"Let her sleep." Lionpaw glanced at Hollypaw's mentor sitting beside Ashfur, sharing a piece of the fresh-kill they'd caught last night. "I'll talk to him."

He padded across the clearing. "I'll help Cinderpaw with the nursery," he offered.

Brackenfur looked up, swallowing. "Is Hollypaw okay?"

"Just tired after the battle." Lionpaw felt his pelt growing hot. No one knew that, after the battle, they'd trekked through half of ThunderClan territory, not to mention ShadowClan's.

"Has Leafpool checked her injuries?" Brackenfur's eyes darkened with worry.

"It's just a few scratches." Lionpaw groped for an excuse for Hollypaw's tiredness. "But she didn't sleep well because she was worried about Squirrelflight."

Brackenfur nodded. "Well, let her sleep now. You can help Cinderpaw instead."

Ashfur twitched his tail. "But don't dawdle. We're going on the next border patrol."

"Okay." Lionpaw hurried back to Cinderpaw. "You go and find fresh moss," he mewed. "I'll start clearing out the old bedding." He glanced at her injured leg. "Can you manage by yourself?"

Cinderpaw rolled her eyes. "Of course." She turned to the entrance, muttering under her breath. "I wish everyone would stop treating me like a three-legged cat."

Foxpaw was outside the nursery showing Icepaw a battle move. He rolled onto his back and kicked out with his hind legs. "Then a RiverClan warrior tried to leap on top of me, but I rolled out of the way." He jumped to his paws. "And I gave him a real nip on his hind leg. I bet he can still feel it."

Icepaw looked impressed. "I wish I'd been in the battle."

"Someone had to guard the camp," Foxpaw mewed kindly.

Lionpaw squeezed through the nursery entrance, the prickers scraping his pelt.

Daisy looked up, her eyes flashing with worry. "It's only you." She sighed as she recognized Lionpaw.

Toadkit and Rosekit tumbled toward him.

"Will you teach us some battle moves?" Toadkit begged.

Rosekit churned her paws as though she were fighting off an enemy. "We need to be ready if WindClan invades again."

Daisy's fur bushed out. "They won't, will they? Not after the sun vanished like that."

"I doubt it." Millie was lying on her side while her kits fed. A cough shook her body, startling the kits away. Briarkit mewled angrily and squirmed back for more milk. Bumblekit sat up and yawned, his eyes hardly open, while Blossomkit snuggled into the moss and fell asleep.

"You should see Leafpool," Daisy advised. "You've been coughing all night."

"It's just something tickling my throat," Millie meowed. "I probably swallowed a feather."

Daisy leaned forward and sniffed at Millie's muzzle. "You feel a bit feverish."

"I'll fetch Leafpool once I've cleaned out your bedding," Lionpaw offered.

Toadkit looked crestfallen. "I thought you were going to teach us battle moves."

"Sorry, Toadkit. I've got to go on patrol after I've finished here."

"It's not fair," Rosekit complained. "You get to do all the fun things, while we're stuck in here."

Lionpaw sighed. Cleaning out dens and patrolling borders wasn't fun. He wished he were back in the battle, fighting for his Clan with the power of the stars pulsing in his paws. "Why don't you ask Foxpaw to teach you?" He glanced at Daisy. "I need to clean out your bedding anyway."

Daisy got to her paws slowly, as though reluctant to leave the nursery. "I suppose we all need some fresh air." She glanced at Millie, who was coughing again. "You should stay inside."

Millie nodded. "I *am* rather tired." She curled around her kits and closed her eyes.

As Daisy followed Toadkit and Rosekit out of the den, Lionpaw began picking through her bedding, pulling out stale scraps of moss. Millie's breathing was hoarse, and the air around her smelled sour.

Lionpaw pawed together the dirty moss and gathered it in his jaws. Then he wriggled backward out of the nursery and dropped it outside. Cinderpaw was trotting through the thorn tunnel, fresh moss dangling from her jaws.

"I haven't done Millie's nest yet," Lionpaw called. "I think she's sick."

Graystripe, sunning himself beneath Highledge, scrambled to his paws. "What's wrong?"

"She has a cough," Lionpaw mewed. "I was just going to fetch Leafpool."

Graystripe was already hurrying toward the nursery. "Be quick," he ordered, his tail bushing out.

Lionpaw padded to the medicine cats' den. A strong smell of herbs drifted through the brambles. He nosed his way in, blinking to adjust his eyes to the gloom.

"Leafpool?"

The medicine cat was crouching beside Spiderleg, her paws green with ointment. "What is it?"

"I think Millie's sick."

Leafpool rubbed her paws on the moss of Spiderleg's nest. "I'll put some more on later," she promised the warrior.

"I'm feeling much better," Spiderleg assured her.

"Good," Leafpool meowed. "But stay in your nest. You're healing quickly, but I want to be sure you're completely healed before you go back to the warriors' den." She turned back to Lionpaw. "Are the kits okay?"

"They seem fine."

Leafpool was rinsing her paws in the pool when Jaypaw padded into the nursery with a bunch of leaves in his jaws.

"Sort them out for drying," Leafpool told him. "I have to check on Millie." The medicine cat pushed her way out through the brambles.

Jaypaw began to lay out the leaves beside a gap in the cave wall.

"Did you sleep okay?" Lionpaw whispered. He wondered if StarClan had told Jaypaw anything about the vanishing sun.

"You mean, did I dream?" Jaypaw snapped. "Why can't you just say what you're thinking?"

Lionpaw blinked, surprised by Jaypaw's tone. "Have you got a thistle stuck in your tail?"

"Sorry," Jaypaw mewed. "It's been a busy night."

Lionpaw glanced at Squirrelflight sleeping in her nest at the back of the den. "Is she better?"

"She's getting there," Jaypaw mewed. "But I have to change the dressing a lot to stop infection."

"Do you want me to fetch some more cobwebs?" Lionpaw offered.

"Cinderpaw brought back plenty this morning, thanks."

While I was sleeping. Lionpaw's pelt prickled with guilt. He should be doing more to help his Clan. He padded to his mother's nest and sniffed at her fur, comforted by her familiar scent.

"Lionpaw?" Squirrelflight opened her eyes. A purr caught in her throat. "How are you?"

"Fine," Lionpaw mewed.

"Firestar said you fought like a warrior in the battle." Squirrelflight lifted her head to look at him through sleep-misted eyes. "You don't seem to have a scratch on you."

Lionpaw shrugged. "Just lucky, I guess." His belly rumbled.

"You should have something to eat," Squirrelflight murmured, resting her head down again.

"I will." Lionpaw licked her ear gently as she closed her eyes.

Jaypaw was still sorting through the leaves he'd brought back.

Had StarClan really not shared anything with him? Or was he just keeping it to himself? "Are you hungry?" Lionpaw asked. Perhaps they could share some prey. It might make him more talkative.

Jaypaw didn't look up. "I've already eaten."

Sighing, Lionpaw headed out of the den.

Hollypaw was stretching outside the apprentices' den. When she spotted Lionpaw, her whiskers twitched. "Why didn't you wake me?" she demanded, trotting toward him.

"You seemed so tired."

"No more tired than you!"

Lionpaw snorted. "I was trying to help!" Why were his littermates so snappy with him? "If you're so desperate to clean out the nursery, then go ahead." He stomped to the fresh-kill pile and picked a shrew from the top. Crouching to gulp it down, he heard Dustpelt.

"We haven't had a battle like that in moons." The brown tabby warrior was sitting beside the halfrock with Ashfur and Poppyfrost.

"It was like the old days back in the forest," Ashfur agreed.

Poppyfrost's eyes widened. "You've had battles like that before?"

"Worse," Dustpelt meowed. "Do you remember the battle against BloodClan, Ashfur?"

Ashfur's tail twitched. "Now, *that* was a battle!"

"Did the sun go out then?" Poppyfrost mewed.

Dustpelt sighed. "No."

"I hope this was the worst battle I'll ever see," Poppyfrost went on. "I was fighting two warriors at a time! I know we'd covered it in training, but I never imagined I'd have to do it."

"You fought well," Ashfur purred.

"Not as well as Lionpaw," Poppyfrost breathed. "Did you see him? And there's not a scratch on him!"

Ashfur stopped purring. "He's ready to become a warrior."

Lionpaw glanced up from his shrew. Ashfur was staring at him.

"There's little else I can teach him." The pale gray warrior got to his paws. "Lionpaw, are you ready for the patrol?"

Lionpaw swallowed and sat up. "Yes."

Ashfur signaled to Sorreltail and Whitewing, who were sharing tongues outside the warriors' den. They leaped to their paws and followed Ashfur to the thorn tunnel. Lionpaw hurried after them.

The forest was brighter now that the leaves were beginning to fall. Sunlight streamed through the branches and pooled on the forest floor. As they padded toward the WindClan border, Lionpaw dropped back. Was he really ready to become a warrior? Since he was a kit, he had dreamed of being the greatest warrior ThunderClan had ever known. But back then it had been a dream. Now the battles were real. He remembered with a shiver the blood pulsing from Crowfeather's neck, and Heatherpaw's terror. He had done that, possessed by some strength he seemed unable to control. Was that what being a warrior meant? Would he ever learn to control the power he felt in his paws?

Lionpaw shivered as the woods darkened. Clouds had

covered the sun. He could hear his Clanmates rustling through the undergrowth ahead, but something moved in the ferns nearer. He paused. A shape rippled between the trees beside him. A dark-striped pelt.

Tigerstar.

The warrior growled from the shadows. "I watched the battle." Tigerstar shouldered his way through the bushes and stepped onto the path in front of Lionpaw. "You fought well. You were a credit to your ancestors." His amber eyes gleamed.

Lionpaw looked past Tigerstar, searching for Hawkfrost.

"I came alone," Tigerstar told him. "I have no patience for Hawkfrost's sneering. He thinks you actually believe this prophecy. But I know you're too smart to believe Firestar's mouse-brained dreams."

Lionpaw shifted his paws, uncomfortable under Tigerstar's unblinking gaze. "Did you see the sun vanish?"

"It seems the Clans have displeased StarClan." Tigerstar's whiskers twitched. "Those starry-eyed fools never had the heart for battle. Unlike you."

"Ashfur says I'm ready to be a warrior."

"Really?" Tigerstar circled him. "You think you have learned all there is to learn?"

"I've learned all Ashfur has to teach."

"You still have plenty to learn from me."

Lionpaw narrowed his eyes. Did Tigerstar really know more? *Does he guide my paws in battle?* Was it only Tigerstar's training that helped him beat every enemy and leave the fight unscathed?

Tigerstar's breath felt hot on his muzzle as the warrior leaned closer. "You have plenty to learn from me, right?"

Lionpaw shifted on his paws. The dark warrior wanted an answer.

"You can teach me more battle skills, I suppose." Lionpaw lifted his chin. "But what's the point when I've proved I can beat any cat?"

Tigerstar's eyes blazed like fire. "You think you're invincible!" A growl rumbled in his throat. "Hawkfrost is right. You *do* believe this prophecy."

"Yes!" Lionpaw dug his claws into the ground. "You saw me fight in the battle. Could you have fought better and come out unharmed?" He flicked his tail. "You were *killed* in battle."

He turned to leave. He didn't need the guidance of this dead cat!

A roar split the air. Lionpaw spun around. Too late: Claws pierced his shoulders as Tigerstar knocked him to the ground. Lionpaw struggled, but Tigerstar held him down, his massive shoulders rippling with the effort.

"You think you don't need me anymore, is that it?" Tigerstar hissed in his ear. "You're a fool! You've just been lucky, nothing more. Firestar's prophecy is blinding you. You're like a kit who still believes in nursery tales." He shoved Lionpaw down harder, pressing his face into the leaves. "You're powerful because of me, and you will only grow more powerful by learning what I teach you." He gave Lionpaw another shake before jumping back.

Lionpaw scrambled to his paws and turned on him, anger

flaring in his belly. But Tigerstar was fading, his shape dissolving in front of him.

"I've not finished with you yet." With a final hiss, Tigerstar vanished.

Lionpaw was trembling with fury. Why was Tigerstar so determined to ignore the prophecy?

"Lionpaw!" Ashfur was calling him from the bushes ahead.

He hurried to catch up, his shoulders stinging where Tigerstar's claws had dug in. He glanced behind him. Was Tigerstar still watching? What did the dark warrior want from him, if he didn't want the power of the stars?

CHAPTER 23

Hollypaw paused from washing herself. "Are you going to the Gathering?"

Jaypaw heard her tongue scrape along her foreleg. "Yes." He rolled onto his side, feeling full.

"Me too." Lionpaw kicked the remains of the squirrel away and stretched out.

The fresh-kill pile had been restocked in the days following the battle, and they had eaten well. Now they lay beside the halfrock enjoying the last of the evening sun.

Hollypaw yawned. "Do you think the other Clans will turn up?" No one had seen any sign of WindClan since the battle, but tension was still high, with continual patrols along the WindClan border.

"They'll be scared of upsetting StarClan if they don't," Jaypaw mewed.

Lionpaw's claws scratched the halfrock. "I hope WindClan is there."

"Don't forget the truce," Hollypaw reminded him.

"Like I would." Lionpaw snorted. "I just want WindClan to see that we're as strong as we ever were, and ready to fight them again if we have to."

ThunderClan's warriors and apprentices were steadily recovering from their battle wounds. Even Spiderleg was taking walks around the clearing. Squirrelflight was still in her nest in the medicine cats' den, though increasingly impatient at being confined there. But Leafpool wouldn't let her move, fearful the wound would reopen before it had a chance to heal properly.

Jaypaw suspected that his mother's injury was the reason Leafpool wasn't coming with him to the Gathering. She didn't trust any other cat to keep Squirrelflight in her nest. She hadn't even been to the Moonpool to share with StarClan yet.

"If StarClan has something to share with me, they'll share it," she had told Firestar.

Jaypaw lifted his head as Graystripe padded out of the nursery. The gray warrior's pelt was prickling with worry.

"Leafpool!" Graystripe called through the brambles at the entrance to the medicine cats' den. "She's coughing again."

"I'm coming." Leafpool hurried out, smelling of tansy.

Millie had whitecough. Daisy had moved herself and her kits into the apprentices' den to avoid catching the sickness, and Rosekit and Toadkit had been strutting around the camp as if they were already apprentices.

Millie was eating well, but her endless coughing was keeping the kits awake and making it hard for them to feed. Hopefully the tansy would help.

Jaypaw laid his head back down and closed his eyes. He must have dozed, because a moment later Hollypaw was shaking him awake.

"The moon's up," she mewed. "Everyone's getting ready to leave."

"Not *everyone!*" Foxpaw's cross mew sounded behind him. "How come you three get to go while me and Icepaw and Cinderpaw get left behind?"

Jaypaw scrambled to his paws. "You'll go next time, I'm sure."

"Maybe." Foxpaw's feet scuffed the ground as he padded away.

While the warriors gathered at the entrance, Graystripe paced around the nursery. Jaypaw could sense that his emotions were torn like fresh-kill. The gray warrior longed to join his Clanmates at the Gathering, but the thought of leaving Millie while she was sick pierced his heart. Jaypaw blinked. An old grief was fanning the flames of Graystripe's unease, lit by the memory of the silver cat on the huge gray rock.

"Graystripe!" Firestar was heading toward his old friend. "Stay here and guard the camp for me. We've a good show of warriors. WindClan won't think they've weakened us."

"Thanks." Graystripe sounded relieved.

Firestar headed for the barrier, where Poppyfrost and Honeyfern could hardly keep their paws still.

"Looking forward to it?" Dustpelt asked them.

"Oh, yes," Poppyfrost meowed. This would be their first Gathering as warriors.

Sandstorm paced restlessly around Brackenfur. "I wonder what WindClan will have to say for themselves?"

"They'll come up with some excuse," Brackenfur muttered.

"Hurry up." Hollypaw nudged Jaypaw. Lionpaw was already waiting beside Ashfur.

Firestar stood at the camp entrance. "We must show WindClan and RiverClan that we are as strong as ever," he reminded his Clanmates. "The moon is bright tonight, and that means StarClan is no longer angry."

"I bet they're still angry with WindClan," Spiderleg called from outside the medicine cats' den.

"*We* were only defending our borders. StarClan would not punish us for that," Firestar answered.

"I should hope not." Sorreltail was sitting outside the warriors' den, her tail swishing over the ground.

"The vanishing sun frightened us all," Firestar went on. "But we must take it as a sign that the battle was wrong. The sun came back when the battle ended. We should have learned by now that the Clans need one another to survive."

Jaypaw tipped his head. The ThunderClan leader's confident words hadn't come from anything Leafpool had said to him. The medicine cat was still baffled and frightened by the vanishing sun, and the silence from StarClan had made her more nervous. But she kept her worries to herself, carrying on as usual, and only Jaypaw could detect the anxiety fluttering beneath her pelt.

"Let's go!" Firestar led his Clanmates out of the hollow.

Leaves crunched beneath their paws. Jaypaw shivered, feeling the first chill of leaf-fall. He pressed closer to Hollypaw as they headed for WindClan territory, following the familiar route down to the lake. They had to cross WindClan's part of the shore to reach the island. If they kept within two tail-lengths of the water, WindClan had no right to challenge them. Yet the warriors fell silent as they crossed the border and hurried over the shingle.

"Any sign of WindClan?" Jaypaw whispered.

"Not yet." Hollypaw's pelt felt spiky against his.

Water suddenly lapped Jaypaw's legs. He stumbled in surprise. They didn't usually skirt the lake this closely.

"Don't worry," Hollypaw soothed. "Firestar's just being careful that no cat can accuse us of straying onto WindClan land."

The warriors splashed through the shallows, and Jaypaw gritted his teeth, hating the feel of the water on his paws. He tasted the air. Fresh WindClan scents were blowing down from the moorland.

"They're coming," Hollypaw warned.

Jaypaw tensed. "Toward us?"

"No. They're far up the hillside and heading toward the island."

At the tree-bridge, Hollypaw jumped onto the fallen trunk first and let her tail dangle down. Jaypaw reached up with his paws, feeling for it. He felt the soft tip brush his pads and knew instantly where to jump.

"Thanks," he puffed, scrambling through the leafless fallen branches.

The trunk was slippery, its bark shredded and peeling away. Jaypaw padded after Hollypaw, putting one paw carefully in front of the other until his nose brushed his sister's tail.

She had stopped where the trunk splayed out in tangled

roots. The shingle crunched as she jumped down onto the shore.

This was the hardest part. Jaypaw took a breath and leaped after her. As always the shingle hit his paws suddenly, but this time he didn't need to stumble to regain his balance.

"Nice landing," Hollypaw purred.

Their Clanmates were streaming through the undergrowth, making it swish as they disappeared into the trees. Jaypaw nosed his way through and followed Hollypaw through the soft swaths of fern. As they emerged on the other side, a barrage of scents hit his nose. WindClan and RiverClan were already here. He wrinkled his nose. No sign of ShadowClan.

The ThunderClan cats padded to one side of the clearing, keeping close together.

"Everyone's keeping to themselves," Hollypaw observed.

Jaypaw tasted the air. She was right: There was no mingling of scents. RiverClan sat upwind in a tight group. WindClan paced restlessly near them, but didn't break ranks.

"I'm surprised RiverClan and WindClan aren't sharing tongues," Lionpaw muttered. His muscles were tight as though ready for battle.

"Where is ShadowClan?" Poppyfrost mewed anxiously.

"I hope they come soon," fretted Honeyfern.

A growl suddenly rumbled in Lionpaw's throat.

"Quiet!" Ashfur snapped.

Lionpaw fell silent, but Jaypaw could sense rage pulsing from his brother's pelt, hot as the sun.

He narrowed his eyes, focusing his other senses on

Lionpaw. He sensed hatred shooting from his brother like a shaft of light, and, concentrating harder, he realized he could follow its path into the defensive cluster of WindClan cats. It ended at Heatherpaw; Jaypaw recognized the tone of her mew and her faint honey scent. He flicked his tail in surprise. Lionpaw's hatred was so strong he was surprised Heatherpaw couldn't feel it burning her pelt. But the WindClan apprentice certainly sensed something; she was weaving self-consciously among her Clanmates, betraying unease with every step.

Bushes rustled at the far edge of the clearing. ShadowClan must be arriving. Jaypaw tasted the air, and was startled by the scent. This wasn't a full-size Gathering patrol. It was just—

"It's just Blackstar and Sol!" Hollypaw's mew was barely more than a whisper.

"Where are the rest of them?" hissed a WindClan cat from the far side of the clearing.

"And who in StarClan's name is that?" came a murmur from the RiverClan cats.

All the Clans shifted anxiously as the ShadowClan leader padded to the center of the clearing. Sol followed, trotting lightly over the sandy earth.

Jaypaw was surprised by the sense of calm flowing from Blackstar's pelt. The ShadowClan leader had seemed so lost and worried when they'd seen him in the camp. What had happened?

"I bring news," Blackstar began.

"I hope ShadowClan's all right," Hollypaw whispered.

"Shh!" Brackenfur silenced her as Blackstar went on.

"ShadowClan will no longer attend Gatherings."

An astonished silence fell on the clearing. Whatever the other cats had been expecting, this wasn't it.

"We no longer believe that StarClan holds all the answers. It was *living* cats who found the lake. It is *living* cats who hunt prey to keep themselves alive, and it was a *living* cat who predicted that the sun would vanish."

He means Sol.

Onestar was stunned. "He predicted the sun would disappear?"

Amazement flooded through the cats like water washing through grass.

"I did no more than warn it would happen." Sol's mew was humble.

"How did you know?" Leopardstar demanded.

"How did you *not* know?" Sol answered. "You, after all, are the ones who share with StarClan."

Barkface stepped forward. "They didn't warn us."

"And they didn't warn me," Sol meowed. "I merely followed my instinct and listened to my own voice of experience. You, of course, are entitled to believe in whatever you want. . . ."

"What's he saying?" Hollypaw gasped. "Does he think beliefs can be chosen like prey from the fresh-kill pile?" Her pelt seared Jaypaw's where they touched. He flinched from her, lost in his own disappointment.

Sol was meant to be helping us! What is he doing with ShadowClan?

There was the sound of soft paw steps padding over the dry ground.

"They're leaving." Lionpaw sighed. "I guess that means Sol isn't going to help us after all."

As Blackstar and Sol swished away through the ferns, frightened whispers broke out among the Clans.

"Who was he?"

"Where did he come from?"

"Can it be true?"

Jaypaw felt his own Clan move restlessly around him, their pelts sparking with fear as they brushed against one another.

Firestar had padded to the middle of the clearing. "We must stay calm," he called to all of them.

"Calm?" Onestar's mew was filled with contempt. "Even you can't change this, Firestar."

Firestar bristled with anger. "I never said I could!"

"We mustn't quarrel." Leopardstar stepped in. "This is too important. We are *three* Clans now."

"Three Clans!" Ashfoot gasped. The WindClan deputy paced around the leaders. "But there have always been four."

"If ShadowClan rejects StarClan," Mistyfoot ventured, "does that mean they can no longer be warriors?"

"Have they given up the warrior code?" Hollypaw's breath was coming in fast gulps.

They've given up more than the code. Jaypaw glanced at the sky. "Is the moon still shining?"

"It's bright and clear," Lionpaw assured him.

What is StarClan doing? Don't they care what has happened?

"These are troubling times," Leopardstar meowed. "We cannot even trust the sun to shine. Is it so surprising that

Blackstar has lost faith in StarClan?"

Her words seemed to fill the clearing with an icy chill. No cat challenged her, tried to say that she was wrong, that their faith was worth fighting for. Sol warned that the sun would disappear, and it did. Where did that leave StarClan? Whispering to one another in frightened mews, the cats began to melt into the undergrowth.

"Come on." Lionpaw was nudging Hollypaw. Thunder-Clan was leaving.

Hollypaw stumbled forward as if she had forgotten how to walk. Jaypaw pressed against her, guiding her path through the ferns.

"Are the cats of ShadowClan really not warriors anymore?" Poppyfrost asked.

"I suppose that's for StarClan to decide," Birchfall told her.

As Jaypaw waited for his turn to cross the tree-bridge, he tried not to let the urgent mews of his Clanmates unsettle him. He had to think this through. But they chattered on, crowding his thoughts.

"If StarClan hid the sun when we fought," Dustpelt growled, "what will they do now that Blackstar has turned their back on them?"

"They haven't covered the moon," Brackenfur pointed out.

Thornclaw leaped onto the bridge. "Perhaps they'll turn their backs on us all!"

As Jaypaw crossed the fallen tree, the warrior's words buzzed like bees in his mind. StarClan had said nothing about the sun, or Sol. Perhaps they *had* given up on watching over the Clans below.

Jaypaw felt Lionpaw's tail touch his shoulder as they padded along the WindClan shoreline. "Slow down," he whispered.

Jaypaw eased his pace and let his Clanmates push on ahead until they were out of earshot. Hollypaw hung back with him, her paws dragging over the shingle.

"I thought Sol had come to help," Lionpaw hissed. "But he's just made things worse."

Hollypaw was still in shock. "He's stopped Blackstar from believing in the warrior code," she mumbled tonelessly.

"Perhaps Blackstar would have stopped anyway," Jaypaw suggested.

"No. It was Sol." Lionpaw was adamant. "He's said something to convince Blackstar that StarClan is worthless."

Hollypaw kicked suddenly at the shingle. "I don't care what Sol says." Her mew was shrill. "They can't stop believing in StarClan. That's what Clans *do*! The warrior code brought us here; it gives us food and shelter." Her fear had turned to rage. "It keeps us safe!"

"But Sol predicted the vanishing sun," Lionpaw reminded her. "StarClan didn't."

"Does that mean you're going to give up StarClan too?" Fury flashed from Hollypaw so fiercely that Jaypaw wondered for an instant if she were going to lunge at Lionpaw. But she only stalked ahead, her breath rasping with emotion.

Lionpaw hurried after her. "That's not what I meant."

Jaypaw let them go. The shingle was soft here, dimpling

around his paws. The lake whispered on the shore. A cool breeze blew off the water, and Jaypaw turned his head, feeling it ruffle his whiskers.

Broken moonlight shimmered on the surface of the lake.

He could *see* it.

I must be dreaming.

The shingle shifted beside him. A cat was walking with him.

Yellowfang.

Her breath fouled the air, but Jaypaw was pleased she had come. "Did you see what happened?" he mewed.

"Of course."

Jaypaw's heart quickened. "What are you going to do?"

Yellowfang's paws scrunched on the shingle. She sighed, and when she spoke again, she sounded old and tired. "We must choose our battles carefully."

Was StarClan admitting defeat without even trying to fight for ShadowClan? Jaypaw turned to her, panic coming in waves. But Yellowfang had faded from his sight. Everything had clouded over, and soon the world was black once more. He could hear the voices of his Clanmates ahead, and pushed on after them.

His thoughts whirled and collided like leaves caught in a storm. At last Yellowfang had told him what he needed to know.

StarClan has surrendered. Their end is drawing near.

Jaypaw, Lionpaw, and Hollypaw would fulfill their destiny at last.

CHAPTER 24

Lionpaw was dreaming.

Blood flooded over him, around him, washing through his fur, thick and warm, filling his nostrils, tumbling him onward until he was buffeted against rough stone walls.

Help!

He fought the crimson tide, churning his paws, his muscles screaming as he struggled against the weight of the flood. His lungs were bursting, and the iron tang of blood filled his mouth.

The wave dragged him across jagged rocks, then swept on without him, leaving him soaked and gasping for breath. He blinked open his eyes and saw a stone roof arching high above him. Silvery light filtered through a crack, dimly lighting the stone walls of the cave. Lionpaw struggled to his paws, his sodden pelt heavy. He stared at the blood pooled in the cracks and crevices of the wide stone floor and glimpsed a shape—a body—lying awkwardly on the stone floor, paws twisted, tail limp, head thrown back, blood dripping from its whiskers.

Heatherpaw!

Lionpaw stumbled toward her, rage surging beneath his

pelt. Growling, he pawed at her, but she lay heavy and motion-less.

She was already dead.

He glared at her, satisfaction welling in his belly.

You deserve it!

She had caused the battle that had made the sun vanish. And now the Clans were falling apart, turning away from StarClan as StarClan turned away from them.

His claws slid out, curling from his paws, longer and sharper than blackthorns. They scraped the cave floor, gouging furrows in the stone. Blood pounded in his ears, heat surging through him as though he were in battle. No enemy could beat him; no foe could spill his blood.

Let the battles come. Nothing can harm me. I am more powerful than StarClan!

"Get off!" Foxpaw's indignant mew woke him. "You're digging your claws into my back!"

Lionpaw rolled away and stumbled out of his nest. "Sorry." His mind was fuzzy with sleep, but the dream still haunted him. He staggered out of the den, feeling sick.

I was glad she was dead!

Horrified, he padded into the clearing.

I loved her once.

The morning sun streamed onto his pelt, but he shivered. Fear spread like ice through his bones. He licked at his chest, relieved to find it didn't taste of blood and his fur wasn't stained red.

"Good morning, sleepyhead!" Hollypaw was carrying

moss to the elders' den.

Lionpaw didn't reply. He kept washing. He felt his dream had tainted him. Did he really want to become more powerful than StarClan if it meant spilling so much blood?

Cloudtail was putting Cinderpaw through her paces below Highledge. "Jump, duck, and roll," he ordered.

She practiced the battle move, landing perfectly on all four paws.

"How did your leg feel?" Cloudtail prompted.

Cinderpaw purred. "Like all my other legs!" She trotted around her mentor with her tail in the air. "Absolutely fine."

Millie was coughing in the nursery, her kits mewling while Daisy tried to soothe them. "It's all right, my sweets. Try feeding again."

Sandstorm began rattling the branches of the apprentices' den. "Wake up, Foxpaw, you dormouse!"

The thorn barrier shivered as Graystripe pounded into camp.

Cloudtail looked up. "Any sign of WindClan?"

"No," Graystripe answered. "The borders are freshly marked, but no cat's crossed them."

Dustpelt and Whitewing followed him in and padded to the fresh-kill pile.

Whitewing picked through the prey left from last night. "Has the hunting patrol left?"

"Not yet," Sandstorm called. "We're heading out shortly." She rattled the apprentices' den once more. "Once I can get Foxpaw out of his nest. He thinks he's allowed to miss all his duties while Squirrelflight's sick." She looked at Lionpaw. "Do you want to come hunting?"

Lionpaw paused in his washing. "Yes." Perhaps a run in the woods would clear his mind. He could pretend he was like any other apprentice—for a short time, at least.

Leafpool slid out of her den. Jaypaw padded after her, yawning.

"We need more marigold," she mewed. "Squirrelflight's wound is healing nicely, but I want to be ready for any late infections. We can't risk taking anything for granted." She glanced nervously up at the sun, rising over the trees at the rim of the hollow.

"I'll fetch some this morning," Jaypaw offered. He stretched, his tail quivering with the effort. "There's a patch beside the shore."

"It'll be the last of the season, I expect." Leafpool sighed.

"Then I'll get as much as I can."

Grit sprinkled down from Highledge. Firestar was sitting outside his cave, washing. His orange pelt turned to fire as the morning light caught it. He gave each ear a quick rub, then gazed down at the camp. "Let all cats old enough to catch their own prey gather together!" he called.

Sandstorm looked up, surprised.

Lionpaw straightened. *What about the hunt?*

The warriors' den shivered as Brackenfur and Birchfall padded out. Poppyfrost and Berrynose followed, their eyes bleary with sleep. Foxpaw stumbled dozily from the apprentices' den.

"About time, too!" Sandstorm chided. "I was about to come in and drag you out by your tail."

Icepaw trotted out after her brother. "Sorry," she apologized. "I kept him awake last night. We were trying to stay up till you got back from the Gathering."

Sandstorm glanced at Firestar. "You'll hear about it soon enough."

Lionpaw padded beneath Highledge as the Clan gathered. Dustpelt shook sleep from his whiskers, while Thornclaw sat beside him and picked moss from his pelt. Squirrelflight had padded to the edge of the clearing. From the stern looks Leafpool was flashing at her, she was meant to be in her nest.

Hollypaw slid in beside Lionpaw. "What do you think he's going to tell them?" she whispered.

Lionpaw guessed she was talking about the Gathering. How would Firestar break the news of Blackstar's revelation to his Clan?

Jaypaw weaved his way among his Clanmates and sat down beside Lionpaw. "I hope you slept better than me."

Lionpaw stared at his paws, feeling hot, as Heatherpaw's motionless body flashed behind his eyes.

"The Gathering was not what we expected." Firestar's mew jolted him out of the hateful vision. "ShadowClan didn't come."

Mews of shock erupted through the Clan.

Brightheart pricked her ears. "What was wrong with them?"

"Is there sickness in ShadowClan?" Cloudtail called.

Firestar ignored the questions and pressed on. "Blackstar came with the loner, Sol, and told us that ShadowClan is turning their backs on StarClan."

Mousewhisker looked puzzled. "What do you mean?"

Firestar stared down at the young warrior. "ShadowClan no longer believes that StarClan holds all the answers. They have lost faith in their warrior ancestors and will not be attending any more Gatherings."

He raised his voice over the murmurs of alarm speeding through the Clan. "The loner Sol appears to be encouraging this belief. But I hope StarClan will have a greater influence over ShadowClan in the end. I believe they will speak through Littlecloud and to Blackstar himself. StarClan has never let us down before. Perhaps they let Blackstar stray for a reason. But I'm sure they will bring him back to the Clans. All will be well. Remember how the sun disappeared? But then it came back again, as warm as ever. This darkness will pass too, I'm sure."

As the Clan stared up at their leader, Lionpaw remembered Sol's words: *The light will return, just like the sun came back, but it will be your light, and yours to control.*

His blood-soaked dream lingered in his mind. Was he ready for such power? Did he even deserve it?

CHAPTER 25

❧

He doesn't believe what he's saying.

Jaypaw lifted his muzzle toward Firestar. *He's not sure at all that this darkness will pass.*

He felt Lionpaw tense beside him, uncertainty prickling beneath his brother's pelt. Hollypaw's tail whisked the ground.

"Can't we get rid of Sol?" Dustpelt called.

"Blackstar has to make his own choices," Firestar answered.

"Even if it affects all the Clans?" Sandstorm demanded.

"We shall go on as usual," Firestar declared. "We shall hunt and take care of our kits and our elders. We shall patrol our borders the same way we did in the forest. The same way we have done here. Whatever change comes, we will listen to StarClan and use the warrior code as our guide."

Hollypaw let out a slow breath. "The warrior code," she murmured. "The warrior code." She repeated it as though it were the answer to everything.

Jaypaw envied his sister's faith. And her ignorance. She didn't realize that Firestar was taking as much comfort from his words as his Clanmates.

He has to believe things are going to be all right, for the sake of the Clan.

Firestar shifted on his paws. "I have good news to share today as well as bad."

Jaypaw looked up, surprised. *What good news?*

"ThunderClan is still strong. We have proved ourselves in battle, and we know that StarClan still watches over us." His tail brushed the ledge. "There are three new warriors to be named."

Jaypaw flinched as excitement blazed from Lionpaw and Hollypaw. It was like sitting between two suns.

"Lionpaw, Hollypaw, and Cinderpaw."

Pebbles cracked as Firestar bounded down the rocks and into the clearing, where the Clan was already making space for the naming ceremony.

Brackenfur darted over to Hollypaw and smoothed her fur with his tail. "Well done," he purred.

Ashfur weaved past Lionpaw. "You'll be a fine warrior."

"I'll make you proud of me," Lionpaw promised.

Squirrelflight was shining with happiness. Leafpool sat beside her, a purr rumbling in her throat. *She must be pleased for Cinderpaw,* thought Jaypaw.

Cloudtail weaved around his apprentice. "I told you it wouldn't be long before you joined your denmates, Cinderpaw."

Jaypaw closed his eyes. It was a long time since he imagined he could be a warrior. But the dream had never left him. He let jealousy surge and ebb away. Then pride blossomed inside him. His littermates would be warriors!

"Congratulations," he purred.

Hollypaw rubbed her muzzle against his cheek. "Thank you."

Lionpaw flicked Jaypaw's ear with his tail. "I hope Icepaw keeps her promise to Mousefur, because I'm not cleaning out the elders' den anymore."

Ashfur's tail twitched. "If your Clanmates' bedding needs changing, then you'll change it."

Brambleclaw padded toward them. "Does Lionpaw think that Firestar's making him leader already?" he purred.

"I was just joking!" Lionpaw protested.

"Of course." Brambleclaw circled his kits and stopped beside Jaypaw. "I'm proud of you *all*."

Hazeltail and Berrynose came bouncing toward them.

"Well done!" Hazeltail mewed.

"I suppose we can make room for you in the warriors' den," Berrynose teased.

"I'm glad I'm not in there anymore," Mousefur called. "It'll be noisier than a nest full of starlings." The old warrior was sitting outside the nursery while Toadkit and Rosekit skittered around her. Warmth glowed from her pelt as Millie squeezed out of her den behind her. Jaypaw smelled the fresh scent of a kit dangling from the queen's jaws.

She dropped Briarkit between Mousefur's paws. "Will you watch this one while I fetch the other two?" Millie's mew was husky, as if her throat was sore. Jaypaw reminded himself to fetch the last of the honey for her after the ceremony. "I thought they might want to see their first naming ceremony," Millie added.

"I'll make sure Rosekit and Toadkit don't trample him," Mousefur rasped.

"Hey!" Toadkit objected. "We're not that clumsy. Anyone would think we were always . . ."

He fell silent as Firestar addressed the Clan from the middle of the clearing.

"I, Firestar, leader of ThunderClan, call upon my warrior ancestors to look down on these three apprentices." Lionpaw clawed at the ground as Firestar went on. "They have trained hard to understand the ways of your noble code, and I commend them to you as warriors in their turn."

Hollypaw was already padding into the clearing, and Lionpaw hurried after her. Cinderpaw followed, her paw steps even and strong.

"Hollypaw, Lionpaw, and Cinderpaw, do you promise to uphold the warrior code and to protect and defend this Clan, even at the cost of your lives?"

"I do," Hollypaw breathed, quivering.

Lionpaw stiffened with determination. "I do."

"I do." Cinderpaw sounded as relieved and excited as a cat that had just caught its first prey.

Jaypaw held his breath. They were closer than ever to their destiny.

"Then by the power of StarClan I give you your warrior names." Firestar's fur brushed Hollypaw's. "Hollypaw, from this moment you shall be known as Hollyleaf." He stepped back. "StarClan honors your thoughtfulness and loyalty."

Lionpaw padded forward.

"Lionpaw, you shall be known as Lionblaze. StarClan honors your courage and skill in battle. And Cinderpaw." Firestar paused as Cinderpaw approached him, trembling with excitement. "You shall be known as Cinderheart in honor of those warriors who have gone before." Jaypaw detected sadness beneath his mew. Was he remembering Cinderpelt? If only he knew that her spirit stood before him, shining beneath Cinderheart's pelt. "StarClan honors your bravery and your determination. You are a warrior at last."

"Lionblaze! Hollyleaf! Cinderheart!" The Clan raised their voices defiantly as they welcomed the new warriors. Despite the vanishing sun and Blackstar's devastating decision, ThunderClan would go on.

Jaypaw cheered with them, proud of his littermates and of Cinderheart, who had fought so hard to become a warrior. Cinderpelt's destiny had been fulfilled.

But what about our destiny?

Jaypaw shivered. Defiance against the vanishing sun was not enough. He knew better than his Clanmates what its disappearance had meant. The time of the Clans was coming to an end, and he, Lionblaze, and Hollyleaf were the only ones who could save them.

ERIN
HUNTER

is inspired by a love of cats and a fascination with the ferocity of the natural world. As well as having great respect for nature in all its forms, Erin enjoys creating rich mythical explanations for animal behavior. She is also the author of the bestselling Seekers and Survivors series.

Download the free Warriors app and chat on the Warriors message boards at www.warriorcats.com!

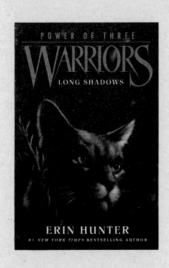

CHAPTER 1

The moon was huge, a golden circle resting on a dark ridge of hills. Stars blazed above Hollyleaf's head, reminding her that the spirits of her ancestors were watching over her. Her fur prickled as something stirred on the ridge. A cat had appeared there, outlined against the moon. She recognized the broad head and tufted ears, and the tail with its bushy tip; even though the shape was black against the light, she knew the colors of its pelt: white with brown, black, and ginger blotches.

"*Sol!*" she hissed.

The outlined shape arched its back, then reared up on its hind paws, its forepaws stretched out as if it was about to rake its claws across the sky. It leaped upward, and as it leaped it swelled until it was so huge that it blotted out the moon and the blazing stars. Hollyleaf crouched, shivering, in darkness thicker than the deepest places of the forest.

Screeches of alarm rose up around her, a whole Clan of hidden cats wailing their fear of the shadow cutting them off from the protective gaze of StarClan. Above the noise, a single voice rang out: "Hollyleaf! Hollyleaf! Come out!"

Hollyleaf thrashed in terror and found her paws tangled in

soft moss and bracken. Pale gray light was filtering through the branches of the warriors' den. A couple of fox-lengths away, Hazeltail was scrambling out of her nest, shaking scraps of moss from her pelt.

"Hollyleaf!" The call came again, and this time Hollyleaf recognized Birchfall's voice, meowing irritably outside the den. "Are you going to sleep all day? We're supposed to be hunting."

"Coming." Groggy with sleep, every hair on her pelt still quivering from her nightmare, Hollyleaf headed toward the nearest gap between the branches. Before she reached it, her paws stumbled over the haunches of a sleeping cat, half hidden under the bracken.

Cloudtail's head popped up. "Great StarClan!" he grumbled. "Can't a cat get any sleep around here?"

"S-sorry," Hollyleaf stammered, remembering that Cloudtail had been out on a late patrol the night before; she had seen him return to camp with Dustpelt and Sorreltail while she was keeping her warrior's vigil.

Just my luck. My first day, and I manage to annoy one of the senior warriors!

Cloudtail snorted and curled up again, his blue eyes closing as he buried his nose in his fur.

"It's okay," Hazeltail murmured, brushing her muzzle against Hollyleaf's shoulder. "Cloudtail's mew is worse than his scratch. And don't let Birchfall ruffle your fur. He's bossy with the new warriors, but you'll soon get used to it."

Hollyleaf nodded gratefully, though she didn't tell Hazeltail the real reason she was thrown off balance. Birchfall didn't bother her; it was the memory of the dream that throbbed through her from ears to tail-tip, making her paws clumsy and her thoughts troubled.

Her gaze drifted to the nest where her brother Lionpaw—no, Lion*blaze* now—had curled up at the end of his vigil. She wanted to talk to him more than anything. But the nest was empty; Lionblaze must have gone out on the dawn patrol.

Careful where she put her paws, Hollyleaf pushed her way out of the den behind Hazeltail. Outside, Birchfall was scraping the ground impatiently.

"At last!" he snapped. "What kept you?"

"Take it easy, Birchfall." Brambleclaw, the ThunderClan deputy and Hollyleaf's father, was sitting a tail-length away with his tail wrapped neatly around his paws. His amber eyes were calm. "The prey won't run away."

"Not till they see us, anyway," Sandstorm added as she bounded across from the fresh-kill pile.

"If there is any prey." Birchfall lashed his tail. "Ever since the battle, fresh-kill's been much harder to find."

Hollyleaf's grumbling belly told her that Birchfall was right. Several sunrises ago all four Clans had battled in ThunderClan territory; their screeching and trampling had frightened off all the prey, or driven them deep underground.

"Maybe the prey will start to come back now," she suggested.

"Maybe," Brambleclaw agreed. "We'll head toward the ShadowClan border. There wasn't as much fighting over there."

Hollyleaf stiffened at the mention of ShadowClan. *Will I see Sol again?* she wondered.

"I wonder if we'll see any ShadowClan cats," Birchfall meowed, echoing her thought. "I'd like to know if they're all going to turn their back on StarClan, and follow that weirdo loner instead."

Hollyleaf felt as if stones were dragging in her belly, weighing her down. ShadowClan had not appeared at the last Gathering, two nights before. Instead, their leader Blackstar had come alone except for Sol, the loner who had recently arrived by the lake, and explained that his cats no longer believed in the power of their warrior ancestors.

But that can't be right! How can a Clan survive without StarClan? Without the warrior code?

"Sol's not such a weirdo," Hazeltail pointed out to Birchfall with a flick of her ears. "He predicted that the sun would vanish, and it did. None of the medicine cats knew that was going to happen."

Birchfall shrugged. "The sun came back, didn't it? It's not that big a deal."

"In any case," Brambleclaw interrupted, rising to his paws, "this is a hunting patrol. We're not going to pay a friendly visit to ShadowClan."

"But they fought beside us," Birchfall objected. "WindClan and RiverClan would have turned us into crow-food without the ShadowClan warriors. We can't be enemies again so soon, can we?"

"Not enemies," Sandstorm corrected. "But they're still a

different Clan. Besides, I'm not sure we can be friends with cats who reject StarClan."

What about our own cats, then? Hollyleaf didn't dare to ask the question out loud. *Cloudtail has never believed in StarClan.* But she knew without question Cloudtail was a loyal warrior who would die for any of his Clanmates.

Brambleclaw said nothing, just gave his pelt a shake and kinked his tail to beckon the rest of the patrol. As they headed toward the thorn tunnel they met Brackenfur pushing his way into the hollow with Sorreltail and Lionblaze behind him. The dawn patrol had returned. As all three cats headed for the fresh-kill pile, Hollyleaf darted across and intercepted her brother.

"How did it go? Is there anything to report?"

Lionblaze's jaws parted in a huge yawn. *He must be exhausted,* Hollyleaf thought, *after keeping his warrior vigil and then being chosen for the dawn patrol.*

"Not a thing," he mewed, shaking his head. "All's quiet on the WindClan border."

"We're going over toward ShadowClan territory." Alone with her brother, Hollyleaf could confess how worried she was. "I'm scared we'll meet Sol. What if he tells the other cats about the prophecy?"

Lionblaze pressed his muzzle into her shoulder. "Come on! Is it likely that Sol will be doing border patrols? He'll be lying around the ShadowClan camp, stuffing himself with fresh-kill."

Hollyleaf shook her head. "I don't know. . . . I just wish we'd never told him anything."

"So do I." Lionblaze's eyes narrowed and his tone was bitter as he went on. "But it's not like Sol is bothered about us. He decided to stay with Blackstar, didn't he? He promised to help us after we told him about the prophecy, but he soon changed his mind."

"We're better off without him." Hollyleaf swiped her tongue over her brother's ear.

"Hollyleaf!"

She spun around to see Brambleclaw waiting beside the entrance to the thorn tunnel, the tip of his tail twitching impatiently.

"I've got to go," she meowed to Lionblaze, and raced across the clearing to join Brambleclaw. "Sorry," she gasped, and plunged into the tunnel.

The morning had been raw and cold, but as Hollyleaf padded through the forest with her Clanmates the clouds began to clear away. Long claws of sunlight pierced the branches, tipping the leaves with fire where they had changed from green to red and gold. Leaf-fall was almost upon them.

Brambleclaw led his patrol away from the lake toward the ShadowClan border, keeping well clear of the old Twoleg path and the abandoned nest where the Clans had fought their battle.

Tasting the air in the hope of finding a squirrel or a plump mouse, Hollyleaf caught a stale trace of her own and her littermates' scents, lingering from their trek across the forest to find Sol. She hoped that none of the patrol would notice, especially not Brambleclaw or Sandstorm, because that would mean awkward questions she wasn't sure she could answer.

To her relief, the other cats seemed too intent on tracking prey to notice. Sandstorm raised her tail for silence, and Hollyleaf could hear the crisp sounds of a thrush knocking a snail shell against a stone. Peering over a clump of bracken, she spotted the bird: a fine fat one with its back turned to the group of cats, too intent on its own prey to realize that hunters were creeping up on it.

Sandstorm dropped into the hunter's crouch and glided over the forest floor, pausing to waggle her haunches before the final pounce. The movement alerted the thrush; dropping the snail, it let out a loud alarm call and launched itself into the air.

But Sandstorm was too fast for it. With an enormous leap she clawed it out of the air in a flurry of wings; it went limp as she bit down hard on its neck.

"Brilliant catch!" Hazeltail mewed.

"Not bad," Sandstorm purred, scratching earth over her prey until she could collect it later.

Hollyleaf picked up the scent of mouse and followed it along a bramble thicket until she spotted the little creature scuffling among the debris beneath the outer branches. A couple of heartbeats later she had her own prey to bury beside Sandstorm's.

Brambleclaw was clawing earth over a vole; he gave her an approving nod. "Well done, Hollyleaf. Carry on like this and the Clan will soon be full-fed." He stalked off into a hazel thicket, his jaws parted to pick up the faintest trace of prey.

For a few heartbeats Hollyleaf stood looking after her father, his praise warming her. Casting about for more prey, she picked up the trail of a squirrel, but as she rounded the trunk of a huge oak she spotted Hazeltail ahead of her, following the same scent. There was no sign of the squirrel, but the trail led straight toward the ShadowClan border. Hollyleaf could already make out the scent of the border markings, but Hazeltail seemed too preoccupied with her hunt to notice.

"Hey, Hazeltail, don't—"

Hollyleaf broke off as three cats emerged from a clump of bracken on the other side of the border. Hazeltail was only a couple of tail-lengths away; startled, she halted, her ears flicking up in surprise.

Relief surged through Hollyleaf as she recognized the newcomers: Ivytail, Snaketail, and his apprentice, Scorchpaw. All three of them had fought on ThunderClan's side in the battle; Hollyleaf could still see gashes along Ivytail's side, and Scorchpaw's ear was torn. They surely wouldn't be angry with Hazeltail for coming right up to the border.

"Hi," she meowed as she bounded up to stand beside Hazeltail. "How's the prey running in ShadowClan?"

"Keep back!" Ivytail spat. "You've no right to come into ShadowClan territory. Just because we helped you in the battle doesn't make us allies."

"Typical ThunderClan," Snaketail added, his voice a low snarl. "Thinking every Clan is their friend."

"And what's wrong with that?" Hollyleaf demanded, stung by their hostility.

No cat answered her question. Instead, Ivytail stalked up to the border until she was nose-to-nose with Hazeltail. "What do you think you're doing, this close to the border?"

"I was tracking a squirrel." Hazeltail sounded bewildered. "But—"

"Prey-stealing!" Snaketail interrupted, the fur on his shoulders fluffing up in anger and his striped tail lashing.

"We were not!" Hollyleaf mewed indignantly. "We're still on ThunderClan territory, in case you hadn't noticed. Hazeltail hasn't crossed your border."

"Only because we turned up in time to stop her," Snaketail growled.

Rustling sounded from the undergrowth behind Hollyleaf; she whipped around to see Brambleclaw and Sandstorm approaching, with Birchfall just behind. "Thank StarClan!" she murmured.

Brambleclaw padded forward until he stood beside Hollyleaf and Hazeltail. "Greetings," he mewed, dipping his head to the three ShadowClan cats. "What's going on here?"

"We had to stop these warriors of yours," the ShadowClan cat explained. "Another couple of heartbeats and they would have crossed our border."

"That's not true!" Hollyleaf exclaimed hotly.

"I was tracking a squirrel." Hazeltail faced the ThunderClan deputy with an apologetic look in her eyes. "I did forget where I was for a moment, but Hollyleaf warned me, and then the ShadowClan patrol appeared. I promise, I never set paw over the border."

Brambleclaw nodded. "You're as close to the border on your side as we are on ours," he pointed out to the Shadow-Clan cats. "But no cat is accusing you of trying to cross."

"We're a border patrol!" Snaketail flashed back at him. "And it's just as well we came along when we did."

"No cat can trust ThunderClan," Scorchpaw added, padding up beside his mentor.

Birchfall let out a hiss of fury; thrusting his way through the long grass he halted beside the ThunderClan deputy. "Brambleclaw, are you going to stand there and let an apprentice insult our Clan? When we haven't even done anything?"

Sandstorm flicked his shoulder with her tail. "That's enough, Birchfall. Let Brambleclaw handle this."

The younger warrior let out a snort of disgust; he said nothing more, but stood glaring at the ShadowClan patrol.

"Birchfall's right!" Hollyleaf protested. "These cats are just trying to make trouble. We haven't broken the warrior code."

"Oh, the precious warrior code!" Ivytail's voice was full of scorn. "You think it's the answer to everything, but you're wrong. The warrior code didn't stop the sun from vanishing, did it?"

"Right." Snaketail supported his Clanmate. "Maybe it's time the Clans stopped being so obsessed with dead cats, and started looking for other answers instead."

Hollyleaf stared at them in dismay. She knew that these thoughts came from Sol. Was this what the strange cat had wanted all along—to destroy the warrior code from inside the Clans?

He meant to start with us. Hollyleaf remembered how friendly and helpful Sol had seemed. But maybe ShadowClan had been an easier prospect; Hollyleaf couldn't imagine Firestar abandoning his beliefs as easily as Blackstar.

I have to save ShadowClan! In her desperation Hollyleaf was scarcely aware of the cats around her any longer. *They can't turn their backs on StarClan and the warrior code! There have to be four Clans!*

"Hollyleaf, calm down," Brambleclaw murmured beside her.

Hollyleaf realized that her pelt was fluffed out and her claws were digging into the damp earth. The three Shadow-Clan cats were staring at her, fur bristling as if they expected her to leap on them. Taking a deep breath she sheathed her claws and tried to make her fur lie flat again.

"I'm okay," she muttered to her father.

"This is Sol talking, isn't it?" Birchfall jeered, taking a pace forward so that he stood right on the border. "You're all crazier than a fox in a fit! It's mouse-brained to listen to a cat that no Clan cat has ever met before."

"We listen because Sol talks sense," Snaketail retorted, stepping forward until he faced Birchfall. "He knows what to do to give ShadowClan a better life for the future. Maybe if ThunderClan listened they would be able to fight their own battles. Maybe that's why the sun vanished, to tell us that the time of the Clans is over, and cats have to work out how to live on their own. If ThunderClan is too cowardly to face that—"

With a screech of fury, Birchfall leaped on Snaketail.

The two cats rolled over in a spitting knot of fur. Scorchpaw jumped on top of them, clawing at Birchfall's shoulder. Hazeltail launched himself onto the apprentice, trying to thrust him away from Birchfall.

"Birchfall, Hazeltail, get back here *now*." Sandstorm took a pace forward, only to find her way blocked by Ivytail.

"Can't your young warriors fight their own battles?" the ShadowClan warrior sneered. "A battle *they* started?" She unsheathed her claws and drew back her lips in a snarl.

Brambleclaw bounded forward to stand at Sandstorm's side. "No. This battle was provoked by ShadowClan."

Another yowl split the air from the fighting cats. Hollyleaf cringed at the sound of ripping fur, as if the claws were raking her own pelt. "Stop!" she screeched. "What are you doing?"

To her surprise, the battling cats fell apart, panting. At once Brambleclaw stepped forward and thrust Birchfall and Hazeltail back across the border onto their own territory.

"There's been enough fighting," he meowed. "Come on, ThunderClan." As they started to leave, he paused and looked back over his shoulder at the ShadowClan patrol. "You can believe what you want, so long as you stay on your own side of the border."

"We weren't the ones who crossed it in the first place," Ivytail hissed.

Brambleclaw turned his back on her and bounded ahead to lead the patrol away.

"Are you okay?" Hollyleaf murmured to Hazeltail; her

Clanmate was blundering through the woods, stumbling over branches and letting trailing brambles rake her pelt.

"I'm a little dizzy," Hazeltail confessed. "I hit my head on a branch when I was trying to pull Scorchpaw off Birchfall."

"Here, I'll guide you." Hollyleaf rested her tail on Hazeltail's shoulder. "We'll let Leafpool take a look at you when we get back to camp. Birchfall was lucky that you did help him," she added. "He would have got an even worse clawing without you."

The young ThunderClan warrior was limping along with blood oozing from a gash on his shoulder. When the patrol paused by the bramble thicket to collect Sandstorm's thrush and their other prey, he sat down and began to wash the wound with vigorous strokes of his tongue.

"Birchfall, you asked for that." Brambleclaw paused in digging up his vole. "ShadowClan shouldn't have accused us of trying to cross the border, but you put us in the wrong when you started the fight. Warriors should know how to control themselves."

"Sorry," Birchfall mumbled.

"So you should be."

When the patrol set off again, Brambleclaw and Sandstorm remained grimly silent. Birchfall padded after them with his head down.

Hazeltail was beginning to recover. "Thanks, Hollyleaf," she mewed, shaking off her friend's tail. "I can manage now. Don't you think Brambleclaw was hard on Birchfall?" she went on. "ShadowClan was asking for a fight."

"That doesn't mean we were right to give them one," Holly-leaf replied absently. She was finding it hard to pay attention to anything. Horror gripped her like an extra pelt, thick enough to choke her. ShadowClan believed that Sol held the answers to a better future, but they were wrong.

He'll destroy the Clans, she thought, terror freezing her limbs until she could barely set one paw in front of another. *Somehow, we have to find a way to stop him.*

THE TIME HAS COME
FOR DOGS TO RULE THE WILD

SURVIVORS

BOOK ONE:
THE EMPTY CITY

Lucky is a golden-haired mutt with a nose for survival. Other dogs have Packs, but Lucky stands on his own . . . until the Big Growl strikes. Suddenly the ground splits wide open. The longpaws disappear. And enemies threaten Lucky at every turn. For the first time in his life, Lucky needs to rely on other dogs to survive. But can he ever be a true Pack dog?

DON'T MISS

RETURN TO THE WILD

SEEKERS

BOOK ONE:
ISLAND OF SHADOWS

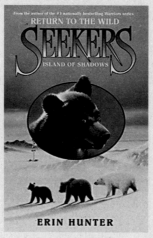

Toklo, Kallik, and Lusa survived the perilous mission that brought them together, and now it's time for them to find their way home. When the group reaches a shadowy island covered in mountains and ice, Kallik is sure they're almost back to the Frozen Sea. But a terrifying accident leads them into a maze of abandoned tunnels, unlike anything they've ever seen before—making them question their path once again.

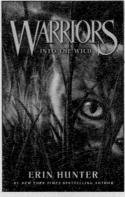

WARRIORS: THE NEW PROPHECY

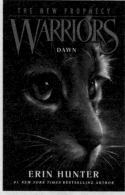

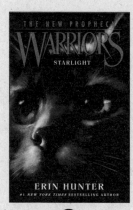

In the second series, follow the next generation of heroic cats as they set off on a quest to save the Clans from destruction.

HARPER
An Imprint of HarperCollinsPublishers

www.warriorcats.com

WARRIORS: POWER OF THREE

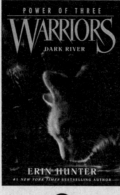

In the third series, Firestar's grandchildren begin their training as warrior cats. Prophecy foretells that they will hold more power than any cats before them.

HARPER
An Imprint of HarperCollinsPublishers

www.warriorcats.com

WARRIORS : OMEN OF THE STARS

1

2

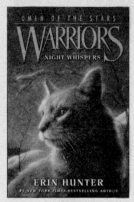

3

4

5

6

In the fourth series, find out which ThunderClan apprentice will complete the prophecy.

HARPER
An Imprint of HarperCollinsPublishers

www.warriorcats.com

WARRIORS: DAWN OF THE CLANS

1

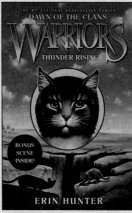

2

3

4

5

In this prequel series,
discover how the warrior Clans came to be.

WARRIORS: SUPER EDITIONS

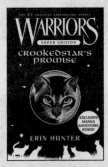

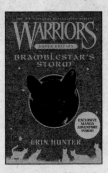

These extra-long, stand-alone adventures will take you deep inside each of the
Clans with thrilling adventures featuring the most legendary warrior cats.